TIM LEBBON is a New Y... from South Wales. He's had ... to date, as well as dozens of novellas and hundreds of short stories. Recent books include *The Secret Journeys of Jack London: The Wild* (co-authored with Christopher Golden), *Echo City, The Island, The Map of Moments* (with Christopher Golden), and *Bar None*. He has won four British Fantasy Awards, a Bram Stoker Award, and a Scribe Award, and has been a finalist for International Horror Guild, Shirley Jackson, and World Fantasy Awards.

Fox 2000 recently acquired film rights to *The Secret Journeys of Jack London*, and Tim and Christopher Golden have delivered the screenplay. Several more of his novels and novellas are currently in development, and he is also working on TV and movie proposals, solo and in collaboration.

Find out more about Tim at his website www.timlebbon.net.

COLDBROOK
TIM LEBBON

HAMMER

AN EXCLUSIVE MEDIA COMPANY

This edition published by Arrow Books in association with Hammer 2012

1 3 5 7 9 10 8 6 4 2

Published in Great Britain in 2011 by Arrow Books in association with Hammer
The Random House Group Limited
20 Vauxhall Bridge Road, London, SW1V 2SA

www.randomhouse.co.uk

Addresses for companies within The Random House Group Limited can be found at:
www.randomhouse.co.uk/offices.htm

The Random House Group Limited Reg. No. 954009

A CIP catalogue record for this book
is available from the British Library

ISBN 9780099571568

The Random House Group Limited supports The Forest Stewardship
Council (FSC®), the leading international forest certification organisation.
Our books carrying the FSC label are printed on FSC® certified paper.
FSC is the only forest certification scheme endorsed by the leading
environmental organisations, including Greenpeace. Our paper procurement
policy can be found at www.randomhouse.co.uk/environment

Typeset in Fairfield by Palimpsest Book Production Limited,
Falkirk, Stirlingshire

Printed and bound in Great Britain by
CPI Group (UK) Ltd, Croydon, CR0 4YY

This one's for Adam Nevill —
great friend, fantastic writer, wise man.

Somewhere, in the infinite sea of universes,
this is a true story.

Prologue

Quantum mechanics: the dreams that stuff is made of.

Wednesday

S ix hours after forging a pathway from his own reality to another, Jonah Jones closed his eyes to dream. But he doubted that sleep would come. His mind, Bill Coldbrook had once told him, was far too busy dancing. The moment he laid down his head he always knew whether the night would usher in a few blessed hours of rest or a long wakeful period of silence, as he stared at the patterns that darkness painted on the ceiling and thought about what might be.

Tonight he no longer needed to dwell upon what might be. It was time to think further ahead than that.

We did it! he thought. *We bloody well did it!* He'd left a night light burning in his small room as always, and it cast a subtle background illumination as he lay with his eyes closed. He watched the arbitrary shifting of his eye fluids, blood pulsing, and wondered just how random anything could be.

He'd wanted to remain in Control, close to the breach. And he'd stood his ground even when Holly sat him down, asked him to drink a glass of water, and mopped up after his shaking hand spilled it. He'd seen the glance she swapped with Vic Pearson – the sort of concerned look a daughter and son might share for their failing, elderly father – and it had galvanised him, driving him to his feet in denial of what he already knew. He had been awake for thirty hours by then, and at seventy-six years old his body was beginning to flag far behind his startling mind. So eventually he had relented and promised that he'd sleep, and dear Holly had threatened to check in on him every hour.

Leaving Control, sensing the staff staring at him as he tore himself away, he'd glanced back one last time. Jonah had smiled, and nodded, and said that he was proud.

What are they doing right now? he wondered, but of course he knew. *Looking at the breach. Looking* through *it at an alternate Earth.* Everett's many-worlds theory suggested this other Earth inhabited the same quantum space as Jonah's Earth, as well as countless others. Another concept was that there were infinite Hubble volumes, each a universe – a number given the name googolplex – and that the similar alternate Earth they could see was so far away that it would take longer than the age of our universe to write that distance down. Both incredible ideas and, for Jonah, both beautiful.

He breathed deeply, ignoring the occasional flutters from his ageing heart, and started thinking about everything that needed to be done. The breach was the culmination of decades of experimentation and centuries of postulation, and now it was time to explore.

He sighed, smiling at the sheer staggering scope of what they had achieved, and experienced a chill of anticipation at what was to come. Sometimes he'd believed that he would die before they succeeded and he would never witness the result. Now, though, here he was at a defining moment in history. One of the greatest days in the annals of science, it would change the way humanity perceived itself in its own universe, and in limitless others . . .

As consciousness faded and Jonah felt himself sinking towards an exhausted sleep, a shadow formed in his mind. It was too vague truly to trouble him, too remote to register as anything more than a shade against the night, but he was aware of it as a weight where there should be none, a presence that had previously been absent. He considered opening his eyes but they felt heavy. He took in a breath and smelled nothing unusual. *Spooking myself*, he thought, and then—

He is in the familiar little North Carolina town of Danton Rock, in the Appalachian mountains a mile north of the subterranean Coldbrook facility. A dozen military trucks are parked in the square, and lines of nervous people are waiting to board. A soldier shouting orders through a bullhorn is not speaking English. Other soldiers are spaced in pairs around the square, each carrying a rifle or sub-machine gun, and there is an air of panic about everyone: soldiers alert, civilians twitchy. Jonah does not recognise the shops – their names are different, and written in a language he cannot *quite* identify – and knows that he is dreaming. He's had frequent bouts of lucid dreaming since his wife's death, and sometimes he can steer the visions, using them to meet dear Wendy again. But though he is aware now, that element of control is absent, as if the images are being projected by some outside agency, onto the screen of his mind. They are not his own.

The trucks are almost fully loaded when a short, attractive young woman slips from one line and runs for an alleyway between buildings. Jonah knows what is coming almost before it happens, and there's a terrible inevitability to the soldier's electronic shout and the gunfire that quickly follows. *No!* Jonah screams—

—and he is somewhere else, a hundred people turning tiredly to look his way, the sad knowledge of what they will see obvious in their eyes. They have the slumped shoulders and defeated gazes of people who will never intervene. The camp is huge, stretching as far as he can see into the distance, a shanty town of polythene, steel tubular shelters, and open sewers. Wretchedness and death hang heavy in the air. It's a sight familiar from disaster areas and war zones around the world, but he recognises Seattle's skyline. Aircraft like none he has ever seen before hover silently above the crowds, their fuselages smooth and pale as bone. One of them is sweeping down, zoning in on the scream even as it comes again. Jonah sees a man, hand clasped to a wet, leaking wound on his arm. Other people are pressing back from him, and the man is turning in slow circles, his eyes wide and pleading. *No!* he cries. *No, it's okay, really, it's clean, it's* clean! But it is *not* clean, and in this vision Jonah understands that. It is unclean, and requires purifying.

Something whispers through the air and the man is whipped from his feet, borne aloft by a flexible arm slung below the aircraft. As it climbs again the people are still pulling back, the circle of bare ground widening, and—

A wide wall of fire reaches fifty feet into the air, and between it and Jonah – a distance of maybe half a mile – thousands of people are staggering from left to right, silhouetted against the flames in their shambling efforts to escape incineration. He is aware that this is another place that is not quite right. The open fields are painted gold by a familiar barley crop, but on a distant hillside stand several tall, weird structures, huge glass globes at their pinnacles seeming to catch light and haze the air around them with shades of darkness. They hint at a technology he does not know, and close to where that hillside smooths out into a valley a group of vehicles are screaming across the ground, bouncing with beautiful elegance. They each fly a stars-and-stripes pennant, but there are too few stars on them.

The sound when it comes is almost soporific, a series of gentle pops like bubbles bursting in a freshly run bath. The people start falling in their hundreds, and Jonah can see parts of their bodies erupting in gouts of black blood and flesh. It's this death that draws and focuses his attention, because then he realises that not only are the buildings disturbingly unfamiliar but the people being mown down are themselves strange. He'd thought that perhaps they were refugees like those from the previous strand of his dream but their movements are wrong – the way they run, the expressionless faces. Even those as yet unaffected by the attackers' weapons seem to be bleeding, and their mouths—

The man's mouth hangs open as he screams at the woman to run. They're in a modern building, the huge open-plan room well furnished, and one glass wall offers views out across a complex of some kind. There are several large featureless buildings, and a place that might be a power plant. The ground is flat, a few benches dotted here and there in the shade of black oak trees. It is sunny: springtime. Beside one bench, three people in red-splashed lab coats are attacking someone squirming on the ground. One of the large buildings is on fire. And inside the room, something is coming to an end.

Run! the man screams again. He is tall and familiar, and it's not until Jonah is mere feet away that he realises why. The man is him . . . although not quite. He's slimmer and fitter than Jonah, his eyes are green rather than blue, and his facial structure is not identical — heavier cheekbones and brow, a longer, flatter nose. But the similarity is shocking, like looking in a subtly distorting mirror. This is not just someone from the same family or even the same parents, but rather a different version of him. *This is what I might have been*, Jonah thinks.

The man grimaces as he raises a heavy pistol and points it somewhere past Jonah, and there is the look of inevitable defeat in his eyes. *Hopeless*. The gun has a small circular magazine and the wisp of a blue pilot light below its barrel, and as the man pulls the trigger the room lights up, splashing fire and heat—

Someone opened his left eyelid.

Jonah's heart fluttered in shock, and his breath locked in his lungs. He clenched his fist and felt sheets crumple between his fingers. He was frozen, motionless, and though the vivid dreams were already fading to mono-chrome he smelled the rot of dead things, the sweet stench of old decay, and felt an intense heat across his face. *That's what those people on the burning plains smell like*, he thought, *and the wound on that man's arm, and the heat is fire eating at my flesh.*

He tried to speak, but breathed out only the faintest of gasps.

The thing leaning over him was poorly illuminated by the night light. It was humanoid, with a smooth head and bulging eyes, and a bulky protuberance where its nose and mouth should be. A mist of steam hung around this strange mask. *Protective suit*, Jonah thought, and for an instant that tempered his fear. But then he saw the redness around one swollen eye, the moisture collecting on one edge of what he'd thought of as breathing appa-ratus, and realised that what he'd believed at first was material stretched across the dome of its head was actu-ally spiked with countless short, thick hairs. It held something, a red object from which a network of slick threads protruded and kissed gently against Jonah's scalp. They might have been wires but for the feel of them there – like cold, dead worms. Still the scream would not come.

It leaned in closer, looking, and Jonah could smell its stale fish-breath.

Then it let go and his eyelid twitched shut, and Jonah

exhaled a breath he didn't know he'd been holding. Sucking in air, filling his lungs again, he knew he *had* to look, *must* look . . . but for a couple of seconds he kept his eyes squeezed closed. He heard no movement, and intuited nothing in his small room; the shadow he'd sensed while falling into sleep had gone.

Jonah sat up and opened his eyes, letting out an involuntary gasp when he realised that the room was empty. The door was closed, and he would have heard the catch clicking. In his sparse room, with its bed, chair, desk, clothes rail, chest of drawers and haphazardly stuffed bookshelves, there was nowhere to hide.

'Bloody hell,' he muttered, pressing his right hand to his chest and trying to calm his galloping heart. He slipped from the bed and rubbed his eyes. If that was what sleep brought, then he was going straight back to Control. Holly could berate him all she liked. He wasn't going to shut his eyes again any time soon.

He dressed and paused with his hand on the door handle, thinking of sleep deprivation and how the significance of what they had achieved might take some time to truly dawn. And then Jonah cast this new dancing partner aside and went to gaze once again upon another universe.

Part One

SPREADING THE DISEASE

The universe is not required to be in perfect harmony with human ambition.

Carl Sagan

Saturday

1

'This is the last of my Penderyn whisky.' Jonah nursed the bottle in his hands, turning it this way and that so that light caught the fluid inside. He swore that in sunlight it was the colour of good Welsh soil, but he rarely saw the sun.

'Been saving it for a special occasion?'

'I have,' Jonah said. 'And in the chaos of the last three days I've been waiting to put it to use.' He looked at the man sitting across from him. Vic Pearson was not someone with whom Jonah would have made friends if circumstance had not thrown them together. He still didn't think they could really call each other friends – when one of them eventually moved on, he doubted that they'd remain in touch – but they were certainly respectful colleagues.

Vic smiled, tapping his fingers on the table.

Jonah turned the bottle again and thought of home.

'So . . .?' Vic said, and Jonah heard the familiar impatience in his tone. Jonah was used to existing far more inside his own mind than outside, and sometimes, so his sweet departed wife used to tell him, it was as though he disappeared altogether. It was said that Isaac Newton would often swing his legs out of bed and then instantly be overcome by a flood of waking thoughts, and that he'd often still be there an hour later staring at the wall, thinking. Jonah had always understood Newton's distractions.

'So,' Jonah said, 'perhaps our first drink should be to Bill Coldbrook.'

Vic leaned forward in his chair, folding his arms on the polished oak desk and looking down. When he glanced up again he was still smiling. But now tears were coursing down his cheeks.

'Vic?' It shocked Jonah. He'd never seen Vic as the crying type.

'Three days since breach. It feels like three years. We're in the middle of forging history. But when times are quieter, I wonder what the hell have we done down here . . . what have we done?' He was still smiling through the tears, because he knew well enough that their names would soon be known. Theirs, and Bill Coldbrook's, may he rest in peace. But here were Vic's damn doubts again, and Jonah was buggered if he was going to let them spoil the moment.

He pulled the cork and breathed in the whisky fumes. Heavenly. Closing his eyes he tried again to think of home, but Wales was far away in distance and memory. Twenty-seven years since he'd left. Perhaps now he could make that journey again.

'We've made history,' Jonah said. 'We've changed the world.'

'Don't you mean "worlds"?' Vic's tears had ceased, and he absent-mindedly wiped at his face, unconcerned that Jonah should see him like this. That made Jonah respect him a little bit more. They both knew that what they'd achieved was much larger than either of them, and that history was being made with every breath they took, every thought they had. *I'll write a book about this one day*, Vic had said after another failed attempt several years before, and Jonah had smiled coolly and asked if that was all he wanted.

Now he knew that within a couple of years what they'd done would fill whole libraries.

They'd drunk together many times before, discussing the day's work and speculating about the future. They'd been accepting of each other's differences, and over time had developed a mutual respect. But Vic's lack of passion – his doubts and concerns, which Jonah had always taken as a lack of confidence – had always formed a barrier.

Vic picked up one tumbler and raised it. Jonah clinked glasses with him.

'A toast,' Jonah said, 'to Bill Coldbrook. I wish he could have been here to see this.'

'If he was, you wouldn't be.'

Jonah ignored the quip and drank, closing his eyes and savouring the smooth burn of the whisky through his mouth and down his throat. It never failed to warm the depths of him. His eyelid twitched and he thought of the terrible nightmares, the thing he'd dreamed staring down into his face. He opened his eyes again and Vic was staring at him. He hadn't touched his drink.

'Don't you *realise* what we've done, Jonah?'

'Of course. What we've been trying to do for two decades – form a route from this Earth to another. We've tapped the multiverse.' He laughed softly. 'Vic, what's happened here might echo across reality. Somewhere so many miles away there's not enough room in our universe to write down the distance, there's another you, toasting our success with another me, and the other you is pleased and happy and confident that—'

'Don't give me that bullshit!' Vic snapped. And Jonah could see that he was genuinely scared. *He has family up there*, he thought, and for a second he tried to put himself in the other man's place. Yes, with the enormity of what they'd done he could understand the worry, the tension.

But there were safeguards.

'Remember Stephen Hawking's visit?' Jonah asked.

'How could I not?'

'He and Bill admired each other greatly, and he gave us his blessing. Said we were the sharpest part of the cutting edge.'

'You say that as if you were proud.'

Jonah laughed softly. Vic above everyone knew that Jonah's pride was a complex thing, untouched by fame or its shadow and more concerned with personal achievement.

'He said we were the true explorers, and gave that plaque as Stephen Hawking's stamp of approval. *We are just an advanced breed of monkeys on a minor planet of a very average star. But we can understand the Universe. That makes us something special.*'

'Just because we pretend to understand doesn't mean we're special. Doesn't mean we shouldn't be *scared*.'

'You should be pleased,' Jonah said, sounding more petulant than he'd intended. But damn it, down here in the facility they weren't walking in the footsteps of giants. They were *making* the footsteps.

19

'Don't tell me,' Vic said, sounding tired rather than bitter. 'It's something I'll be able to tell my grandkids.'

'If you're lucky enough to have them,' Jonah said, 'then yes, of course. You can tell them you were part of the most startling, audacious experiment in history. At Fermilab and CERN they're knocking protons together to look for the Higgs boson particle and mini black holes. Theorists discuss Planck energies, and waste time arguing about Copernican and anthropic principles with those possessing narrow vision or blind faith. But here . . . here, we've made much of theoretical physics redundant. Here, we have *proof*.'

Vic remained silent, turning his glass this way and that, catching the light and perhaps trying to see what Jonah saw in it.

'What were you doing here, Vic?' Jonah asked. 'If what we've done makes you like this, why were you even here?'

'I wanted it as much as everyone else did,' Vic said. 'But the reality is . . . more massive than I ever imagined. The impact of what we've done here . . .' He trailed off, still staring into his glass.

'Will be felt for ever,' Jonah said.

'We've changed the whole fucking world,' Vic said softly. Then he put the glass down without drinking, stood, and leaned in close to Jonah as if to look inside him.

'Vic?' Jonah asked, for the first time a little unsettled.

And before leaving Vic Pearson spoke the stark truth. 'Things can never be the same again.'

2

Holly Wright should have gone to bed hours ago. It had been like this since breach three days before, with her desire for sleep driven out by the unbridled excitement at what had happened. They would sit here together when others were sleeping, her and Jonah, analysing and theorising, speculating and sometimes just staring at the thing. But most of the time Control was buzzing, there was still much to be done, and staring had to be kept to a minimum.

She missed that time. For her, being a scientist was all about dreaming. Which was how she survived on two hours of sleep per night, and why she was here now. Staring and dreaming.

With her in Control were three guards and their captain, Alex. She had trouble remembering the guards' names – she blamed the hats and short haircuts. They paced and talked, chatting into communicators, and she found their presence comforting. Jonah had once commented that their minds were too small to appreciate what was being done here, but she'd long known that attitude as a fault of his. He never suffered fools gladly, and as he was a genius most other people were fools to him.

Taking up most of the lowest of Coldbrook's three main levels, Control was laid out like a small theatre. On the stage sat the breach, its containment field extending several metres in an outward curve. And where the seats should have been were the control desks and computer terminals, set in gentle curves up towards the rear of the room. The floor sloped up from the breach, set in four terraces, and the doors at the rear of Control were ten feet above the breach floor. The walls, floor and ceiling were constructed of the same materials as the core walls, and sometimes Holly felt the weight of everything around her.

Behind Control, the corridor curved around the one-hundred-feet-diameter core until it reached the staircase leading up to the middle level. In this largest level the corridor encircled the core completely, and leading off from it were the living quarters, plant rooms, store rooms, gym, canteen and common room, and beyond the common room the large garage area. The highest level – still over a hundred feet below ground – contained the medical suite and Secondary, the emergency control centre in case something happened in Control.

And in an experiment such as this, 'something' could mean anything.

The cosmologist Satpal was working at his station across the room, and though they chatted occasionally he was much like Holly – too excited to sleep, and when he was here, too wrapped up in what they had done to engage in small talk. One thing he'd said stuck with her. *I can't wait to see their stars.* In an alternate universe where different possibilities existed, it was feasible that those possibilities had extended to the heavens.

Down on the breach floor – and closer than Vic would have allowed, had he been there – sat Melinda Price, their biologist. She had chosen the graveyard shift on purpose as her time to be down there. Since the formation of the breach she had been filming, photographing, and running tests with an array of sensors that had been pushed as close as Jonah would permit, and Holly knew that Melinda itched to go through. So far she'd recorded seventeen species of bird – both familiar and unknown – over a hundred types of insect, trees and flowers, some small mammals, and one creature that she had not been able to categorise. Her breathless enthusiasm was catching. If there was anyone who was going to quit their post and just run, it was Melinda.

Her favoured instrument was the huge pair of tripod-mounted binoculars. She spent so long looking through them that she had permanent red marks around her eyes from the eyepieces. That never failed to amuse Holly. Melinda used simple binoculars to view across distances that philosophers and scientists had been contemplating for millennia.

The graveyard shift. Holly still smiled when the

biologist called it that. After so long working at Coldbrook – and Melinda was the newest scientist here, having arrived eight years before – none of them had ever felt so alive.

Holly glanced at the younger woman now, watched her watching. Melinda was a natural beauty who paid little attention to what God had given her and, even though she rarely made much of an effort, she always exuded sexiness. It was partly her looks, but mainly the intelligence that resided behind her eyes. Some men would have found it threatening. But to most men working at Coldbrook, it was a draw. *Oh yeah, Melinda's my freebie*, Vic Pearson used to say to Holly. Which made Holly wonder whether he'd once said the same about her, Holly, to his wife Lucy.

A blue light flowed from the breach, accompanied by a brief, low sizzling sound. A spread of lights on Holly's control panel lit up, and she leaned forward and accessed a program on her laptop. A few keystrokes and the viewing screen to her left flickered into life. It was a focused view of the breach, fed from a camera set up inside the containment field, and she swept it slowly from left to right until she found what she was looking for.

Melinda was already standing and looked at Holly expectantly.

'Small winged insect,' Holly said. 'I'll file it as sample two-four-seven – you should be able to access it now.'

Melinda nodded and, without saying anything, turned to her own laptop, propped on a chair beside where she'd been sitting. *Can't we bring something through alive?* she'd been asking Jonah ever since the stability of the breach had been established. But his response had always been the same. Until they'd run a full cycle of remote tests on the atmosphere beyond the breach, the eradicator would remain switched on.

Holly zoomed in on the dead insect and scanned for any signs of damage. There were none. It gave her a deep sense of satisfaction that her contribution to the experiment was working so well, though she could sense Melinda's coolness growing day by day. For three years it had been Holly's task to create a safety barrier that would prevent the ingress of anything living from another world into their own, whatever its size, phylum, composition, or chemical make-up. Her previous work in force-field engineering had seemed like child's play compared with the task facing her, but she had relished the challenge. Upon detecting something penetrating the field, the programs she had devised took three millionths of a second to establish the nature of the incursion and deliver a delicately measured electromagnetic shock to halt its life. The device would kill anything from a microbe to an elephant, and way beyond, with minimal or no damage to the bodily tissues.

Within the breach, several robotic sample pods took

turns collecting these samples, isolating them, then retreating to the extremes of the containment field. They were rapidly filling up.

'Zapped another alien?' Vic Pearson asked. He'd crept up on her again, as was his wont. *Ninja Vic*, she'd once called him, when she'd only become aware of his presence when his hands had reached around to cup her breasts. But that had been years ago.

'Small fly of some kind,' she said, pointing at the screen. 'Four wings. See the colouring? It's gorgeous.'

'It's a fly.'

'From an alternate universe.'

'Whoopie-fuckin'-do.' He sat heavily in the chair beside her and sighed.

'You been drinking?' she asked. She kept her voice down; with some staff sleeping, Control was a quiet place, and without Satpal's soft music the silence might have been unbearable. Even the air conditioning was all but silent.

'Jonah asked me to his room,' he said. 'Raised a toast to old Bill Coldbrook.' He drummed his fingers on the desk, staring at the breach. 'Night over there, too.' His voice had dropped.

'Jonah got you drunk?'

'I'm not drunk!' he protested too loudly. 'And no, he didn't. We chatted, I left.' He waved a hand. 'Had a few on my own in the canteen.'

'You didn't argue with him?'

'No, no. We didn't argue. Not this time. But he's completely . . .' he smiled, grasping for the word '. . . unaware, you know?'

'As you keep saying. I think you're unfair on him.'

Vic snorted, and Holly knew what was coming next. She didn't like it when he drank and she never had. Alcohol didn't suit him.

'You say that, and you still balance your religion with what we've done here.'

'Yeah,' she said. 'But my beliefs aren't tested at all by this. If anything—'

'Maybe,' he said, shaking his head. 'Maybe.' And that was what she hated most about Drunk Vic. With alcohol in him, he'd only listen to himself. He stood and skirted her station, descending two wide steps and standing halfway between her and Melinda. And he just stared at the breach for a while.

One day soon, someone would have to go through.

'You know,' he said, returning to lean on her desk and look her in the eye, 'if your God's on the other side as well—'

'Of course He is. The other side is just another here.'

'Right. Well, if He is, don't you think He'll do his best to stop us going through?'

'Why?'

Vic held out his hands as if it was obvious. 'We're fucking with His stuff.'

'What did you come down here for, Vic?'

He shrugged, touched her hand briefly – a surprisingly intimate gesture from someone she'd once loved – and left Control for his bed.

After Vic had gone and the guards had locked the doors behind him, Holly ran a diagnostic on the eradicator as she did every time it had been activated, checking systems and charges, running three virtual trials and then accessing its automatic log. All the while she tried to ignore what Vic had said. But it wasn't so easy, because she'd been thinking much the same herself.

Diagnostics run, she went down the three wide steps onto the breach floor and stared. Contained within a large hexagonal frame was a window onto somewhere else, the thickness of the window itself mere steps away. *Night over there, too*, Vic had said, but the darkness of that other Earth seemed subtly, beautifully different. There was a glow to the sky that Satpal thought might be due to layers of dust or moisture in the atmosphere. It cast a faint red light across the night-time landscape, painting the triangle of visible sky with an arterial-blood smear. Below that, the hillside was the colour of good port, shadows hiding behind boulders and short, squat trees. They'd broken through (*Eased through*, Jonah would have said, *probed through, nothing's broken*) into a small valley, and the hindered view they had of this place gave little away.

There were no signs of habitation. That had disturbed Holly to begin with, but the idea of the multiverse allowed for all possibilities. Just as there were other Earths that would be inhabited by people very much like them, so there would be worlds where life had never begun, or had evolved differently, or where the subtle leap to intelligence and consciousness had not been made. *There are countless possibilities*, Jonah had told them all weeks before. *And we have no way to steer*. What they had accomplished was the crowning achievement in humankind's technical exploration of existence, but Jonah likened it to walking blindly onto a beach at night and plucking up a grain of sand at random. There was no way they could target a particular particle, especially as they had no idea which grains existed.

This grain, Gaia, might be paradise, she thought. Soon after making their first observations, Melinda had named the world Gaia and it had stuck. And for Holly, the idea that beyond the breach was just one possible Mother Earth out of a limitless number did not detract from its wonder. If anything, it was *more* wondrous, and it got her to thinking about why they had forged through to this particular possibility.

During the day the distant hillside was a flower-speckled wonderland, with swathes of purple and pink blooms huddled low among the larger bramble and wild rose bushes and the graceful curls of tall ferns. Birds fluttered from tree to tree, and higher up they'd seen larger, more obscure shapes gliding on thermals, barely flapping their wings. Small rodents rooted around in the vegetation. A stream flowed through the shallow valley, turning left a hundred feet from the breach and continuing out of sight. It was beautiful, and though no one had seen anything shockingly alien or unknown all of them could sense a difference about the place. This was somewhere further away than anyone could imagine or even conceive, brought close enough to touch. When Vic had shown a smuggled-out photograph of the place to his six-year-old daughter Olivia, he said she'd called it 'all wrong', broken out in goose bumps, and started crying.

Out of the mouths of babes.

It's somewhere else entirely, Holly thought. A chill went through her. And the familiar conflicting desires arose to tell her father and brother all about this, or protect them from it.

Melinda glanced back at her and offered a half-smile. The biologist now seemed to occupy a state of permanent distraction.

'You should go get some sleep,' Holly said.

'So should you.'

Holly nodded and sat in a swivel chair without taking her eyes off the breach. Staring into a world so far away, yet alongside their own, gave her mind a surprising freedom and focus. As she watched darker colours in alien skies, she thought about Vic and that touch on the back of her hand. However much she tried to delude herself, she could not deny that she thought of him every day. And memories of their affair were elusive things. When they were working together in Control or sharing a meal in the canteen, he was a colleague and a friend, somewhat volatile but marked by genius. His background in military research and development had given him access to the forefront of technological progress, and he was the most brilliant engineer working at Coldbrook. The science might elude him sometimes — even after all this time, Holly believed that only Jonah came close to *really* understanding — but he could strip and reassemble any piece of equipment they used, and make it perform better in the process.

It was when they weren't working together that she dreamed about those two years when they had been lovers. It had ended seven years before when Vic's wife Lucy had fallen pregnant, a mutual agreement that had hurt them both. But Holly had been pleased that they'd remained close friends. That was important.

Coldbrook was filled with memories for them both. They'd once made love in Control behind her work station, a quick, giggling liaison back when the place

had been empty at night. And her own quarters still sang
with the cries of past pleasure, sometimes breathed again
in the dark as she remembered.

We're grown-ups, Vic had said when they'd ended it.
And we'll always be friends. He had been right. But there
were times . . .

Like when he touched my hand, she thought.

'Holly.'

Her eyes snapped open, she jerked, and the swivel
chair slipped a foot to the right. 'Wha—?'

'Wake up, Holly. There's something . . .'

Holly blinked the brief sleep away, looked into the
breach – and squinted as she saw movement.

She gasped and felt the hairs rise all across her body.
The conviction she'd been feeling for three days pressed
on her again: that they were balanced on the precipice
of change. She focused, glancing to the left and right to
give her eyes time to work in the dark.

There was a weak moon-cast shadow that should not
be there, because there was no tree or rock to form it.
Once again, it moved.

'Melinda?' she said quietly. 'What do you see?'

The other woman took another step across the breach
floor and lifted her binoculars. *No closer!* Holly thought,
panic prickling her scalp.

'Something coming,' the biologist confirmed. 'Can't
see what. But . . . it's bigger than anything we've seen.'

She looked back at Holly and her eyes were alight with excitement.

Holly dashed up the two steps to her desk and initiated another systems check of the eradicator. 'Let's get ready,' she said, louder than she'd intended. She watched the viewing screen, waiting for the shape to arrive. Satpal glanced over, then turned back to his own bank of computers. The four guards stood in their assigned positions, in two pairs. All was well.

Down by the breach, Melinda crouched with her camera.

I wish Vic was here, Holly thought. She should have contacted Jonah then, told him that something unusual was happening. This was no bird or insect. She should have called Vic as well, but there was no guarantee that he had even arrived back at his room. He might have returned to the common room to find another drink from the canteen's small bar. So she waited instead, ignoring established protocol to give her old boss the sleep he so needed, and to avoid possible conflict with the man she probably still loved.

3

Even a third of a bottle of good Welsh whisky couldn't grant him sleep.

Jonah lay back on his bed and stared at the ceiling. He

hadn't turned out his light when Vic had left, and the room was bathed in sterile fluorescence. The crystal tumbler was propped against his side, empty, and the bottle on his bedside table taunted him with its liquid gold.

He'd left Wales the year his dear Wendy had passed away, taken from this world by a cruel cancer that none of his love or anger could counter. He had raged and railed against such unfairness when he was alone, maintaining his composure when he read aloud from the newspaper as Wendy drifted in and out of a morphine-fuelled sleep. And when she was gone he had continued to rage on his own, except this time there had been no one to compose himself for. Three months later he was living in the USA, and three months after that he met Bill Coldbrook.

Coldbrook had already received approval for his project by then, and while politicians politicised and funding bodies negotiated funding, Bill was already setting up temporary base in a trailer high in the Appalachians, collecting together his books and documents, planning the project scheme by scheme, and contacting people who he wanted to poach from other projects to help him. Jonah came to meet Bill through a mutual friend of theirs at the Harvard-Smithsonian, and the thought of retiring to the mountains – immersing himself in such radical physics that many regarded it as science fiction – had appealed to a grieving Jonah.

From the day when he and Bill met, their relationship had felt like that of two brothers. They'd bickered and argued, brought out the best in each other, drank and raged, and sometimes Jonah had believed they were two elements of the same mind. Yet, ironically, the catharsis that Jonah had believed he might find in such a project was not forthcoming.

His disbelief in an afterlife had never pained him until he'd met Bill. The American had seen a like mind in Jonah, not only a brilliant scientist but a man with passion in his heart and disaffection simmering just below the surface that he presented as a public front. And Bill's talk of the multiverse and all it might be – world upon world, a perpetual variation of quantum universes echoing with each and every decision taken or moment passed – had fuelled a frustration in Jonah's heart. His religious friends were content in their beliefs, and Jonah slowly found himself seeking his own. This was no deity that lured him, or teased him, or subjugated him with promises of pain and pronouncements of sin. It was a faint hope – vain, though he knew; naive, so Bill told him – that, in one of those endless worlds, Wendy might live still.

It's not like that, Bill would say, and Jonah would nod because he knew his new friend was right. But at night, lying alone in bed in a nearby hotel and nursing the early insomnia that would grow to haunt him, he couldn't convince himself that possibilities were not endless.

Jonah was no romantic. He was no crazed Ahab, seeking the impossible in an ocean of infinities. But his long-dead wife was still with him in a way that his atheistic heart had never dreamed possible.

He sighed and sat up. If he couldn't sleep, he might as well have another drink. He picked up the bottle and poured, and it took a few seconds for him to register that the soft chiming came from his bedside phone, not the glass.

'What?' he snapped, snatching up the receiver. He fumbled and dropped it, having to lean over and retrieve it from the floor. His vision swam. Damn it, he was more drunk that he thought. 'Yes?' he asked again, holding it to his ear.

'—coming through, and it's the biggest yet. I wasn't going to call you, didn't want to cry wolf, but . . .'

'Holly?'

'Jonah, did I wake you?'

'Yes,' he said, trying to focus. He placed his tumbler on the table and stood, leaning against his bookcase. 'What's coming through?'

'Sorry. I wanted you to sleep . . .' Holly trailed off, but in the background Jonah heard activity in Control. Someone shouted something – Melinda, he thought – her voice excited and loud. Someone else spoke in the distance, his voice calmer and more troubled.

'Holly, what's going on?'

'—eradicator is fine, fully charged,' Holly said, though it wasn't to him.

'But it should have fried it a couple of seconds ago,' a male voice said. It sounded like Alex, the guards' captain.

'Holly?' Jonah said.

'It doesn't *fry* things,' Holly said, and Jonah smiled because she was so defensive of her work. 'Melinda, can you see—?'

'Biped,' Melinda said, her voice high and shrill.

Biped, Jonah thought. Jesus Christ, a *human* might be coming through, and she'd held back calling him because she wanted him to bastard *sleep*?

'Holly!' he shouted, and he heard fumbling as she brought the phone to her ear again.

'Jonah, it's okay, everything's fine. Can't make it out yet, it's dark, moving strangely, some sort of ape, I think, and—'

'That's no fucking ape!' another guard said.

'—and it's almost at containment. Melinda's trying to wave it back, doesn't want it eradicated because—'

'Trying to wave it back how? Just how close is she to the breach?'

'She's . . . it's all under control, Jonah. But you might want to get here.'

'Apes don't walk like that!' the same voice shouted.

'Holly, *how* is it walking?' There was a thud as the

phone was placed on a desk, then the unmistakable rattle of a keyboard being worked. '*Holly*? Do you need to sound the alarm?' But she did not reply.

'Melinda, not so close!' Holly called. And then quieter, to someone standing close by: 'Yeah, look, it's okay, fully charged and operational.'

'Then why hasn't it fried it?'

'I *told* you, it doesn't—'

'Positions!' Alex shouted, and Jonah heard a metallic click. Gun being cocked?

'Holly?'

A rattle, then Holly's excited breathing. 'It's fine, Jonah. Melinda's waving it back. I think it sees her! I think it understands!'

'You should have called me! I'm coming to Control now.'

'Okay, but it's fine, Jonah.'

In the background, running feet and more excited chatter.

'You'll have to contain it!' Jonah said. There was no answer, because Holly had put the receiver down again. And as he hung up on his end, he wondered why he'd felt the need to say that. The eradicator would kill any living thing that attempted to ford the breach. The robotic sample pods within the containment field would gather it. There was nothing to contain.

* * *

Outside, Jonah clicked his door shut and hurried along the corridor, joints aching. He was angry at Holly for not calling him but it was mixed with a flush of excitement. *Biped*, Melinda had said, and that implied so much. For three days he'd been monitoring the samples collected and classified by Melinda, and most of them had been, if not completely familiar, then at least recognisable. And for those three days he had been wondering, *How similar is that Earth to our own?* He'd seen the same look in everyone's eyes at some point, the same question: *Is there anything like us?* It was an idea both terrifying and thrilling, and it was the one answer he sought before he'd even consider authorising extraction of any of the samples.

After that, of course, would come the preparations to send someone through.

He hurried along the corridor curved around the central core, his footsteps echoing. There were no other sounds. Most staff were sleeping right now, those of them who weren't were down in Control. He passed the side corridor that housed Vic's room and paused, wondering if he should wake him. Probably. But he moved past and entered the staircase instead. Holly had probably called Vic already, and Jonah wanted to reach Control as quickly as possible.

At the bottom of the stairwell he accessed a security door, leaning his chin on the eye-scanner rest. The door hissed as it opened and the air quality suddenly felt different.

More loaded.

He paused inside the door and looked along the hallway. It was twenty yards long, and for the final five yards one wall was made of solid glass, offering a panoramic view of Control's curved, terraced layout and the breach floor below. The light flickering at that window was the dancing electric blue of the eradicator.

As Jonah's heart skipped a beat, Coldbrook's main alarm began to sound.

4

Holly felt as if she were being watched. It was probably the phone she hadn't hung up again, with Jonah on the other end. And even though she knew he'd be on his way by now, still the feeling remained until she hit the alarm button. But by then everything had gone wrong.

The thing stood on their side of the breach, within the containment field and the influence of the eradicator, but still standing as well. *Maybe it's dead and just won't fall down*, Holly thought, but she could see movement in its limbs, and its lank hair swayed as it swung its downturned head a few degrees in either direction. It was naked, its exposed skin dark and cracked. Clumps of hair clung to its body and its genitals, though shrivelled, were obviously a man's.

When it had first come through, Satpal – standing close to Holly now, eyes wide in wonder – had called it humanoid.

'No,' Melinda had said, 'it's *human.*'

But there was something so very wrong with that assessment.

As the intermittent wail of the alarm filled Control, Holly's hand hovered over the manual eradicator controls which she'd already turned to full charge. Enough to kill a rhino five times over. *One more time*, she thought and she pressed the round red button. The breach flashed as the eradicator discharged. Sparking blue light wormed through the thing's hair and illuminated the deep dry cracks in its skin, a jigsaw of wounds and fractures. It should be dead, if not from the eradicator then—

Because of those wounds.

'Charge it again!' Alex shouted, gun aimed.

'That was full charge,' Holly said, and Melinda turned to her, wide-eyed. *Full?* her look said. Holly nodded, then looked back at the intruder. The eradicator was designed to cease brain activity and negate electro-magnetic function, halting hearts, freezing muscles, shifting a thing from living to dead in a matter of seconds.

Their intruder had taken three full charges, and still stood.

'It takes one more step, open fire,' Alex commanded the other three guards. Holly knew that they wore throat mics and inner-ear receivers, so their voices would easily carry over the harsh noise of the alarm.

Jonah and the others will come running, she thought, glancing back at the glass wall beside the main entrance door.

And Jonah was there, pressed flat against the glass like a kid at a sweetshop window. He looked past her and Melinda at the intruder, and in his eyes Holly could make out the sudden terror that they had done something dreadful. By pressing the alarm she had initiated a partial lockdown of Coldbrook, securing Control and the breach floor within it from the rest of the facility. Jonah could look, but he couldn't touch.

'It's *not* human,' she said. 'It can't be.'

'Stay back!' Melinda said, holding up her hands in a warding-off gesture. She was ten steps from the visitor. 'Stay *away!*' And as though taking her words as a signal, it started forward again. A dry rasping sound accompanied its movement. It shambled, feet dragging, head down, hands barely moving, as if at the end of a walk hundreds of miles long. The intruder had not seemed a threat until the eradicator failed to stop it, and even then Holly had frantically checked the settings and levels of the device she had designed and built. But pressing the alarm button had felt like an admission, and from then on Holly's fear had been building. Charging, like the eradicator. Ready to burst.

Melinda did not move back and, as the man from the other world came within three feet of her, gunfire erupted.

Bullets thudded into the shape, its face still turned down but hands raised, reaching for Melinda as if she had always been his goal. Holly saw the bullets flick at his hair and blast bits of him across the breach floor, shattering him as he moved between this universe and another, and she thought, *Have we just declared war?*

But then he reached Melinda, and in a surreal gesture she held out her arms as if to prevent him from falling. He bore down, driving her to the floor beneath him. He started to scratch and bite. And when Melinda's scream came it echoed Holly's, their own alarm filling Control with a very human fear.

'Oh, God!' Holly said, a plea in her voice because she didn't know what they had done. *The bullets hit him and ripped him, but he's still—*

The shape, previously slow and lethargic, was now frenzied in its movements. It used both hands to bat away Melinda's arms, which she had raised over her head to protect her face, and darted its head down at her like a bird pecking seed. Even behind the shouting and gunfire, Holly heard the unmistakable sound of teeth clacking together.

'Help her,' she said hopelessly, and the guards were doing their best. Alex and another had advanced and were kneeling, trying to adjust their angle of fire so that they didn't strike Melinda. The other two were carrying a long table down the steps towards the breach floor.

Melinda screamed as the man bent his face into her chest and starting biting. He shook her like a dog, lank hair flailing, and Holly closed her eyes and looked away as she saw blood flying, spattering down across the floor from his teeth. *Why don't they just shoot?*

Gunfire erupted again, several short bursts from two weapons, and when Holly opened her eyes she looked directly up at Jonah. He was still pressed against the window, his face slack. He looked from her to Melinda and back again, and Holly wanted so much to tell him that it wasn't his fault.

Protocol dictated that Control must now remain sealed for three days. All functions would be transferred to Secondary, a room two floors up on Coldbrook's top level that had full audio and visual access to Control and the breach, and from where Jonah and the others would be able to monitor what happened. And however appalled and guilty Jonah looked, Holly knew that he would follow protocol.

The gunfire ceased, and for a moment Holly could not turn around because she was terrified of what she would see.

'Ohshitohshitohshit,' Satpal said. She glanced sidelong at him, saw his hands pressed to his face, fingertips trying to massage the truth from his mind. He looked at her and his expression did not change.

She turned around. The man was slumped on top of Melinda, unmoving. Part of his head had been blown away. There was blood splashed across the concrete floor, and bullet holes pocked the framing around the breach. *Did we shoot into there?* she thought, and she looked everywhere but at Melinda, because she didn't want to see. Though the man bore terrible wounds, only his ruptured skull seemed to bleed.

The two guards with the table used it to shove the dead intruder to one side. Holly heard him hit the floor, a sibilant sound like something dry, not wet. His head looked like a ruined coconut.

'What do we do?' one of the guards asked. 'Do we . . .?'

'Not sure there's much point,' Alex said. 'She's already stopped moving.'

Oh no, Holly thought, and she looked directly at the biologist for the first time. The man had made a mess of her, and from twenty feet away she was glad she could not make out the details. Melinda's face had vanished in a mess of meat, her throat had been ripped out, and the pool of blood beneath her was spreading.

'Holly!' Jonah's electronic voice said. He was using the

intercom. There was a button on Holly's desk, but right now she didn't know what she could say. Melinda was dead. Blood still trickled from her ravaged throat, but it no longer *flowed* because her heart had stopped.

'Miss Wright,' Alex said, 'we need to see if anything else is coming through, check the status of the—'

'Okay!' Holly said, pleased to have something to do. She sat at her station and looked at the large high-definition viewing screen to her left. She used her computer keyboard to run through all eighteen views available to her and, when she was confident there was nothing large moving over there, she set about checking the breach containment. All appeared well. The eradicator was back to full charge, sensors were all online, and the robot pods were fired up to collect anything.

But the man had still come through.

We've got to shut it down, she thought. *Seal the breach and* . . .

But that was something for Jonah to decide. And it was nowhere near as easy as simply closing a door.

'Looks clear,' Holly said, and when she looked up Alex was already moving forward. The other three guards covered him. He shouldered his gun and stepped into the puddle of blood. His boots made a slight splash in the congealing fluid and sluggish blood flowed in to fill his footprints. He edged around the dead man and skirted Melinda's head, approaching from the other side, checking his men's field of fire and squatting beside her.

Melinda groaned.

'She's alive!' Holly said. 'She's *alive*?' She spun around and looked up at Jonah, already seeing the hopelessness in his expression. *He'll still have to leave us in here*, she thought.

'But she can't be . . .' Satpal said. And Holly turned around again, because something about his voice seemed so sure.

Alex was still squatting beside Melinda, both hands held out as if unsure if or where he should touch her. She was moving slightly, groaning, limbs flexing, and when her face turned towards Holly she realised what Satpal had meant. She was all raw meat and teeth.

'Get me some dressings!' Alex snapped. One of his men dashed to the guard station by the main door.

'Is it just—?' Satpal said, and then Melinda sat up.

'Just what?' Holly asked.

A soft, ghostly sound filled the room, like a breeze blowing through weathered rocks.

Alex was looking at the biologist in amazement. He was still holding his hands out to either side, not wanting to touch her anywhere, when she grabbed his head, pulled it towards her face – and bit him.

5

Vic Pearson dreams of his dead sister. It is the worst kind of nightmare, one where he knows what is to come but cannot wake up or change its course. And in the waking hours to follow, he will think that quite appropriate. Charlotte's real life had gone the same way, with him as a passive but supportive observer, unable to nudge her from the track of self-destruction that had finally taken her from him. He'd loved her and hated her, but in the nightmare she terrifies him.

Charlotte died at nineteen, but in the dream she, like Vic, is in her forties. She has hair greying at the temples and a face pinched by her troubled life. Stone-cross gravestones have been tattooed onto her forearms by blunt, infected needles, and he follows her through their Boston suburb as she goes from house to house, gathering the paraphernalia of her demise from people who should know better. At one house their mother opens the door and hands Charlotte a family heirloom to sell for drugs, and as Charlotte walks away without saying thank you Vic rages at his mother, shouting. But he has no voice – she does not hear. She averts her eyes and closes the front door on the smell of baking and despair. At the next house, Charlotte's teenaged school friend answers the door and starts nodding, agreeing with every mad thing that Charlotte says. Satisfied, she walks on to the next house, and the next, and each time Vic tries to plead with the person who answers the door to make a stand against his sister's downward spiral.

He knows what is coming and whose the last house will be, but it is still a surprise when he spies the toys scattered across the lawn and his own car in the driveway. It's a house that he has never lived in, but which feels more like home than the Danton Rock bungalow he has shared with Lucy since their marriage.

This is the only part of the nightmare where he actually hears the words being spoken.

Lucy answers the door when Charlotte knocks.

'Charlotte! You're looking well. Death becomes you.'

'Hi, Luce. My loser brother at home?'

Loser! Vic thinks. *She dares call me a loser!* He hears Olivia's sweet girly voice from inside the house, and he starts to loathe himself as his hatred grows for his sister, dead for over two decades but alive and ageing along with him right now, because of the sense of dreadful loss she's instilled within him. When she died he felt the guilt resting squarely on his shoulders, and though he'd seen the same responsibility crushing his parents and her friends as well, he'd never been able to shake it. His unrelenting and almost painful love for his wife and daughter is fed partly by that guilt, and partly by the hopeless loss he still feels for Charlotte.

And the dream turns to nightmare.

'Vic's not in right now,' Lucy says. 'He's at work.'

'Right, yeah. At *work*.' Charlotte leans against the wall and rubs a powder into her gums and stabs her forearm with a hypodermic that instantly vanishes. 'He's fucking Holly Wright, you know. Any chance they get. They're down there for days on end sometimes, and she likes him to eat her out in her shower cubicle. She sucked him off in the canteen's kitchen once. She doesn't like to swallow, but she takes it over her tits.'

'Vic's not in right now,' Lucy says again, apparently not hearing.

'He says he loves her,' Charlotte says, and her skin starts changing, hanging slack from her frame as death catches up with her. She turns and acknowledges him for the first time. 'When we were kids he said he loved me, too.'

I did, Vic screams, but no sound emerges. And then to feed his guilt comes Charlotte's denial of what he is trying to say. She opens her mouth and starts screeching at him, an intermittent cry that raises the hairs on the back of his arms and neck and makes his balls quiver, just as thoughts of Holly used to. They sometimes still did.

Lucy smiles uncertainly at the terrifying sound, glancing around her front lawn, not seeing Vic but carrying in her eyes a suspicion that he has spent years trying not to see for real.

Vic snapped awake and sat up in his small room. He sighed, wiped a hand across his face, and fell out of bed. He looked around for Charlotte, but she was only ever in his dreams. The sound was something else. The sound was—

"'Fuck me, it's the alarm." He stood and tried to shake the last remnants of the nightmare, knowing from experience that it would haunt his mood and mind all day. The nearest sounder was at the corridor junction a dozen steps away, but the sound was designed to penetrate every corner of Coldbrook. Already he could hear running feet outside. They'd rehearsed for this; it was one of the safeguards that Jonah insisted upon. What they'd never designed was any method of communicating just what the emergency was.

He looked around his small room. It was a stopover place, because his main home was up in Danton Rock with Lucy and Olivia. They had always been the most important things in his life, despite what Charlotte might have to say, and he'd die or kill to protect them. If necessary, both.

He groaned, squeezed his eyes shut and tried to shake off sleep. Dream and reality were still bleeding together, the nightmare tenacious, so much so that he expected to see Charlotte in front of him when he opened his door. But out in the corridor a technician ran by, dressed in boxers and boots and a scruffy Motörhead T-shirt.

'Andy! What's up?'

He skidded to a stop past Vic's door and looked back. 'Dunno. Alarm woke me so I'm off to my station.'

'Yeah,' Vic said, and Andy turned and hurried on. *Off to my station*. They all knew what to do should the alarm sound. It had been drummed into them enough.

Vic slipped back into his room and closed the door, searching through the mess of clothes on the floor for his satphone. He was one of several in the facility who kept them on their person at all times – him, Jonah, Holly, the guards' captain Alex – and it was also a direct link to outside. His priority now was to find out what had gone wrong, and then decide what he should do about it. *Gotta get to my station in Secondary*, he thought. That was what procedure said – the alarm would initiate Control lockdown, and Secondary should be his aim. But that was not what his heart said, and never had been. He'd always promised himself that if things went badly wrong down here, his family would come first.

He dialled Holly but received an unavailable signal. What the fuck . . .? He cancelled, and dialled Jonah. It was answered in three rings.

'Vic . . . something came through.' The old man sounded breathless and panicked, and Vic had to close his eyes for a moment, sick at the knowledge that this was not a false alarm. He'd always had his doubts and fears, but even then he hadn't really believed that something would go wrong. Not really.

'Jonah, what was it? Where are you? Where's Holly? I can't reach her.'

'I'm going for Secondary. Control's locked down.' He panted, running as he spoke. 'Something came through.'

'*What* came through?' Vic asked again, cursing the continuing alarm that stole some of his words.

'Don't know . . . a creature, but . . .' Gasping, coughing.

'Where's Holly?'

'Control.' Vic stared at the narrow cot where he and Holly had made love so many times, felt her breath on his neck and her fists squeezing his shoulders as she came, and his sister's voice echoed from his dream. *Right, yeah. At* work.

'How did something get past the—?'

'Vic, it attacked Melinda.'

'What? How?'

'Bit her. Bad. But then she . . . I thought she was *dead*, but she . . .'

'Jonah?'

'Need to control this until we can . . .' He was panting harder now, each breath a gasp. '. . . can figure out . . .'

'Is Holly safe?'

'Don't know. Meet me in Secondary.'

'Okay.' And before he could say anything else Jonah

signed off. Vic stared at the satphone for a few seconds as if expecting it to buzz into life again.

He snapped up his palmtop computer, patched into the wireless network and then accessed the facility's remote cameras. It took two attempts to enter the correct password, and for a panicked moment he feared that some security-conscious employee had changed it. But then the thumbnail images sprang up, and he scrolled across to Control.

Even before maximising the image, he could see how bad it was.

Control was in chaos. Someone was shooting, the gunfire somehow seeming even more violent without sound. Blood was splashed across the floor, pooled around a prone shape.

Vic gasped, looked for Holly, brought the palmtop closer to his face. But he couldn't make anyone out.

'Fuck. Fuck.' *Something came through* and Vic couldn't see what that something might be. Whatever it was, it had brought death.

Shaking, he dropped the palmtop face-down on the bed and dialled the first few numbers of his home landline. He paused, cancelled. It was four a.m. If he told Lucy that something was wrong, she might panic and let it slip to someone else. And he needed his family exactly where they were.

He paced his room, uncertain, clasping the phone,

glancing again at the palmtop. *Something came through, something attacked, and Holly was somewhere in there.* His family would be asleep, Lucy lonely in the marital bed he had betrayed so much. His long-dead sister was right, he had told Holly that he loved her. But it was an illicit love, passion-driven, and nothing compared to what he felt for his family.

Vic was shaking.

As he blinked, he saw Lucy's expression in his dream as Charlotte spewed out the sordid truth. The suspicion that existed in nightmare, and which perhaps he'd spied several times in the years since the affair had ended.

In the echo of Jonah's gasping, panicked words, duty called. But Vic could only heed a far greater duty.

Panting, he dragged the gun box from beneath his bed and clicked though the numbers on the coded lock. The M1911 pistol went into his belt, along with three extra magazines. He hadn't fired it for almost a year, when he'd hiked to a range high in the Appalachians to see how stale his shooting had become. He'd still been pretty good. Holding the pistol, feeling the rough grip, smelling the gun oil: it felt like a statement of intent.

The siren screeched again and again, and it could only be turned off from Control or Secondary. Jonah hadn't reached Secondary yet, though it must only be a matter of seconds. And in Control, perhaps they were too busy.

'Holly,' he said out loud, and he thought back to the

last time he'd spoken her name in this room. She hadn't been here since the evening they ended their affair, when they'd sat together for half a night and had drunk three bottles of wine. *Holly, you're too special for me to lose*, he'd said, *and if we carry on I will lose you.*

But your family are more special, she'd said. And she understood fully, she really did. That was why he still loved her. The sex was no longer there, but the friendship was priceless. Vic hoped that, if she was still alive, she would understand what he had to do now.

He had to abandon her.

'Control's locked down, can't get in anyway,' he whispered, justifying this new betrayal, thinking of the silent image of blood and shooting. 'Whatever came through is trapped.' And despite trying to convince himself that was true, his need to get his family as far away from here as possible was so pressing that it made him dizzy. Because he had always been afraid that something terrible might happen, and there was no telling what had just been released.

Vic left his room and slammed the door. At the junction, he looked left at where the corridor curved around towards the staircase leading down to Control and up to Secondary, and right at where it dog-legged away from the core and towards the common room and garage. He hesitated for only a second, and then turned right.

With every step he ran further from his professional responsibilities and the alarm screamed at his betrayal.

6

Alex shot Melinda five times. She fell back still biting, and the guard captain yelled as her teeth tugged away part of his face. She flipped onto her back and writhed for a second, bloody hands shoving at the motionless intruder from beyond the breach, and Holly thought, *That's it, she's dead now, I'm sure I saw her spine—*

Melinda sat up again, pushing with one hand and seemingly unaware of her new, terrible wounds.

'Alex!' Holly shouted, as if the captain would need warning about this pitiful, bloody wreck. But Alex was leaning back on his knees with a terrible, disbelieving look on his face. One hand still aimed the pistol at Melinda, the other was pressed against his cheek and jaw where she'd bitten him. He leaned further back, legs bent almost in half at the knee now, head almost touching the floor, and the gun made a metallic *tink* as it dropped from his hand. He grew still.

'Sir!' another guard said, moving closer.

'Back,' Satpal said. 'Stay back! Can't you see . . .?'

'See fucking *what*?' Holly said, and then the cosmologist was at her side. She could smell the sweat on him, the fear. She wondered if she smelled the same.

'She *can't* be getting up,' he said softly. And Holly knew that he was right. *No one leaks that much blood and lives. No one . . .*

'Sir!' another guard shouted, the one that Alex had sent away to fetch dressings to tend Melinda's wounds. He stood close to the breach floor now, staring down at the massive pool of blood and the figures at its centre: the intruder, motionless with most of his head missing; Melinda, sitting up fully now, one arm propping her as she tried to get to her feet; and Alex, hand fallen from his face, horribly contorted and motionless.

'What the fuck do we do?' another guard said. He was standing ten feet to Holly's left, pistol aimed at Melinda, his face pale. 'Sir, what do we do?' Holly realised that he was directing his questions at Alex.

The captain suddenly tensed, then raised himself back to a kneeling position. His mouth worked, but only a soft humming sound emerged from it. Holly could see his teeth through the wound in his cheek.

'Shit,' someone muttered. They could all see that the soldier's movements were wrong.

'We're locked down in here,' Holly said. 'Two of you keep watch on the breach in case . . .' She shook her head. 'You.' She nodded at the guard with the field dressings. 'What's your name?'

'Neil.'

'Neil, I think Alex is . . . is in shock.' Alex was on

his feet now, swaying forward and backward and looking around the room. There was something about his eyes . . . They didn't look shocked to Holly. They looked *different*. He looked at her, then at Satpal, then at the three other guards, two of them pointing guns at him. Blood spewed from his face, and Melinda was behind him now, a bloody, meaty mess who should have been . . .

'Melinda?' Holly said softly, between a blast of the alarm's loud siren. But the biologist did not seem to hear, and her previously beautiful face was gone, home now to red.

Alex hooted softly like a dove, a strangely beautiful sound. Then he ran at Neil, the guard holding the dressings, and Neil didn't even manage to gasp before his captain shoved him backward onto a step and fell on him.

'Shoot him!' Satpal screamed, but neither of the other guards moved.

'Oh dear God, what have we done?' Holly said.

'I can get us out,' Satpal said, leaning in close to whisper his secret.

'No. Lockdown.'

Neil screamed. Alex was biting him, his head thrashing. The other two guards were shouting at each other and at their captain, but still neither of them fired.

Holly glanced at the breach and the darkness beyond.

'I can get us out,' Satpal said again. Holly frowned. He snorted, then ran up towards the main doors.

'We're in lockdown!' Holly shouted, and someone started shooting. She ducked down beside her desk, not sure where the gunfire was coming from or whether the workstation would shield her or not. The sound was horrendous, smothering the alarm, and she pressed her hands to her ears and cried out. When the shooting ended she looked up the terraced room at Satpal. He was doing something with the door control, sweat patches spreading from beneath his arms and across his back, and she thought, *No, Satpal, we can't let them out*. He glanced back, caught her eye and then looked beyond and behind her. His eyes opened wide.

Holly raised herself and looked across the top of the control panel. Her computer screen had been shattered by a bullet. Past that she saw Melinda, bloody red Melinda, clawing at a guard's face and chest even as he backed away from her, pulling her with him. He must have dropped his gun because he was now stabbing at her with a short knife, plunging the blade into her back again and again. It had no effect. Holly saw the terror in his eyes, and then the pain as her nails opened him up and her face pressed in to gnaw at the wounds.

Alex was standing again, and another shape was pulling itself up the front of a solid desk beside him – Neil, the guard he'd attacked, hat knocked off, a smear of blood across one cheek, red patch spreading across his shoulder and down his chest. He held himself still against the desk, the fear gone from his face, and it was that more than anything that told Holly how little time she had left. The guard was no longer afraid. His mouth opened and his eyes grew dark as all expression left them.

The last guard had climbed several steps and was making his way around Control to the main doors – and Satpal.

'You can't open that door!' Holly shouted. 'It's a disease, *something*, and you *can't!*'

Satpal glanced back at her, and the guard paused behind a bank of desks to look as well. He was terribly young, perhaps no more than twenty, and his fear was that of a child. *Of course, he's seen stuff that shouldn't be, and that's just the reason why Satpal* must not open—

She heard the hiss as the door's hydraulics engaged. Satpal took one last look back at her and then left Control, and the last that Holly saw of him was as he ran past the glass-block wall. *They can get out now*, she thought. She looked up at one of the cameras mounted high on the ceiling and wondered how many people were watching this. Jonah, almost certainly. Some of the others.

Vic? Maybe.

The guard tripped as he ran for the door. Alex and the other guard, changed now, were going for him, scrambling across desktops and leaping the spaces in between, both of them emitting that strange hooting sound.

The alarm ceased, and in the sudden silence everything that Holly could hear was terrible.

Melinda was advancing on her, dragging one leg because Alex's bullets had shattered her hip.

Oh sweet Jesus, Holly thought, because she suddenly knew what she had to do. She looked up at the camera again and drew her hand across her throat, hoping that whoever was watching would understand. And she hoped also that they would have the courage to do what needed to be done. Satpal had betrayed himself. It was understandable, but it didn't make things any easier. *If it weren't for him* . . . she thought. If it weren't for him, they could have sealed Control and gone about closing down the breach remotely from Secondary.

But now that Satpal had somehow managed to open the door – through sabotage, or prior agreement with some of the maintenance engineers working here – they were *all* finished.

Unless.

Holly closed her eyes and breathed deeply, wondering if she could really—

The young guard screamed, the sound suddenly becoming muffled as he slipped through the doors and out into the corridor. She looked just in time to see Alex grab him, press him against the glass wall and bite into his throat.

Oh God, don't let me go like that, not like that, not eaten.

Melinda was close now, and the other guard also came for Holly, taking away any chance she might have had to consider more fully the threat she faced. In that instant her survival instinct took over. Instinct, and her scientist's mind, because fascination still bubbled below the surface.

She slapped her hand on the eradicator power button on her desk and sprinted for the breach. As Holly ran she had time to think, *What will it be like, walking in another Earth?*

Then she entered the space between.

7

Secondary was on Coldbrook's level one, the highest level, still well over a hundred feet below ground. Jonah had rushed along corridors and climbed stairs from level three in Control. And he was almost an old man. Sometimes he forgot that, but not today.

He arrived just as three other people reached Secondary. He was sweating, gasping, and clamping a hand to his chest. He didn't know the guard's name, but the other two arrivals were Uri, their communications technician, and Estelle, the brilliant anthropologist from France. He nodded at them, and once inside Secondary the guard closed the door. As it clicked shut Jonah glanced through the reinforced viewing glass at the empty corridor beyond, his breath misting the window.

'What's happening?' Uri asked. He'd obviously been asleep and was still shaken at being woken by the alarm.

'Kill the alarm first,' Jonah said. 'Then wind up the cameras.'

Secondary was a much-compacted version of Control, with one long desk holding an array of computer monitors, keyboards, switches and levers, and four large screens on the facing wall through which could be accessed any remote-viewing camera in Coldbrook. The rear wall was home to a schematic of the facility. It showed the circular central core, a hundred feet across and rising the full depth of Coldbrook, and the three main levels that were set around the core. There were digital indicators at door-ways, change of levels and access points to the surface, and it worked as a security map, as well as an indicator of system functionality. Right now it was unlit. Also along the back wall were two rows of chairs. At present they were folded and stacked, and Jonah nodded at them and looked at the guard.

'Can you—?'

'Sure.' The young guard went about opening the chairs, and Jonah took some small comfort from the sub-machine gun slung across his shoulder. There would, with luck, be others here soon, and they'd all need somewhere to sit.

Estelle switched off the alarm, and Jonah sighed in relief.

'Please keep an eye on the door when you've done that,' he said to the guard. 'Don't let anyone in if they don't seem . . .'

'Don't seem what?' the guard said, still placing chairs.

'Just . . . normal.' Uri and Estelle were both looking at Jonah, and he pulled across a chair and sat between them. He was still shaking and breathless from rushing here. The alarm had chased him all the way, and the fear of what was happening, and the certainty that he was to blame. *There are safeguards*, he'd used to think whenever anyone expressed doubts about what they were doing. But safeguards were only as effective as the minds that created them.

'What's happened, Jonah?' Estelle asked.

'Something came through the breach. Holly called me. By the time I got there the alarm was sounding and Control was locked down.' There was so much more to say, but he didn't know where to begin.

'What something? What about the eradicator?'

'A person. And it didn't work.'

'So . . .?' Estelle asked, her professional interest piqued. Jonah glanced at her. They'd known each other for ten years, and she knew without him saying anything that there was worse to come. But her eyes were wide with excitement. He'd been aware of her growing disappointment that there were no obvious signs of human habitation or influence beyond the breach, and now . . .

'I think it was a man,' he said. 'And he killed Melinda. And then Melinda bit Alex Maxwell on the face.'

'She . . .?' Uri said. 'You said it killed her.'

'Melinda?' Estelle gasped. They had been good friends.

'I ran,' Jonah said, remembering the last terrible thing he had seen as he'd torn himself away from the glass wall. Part of him had wanted to stay, hoping that the situation would be resolved and that things would be safe again. But he had already been locked out of Control, and Secondary was the only place for him to go. And even if they did manage to restore calm to the chaotic situation, everything had gone too far. He was aware of the selfishness of his thought, now as he had been then, but he couldn't help it. This place was his life. From the glimpse he'd had down at the breach, it was close to ending.

'But what do you mean—' and then the three of them were talking at once.

'Can we have some order, please!' Jonah said coldly. 'Bring up Control on screens one to three, and the corridor outside the main doors on four.' He glanced at the guard. 'Anyone else coming?'

'No,' he said. 'I thought I heard a scream.' Jonah had often wondered how many of the ex-military guards they employed had killed. He'd never really wanted to know, but now he did. The guard's face was pale, but he was not panicking. Not yet.

'A scream?' Uri whispered.

'Oh my God!' Estelle gasped, because the screens had flickered into life. And it was worse than Jonah could ever have imagined.

Control was smeared and splashed with blood, but he could see only one body: the intruder that had come through the breach. He lay motionless in a wide pool of Melinda's blood just outside the breach boundary. On screen four, a guard lay dead outside the open door to Control.

'Someone's opened the bastard door,' Jonah said softly, his heart pounding. 'Someone's . . .'

'There!' Estelle said. 'Movement, screen three. Look! Can't you zoom in, or . . .?'

Uri worked his control desk expertly and the image on screen three grew. Holly was cowering behind her desk, and Melinda was advancing towards her. She dragged one leg, and it looked loose. Her head and back were a mess, and Jonah shivered, glad that he could not see her face and the damage that the thing had done. A guard was standing behind her, swaying slightly as if he'd been knocked over the head.

'Melinda's not dead,' Uri said. 'But . . .' *But*, Jonah thought. *But indeed*. She trailed a slick of blood behind her, and the back of her lab smock was torn with what appeared to be bullet holes and knife slashes.

'Where's everyone else?' Estelle asked. Jonah could see that she was staring at screen one, where the intruder from beyond the breach could be seen most clearly.

'Who else was down there?' Uri asked.

'Satpal,' Jonah said. 'The standard four guards, including Alex.'

'He's alive!' Estelle said.

On screen four, another guard was getting to his feet, inching slowly up the glass wall until he stood upright. Blood had sprayed the opposite wall and, though it was unclear on the image, Jonah thought he could see a dark mess at the guard's throat. *That's arterial*, he thought. The guard stood with his hands by his sides, not pressed to his wounds. Then he turned and started walking along the corridor towards the camera.

'Fucking hell,' Estelle said.

'His face!' Uri said.

The wounded man passed below the camera, and he was not wearing the expression of someone in pain or close to passing out. Instead, his teeth were bared and his pupils completely dilated. He looked predatory, sharklike. He was barely out of his teens, and the most frightening thing Jonah had ever seen.

'Holly,' Jonah breathed. She stood slowly from behind her desk and looked up at a camera, drew her hand across her throat – and then the last guard remaining in Control ran at her. His uniform was splashed black and torn in several places. He had dropped his gun, and his hands were held out, clawed, in front of him, ready to rip and tear. He leaped onto a desk and jumped over Melinda's head onto another work surface. Holly slammed her hand down onto a button and ran.

Directly at the breach.

'No!' Estelle gasped.

Jonah caught his breath, heart thudding. Her disappearance into the breach was such a simple thing, so soundless and fast, that he was not sure he'd seen it at all. One moment she was there, the next she was gone, and he sat back in his chair and took a deep breath. *Where are you now?* he thought, and though he was not a believer he prayed to something, anything, that she was still alive. Then at least something might be saved from this disaster.

'She'll see it all,' he said. His powerful sob surprised him.

The pursuing guard hit the floor where Holly had crouched moments before and stared after her. He swayed left to right, apelike, as if searching into darkness. Then he tilted his head to one side as though he'd heard something, and ran from Control, a fleeting shadow across screen four as he too disappeared into Coldbrook.

'She's gone through,' Uri said. 'I can't . . . can't access all of Control's sensors to see if . . .'

'I know,' Jonah said. 'But it doesn't matter. She's on her way to another Earth.' He watched Melinda pause in front of the breach, her head raised slightly as if sniffing the air, and then turn away and stagger towards Control's open door. He sighed in relief, glad that she had not followed Holly. Perhaps she had sensed closer prey.

'Holly's on her own through there. And we have to commence lockdown.'

Secondary fell silent as his words sunk in. None of them spoke, all thinking their own thoughts. When no one objected Jonah sobbed again, quieter this time, because of everything they had done.

'Still no one approaching,' the guard said.

From the distance, gunshots. And screams.

'Jonah, this doesn't mean we were wrong,' Estelle said.

'Thank you,' he said, and he had never meant the words so sincerely. 'Now, Uri, if you'd prepare the lockdown orders, I think I should initiate it myself, and I'll remain here to ensure it's worked. You all go and find somewhere safer. I'll see you on the screens.' He nodded up at the view of Control, free of all movement now apart from Melinda's shuffling figure. 'I'll join you later.'

Uri nodded and started tapping some keys.

'Sir, you don't have to stay on your own,' the guard said.

'I appreciate that,' Jonah said. 'But that's what I'd rather. And these two will need you to protect them. Secondary was never designed to be a refuge. I have to lock down and tell the surface what's happening. We need to let people know. And then . . .'

'And then?' Estelle asked.

Jonah shrugged. And then? He didn't know. Their absolute priority was to stop any danger reaching the surface. Beyond that, he could not yet think.

He closed his eyes. He was old, and that was fine, and he had lived a life. But others in this place had people up there, many of them living in the nearest town, Danton Rock: wives, husbands, kids.

Like Vic Pearson. A family.

And then Jonah wondered where the hell Vic Pearson had gone.

'Uri, quickly,' he said. '*Quickly!*'

Uri worked fast, and half a minute later he slid the wireless keyboard across to Jonah. 'Hit enter to initiate automatic lockdown. You can monitor all lockdown procedures – or switch it to manual – on the schematic behind you.'

'Thank you,' Jonah said. But he didn't look up as they left, and was glad that none of them offered a final comment. As they closed the door he pressed enter, and Coldbrook began closing itself off from the only world any of them knew.

8

As Vic entered the vehicle garage he heard a distant shout, and then a noise like doves cooing. He paused, pressed flat against the wall with his head tilted to one side. Had he *really* heard that? Birds, underground? He couldn't be sure – there wasn't even an echo now. He released his held breath, the sigh making the garage's silence seem even more eerie.

There were three vehicles in the large garage area – two SUVs and a military Hummer – and the smell of fuel and spilled oil hung in the air. For a moment the idea of taking an SUV crossed his mind, but he knew that the wide door at the far end of the garage was always kept electronically locked, and that on the slowly curving ramp that rose two hundred feet to the surface there were three other security doors.

He had criticised several times Coldbrook's design, suggesting that there should be at least two independent escape routes to the surface in case of an accident. To begin with, Jonah had reasoned with him – nothing would go wrong, they were cautious when they built it, there was no risk. But after a while he had simply chosen to respond with the stark truth: if the core was ever breached, none of them would have to worry about escape.

Vic could open the doors on the vehicle ramp but it would take time. And, of the escape routes he'd considered as he made his way here, it was the most observed and the least likely to be successful.

He had somewhere quicker in mind.

'So long as they don't go for complete lockdown,' he whispered to himself, listening again for more voices, and deciding it must have been his own guilt calling after him. He looked around the garage, checking for movement or the dark blue of a guard's uniform. He was sure that he was alone, and since the alarm had switched off he'd started to wonder just how serious the situation was. If they had it contained in Control, it wasn't certain that Jonah would seek to lock down the whole facility, because if he did—

Vic . . . something came through.

'Shit.' Vic shook his head and checked his palmtop. The camera view of Control showed no activity now. He switched back to the thumbnail views and saw a flash of movement in one of the accommodation corridors. The image was too small to make out any detail, and by the time he enlarged it whatever had moved was gone. But . . .

Blood on the wall – and his own ran cold.

He switched programs to the schematics of Coldbrook that he'd stored on the computer. He was responsible for the maintenance and adjustment of the unique core containment and, in turn, the breach generator. But he'd made sure that he knew as much as possible about the rest of the facility. He'd never really believed that something would go so catastrophically wrong, but it was always good to be prepared.

Holly, he thought, but he tried to blink her away.

Vic shifted the plans on his palmtop screen. Behind the garage lay one of the three main plant rooms serving the facility, this one dedicated to the air-conditioning systems. Every single external access point would be affected by a lockdown, but if he was fast enough now maybe—

From the main door across the garage he heard the click and snap of metal. He dashed between the Hummer and an SUV and watched from there. He should have known what was happening from the first instant, but his mind was fogged by the stark fact of his betrayal. He was running just when Jonah needed him most, and if he dwelled on that for more than a second he felt physically sick. So he did not dwell on it at all. He focused on Lucy and Olivia.

Across the garage a wisp of smoke rose from the huge door's securing mechanisms as they melted into lockdown. The smell of burning filled the air, and the acrid whiff of hot metal. The clicks and clanks of warping locks echoed through the space. Vic had always thought such a process was overdramatic, and that secured locking of the exits would be enough in any emergency. But his boss had always been keen on his safeguards.

Jonah's started! he thought, and he ran for the doors to the air-conditioning room. Once inside he consulted the palmtop again, then dashed for the largest duct that led up through the mountain. There was a maintenance-access point at the base of the duct, sealed with three coded locks. He tapped in the codes and breathed a sigh of relief when he heard the quiet clicks of release.

The metal duct was a little over five feet wide, with a vertical ladder bolted into the inner wall. Vic pulled a head torch from his tool belt and flicked it on, securing it on his forehead before beginning the climb. He went as fast as he could, knowing that he would tire quickly but desperate to get as high as possible before lockdown of the duct commenced. The idea that he might become trapped in here had not even crossed his mind: concern for his family drove him on, and he had confidence in his ability to bypass any secured barriers.

As he climbed he wondered what was going on down below. He knew so little, and that made the fear stronger, a sense that the vast extent of the facility was loaded with threat. Once he was out and with his family he would use the satphone to find out what was happening.

75

Jonah would hate him for running. And Vic was certain that the old man wouldn't even understand. But they had worked together for eight years and he was confident that Jonah would talk to him.

As he approached the first of the duct's three fire dampers – an automatic divider that would double as a security barrier during a facility lockdown – it started sliding shut. He speeded up but was too late, reaching the damper just as it snicked closed and its internal mechanisms started overheating and warping. He winced at the acidic odour of superheated metal, but being poisoned was just something else to be afraid of.

So this would be when he'd test how good he was. There were three dampers in the vertical duct to make his way past, all of them now probably sealed shut. Beyond that, he would have to open the surface hatch from the inside and then sneak past the compound guards. And then he'd have to run a mile across the dark mountainside to Danton Rock, and his family. Perhaps once he got there he might allow himself a few seconds to relish the fact of his escape.

Vic braced himself on the ladder, and as he caught his breath he consulted the Palm Pilot. The best way past the barrier was around, not through it. As he plucked items from his tool belt, his satphone started chiming. He plucked it from his pocket and glanced at the screen: Jonah. He turned it off and set to work.

It took three minutes to create the necessary opening in the duct wall and start on the still-hot damper mechanism, and another two minutes to dismount the mechanism itself. Vic twisted and slid it out of sight on top of the damper, then squeezed through the gap. It was a tight fit. His tool belt caught and caused him a moment of panic, but then he was through. Two more to get past, and fifty feet of climbing in between. He hoped to be out of Coldbrook and into the cool night air within fifteen minutes.

He slid the mechanism back into place to block the opening, a fresh surge of guilt making him feel queasy again. And as he climbed, Coldbrook pulled at him, with its terrible gravity and the implications of what they had done there. He resisted, sweat running down his sides and teeth gritted against the pain in his arms and legs. He wasn't used to physical exertion. They had a small gym down in the living quarters – a few treadmills and exercise bikes squeezed into an unused suite – but it was rare that he spent any time in there. Vic was naturally skinny, but that didn't mean he was fit. He regretted his laziness now.

The second damper took longer to get past, and the third one longer still. Maybe it was exhaustion, or panic, but the head torch started slipping on his sweaty skin, and he dropped three screwdrivers back down the duct. He held on tightly to the fourth – it was his last. Drop that one and he'd have to climb back down to retrieve it . . . he was starting to fear that Coldbrook would never let him out. It had its claws in him, and Jonah had called him four more times. He was tempted to answer and find out exactly what was going on, but he had gained a momentum now. Jonah's voice might be enough to change his mind. *Ignorant old bastard*, Vic thought, surprised at the affection he suddenly felt for the old man. He hoped Jonah was safe.

And Holly. But he was trying not to think of her, and when she did cross his mind it felt as though she was strangely far away.

As Vic climbed, he tried to ignore the fact that he was leaving an open route behind him. He shoved the mechanisms back into the openings he'd crawled through, though he could not secure them again from above. *Jonah will lock it all down*, he kept thinking, a mantra to persuade himself that security would be maintained. And he willingly let panic conceal the illogicality of that idea. What was ahead mattered more.

Reaching the head of the duct, he squatted on the small maintenance platform and started immediately to undo the access hatch that led outside, working quietly in case the compound guards were nearby. His nostrils stung with the acrid stink of melted metal and plastics, his hands shook from exertion, and for the last fifty rungs of the ladder he'd been desperate to breathe in the air outside the duct, a desperation that had grown the higher he climbed. He tried to calm himself, but as he scrambled out of the hatch and dropped into the cool night he sobbed.

The grass was damp and cool, the fresh air a gentle caress across his sweat-soaked clothing. Above Vic a thousand stars speckled the sky, all of them ancient history. To the east a smudge of light smeared the summits of the mountains as dawn began to break. The compound was quiet, motionless. He quickly flicked off his head torch, cursing his clumsiness, and ran crouching to the corner of a low supply building.

Does anyone up here even know what's happening? he wondered. The only reason that they would not know was if Jonah was too busy to have informed them. Or if he was . . .

For a second Vic thought again of calling Jonah. But not yet. He wasn't away *yet*. When he reached home and saw Lucy and Olivia, then he would allow himself that call.

Right now he had to run.

9

As Holly fled into the breach she thought of the man who had come through, and wondered whether he had been like her when he'd stepped past the threshold. She could see through – the dark valley, shadows of plants and boulders across the hillside, the red sky brightening as the sun slowly rose – but that didn't mean it was as close as it seemed. Distance and direction were concepts that lost meaning in the science of the breach. *It's exactly where we are and a trillion light years away*, Jonah had whispered once as they'd sat drinking and musing upon their efforts. Maybe now, she would be walking for ever.

And then she felt the breach's clasp.

Holly would have gasped, had she still been breathing. Her legs moved and her arms swung by her sides, but it felt like the processes of her body were frozen in the moment. Her skin chilled, as if it had been exposed to an open freezer. Thoughts jumped and scattered, formed and shattered: perhaps this was how everyone felt at the moment of death.

A slew of random memories erupted all at once, each of them richer in tone and sense than memory should normally allow. Holly at four years old, making mud pies in the back garden with her brother Angus, parents looking on with indulgent smiles, the wet soil warm between her fingers, the smell of dirt. The time in school when she had told her friends that she was seeing Ashley, the boy who'd been the object of her desires for months; their jealousy, and her certainty that the relationship would be short and precious. Her drunken eighteenth birthday when her mother had cleaned up her vomit and gently chided her, then sat on her bed and reminisced about her own youth for an hour while Holly sobbed herself to sleep, the acid smell, of puke tingeing the air. A long afternoon in college when the sun shone and she was filled with an unaccountable sense of joy; the death of her mother, withered and faded yet still smiling; one mealtime at Coldbrook when Vic had smiled at her and she'd truly noticed him for the first time, burning her finger with the coffee she'd spilled.

And many more memories came and went, each of them so intense that she relived them all again, crying and laughing, smelling and tasting, sighing with pleasure and cringing in pain. Then the brief yet endless moment of pause passed and she ran on, swinging her arms through air that felt heavy with potential. She experienced a momentary tug as the world she was leaving urged her back, and then the sensation suddenly shifted and she was drawn forward. She was aware of every movement of her body, every muscle stretching and contracting, and the first touch of somewhere else brought the smell of spicy heather and the taste of cool fresh air.

What was that? she thought, the scientist in her trying to make sense of what had just happened to her, and why. But Holly ran on. It was a few seconds before she realised that tall wet grass was whipping at her trouser legs, and that her boots were impacting on soft ground, not the uncertain hardness of the breach. She skidded to a halt, and when she blinked she saw red. She gasped in fear and fell onto her back, kicking out at anyone or anything that might have followed her through. But she was alone. Melinda's bloodied face was not staring at her, and the guard's ravenous jaws were no longer gaping at the thought of rending her flesh.

Tears burned in her eyes but she wiped them away. She was shaking. Holding up her hand, she saw that it was jittering uncontrollably, and she clamped her mouth shut to stop her teeth from chattering. *I'm through*, she thought, and what had happened so recently in Control began to retreat into the realms of memory. Holly welcomed the dimming of the terror.

Perhaps the dawning sense of wonder was drowning it out.

She closed her eyes and stood still, holding her breath, hearing her heart thudding and blood pulsing. *I'm elsewhere*, she thought, and she breathed out and inhaled again, slowly. Definitely heather, wet and somehow spiced, and below that she could smell damp soil and something like old chocolate. She held out her hands and felt a brief misty rain cooling her skin. She stuck out her tongue and tasted moisture on the air, frowning as the tang of something unknown played across her taste buds. She didn't like it, but perhaps only because it was a mystery.

Silence hung around her.

And then she opened her eyes and gazed upon this distant Earth. She saw trees and grasses and plants and hillsides, and a stream running through the small valley, and a sky smeared with the gorgeous colours of an extravagant dawn. The alienness was staggering.

Holly looked for anything she might recognise – Coldbrook's structure, its surface buildings, or the Appalachian mountain landscape that surrounded it. Even if she saw something familiar and identical to how it appeared on her Earth, counterpart theory suggested that it could only be regarded as similar, a separate form of the same object. But what she saw was unfamiliar, and though she could not pin down why, it seemed wild.

'I'm somewhere else . . .' she gasped, aware that these could be the first words ever spoken here.

This could have been a place on her Earth, but her knowledge that it was not hit hard. The small valley was home to several types of plants, not all of them completely familiar. Higher up the valley a clump of black oaks hid darkness beneath them, and closer to her a single tree bore what might have been apple blossom. The heather she could smell was soft and silky to the touch, but the flowers were unfamiliar, and Holly was not sure she'd ever seen their like before. The stream gurgled merrily by to her left, whispering past rocks protruding from its bed, and a thousand small plants grew along its bank on tripod-like stalks. They unnerved her. They seemed to be waiting for something.

Dawn was peering over the hillside to her right. The colours were stunning, smears of yellow and orange merging into a deeper red higher up, though the clouds must have been high indeed, because she could not make out any texture to the sky. High up, a few hawks circled slowly on morning thermals.

A fly landed on the back of her hand. She studied it, the first time she'd seen a living insect from this world, and did not recognise it as any of those caught by the eradicator. And prompted by this thought she turned around again to see from where she had emerged.

The breach sat in a hollow in the hillside, a fresh wound in the land. Shards of stone and clumps of soil were scattered around the hollow, and the breach itself existed as a vaguely wavering smudge of light ten feet across, opaque and mysterious. Holly squinted, but could not see within. There was no framing to it on this side, and she remembered Jonah saying something about it mirroring itself in the target area. It held a hypnotic power. She closed her eyes and a staggering loneliness hit her. Would she ever be able to go back through? *Could* she?

She muttered to herself, 'What have I done?' She looked up at the brightening sky, stars still just visible but fading quickly, half-moon sitting low above the valley.

Satpal had so wanted to see the alternate world's stars. She tried to spot a constellation she knew, but there were too few now, and she looked away, afraid of seeing nothing, afraid that—

Something called softly. She turned back to the breach, terrified that Melinda had come through. But there was no movement there, and when the call came again she looked up at the hawks, swooping now instead of circling.

'Gaia,' she said. The breach was too close. Terror had already stepped between worlds. She could not stay here.

Holly started walking. She followed the stream and aimed for one of the ridge lines. From there she hoped she would have a good view across the surrounding countryside. She had no idea what she would see. As she went she assessed what she had come through with, and it was not much. The clothing she wore – casual shirt, trousers, boots, none of it heavyweight. There were two pens in her pocket, and her satphone. She checked it: no signal. She gave a short bark of laughter: of course not. As she walked, she checked behind her regularly. She kept her eyes peeled for movement because she knew for sure that this world was inhabited. The man who had come through had brought some unknown, sickening danger with him, and now she was stranded in *his* world. She would have to be careful every step of the way.

The loneliness was constant and bruising, and several

times she found herself singing childhood songs under her breath as she climbed over rocks, skirted marshy areas of ground, and passed into a heavily wooded area. Her clothes were damp from the earlier misty rain, but she was not too cold. *What will happen when I do get too cold?* she thought. *Or if I fall and break my ankle? Or if I get lost and can't find my way back here?* At the back of her mind was the idea that she was still within reach of home, however different the breach looked from this side, and however terrible, however *unbelievable* the events that had happened in Control. She would have to give them time to get some kind of order restored and perhaps then they'd send someone through to find her. But the ridge and whatever might lie beyond beckoned, and she could not ignore the call.

'Just be careful,' Holly whispered to herself.

As she climbed slowly out of the small valley, dawn brought this new world – this Gaia – to life around her. Crickets scratched in the grasses and heather, birds welcomed in the dawn from the tree canopy with songs she knew and some she did not, and a muted sunlight touched the hilltop above her. She emerged from the woodland onto a bare slope, still in the opposite ridge's shadow, but a growing feeling of warmth was close and inviting.

A few hundred feet from the ridge she passed into sunlight and turned to stare back at the sun. It was a yellow smudge against the clouds, still splaying exotic colours across much of the sky before her. She'd never seen such a gorgeous sunrise. Looking back down along the valley she could still just make out the shimmer of the breach, a slightly blurred area against the valley floor. It was the only familiar sight in this new world, and she was keen to keep it in view.

Holly had left the stream behind now and was climbing directly for the ridgeline. The closer it drew the faster she moved, spurred on by the thought that she was the first person from her Earth to witness this world. The sunlight felt both familiar and shatteringly alien across the back of her neck, like a surprise kiss from a stranger. *That's* our *sun*, she thought, but of course that was not quite true. She had already seen, and felt, and smelled this world's subtle differences, and witnessed the horror of a more extreme divergence. There really was no telling how unlike her own planet it might be.

There might be mountains up here, she thought, *or lakes, or cities or ruins, or something unrecognisable.* And when at last she reached the top of the ridge and stood staring out over the vista ahead of her it took her breath away.

The mountains stretched to the horizon, as they did at home, and beyond the valley the landscape was more familiar. The muted sunlight bathed its features, forest and bare slopes alike, and the darker depths of the valleys could have held any number of mysteries. What disturbed Holly so much was the mystery of what might lie beyond them.

Exhausted, scared and feeling more lost and alone than ever before, she managed to walk a dozen steps to a small mound of rocks. Here she sat, leaning back with her eyes closed to catch her breath. The breeze was stronger up here, and it was fresh and untainted by the tang of industry. *That doesn't mean anything*, she thought, and she pictured that shuffling, monstrous thing once again. She opened her eyes and stared directly at the sun. She'd never been able to do that at home. The whole sky was tinted a faint pink. *Maybe this sun is dying*, she thought, and she wished Jonah were here to tell her why that might or might not be possible. The last time she'd seen him was when he'd been pressed against the glass wall, his face slackened by hopelessness as he watched events unfolding in Control. She looked into the valley as if those things had happened down there, but the breach was hidden from her now by the curve in the hillside.

'I'm so far away,' she said, her voice surprisingly loud. She rested her elbows on her knees, her head on her forearms, and then she saw the single word carved into a smooth rock at her feet.

Exit.

The word seemed to pin Holly to the rocks. She

glanced to the left, and saw that another of the seemingly random stones had a sharp, regular edge. She hadn't
looked for it before, but now she could see.

Exit.

She heard movement behind her, sliding, slithering,
skin over wet stone. And as she stumbled from her perch
and turned around she realised that she was not alone.
The thing was rising from beneath thick vegetation atop
the stones, lifting through twisted roots, parting leaves.
It looked old and withered, similar to the man in Control,
except this being had once been a woman. And she wore
the scrappy remnants of clothes.

As the gaunt thing reached out something flicked at
Holly's hair, whistling past her ear, and an arrow buried
itself in the woman's face.

Sunday

1

Just before dawn on the day when the world changed for ever, Jayne Woodhams wished that she could die. For her it was not an unusual thought, and neither was the anger that followed.

'Okay, babe,' Tommy said. 'It's okay.' And she groaned some more because it never was.

Dawn made the Knoxville skyline beautiful. Their second-floor apartment looked out over Fort Dickerson Park, and the Appalachian Mountains were silhouetted against the sky by the new day emerging from beyond. Such beauty sometimes held Jayne entranced and gave her every reason to live, but some mornings – like this one – it passed her by. The first pains of the day forbade beauty, and today the agony seemed worse than usual.

Tommy knelt beside her on the bed. He'd thrown back the covers even as she stirred, and now he was slowly massaging her feet and lower legs, working the feeling back in, pressing away the nightly muscle paralysis that her condition brought on. A year ago they'd seen a consultant in Cleveland who'd told her to wake every hour and exercise for five minutes. That had reduced the pain by maybe a fifth, but she spent her life exhausted, and the tiredness brought on a more fiery discomfort later in the day. Two years before that, a herbalist in Nashville had prescribed a paste to be applied to her worst-affected parts every night before bed. For three weeks Tommy had followed the herbalist's instructions, mixing the gloop and smearing it across her lower legs and knees, elbows, shoulders and hips. There had been no obvious change, and at the beginning of the fourth week Tommy had shown her the weeping sores between his fingers from where he was having an allergic reaction to something in the paste. Medicines, muscle relaxants, hypnosis, acupuncture, a hydrotherapy bath, and more: they had gone from consultant to doctor to quack in their search for something that would ease her pain. And, in the end, they had learned to trust themselves.

Jayne slept badly, woke in agony, and Tommy was

there every morning to massage her back to life. In the last six years, since she was sixteen and he fifteen, there had been perhaps twenty mornings when he had not been there to welcome in the dawn – and its pain – with her. His devotion had precluded college, and a job which meant frequent travelling, and he had settled into an easy, unfulfilling office job just so that he could be with her. She'd protested every step of the way, but her protestations made him angrier than she had ever seen him. They had soon stopped. *I've never done anything I didn't want to do*, he'd told her, as if that made the limiting of his life for the sake of hers more acceptable.

She felt his hands moving up towards her knees and winced in readiness.

'Knees now. Ready?'

'No.'

'Here we go.'

'Touch me there and I'll fucking kill you, you fucking torturer.'

'Big talk.' Tommy started working the area around her knees with his fingertips, a steady pressure to start with, growing harder and stronger as he plumbed the depths of her pain.

Jayne gritted her teeth, but she had long ago given up trying to hold back her tears.

Though treatment of her condition had varied with everyone she had consulted, at least three doctors had agreed upon a name: *churu*. One of them told her he had never seen a case, and that when he researched it he found only sixteen recorded cases. He said he was surprised it even *had* a name. It was a condition of the brain and nervous system. No one knew where it originated, or why it happened. Of the previous sixteen cases, the oldest to die had been a man in Argentina – at the ripe old age of twenty-six.

'I'm going to rip your fucking *head* off!' she growled as Tommy ground his thumbs around the tops of her knees. She had never loved him so much.

Tommy, grim-faced as ever at the pain he caused, worked on while Jayne lived through it. It usually took half an hour before she could sit up on her own, but this morning she felt stiffer than usual, and even flexing her arms and turning her head sent bolts of pain through her body. The sun would be up and the streets outside buzzing before she felt even half-human.

After her knees, he moved on to her hips, grinning as he pulled up her nightshirt.

'Helpless before me,' he cackled, running his hands up her inner thighs.

Jayne kneed him in the side, grimacing at the flaring pain but finding his gasp worth it. 'Later, slave,' she said, 'if you perform your duties well.' She settled again, hips on fire, legs now merely simmering after Tommy's ministrations, but she could never feel angry at him. Not after what he had done. He was a young guy devoted to a young woman in an old woman's body, a woman who could sometimes barely walk, who could well be dead in the next few years. Every morning she woke up and wished for death, and Tommy was there to save her life.

'Thought we could go down to the park later,' he said, working his thumbs across her hip bones as his fingers pressed beneath. 'Picnic, couple of books, bottle of wine.'

'Feeling all horny now you've spent half an hour touching me up?'

'Always horny,' Tommy said.

Jayne frowned as he worked harder around her hips, but as his hands moved on the pain was lessening to a background glow, and movement returned. It was as if he brought her back to the world every morning, and sometimes she laughed at people's perception of their relationship. Everyone saw Jayne as the strong one – the sufferer, the fighter – but Tommy was the rock to which she clung.

'Park sounds good,' she said.

He sat back on his haunches and she saw the beads of sweat on his brow. He swept his long hair back from his face, blinking faster, and she knew he wanted to get finished.

'I'll do my shoulders,' she said.

'Sure?' He pretended to be hurt, but she could read him so well. He never complained, but that didn't mean that he enjoyed this morning ritual. She could hardly blame him. And she saw, and understood the need. *He* was her addiction.

'Sure.' She reached up with her left hand and started massaging her right shoulder, biting back a gasp at the pain it caused her. No one could tell her why the churu affected muscles around joints more than anywhere else. One of the more honest consultants had said that it was such a rare disease. Certainly no one really knew much about it, and no one was willing to spend the money to research it. He'd finished with, *If what you're doing works for you, keep doing it*.

Well, fuck them.

'Okay,' Tommy said, standing beside the bed, stretching, watching her, when all he really wanted right then was to go out into the small kitchen. 'Well, I'll have a smoke, then.'

'Okay. Thanks, babe.'

'Don't call me babe.' He delivered the familiar line with the usual sternness, then breezed through to their kitchen. Moments later Jayne heard the scratch of a match and Tommy's satisfied sigh, and soon after that the first whiff of pot hit her. *He's started rolling them ready the night before and he'll have two before we leave the apartment*, she thought. But she couldn't judge him. It was only pot.

She worked at her shoulders, left and right, and soon

she would be able to rise, shower and dress. Sunday was her favourite day.

2

It was vital that Jonah should alert the surface about what was happening. He was berating himself for not having done so sooner. Those afflicted – or infected, which was how he was viewing them now – were secure down here with Coldbrook closed down, but the news must be broken.

The project's influence spread across the globe. Two thick tentacles reached out to the US and UK governments, their funding for Coldbrook hidden away through complex paths of finance and banking, two-decade-old signatures on yellowing sheets of paper in files in locked storerooms, and his call would reach those countries' security agencies in a matter of minutes. And then there were links that were less substantial finance-wise though perhaps stronger in their commitment. These led to private individuals and organisations, ranging from billionaire entrepreneurs who gifted their money to fund their appetite for amazing things to oil barons and shareholding companies with high-risk portfolios, their real object hidden from bond holders by an almost insanely intricate web of investments.

Jonah's call would cause a huge splash, and that splash

would make waves. By the time he hung up, people across the world would be woken, called out of meetings or interrupted on their yachting holidays to be told that Coldbrook's recent astounding success had been followed by catastrophic failure. Jonah knew of the safeguards in place down here because he had insisted on many of them himself. But he had no idea what measures had been set up beyond these walls and a thousand miles away. His call might piss off investors or start an avalanche of military intervention, and he would have influence over neither outcome.

I'm going to die and stay down here for ever, he thought. But, right now, for ever did not concern him unduly.

Satphone in hand, he swivelled in his chair and briefly examined the schematic on the wall behind him. Yellow lights indicated where internal lockdown measures had taken place, and the light over Control's door was blinking. Failure. But Satpal's escape was no longer important. What *was* important were the red lights, showing Coldbrook's outer containment. All remained steady but one: a ventilation duct.

That one also blinked.

Jonah stood up from his chair and walked closer. His eyes weren't what they used to be and perhaps they were watering, causing the image to flicker. But no: the light was flashing. He tapped the vent reference code into his laptop and read the information presented there. All three dampers had been closed and their mechanisms destroyed, as expected.

'Malfunction,' he muttered looking back at the light. 'Melting caused a short. Has to be.' But he had not seen Vic Pearson on any screen, in any room, dead or alive – or walking the line between.

'Vic, I hope you haven't done something stupid,' Jonah said, and he dialled Coldbrook's above-ground administration and guard block. The call rang several times before it was answered.

'Asleep on the job?' Jonah asked as soon as he heard the click of connection.

'Not at all, no,' a voice said, flustered. 'Who is this?'

'Jonah Jones. Is that Rick Summerfield?'

'Yes, professor. Er . . . it's early.' Jonah felt a shred of relief. Summerfield was a manager rather than a scientist, but he and Jonah had always seen eye to eye, and he possessed that spark of imagination and wonder that made him a true part of Coldbrook like many others. He saw not just an experiment but something more meaningful. Jonah closed his eyes.

'You haven't seen that we're in lockdown?' he asked.

'What? Why? There's nothing . . . hold on.' Jonah heard keyboard keys being tapped and the rustle of Summerfield pulling on headphones. 'We're showing nothing. All boards clear up here.'

'It doesn't matter,' Jonah said. He knew that the small

surface compound – four buildings, a car park and a perimeter fence – was linked into Coldbrook's network, but something must have gone wrong. He didn't know how recently the systems up there had been checked, and the ongoing endless modernisation of the facility's IT equipment often favoured the subterranean area where the real work was done.

Unsettled, Jonah watched the three flashing LEDs as he continued. 'Rick, something came through.'

'What something?'

'It doesn't matter. Patch in to email and I'll send you what you need to see. But . . . we have to sound the alarm. You have the protocols, a list of who to contact.'

'Yes, I have it here. But the breach was stable! Everyone's probably still celebrating, Jonah.'

'Something came through. People are dead. Maybe everyone.' There was no response to this, only a shocked gasp. 'Except . . . before you do that, I need you to check the ventilation-duct housing on the services block.'

'Why?'

'I can't find Vic Pearson. I'm afraid he might have made a break for it.'

'It's fine,' Summerfield said. 'I can see the cover from here, it's intact, and Vic wouldn't—'

'Will you just check the bastard for me!' Jonah said, anger creeping into his voice. It was shock and grief that were causing it and he reined it in. 'Sorry, Rick. Please check. For this old Welshman.'

'Okay, hold on.' He heard mumbling in the background as Summerfield used a walkie-talkie, then he was back online. 'Moore's going to look right now.'

'It's a contagion,' Jonah said. 'Something I've never seen before. Never imagined. I'll send the info but access the security cameras for the last hour, if you can. You'll see. All of them. It's horrible.' He trailed off, shaking his head as if Summerfield were in the room and could see him.

'Jonah?'

'All of them, dead – but not lying down.' And he had stated the truth of it at last, though he could not understand.

'That doesn't make sense.'

'I know.'

'Melinda? Satpal? Holly?'

'No,' Jonah whispered. He sat down and stared at the breach on the screen. *What's she doing now, and where, and is it even* now *for her?* 'Not Holly. She went through the breach.'

'Holy shit,' Summerfield said.

'I know. Wherever she is now—'

'I can see Moore at the duct housing,' Summerfield cut in. 'He touched the maintenance hatch and it fell off. It's open, Jonah.'

Vic, Jonah thought, *what the hell have you done?* But he knew. Vic Pearson had stayed true to everything he believed in – his family.

'Close it,' Jonah said urgently. 'Rick, seal that hatch, weld it, bury it in fucking concrete but—'

'Oh, hang on. Someone's . . .'

'Rick?'

'It's . . . it's okay, it's Alex. He looks—'

'Rick!' Jonah shouted. 'Tell Moore to get back, tell him—'

Jonah heard the distant rattle of gunfire, and then silence, and then Rick Summerfield screamed, 'Oh my fucking Christ.'

'Rick? Rick!' But Rick had gone. Jonah closed his eyes but he couldn't think straight. *Got to contain it, keep them in, maintain the perimeter*. Already he could hear the static-filled thumping and smashing of glass, as somewhere directly above him the disease spread itself.

He disconnected, but kept hold of the satphone. After so many congratulatory phone calls over the past three days, he would now be the one to spread the devastating news. 'Contagion,' he said, practising the word again, and then he dialled.

After breaking the news to three key people on three continents, Jonah switched off the satphone and watched another friend die. Though he tried to he could not close his eyes. He saw Andy tripped and then pushed against a wall in the electrical plant room, arms thrashing at the mutilated guard holding him there, Motörhead T-shirt slashed and torn and darkened with his blood, eyes wide with panic and terror and disbelief as the guard pressed forward and closed his mouth on Andy's nose and ripped his head to the side . . . and Jonah could not close his eyes. Here was his legacy, in blood. Here was the result of everything he had thrown himself into for years. The guard bit again and again, and then moved away to let Andy slump to the floor, dead.

It was only as Andy shoved himself upright again, half a minute later, that Jonah looked away.

The temptation to turn off the viewing screens was great. In his seventy-six years he had seen two dead bodies: his dear wife Wendy, prepared and laid to rest, her hair brushed the wrong way and her visage so painfully, terribly still; and Bill Coldbrook, his old friend and boss, whom Jonah had discovered hours after his suicide. Death was no stranger to him, yet it had always been distant.

But he berated himself for his cowardice. He was responsible for Coldbrook, and he had a responsibility for almost forty staff members down here, from the most talented scientist to the canteen cook. He *had* to keep watching the screens to see who would survive and where they would find shelter. After that . . . he did not know.

Jonah kept two of the four screens focused on Control, one zoomed in on the breach, the other encompassing the whole room. It was a dead place. Since he'd locked himself in Secondary fifteen minutes ago he had seen no movement there, though his attention flickered back to those screens every few seconds, drawn by the breach. It looked so harmless. So benign.

What had come through now lay dead on the floor of Control, one of the few motionless bodies he could find. Others, like Andy, moved on, perpetuating the violence and hunting down those as yet untouched. Shocked and confused though he was, Jonah was a scientist, someone who had always retained his sense of wonder. And already he was analysing what he was seeing.

The bites stopped them, they fell, and then they rose again, usually within a minute. The infection – because that was what it had to be – changed them. *Kills them*, he kept thinking, but he was not certain of that yet. Not definite. *Melinda, Satpal* . . . He shook his head. Perhaps the infection dulled pain receptors, did something to their sense of self, and drove them on through pain to . . .

'Jesus,' Jonah muttered, because it seemed the horror would never end. There were no microphones on the facility cameras and silence made the carnage more shocking somehow. The picture flickered and settled on the canteen, apparently still and peaceful until a naked man pulled himself up on one of the dining tables, his throat a ragged mess, his chest scored by scratch marks, and ran quickly from the room.

The image flicked to the kitchen. There was no one there and no movement, and then there was a thrashing at one edge of the screen, someone moving just out of shot, their shadow thrown across the room by harsh fluorescents, and a spray of blood splashed across the previously pristine food-preparation surface.

The large garage area: unsettlingly still, three big vehicles sitting like soldiers awaiting orders. He scanned the image, trying to work out what was wrong with what he saw but unable to find anything. *Just that it's so still.*

One of the accommodation hallways: no movement, but a heavy smear of blood along one wall, and something that looked like bloody clothing piled against a closed door. Jonah counted three out of eight doors that were still closed. There were no cameras inside the rooms. Invasion of privacy. He wished he could reach through and knock on those doors, but if there was anyone inside left alive they would surely not answer.

A second accommodation hallway: and the shock of what he saw made him flinch back in his seat. At the far end of the hallway, thirty feet from the camera, bodies thrashed and fought, maybe seven or eight of them. He saw the flash of several gunshots and one body flipped back. A man leaned from a doorway and aimed down at the body, shooting three more times. He retreated back into the room and the light changed as the door slammed, and then the body stood again and started throwing itself against the door. Its chest was a ragged mess. It wore a nightdress, and Jonah thought its foot had been torn apart until he realised it was a fluffy rabbit slipper.

Jonah changed views to a storeroom close to the gym. Estelle and Uri were huddled together in a corner, the guard who'd left with them crouching behind the locked door. Jonah could see their careful movements to ease pressure on bent limbs, their heavy breathing as fear refused to loosen its grip on them. Uri glanced up at the camera, then back at Estelle. He was holding her tightly. She held him too. Uri used to juggle during his lunch breaks to settle his nervous disposition, and Estelle had a quotation handy for most occasions. Jonah wondered what she would come up with for this one but he could see that she was silent.

He checked the list of camera locations displayed on the laptop before him and entered a code for the fourth screen. It was a view of the short storage-area corridor, and it was full of dead people.

Dead people, Jonah thought. *Is that right? How can they be dead? They're not fucking zombies, so they must be . . .?* But he had seen the damage inflicted on some of these people. Even if they *were* infected with a contagion that subdued pain and turned them into berserkers, they could not function drained of blood, or with shredded muscles or cracked bones, or—

Leave that for later, he thought.

There were seven people in the corridor and all of them were standing still. Their wounds flickered slightly on-screen: wet, open, but no longer bleeding. He knew all their names but tried not to think of them. They seemed to be listening, waiting. They knew what was behind the door.

In the storeroom, the guard seemed to be whispering to Uri and Estelle. Jonah wished he could hear, because he had a terrible sense of what was about to happen.

How the hell can I speak to them? he wondered. He tapped at the laptop, bringing up schematics of the facility and turning around to view them on the large wall behind him. He glanced at some of the folding chairs the guard had opened up, thought, *There should be people sitting there now*, and then tried to concentrate. Fire alarm? Lighting system? Anything he could control from here to give them warning, because the guard was growing impatient.

Jonah thought he might open the door.

'Damn it, *damn* it!' His heart fluttered and he coughed, and he cursed his *advancing years*. He'd never thought of himself as infirm, though he had never been one to deny the onset of age. Now, though, he wished he were a younger man. A younger man might leave the room with a makeshift weapon – a chair leg, or a strut from beneath the table – and try to fight his way down one level to the storeroom, stop whatever was about to happen. But Jonah didn't think his heart would take it.

Besides, his was a greater responsibility. He glanced at the breach again and guilt weighed heavy on him. All that planning and all those precautions – and Control's lockdown had still failed.

On the screen, the guard rested his hand on the door handle. Uri was shaking one hand at him, leaning forward to speak in his ear, but Estelle held him back, not wishing to relinquish contact. The guard waved them away without even looking. In his right hand he held his sub-machine gun, aimed directly at the door.

On the next screen there was a shimmer of movement through the assembled bloodied people, as if the picture had skipped several frames.

'No!' Jonah screamed. 'Leave the door alone!' It was a cry of impotence, a useless gesture, and he was not used to such things. His blood raged, and he clenched his fists and thumped the desk as the guard worked the handle.

The sudden movement on the next screen was startling. Any suspicion that Jonah had about them waiting together as a group vanished instantly when all seven people surged at the door. They clawed past each other, shoving, thrusting forward, and on the storeroom screen he saw the door burst open and the guard disappear beneath an avalanche of bodies.

Estelle and Uri drew back, pressing past boxes and causing them to tumble down around them. For a moment Jonah was unsure what the falling, streaming things were, but then he knew: toilet paper, a hundred rolls unfurling and bouncing around the small room, quickly turning dark as they soaked up the blood already being spilled.

Uri kicked and punched, Estelle grabbed someone around the throat, and there was a flash as a gun fired. Jonah did not want to see, but he had to watch. He had to learn. Something was happening here that needed witnessing and he concentrated, biting his lip and trying to pretend that the blood and death he saw was only a movie. But Uri was his friend, and seeing him fall beneath two ravening people, seeing their heads darting up and down as they bit, could not be ignored so easily. And Estelle. He saw her throwing toilet rolls at someone so bloodied and mutilated that Jonah could not identify them – and then that someone pressed in and gnawed off part of Estelle's face. He could not pretend that was make-believe. The blood and silent screams were real; the sight of people who should be dead acting like a pack of starving dogs was painfully, impossibly real.

'What have I done?' Jonah said aloud and he thought of Bill Coldbrook slumped dead in his chair, the empty sleeping-pill bottle on the floor beside him. Had he known? Impossible: he couldn't have, because if he had surely he would have—

Jonah thought of the dreams, the thing in his room, how he'd actually felt the feather-touch of its finger lifting his eyelid. 'They were dead, too,' he muttered, remembering the shambling people in his nightmares, the bitten man being whisked away by a machine like none he had ever seen before.

Jonah closed his eyes for a moment, shutting out the terrible images so that he could gather his thoughts. But they were loose and elusive, shocked apart by this terrible reality.

He looked again and the guard was on his feet, backed into the corner beneath the camera. Jonah saw only the sub-machine gun and the man's hand and forearm, and the screen flashed five more times until the bullets ran out. The attackers jerked and danced at the bullets struck them, but only two fell. One stood up again, his hand scratching at his chest as if he was irritated by a fly bite. The other, Estelle, stayed down, the top of her head blown off. And Jonah concentrated on her as the shapes pressed in below the camera and the guard met his end, waiting for her to move again. She did not. Her eyes were open, looking lifeless through the lens.

'Blew her head off,' he muttered.

He steeled himself, then ran through the facility's cameras one more time. Three out of twenty-three had ceased working, but on every other screen he saw only those mad people walking – he could tell by the blood, and their injuries, and their slack faces, and the way their arms failed to swing as they moved that they were not merely survivors – and a few motionless. He tried to zoom in on these, but the angles were wrong, and picture quality worsened the further in a camera zoomed. Only on one of the bodies did he see clear evidence of severe head trauma.

Jonah started to shake. Could they *all* be infected? *Everyone?* There were places to hide in Coldbrook's three levels: cupboards and locked rooms, nooks and crannies, empty spaces left over from construction of the underground facility more than twenty years before. And those three closed doors in one of the accommodation corridors – maybe survivors were hiding in there. If so, he hoped they were people who had seen what those infected – those bitten – could do. Otherwise they might be tempted to open their doors.

He glanced at the reinforced viewing window in Secondary's single door, but there was no face there looking in. *I'll have to leave sometime*, he thought, and fear shivered through him. He breathed deeply and tried to pull himself together. Panic could help no one, least of all him. The news would be spreading beyond

Coldbrook by now. His new aim must be only to stay alive and gather whatever information he could.

3

Vic heard gunshots. They were *shooting* at him! He flung himself into the ditch beside the road and felt cool slick mud closing around his arm and hand. The palmtop slipped from his pocket and splashed into the mud. He panicked, trying to prevent himself sinking deeper. The muck stank, but he welcomed the smell because it meant he was outside. Down in Coldbrook the air was sterile and clean, but to Vic it always smelled artificial. Real air was tainted by life, and he was glad to be free.

He rolled onto his back and sat up, his stomach muscles screaming. *Really should have used that gym*, he thought as he looked back down into the valley. Coldbrook sat further down the hillside, and now there were lights on in the buildings. He realised that the shooting had been distant, gunshots echoing from the slopes. No one was chasing him. His nerves had got the better of him. He tried to breathe calmly, but could not stop panting from exertion and fear. His heart fluttered like a trapped bird. He felt nauseous but it was nothing to do with the stinking ditch he had thrown himself into.

It was everything to do with those gunshots.

Something flashed down in the compound, though it

was too far away to make out any detail, and seconds later more gunfire echoed up to him.

It's out, Vic thought, and his chest and stomach felt heavy. *I should have sealed that duct behind me, even the hatch, even if I'd spent a minute to screw that back properly instead of just propping it . . .* But panic had gripped him, a mortal fear for Lucy and Olivia that had dulled his understanding and made his thoughts race: reach home, at all costs. The idea that the danger could be contained had not occurred to him. Never before had instinct taken him so completely, and as he climbed from that ditch he shivered at the idea.

He stepped back up onto the road and started running again, Coldbrook at his back, the long slope of the ridge ahead of him. Danton Rock was maybe a mile away over the curve of the hilltop. Already he could see the first few farm buildings. To the east the sun was smudging the division between night and morning, and he was beginning to dread what the day would bring.

The satphone shrilled again, but Vic ignored it. He couldn't talk to Jonah just yet. *Whatever the shooting was about, they've got it contained*, he thought, trying to make sense of what he was doing. Trying to divert the blame. He had to keep it at bay until he reached his family. *Then* he could speak to Jonah; *then* he could find out what had really happened and how bad it was.

'I'll be back down there by sunset,' he muttered, his

voice shaking as he ran. 'He'll be fucking furious, he'll dock a month's money, but he'll need me down there.'

The lies kept coming as the road passed by beneath his feet, and the rising sun started to dry the thin, putrid mud coating his right side. He was exhausted but he ran on, ignoring for now his straining lungs and the burning in his knees and legs. His satphone had gone silent and he started to fear what that meant.

The road twisted up towards the ridge, and as it started to level out he passed the small farm on Danton Rock's outskirts. A few cows lifted their heads to watch him pass by, still chewing the cud, uninterested. A dog barked somewhere out of sight, and he could hear the sound of a motor among the farm buildings.

He slowed down, the shaking in his chest forcing him to a walk. He passed several houses on his right and a row of shops on his left, a couple of small restaurants tucked neatly between a baker's, a food store, and a pharmacy. He and Lucy had eaten in the Asian restaurant several times, and once they'd been in there when Holly had walked in. Vic's surprise had been genuine – Holly rarely ventured out of Coldbrook, and when she did she tended to travel to Asheville for a couple of days away from work. It had not been the first time that Holly and Lucy had met, and he'd sat awkwardly while the two women exchanged pleasantries. He and Holly had still been involved then, and the rest of the evening after she joined the friends who'd arrived soon after had been strained. He and Lucy had made love when they returned home, he remembered, and afterwards she had asked him what was wrong.

He started to run again, driven by thoughts of his wife.

'We have to get away. In ten minutes. Pack a bag for both of you, but leave Olivia on the Wii for now. How's the car? Is the tank full?'

Lucy stood at their kitchen counter, still wearing her dressing gown, hair a mess, eyes puffy from sleep. Coffee was brewing, and as she and Vic stared at each other in uneasy silence the toaster popped up three slices. Vic jumped slightly, then looked around their kitchen. He spoke with Lucy several times each day but he had not been home since breach, four days earlier.

'You're covered in mud.'

'Yeah.'

He'd appeared at the back door to see Lucy stretching and yawning, mug in one hand and the other scratching absently below one breast. Then she'd seen him, her eyes going wide and a slick of coffee spilling down her front. It had not been hot.

'I don't understand. Why won't you tell me why?'

'I will. When we're on the road,' he said again. If he started now, he'd have to finish, and he had no real idea how this would end. He'd drive and talk at the same time. And if he was going to scare her he'd rather it were as they were leaving than now, when she had herself and Olivia to get together. And he had stuff to think about, things they'd need to take with them. *Vic, something's come through . . . a creature, but . . .*

'But you're scaring me!' Lucy said. 'You look—'

'Everything's going to be fine. I've been running, that's all.' He moved to the side and glanced at his reflection in the oven door. He no longer looked like himself, and he wondered if mere mud and exhaustion could do that.

'Olivia won't want to go. She's only been up twenty minutes, she hasn't even had . . .' Lucy nodded at the toast, and Vic moved quickly across to her, grasping her upper arms and pulling her close. He stared into her gorgeous blue eyes for a few seconds, seeing how this was upsetting her but unable to change course. Then he hugged her to him, thinking of the dream and his dead sister, and those brief moments of suspicion he'd seen in his wife's eyes.

'Something came through,' he said.

'What?' Her voice was muffled against his shoulder.

'Just trust me. I'll tell you everything I know when we're rolling. But I want to be away from here in ten minutes.' Vic let go and moved back, looking her in the eyes again and loving everything about her. She was scared, but she'd sniffed back any tears.

'Okay,' she said. 'But Olivia will—'

'Daddy!' the little girl shouted as she ran into the kitchen, and Vic's smile as he spun around to sweep her up was genuine. Olivia hugged him tight around the neck and her long hair brushed against his face, tickling his nose. 'Wow, you're all dirty.'

'Yeah, I know, sweetie!' he said, hugging her back. This was everything he had left Coldbrook for. He turned so that he could see Lucy and offer her a smile.

'Hey, honey,' Lucy said. 'Daddy's been keeping a surprise from us.'

'Has he found Rosie?' Olivia asked, so serious. Rosie was a doll she'd lost over a year ago, a ragtag creation that still seemed to visit her dreams.

'Not Rosie, sweetie,' Vic said. 'But we're going on holiday.'

'Yay! No school?'

'No school,' he said.

'How long for?'

Vic glanced at Lucy, and something in his eyes must have struck her for the first time. She leaned gently against the kitchen worktop for support.

'Only a few days,' he said. 'That's all.'

Vic wanted to leave in ten minutes, but it was almost twenty before they were sitting in their RAV4, Olivia strapped into her seat in the back with a Nintendo DS open on her lap, Lucy clicking her seat belt and sitting back, staring straight ahead. When he'd stretched to push several large water bottles behind the front seats, she'd caught sight of the pistol in his belt. She'd hardly said anything since and it was time to tell her what he knew.

'Lucy, everything I'm doing is for—'

'Should I call my mother?' Lucy asked. There was a quiver of fear in her voice. 'Or Richard? He and Rhian are in Seattle, should I—'

'Don't call anyone!' Vic said, more sharply than he'd intended.

Lucy blinked and stared at him wide-eyed.

He sighed, started the car, and sat back in his seat for a moment, eyes closed, trying to remember everything they had packed. *Should have brought more food*, he thought. *And water. Only ten litres of water.* Lucy had thrown a load of clothes into a suitcase and a kitbag, and Vic had added some heavy walking boots, coats and gloves, even though it was still only September. Toys and books for Olivia, a mobile charger for his phone, the spare five hundred dollars he kept in an envelope in his desk drawer. When he'd casually loaded a compact tent and camping stove into the car, Lucy's glare had been thunderous. But he'd ignored it and walked away, because there was so much left to do.

'Where are we going?' Olivia asked, breaking the

awkward silence. Vic looked at her in the rear-view mirror, hunched down over the DS and immersed in her child's world.

'North,' he said. 'Somewhere nice. It's a surprise.'

'You've no idea, have you?' Lucy whispered.

Vic glanced across at her, then squeezed her leg, hoping she'd place her hand on top of his. She remained stiff and upright in her seat, nursing her mobile phone and staring through the windscreen at their house. It was a big family home, double-fronted, small pool out back, hot tub, and entirely the product of Vic's work at Coldbrook. The facility paid their mortgage, and there was the promise of complete ownership of the property upon project completion. *They'll have the house from me*, he thought, and he barked a short, bitter laugh as fear flushed coldly through his veins.

'Shouldn't we be going?' Lucy asked coldly.

'Yeah,' Vic said. He backed away from the house and drove off. As he headed towards the centre of town he looked in the mirror again, but this time not at Olivia. He watched behind them, not sure what he was expecting to see. But he saw nothing.

They drove around the town square where he and Lucy had once sat, Olivia in her pushchair, and talked about having a second child. That had not happened yet, but Vic kept telling Lucy that they had plenty of time. *The world is our lobster*, he'd say, smiling and hugging her tight. The bench where they'd sat had a plaque dedicating it to the memory of a young girl called Alice Klein, the daughter of friends of theirs. She had died three years before at the age of fifteen from brain cancer. She'd been a popular girl, and as she had deteriorated she'd raised many thousands of dollars for the small town hospital where she'd spent her last days. She had been quite a character in town, pushed around in her wheelchair by her older brother, flaunting her baldness and the scars of unsuccessful surgery, demanding men's shoes – just one from a pair – and holding them to ransom for charity. She'd taken Vic's three times, and the last time it had cost him a hundred bucks to get it back. He'd had to collect it from her house, because she'd taken a sudden turn for the worse by then, dying five days later. He still visited her parents every time he was up in town. Her father worked for Coldbrook, though not in the facility – he was one of several accountants of theirs, responsible for dealing with their foreign investors. A good man, a friend to the Pearsons, he had changed since his daughter's death, taking his work more seriously. There had also been rumours that he'd tried to take his own life, though no one wished to explore them too deeply.

I should tell David, Vic thought. He stopped the car to let a postman cross, raising a finger on the wheel in acknowledgement when he nodded his thanks. *I should tell him, because they don't deserve any more heartbreak.*

He drove on, and the atmosphere in the car was thick with tension. Even Olivia seemed to have noticed it; she'd closed her DS and sat staring out of the window, frowning into the sun.

They left the square and passed McCready's, where Vic and his family had spent last New Year's Eve. Old Walt McCready threw a big party every year, charging everyone ten bucks and laying on food, drink and entertainment until the early hours. Adults and kids alike remembered the party for months afterwards, for the quality of the home-catered food and the variety of drinks he'd ordered in for the evening. Vic remembered it most for the ten minutes he'd sat and watched Lucy dancing with some of her friends from town. He'd been gently drunk by then, and he'd realised that he loved his wife more than he ever had before. He'd even muttered a foolish New Year's resolution to himself: *Be better to her this year than you ever have*. As they drove by he realised that he had now broken that resolution. He remembered their friends dancing and eating and laughing with them that night, and knew that he should warn them all.

Olivia sniffed behind him, and Vic realised his daughter was crying.

'So?' Lucy asked beside him, so cold, so afraid.

His guilt scoured deep into him. Before he could change his mind he brought the Rav4 to a halt and pulled out the satphone.

'Honey, I just need to see how bad it is,' he said, pressing Jonah's speed-dial number as he spoke. By the time Lucy began to protest the call was answered, and the old bastard's Welsh accent cut through the static.

4

'Vic, you stupid bastard Yank, do you have any idea what you've *done?*' The phone's ringing had startled Jonah – he was standing at the viewing panel in the door, looking out at the deserted, silent corridor beyond – and his shouted response was partly in reaction to that shock. But it was also provoked by the words that had appeared on the little screen: *Vic calling.*

'Jonah—'

'Today I've seen people dying. Melina. Uri. And Estelle, she had her head . . . it was . . . because of you.' He drew a breath, leaning against the door with one hand.

'Jonah, where are you? How bad is it?'

'Ah, fuck off, Vic,' Jonah said, and he disconnected. His head was spinning, heart galloping, and he sat down gingerly on the edge of the desk. The palpitations made him cough, and for a moment he was sure the dizziness would increase and he'd hit the floor. *Break a hip*, he thought, *and wouldn't that be just fine? Survive all that and then break a damn hip?* Wendy would have laughed at the irony in that, but then she always did have a skewed view of life. Bill Coldbrook had once said, *The more we think we know, the more humble we should become*, and how right he had been. Had Jonah's own pride and arrogance caused this catastrophe? Perhaps.

Jonah dialled Vic back and the call was answered after the first ring.

'Vic, don't talk,' Jonah said. 'I'm not sure I want to hear your cowardly bastard voice right now, but you need to hear mine, and what I have to say. You need to know. Are you listening?'

'Yeah.'

'Good. I've seen people attacked and killed down here, and then get up again to go and attack others. I believe I might be the only one left who's not either dead or infected. I've made some calls, sounded the alarm. And I'm alone in Secondary.' He stared at the door for a moment, sure he'd seen movement beyond. But his view of the corridor outside stayed clear. *Just shadows on my mind.* 'Whatever the contagion is, it's spread by bites. It kills and infects its victims within a minute. I've seen people shot five times and still walking, unless they're shot in the head. You have to shoot them in the head.'

Vic snorted, and it might have been a laugh.

'Funny?' Jonah asked softly. 'You're finding something amusing?'

'No, it's just—'

'I said I didn't want to hear your bastard voice, Vic. There's nothing funny here. Nothing! I saw Estelle have her face bitten off. She fell and bled out, died. And then stood again, and attacked the only guard I believe was left alive. He . . . he blew her head off. That time, she stayed down.'

'You're talking about *zombies*, Jonah.'

'The notion's make-believe. But what it implies fits.'

Vic laughed again, but there was desperation there, a hint of hysteria. And Jonah did not like that.

'Pull yourself together, boy! Think of your family.'

'I *am* thinking of my family. They're here with me now. We're on our way out of Danton Rock, but . . . I heard shooting when I left the compound.' Vic fell silent for a moment, and now Jonah did see movement through the door's glass panel.

A face appeared there, so ruined that he could not possibly identify it, could not even tell its owner's sex. It stared in at him with one good eye, pressed against the strengthened glass and smearing blood. It did not blink. He heard nails drawn across the metal door.

'There's one watching me,' Jonah said, backing away from the door, and the truth of what he saw hit him hard. *Don't give up on me now*, he thought as his heart lurched in his chest, and he closed his eyes to try and calm his body. The thing scratched some more.

'One what?' Vic asked.

'One of them. If you could only see. I'm turning away, but listen to me. This is beyond fault or guilt now – that all comes later, and damn me if I won't punch your lights out when I see you again. But I'm trapped down here. And there's something I need to do, and something you must do, too. You've got to warn people. Visit the station there, speak to Sheriff Blanks. Tell him what happened, tell him everything I've told you. And tell him to shoot them in the head.'

'Can't you tell him—'

'*No*, Vic! You're the one who ran, and you're out there now, boy. So that's down to you, face to face. I've got to stop any more of these bastards getting out.'

'And how the hell are you going to do that?'

'Do you care?' Jonah shouted. 'Just do your part.'

'Jonah. *Everyone* else?'

I don't have to tell him, Jonah thought, but such cruelty was beyond him. 'Holly escaped through the breach,' he said. Then he disconnected, turned the satphone off, and went back to the window.

The face from hell was still there, pressed against the glass, staring at him: jaw moving slightly, tongue squashed, wounds not bleeding. 'Because it's dead,' Jonah said, and he no longer found the idea ridiculous. *You're talking about* zombies, *Jonah*. Yeah, well. *What you see, you see*, Wendy used to say when Jonah tried to impress upon her the question of scientific proof versus spiritual nonsense and he'd held her comment close to his heart. *What you see, you see.*

'Right, then,' he said, looking at the door window but talking to himself. 'Let's see how I can get out of this one.' He returned to the desk and turned his back on the door, tilting the laptop screen so that he could not see its reflection, and accessed two programs. Some of the afflicted had escaped – Alex the guard captain, at least – but the more he could keep down here with him, the better. They'd be contained, and when the time came to start testing antidotes there'd be a supply of captive subjects.

'When that time comes,' Jonah muttered, feeling a chill at the prospect. This was a condition seeded in the other Earth. How would anyone here have a clue how to combat it? And if it spread . . .

After his calls, help would be on its way. But there was no saying what form that help might take.

The scratching at the door became more agitated and Jonah glanced back. There was another face pressed against the glass panel now. Uri. He seemed undamaged, but his eyes had changed. No more laughter or jokes in there. He stared in at Jonah, and Jonah wondered what he saw.

'Damn it!' He turned away again and checked to see if he could do what he had planned. It had been a passing thought but, the more he considered his options, the more likely it seemed to be the only possibility. Better than staying trapped in here, at least. Secondary had always been considered a backup location for control of Coldbrook, not an emergency one, and it was as basic as that consideration warranted. There was access to all systems, air conditioning in case of lockdown, and a small cupboard with dried foods and water to last eight people for two days. There was a small bathroom, but nowhere to sleep.

It also had a gun cabinet. *Only in America*, Jonah had commented to Bill Coldbrook several times during the construction of the facility. *They don't have gun cabinets at CERN.*

Don't they? Bill had replied, and a raised eyebrow had silenced Jonah.

The guns had always been the part of Coldbrook that troubled Jonah most. The argument for them was solid enough, but that didn't mean he had to like them. If and when they did eventually succeed in their experiment, then through and beyond the breach chamber would be another Earth, perhaps with its own geography, flora and fauna. And perhaps with people. There was no guarantee that anything through there would be friendly, but no certainties otherwise, either. He hated the feel, sight, and smell of guns, but he also grudgingly saw the logic behind their presence here. *Should've built this thing in the Welsh mountains. Safer, and would've brought some money to the valleys*, he'd once said to Bill, and Bill had countered with, *And you really think the British government wouldn't station an SAS platoon there?*

Jonah left his desk and went to the gun cabinet, entering his ID code into the electronic lock. The door popped open with a gentle click. Inside, two pistols hung on clips, and a shotgun was strapped in one corner. There were two boxes of shotgun shells, and a dozen loaded magazines for the pistols. He had not fired a weapon for seven years, when Vic had taken him to a range a mile outside Danton Rock. After an hour of shooting Vic had declared, *If I asked you to shoot at the sky I'd lay good odds that you'd miss*. Jonah had taken it as a compliment.

He plucked a pistol from its clips and, after a few moments pressing and prodding, the magazine slipped out. It was fully loaded, so he pushed it back in until it clicked into place. The pistol had a safety built into the grip, he remembered, so he'd have to squeeze tight when he was shooting, and he had to make sure he aimed for—

'What the bloody hell am I doing, Wendy?' It had been a long time since Jonah had spoken to his dead wife aloud. Hearing her name startled him, and he felt a weight in his chest as he thought of her easy smile and intelligent eyes. He laughed out loud, looking at the cool alien object in his hand, thinking how ridiculous this all was. 'Hey, Wendy . . . Jonah Jones, action hero. Think I'll be the next Richard Burton?' His voice sounded loud and flat in the large room, and he glanced back at the door to remind himself where and when he was.

The two faces stared back, and he was sure the scratching sound got louder when he looked at them.

The longer Jonah stayed here, the more difficult his next step would be. He had to go. Now.

'Got to stick to my guns,' he said, but all humour had left him. *Can I really shoot someone?* He thought of everything he had seen and decided that yes, he could. He *had* to. 'You're already dead.' The faces held no expression, and he wondered if they could hear him when he spoke, or would feel anything when he shot them.

Jonah sat down and took several deep breaths. He scanned the viewing screens, checking his route from Secondary down to the next level, then past the offices to the garage area. He remotely locked several corridor doors, watching on the screens as their door closers operated. On the staircase that he'd have to descend there was a body, lying on its front and with its head pointing away from him, and he could see no movement. It was a woman, her nightgown pulled up around her chest and soaked in red. He was glad he could not make out who it was.

He'd have to be cautious there, just in case, though from what he had seen of the afflicted—

Not dead, I can't call them the dead, and calling them zombies . . .

– he didn't think they could scheme or plan. They could not play dead.

Jonah went into the bathroom and urinated, leaning against the wall, supporting himself with one hand and staring into the mirror above the toilet. An old man stared back, and he felt shocked at the image. Seventy-six was the count of his years, but his mind was as vivid and sharp as it had ever been, his heart and soul immersed in Coldbrook and the wonders he was determined it would one day reveal. Ageing was for people who spent mornings at bridge clubs, afternoons strolling in the park with walking groups, and evenings fussing over dinner and deciding what to watch on TV. The fact of his approaching death crept up on him sometimes, surprising him with how close it had come, but he was so involved with his work that mortality seemed to be for everyone else. But now he looked into the face of someone who had seen terrible things, and who had seen death in unreal forms. He had always felt at ease with the prospect of his own demise, but Coldbrook had become a travesty of its original purpose. And a deadly one at that.

Back in Secondary's main room he unplugged the laptop, checking that it still had its wi-fi connection, then moved to the door. With his other hand he held the gun down by his side, safety catch off, hand clasping the grip, finger on the trigger.

In the head, he thought, and this close up the faces

looked less human than ever. Realising he had both hands full he put the laptop down, shaking his head to clear his thoughts. *Got to think clearer than that.* He rested his hand on the door lock, took a few deep breaths, then clicked it open.

They seemed to hear the sound of the lock disengaging. The scratching became more frantic, and they called to each other softly, a haunting hum. Jonah watched for a moment, to see if they remembered how to open a door. The handle flicked down, but they did not depress it fully. Gun ready, Jonah pressed the handle down and opened the door.

A hand came through. Fingers opened and closed, grasping. The little finger was shredded and hanging, though no blood dripped from it. He pulled back as another hand came through, this one with painted finger-nails and a diamond ring shining obscenely amid dried blood. The door swung open and he stepped back, raising the gun and sighting on the woman's head. Two afflicted pushed into the room together, squeezing through the door and reaching for him. Their previously expression-less faces now held a tension that pulled their mouths open and widened their dark eyes.

Their hooting calls could have been tuneless singing, and they smelled like mouldy, wet clothing.

'Wait, wait, hang on,' Jonah said, retreating until the backs of his legs hit the control desk. Although he had the gun raised he could not pull the trigger. Shooting someone in the head, seeing the damage it could do, was beyond his comprehension. 'No, wait, stay back and let me—'

A hand swiped across his face and he jerked his head back, wrenching his neck and feeling a fingernail scrape across his nose. He kicked out and shoved the bloody-faced woman back, but Uri was beside her and he pressed forward, slower, his actions much more controlled.

There was flesh between Uri's teeth, and a clot of blood and blonde hair was stuck to his chin.

'No, we should talk, you need to sit down and—' Jonah stammered.

Uri's face changed as his mouth fell open, lips and cheeks wrinkling into a silent growl, and it was the silence that threw Jonah. On the viewing screens he had seen carnage and shooting and blood, and he had played his own imaginary soundtrack to those sights. He had been wrong. These things were not ravenous slavering animals, not growling roaring things, but some-thing else entirely.

He lifted the gun quickly, its barrel striking Uri's chin, causing is head to flip up, Jonah tucked in his elbow and raised the gun higher – it was only inches from his own face when he fired. The explosion was deafening. His hearing faded instantly, driving all his senses inward for what seemed like minutes but must have been only seconds. When he opened his eyes again there was dust drifting from the ceiling and Uri was slumped against the open door, slowly sliding down to the floor, his head a ruin. And the woman was coming for Jonah again, her mutilated face stretching horribly as her jaw seemed to unhinge, teeth glaring in the wet red mask. The shot's recoil had jarred Jonah's shoulder, but he brought the gun up again and held it in a two-handed grip at arm's length this time, closing his eyes as the woman's forehead struck the barrel. He pulled the trigger, then squinted through the smoke at her thrashing on the floor. He shot her again and again. The gunshots sounded distant, though the recoil forced him against the desk. His ears started ringing as his hearing returned, though beyond the ringing there was only silence and his own panting and groaning, and the gasps as he tried to spit gun smoke from his mouth.

The woman was motionless. Her head was shattered, spilling out a mess of gore. Blood seeped, and Jonah gagged, but he had to look again. It did not gush. *No working heart to pump it*, he thought. Uri was slumped against the open door, chin on his chest, displaying the exit wound on the back of his head just above the neck. Blood and brain matter ran down beneath his collar, but again there was no excessive bleeding.

I shot two people, Jonah thought, but he found himself feeling surprisingly calm. Although his ears were still ringing the stillness seemed a comfort to him. *I gave them peace. I helped them.* He nodded as he knelt, holding on to that thought. The woman's leg was stretched out and her shoe hung off. He touched the top arch of her foot, blew on his hand and touched her skin again. She was cooler than she should have been, her skin paler. She was someone from the kitchen. He had eaten food that she had cooked, and had thanked her for it. Now she was dead.

'Bloody hell.'

He moved backwards until the desk stopped his progress again. He stared, chilled by the bodies' presence. But he had opened the door for a reason. He had to move on. There would be dangers, and part of his scheme relied on pure luck. But it meant taking action. Standing here returning cold dead stares was not meaningful activity.

Jonah dragged the corpses outside, wanting to keep Secondary clear. As he grabbed the laptop and closed and locked the door, he did not take his eyes from the two motionless cadavers. And even as he turned a corner to reach the staircase, he kept glancing back. Though they did not follow him, he knew they would pursue him in his dreams.

He descended the staircase, stepping past the nightgown-wearing woman and almost slipping on the mess that her shattered skull had spilled down the stairs. Heart thudding, he closed the staircase door, gasped, and paused, raising the gun again as a shadow moved away in front of him. It slipped down a side corridor into one of the accommodation wings, seeming to flow rather than walk. An overhead light flickered and a shadow danced again. Perhaps that was all he had seen. Turning the corner quickly he saw nothing but empty corridor, and he hurried on.

Jonah used the laptop to open and close doors remotely, flipping to the other program so that he could use the CCTV cameras to see around the bends in corridors and check his route. He passed the offices and entered the canteen and common room, where pool tables and loungers were scattered around the large room. He'd sat in here often, drinking bad blended whisky from the small bar run by Andy. Jonah had seen the barman die. Andy would laugh and chat with those who spent most of their time in the facility itself – often Vic had been down here as well, even though he had his wife and child topside. For a while he had remained down here a whole lot more, and Jonah was well aware of the intense relationship he'd had with Holly.

The common room had been a place of laughter, but now a monster sat in one of its chairs. Sergey Vasilyev was a particle physicist, seconded to Coldbrook to share in their work and to contribute what he'd learned from research he had been undertaking in Saint Petersburg for the past eighteen years. Russia's own version of Coldbrook had been mothballed due to the massive financial investment required, and Sergey had been invited to represent Russia at the Stateside complex. Some of Coldbrook's backers had been uncomfortable with the Russian's presence but Jonah had been adamant – as far as he was concerned, there were no secrets or borders when it came to science, and Sergey was the best in his field.

Now he sat in one of the leather loungers, watching Jonah with lazy eyes as the older man circled the room's perimeter.

'Sergey?' Jonah asked, though he knew it was useless. It looked as if the tall Russian had taken a sustained burst of gunfire to his stomach and pelvis, and his legs hung at unnatural angles. He lifted one hand, as if to reach across the twenty-foot gap between them. His face was slack, his expression inhuman.

Jonah lifted the gun, then lowered it again. As he left the room he heard a low, sustained moan, and remembered the sound from the first time Sergey had tried proper whisky.

Just leaving a problem until later, he thought, but he could not bring himself to shoot the seated man.

Nerves tingling, limbs shaking even as he walked, Jonah made it to the short corridor leading to Coldbrook's garage. He closed the door, saw no lock, and checked the systems on his laptop. There was no facility to lock this door automatically. Why? Why the hell enable corridor doors to be locked, but not the door to the garage? He almost shouted in frustration, but instead knelt with his back against the door and accessed the CCTV programme.

Perhaps the afflicted really couldn't open doors. The two outside Secondary had been scratching at the door, not clinging to its handle. But maybe they'd known it was locked, and the scratching had been a sign of their frustration.

Breathing heavily, Jonah viewed the garage through its three cameras. One of them did not react to prompts, but the other two swivelled to order, giving him a panning view of the whole area. He saw himself hunkered down by the door, an old man hiding in fear. The three vehicles seemed untouched, and he saw no shadows that should not be there. Behind the parked vehicles to his left was the access door to the air-conditioning plant room. It was open. He flipped the laptop windows again to the security program but this door also was manual only.

'Damn it!' he whispered. At the sound of his own voice, he felt tears welling up and his throat constricting, and as he tried to stand his legs gave way and he slid down the closed door until he was sitting again on the cold floor. The shakes came harder than before, and his vision blurred. His joints ached. He wiped his eyes angrily but more tears came, and he tried to remember the last time he'd cried. He sometimes woke from dreams with tears in his eyes, but he had not cried while awake for some time. 'But I've never shot anyone before,' he whispered, and his voice shook. He laughed softly and let the tears come, because there was nothing else he could do.

Jonah cried for a couple of minutes, not caring what the tears were for. If he wept for those he had seen die, then they deserved this meagre tribute. And if he shed tears over those he had shot, then perhaps that might purge some guilt.

But even as his weeping ceased and he managed to calm his shivers, with every blink of his eyes he saw scenes of devastation that were sensations rather than images, intimations of chaos and death that filled him with a sense of deep, primeval dread. And as he rested his head back against the door and tried to resolve what to do next, the handle above him started to move down, then up again.

He stood and ran, legs shaking beneath him, his heart protesting with stutters and missed beats. The laptop almost slipped from his hand and he grabbed it just in time, pressing it against his chest. If he had a choice of what to drop it would be the gun, not the laptop. *Battery won't last for ever,* he thought, but he was not thinking about for ever, or even the next few hours. This was minute-by-minute stuff.

The handle snapped down with a different sound as the catch clicked open. The door behind him banged open just as he reached the Hummer's driver-side door. Regulations said that keys were to be kept in the vehicles, but they also said that cameras should be regularly serviced and that communication routes to the surface should be maintained at all times. Rick Summerfield had not heard any alarm, and the third camera in the garage did not react to prompts. *Someone's head's gonna roll!* Jonah thought as he stepped up and pulled the door open.

The keys were in the ignition, a Darth Vader key-fob hanging below. He climbed in, slid the laptop across the front seats and slammed the door behind him.

Something hard struck the vehicle on the other side.

Jonah jumped and stared into Sergey's face. The physicist's eyes were wide and staring, his lips drawn back in a grimace. He must have dragged himself through the garage door after Jonah, lifting himself on the door handle and thereby opening it, and climbed onto the Hummer's step. Now he held on to the passenger-side door handle and tugged. Spittle flecked the glass, Sergey's hair shook and tangled, and behind him Jonah saw a shape darting through the open door. This second shape joined Sergey on the step, scratching at the glass with long, delicately painted fingernails. Jonah did not even look at her face before starting the Hummer.

The engine roared to life, startling Jonah but causing no let-up in his attackers' efforts to open the door. *They're fast. And they can open doors, even if it's only by accident. Remember that.* He shoved the big vehicle into gear and then swung it around to the left, clipping one of the SUVs and tearing off its bumper. It was a long time since he'd driven anything. He stamped hard on the brakes, bracing himself against the steering wheel as the dead woman disappeared below the Hummer's door frame. Sergey hung on, tugging, tugging, his teeth still bared. His actions spoke of a need beyond understanding, but his eyes were dead windows onto the void.

Jonah backed up slowly, using both wing mirrors to judge his approach, trying to ignore the raving thing shifting back and forth to his left. He felt the gentle knock of the plant-room door being shoved closed, and even though it was moving slowly the final impact of the heavy vehicle against the wall jarred him in his seat. He revved some more, lifting the clutch but sensing no more backward movement. It was done. Whatever had passed through that way was not coming back, and nothing else could enter.

The woman jumped up at the passenger-side window, scratching at the glass rather than tugging at the handle. Jonah looked down into his lap, twisting his hands and remembering the time almost fifty years before when

Wendy had slipped the ring onto his finger. Then he turned in his seat, held the gun in both hands and shot the woman through the window. She flipped back out of sight and he scooted over the seats, looking down to make sure he'd fired straight.

She slammed into the window again, glass starring and then tumbling into the cab in a hundred diamond shards.

Jonah kicked himself back, aimed again, and shot her in the face. This time she didn't get up. He edged over and looked. She lay on the concrete floor, arms flung back, dead eyes staring at the ceiling, a neat hole in her forehead.

'Good shot,' Jonah said, and his immediate future was suddenly, awfully clear. There was the laptop, through which he could scout his path through the facility, remote-locking doors to secure certain sections. There was the gun in his hand, spare loaded magazines in his pocket. And there were the zombies.

He might be here for days, or weeks. He might be here for ever.

Turning in his seat and telling himself the thing at the driver's window was no longer Sergey Vasilyev, Jonah lifted the gun once more.

5

'Just what the fuck have you freaky fucks gone an' done down there?' Sheriff Scott Blanks asked. He was a big man, carrying a little extra weight but burly enough to get away with it. He was also quietly spoken, but Vic could feel the anger radiating from him. And fear. It was good that he was afraid; that was one less thing Vic had to do.

'I'm just relaying what Professor Jones told me,' Vic said.

'And how come you're not still down there?'

'I was home with my family,' Vic lied. 'Got the call. He says that . . .' He shook his head, because it still sounded too outlandish.

'What, son?' Blanks was maybe a couple of years older than Vic, but it still seemed entirely acceptable that he should call him 'son'. That was the kind of man he was.

'Sheriff, can we talk in private?' They were in the police station reception area and three other people were listening to their conversation, two cops and a desk clerk.

'We *are* in private,' the sheriff said.

Okay, Vic thought. *Olivia and Lucy are waiting, I need to be as quick as possible, and* . . . And the only road leading away from Coldbrook came here. However damaged those infected were – whatever they had become – he thought it likely that they would follow the path of least resistance.

'There's been an accident. There's an infection, and it makes people . . . mad. Murderous. Jonah Jones says that lots are dead down there, and some of the killers may have escaped.'

'Killers?'

'And they may be coming for Danton Rock. So be ready. And Jonah says to shoot them in the head to stop them.' Vic winced against the mockery he expected, but Sheriff Blanks only raised his eyebrows.

'The head?'

'That's what he said.'

'What we got here, zombies?' the woman cop said, chuckling softly. She was short and squat, pretty face, and she'd once let Vic off a parking ticket. The other cop was smiling, but moving nervously from foot to foot. He must have been ten years younger than Vic, and the flicker of uncertainty lit his eyes.

'Yeah,' Vic said, taking a chance, because he really needed to get away. Silence descended for a few long seconds.

'Just what the *fuck* have you guys gone an' done down there?' Sheriff Blanks asked again.

'I've heard talk about what they done,' the young cop said. 'Blasting holes into other places, that's what. Letting stuff out. Just like in *The Mist*.'

'There's no mist,' Vic said, unsure of what he meant.

'Fiddling with stuff you shouldn't?' the woman said. Vic bet she wished she'd given him that ticket now. She'd laughed at the idea of zombies, but she knew there was something very wrong. She was that perceptive, at least. No one could look as shocked as Vic, nor act that edgy, without *something* being wrong.

'You leavin' town?' the sheriff asked.

'Yeah,' Vic said, nodding. 'Had a trip planned for a couple of days, and—'

'Don't bullshit me, son. You're running.'

Vic did not reply, and silence descended again, broken only by the creak of the young male cop's shoes as he shifted left, right, left.

'Okay,' the sheriff said eventually. 'Okay.' And Vic heard the decision in his voice. *He listened, he heard, and now I can go.*

'Might only be one or two of them,' Vic said.

'We'll need a statement,' the woman cop said, and then the phone rang and she snatched it up. 'Sheriff's office.' She was silent for a while, her eyes flicking from Blanks to Vic, back again. 'Okay, keep the doors locked, get upstairs, we'll be right there. Got a firearm? Okay. Okay.' She hung up.

'What?' the sheriff asked.

'Pete Crowther, the farmer. Says two men and a woman're trying to break into his house. Says one of them's had an arm torn off, and the woman looks like she's bin run down.' Her pretty face had paled, and she kept glancing at Vic as she talked. 'Says they're like animals, but quiet. 'Part from the hootin'.'

'Hooting?'

Vic backed towards the door, the sheriff staring at him, and when he felt the cold wood at his back the policewoman came for him, still afraid but with a purpose in mind. She had one arm behind her back, reaching for her handcuffs.

'Let the fucker run,' Blanks said, and he stormed through a door behind the desk.

Vic turned and pushed his way out, feeling the police-woman's stare on his back. When he emerged onto the sunlit front steps, Lucy was leaning from the passenger window of the RAV4, Olivia's small face pressed against the back window.

'What?' Lucy asked immediately.

'Nothing.' Vic ran down the steps and around the front of the vehicle, and as he was opening the driver's door he heard the roar of a motor. He climbed into the car and slammed his door, hitting the central locking button in case the sheriff changed his mind. *If he does, it's pedal down* – the idea of fleeing the law was somehow more unsettling than anything. It was an indicator of how much had changed so quickly. *Three hours ago I was asleep*, he thought, and his dead sister's face loomed at him again.

'I love you,' he said, turning to his wife.

She caught her breath, surprised. Her eyes watered. Vic leaned across to kiss her and, though she barely responded, she didn't pull away.

'Mommy and Daddy, loving it up!' Lucy called, and Olivia's laughter was the greatest gift Vic could have asked for right then.

A police cruiser emerged from beside the station and stopped directly in front of the RAV4. The sheriff sat in the driver's seat, the policewoman beside him, and he stared at Vic as he spoke into the car's radio. As he pulled away and powered off down the street, Lucy asked, 'What was that all about?'

'Out on a call,' Vic said. He started the car and swung it around, and as he headed onto the road leading north out of town he hoped the sheriff had listened to the message he'd relayed from Jonah: shoot them in the head.

Says they're like wild animals, but quiet. Suddenly, zombies no longer sounded so absurd.

'Look, Daddy!' Olivia said, pointing, and Vic skidded to a stop. With the roads still quiet, the *whukka-whukka* sound of three Chinooks heading south-west towards Coldbrook was almost ghostly.

He drove fast and hard, trying to lay down distance between his family and whatever he had let escape.

It was nine o'clock in the morning.

6

Holly rose from her nightmare —

God help me, where did that come from? That thing, Melinda, the blood and screaming . . . Jonah's hopeless gaze through the window. And the breach—

145

– and for a moment before she opened her eyes she believed that Vic was lying beside her. The narrow bed moved as he stirred, and she reached out to touch him, wondering why she couldn't feel his warm naked body pressed close to hers. They were all given single beds in their quarters, and sharing had always been a cramped, sweaty affair. But she had liked it. Waking to Vic, sometimes she believed they could be together.

Her hand closed around something cool and gnarled, and when she opened her eyes she saw a wooden pole slipped through the stretcher's canvas hoops, and remembered where she was.

The realisation struck her with a jolt, unreality flooding in as she struggled to find sleep again. *Back to sleep, escape this nightmare, and Vic's waiting for me if I can only close my eyes and get back to sleep!*

The stretcher shook as those carrying it negotiated uneven terrain, and Holly opened her eyes once again. A thud of pain throbbed through her head. She tried to sit up. Something clicked nearby—

Their fingers, that's how they communicate, I saw that just after—

—and the stretcher was lowered to the ground. She felt the rough ridges and contours of this place pressing through the canvas, spiking her buttocks and hips, and her elbow where she propped herself up. Memory flooded in as she looked around at the people who had saved her.

The arrow had struck the crawling woman just below the left eye, the impact sounding like wood striking wood, flipping her head back and to the side. She'd slumped down on the ruin, and suddenly people were all around Holly. She had not seen them moments before, and wondered whether they had been hiding or had been tracking her since she'd emerged from the breach. She'd barely had her wits about her then, after the violence she had seen. *None of this is real*, she'd thought.

But then a man and woman had approached her, and behind them were six more. They'd all carried weapons: bows and arrows, and crossbows. Most wore their hair braided tight to their scalps, and their clothes were loose and rough and all but colourless. They were utterly silent. Holly heard no breathing, no rustle of leather-bound feet through the long grass, no clink of metal on metal as they moved. And they seemed to communicate entirely by sign language, an incomprehensible twisting, clicking and flexing of fingers, shifting of hands, and facial expressions that might have been a background to whatever they 'said'.

She'd looked at the dead woman, now nothing more than a dried husk, and wondered whether there were more. *One on its own might have been bad luck*, she'd thought, *but two means there* must *be more.*

The man had lifted his crossbow and aimed it at

Holly's face, two fingers held to his lips. He and his female colleague walked slowly around her, looking her up and down, making her feel distinctly uncomfortable. The others stood back, at least two more aiming their weapons in her direction.

And then she'd realised what this was – the first meeting between different universes. This might be a version of Earth, but she was here from somewhere else. Jonah had said *It's exactly where we are and a trillion light years away*. Holly had felt the muscles in her legs turning to water.

'Thank God,' she'd said. 'Thank you. My name is Holly Wright and—' She'd seen the look passing between the man and woman – shock, surprise, fear – and then . . . a faint whistling, like something sweeping quickly through the air. Then nothing else.

As if inspired by the memory, another wave of pain passed through her head. She groaned, lifted her hand and touched the tender bump just above her right ear. It was like setting a burning brand against her scalp. She winced and shivered as the pain lanced into her back and right shoulder. Closing her eyes, she wished it away. *Hit me over the head*, she thought, and she wondered how indifferent they were to hurting or killing her. *Here I am in another world, and—*

There was a slight change in the light beyond her eyelids. Someone was squatting beside the stretcher, she sensed them there, and when she looked a woman was kneeling beside her. She was maybe thirty, black, short and muscled, attractive in a wild sort of way, and Holly's first thought was a surprising *Vic would love her*. That made her smile . . . and the woman smiled back.

'Wh—?' Holly began. But the woman moved quickly, pressing two fingers to Holly's lips and shaking her head.

Holly nodded her understanding and the woman took her hand away. She made several simple hand signals, one eyebrow raised. Holly shrugged and shook her head. The movement set the pain roaring once again. She cringed. The woman, appearing confused, pointed to the stretcher and to Holly. Then she stood.

Four of them lifted the stretcher and carried Holly across the top of the hill.

For the first time she was able to take in her surroundings. The tumbled building with *Exit* carved on one stone was gone, but it was possible that she was now further along the same ridge. She remained propped on both elbows, and they seemed unconcerned at what she saw, only what she said. *Maybe they're mute*, Holly thought. *Haven't ever heard anyone speaking*. It seemed likely, and that produced a feeling of disappointment that she could not shake. Had they really breached into a primeval world where language had barely advanced beyond a few hand signals? But she thought about the way the man had been shaping his hands again, the fingers splayed and clicking, and it seemed easily as advanced as sign language back on her own Earth. The stretcher was rough but serviceable, and their weapons had proved their effectiveness. Surely they were as developed as her.

Holly looked beyond the people to the landscape they were travelling across. The sun was fully up now, and if seasons matched between the worlds she judged it to be early afternoon. There was a light cloud cover that smudged the sun into a yellowed pastel shade, and streaks of colour hung low to the horizon like a forgotten sunset. They were beautiful, but disquieting.

On a hillside far across the valley, picked out by diffuse sunlight, she saw more ruins.

Holly squinted and shielded her eyes, her right eye throbbing with pain. She tried to work out exactly what she was seeing. It could have been an exotic rock formation, limestone corroded by wind and rain into elaborate and misleading shapes. But she thought not. There was an intimation of regularity, though some of the higher structures had obviously fallen, the remains of their walls pointing skyward and piles of broken masonry at their bases. It looked like a collection of structures that had been smudged by a giant hand, their sharp edges blurred and order destroyed.

Close to one wall sat the skeleton of what might once have been a car.

Holly wished she could go closer, but the people were

heading down from the ridge into the heavily wooded next valley, and soon the ruin was hidden from view. Was *that a car?* she wanted to ask, because the possibility meant so much. One fallen building with an 'Exit' sign was puzzling enough but two fallen buildings, the rusted remains of a vehicle, bows and arrows, and shrivelled people rising from beneath undergrowth . . .

She looked at the people, smiling as the short woman who had tended her glanced at her. The woman smiled back distractedly, scanning all around as they walked. The others seemed alert as well, including the two people walking on ahead who had to concentrate on their route. Apart from the four carrying her stretcher, everyone else constantly looked left and right, sometimes turning and walking backwards for a few steps as if expecting to be ambushed at any moment.

Holly didn't know what this meant, but none of it seemed good.

She was amazed at just how silently they were able to move across the ground, and how quickly. Their feet were clad in leather, tied tight so that no loose flaps struck at the ground. They picked their way instinctively, avoiding loose rocks or fallen branches or twigs, and when they traversed a steep slope there was only the slightest whisper of undergrowth. Birds sang all around them, crickets scratched messages from their hiding places in tall ferns, something whistled low and continuously far away, and once Holly heard the patter of small, fast footsteps as an unseen creature fled the party. It was almost as if the land hardly knew that they were there.

The jacket worn by the man holding the stretcher's front right handle had some sort of design on the back. It was a rough garment, its edges frayed and its seams held together by heavy stitching. Whatever was drawn on or sewn into the material had blended into it due to grime and time. Holly narrowed her eyes, squinting as a pulse of pain thrummed through her head once more, then looked away. She could not make it out.

The group paused abruptly and lowered the stretcher to the ground. Her carriers each unslung their primitive weapons – a bow and arrow, a crossbow, a short spear, a heavy spiked mace on a chain – and the several others arrayed around them hid behind trees or ducked into the waist-high ferns. The woman looked over her shoulder at Holly and held her hand out flat, pressing it down.

They waited like that for some time, motionless and silent. When Holly started feeling pressure on her bladder she closed her eyes and tried to will it away. She needed to pee but the feeling wouldn't become urgent for a while.

A bird landed nearby, the size of a blackbird but with a dull orange chest and speckled white wings.

One much like this had been killed by the eradicator and stored in the breach containment area, and Holly thought of Melinda and what had become of her. She'd been passionate about her work, and sometimes when they'd shared a drink and a chat together in the common room or each other's quarters Melinda had been almost unable to contain her excitement about what they were doing.

She held out her hand, hoping that the bird might hop across to her. But it flew away.

One of the two men further ahead stood and ran, crouching, into the forest, disappearing in moments. No one reacted, or moved. The woman looked at Holly again and pressed her fingers to her lips.

Holly nodded, suddenly afraid. *I want to be back in Coldbrook*, she thought. And then a shape appeared through the trees higher up the hillside and slightly ahead of them. It might have been a ghost, a human figure standing motionless while the breeze made waves of its tattered clothing and hair. The hair was long and clotted with mud and leaves. Holly held her breath, and the moment stretched into a painful stillness.

The pressure on her bladder increased and she shifted position, her clothes scraping across the stretcher's rough canvas. Her pulse thumped in her head and lit up the pain there again – and then she saw the shape's head turn, as if sniffing the air. Then it started moving, slowly passing between the trees and swishing through the heavy green ferns, coming right at her.

A whisper in the distance, and then the shape fell with something protruding from its head. The man who had run into the forest minutes before emerged behind the fallen creature. When he reached where it had fallen he pulled a machete from his belt and hacked down once, hard. Then he came back down to them, following the same route that the shambling creature had been taking. When he was closer he held up one thumb – an amazingly human gesture, which produced a shocked gasp of surprise from Holly – and they set off once more.

I want Jonah, Holly thought, shivering even though the day was growing warmer. *I want Vic*. The pain in her head was growing into the worst headache she could remember, and she wondered whether the blow to her skull had damaged her more than she knew.

They reached the valley floor. It was only sparsely wooded here and they followed a track that ran alongside a stream. It was barely a trickle, though its route was marked by a deep gulley with sheer sides, and Holly guessed it must be prone to flooding. The landscape was terribly familiar, its features like an elusive memory. Beside the track at irregular intervals stood the vertical trunks, thin and grey, of what looked like amputated trees. She thought perhaps they were birch or some similar species, but every one was broken off within a few feet of the ground. She stared at each of them as they passed, and then just as they turned from the track that might once have been a road she realised what they were. Telegraph poles.

'I know this road,' she whispered, and the woman glanced back at her. Holly thought she'd be scolded but the woman's face seemed less severe now, and the rest of the party seemed to be moving more casually. *A couple of miles south of Coldbrook, old mountain track, upgraded to cater for the Appalachians' increasing tourist trade. And now . . .*

As they approached a small ravine that joined the valley they passed through more ruins. Holly propped herself up and took notice, because that word from the tumbled pile of rubble where these people had found her kept echoing back: *Exit*. She hoped that the ruins might tell her more. But their plant-clogged windows only prompted endless questions.

Passing into the ravine, Holly looked up at the sloping sides and the segment of sky above. It was darker in here, and she doubted whether the sun's rays ever penetrated this far. The ground was marshy, and a dozen small waterfalls trickled down the sides. Their sound was soporific, and as she closed her eyes she felt the pain easing slightly. To sleep now . . .

But she needed to pee – more urgently now – and to find out where she was. And most of all she had to work out how to get back to Coldbrook.

Something clanked, metal on metal, cutting through her daydream, and it was so loud and sudden that she cried out. Set in the ravine's side was a metal door, its frame an uneven wall of solid concrete. Layers of rust camouflaged the door, but as it swung open she sensed that it was more solid and secure than it looked.

Several people emerged, and it was the last one to come out who commanded her attention. He was tall and thin, and he carried no weapons. A child stood behind him, a little girl, peering around his legs at Holly, fascinated. The tall man was pale, like an underground thing. *Their leader*, she thought, and she smiled softly at wherever that idea had come from. The little girl smiled back. Holly was already starting to suspect that she had been wrong in her assessment of these people.

The woman who had been at Holly's side stepped forward, and she and the man briefly touched hands. He never for an instant took his stare from Holly. He was sizing her up.

'She came through,' the woman said, and Holly caught her breath. She could communicate with these people. Her eyes went wide and she could feel tears prickling their corners. She looked around at the others – still silent, watching. Then she stood up slowly from the stretcher, biting her lip against the pain singing through her skull. She smoothed down her clothes and opened her mouth to speak, but thirst had dried her voice.

'So I see,' the man said, and there was something about the voice that Holly recognised. This all felt suddenly dreamlike, and for the first time in her life she put the cliché into action and pinched the back of her hand. But she did not wake up.

'How do you feel?' the man asked.

'Head hurts,' Holly said. 'And I need to pee.' She almost smiled. What an auspicious introduction to another world.

'Sorry about your head,' the man said. 'Precautionary. We'd been watching, and we didn't know quite what to expect.' He stood to one side as if allowing her to pass, and the little girl fled back through the doorway.

'In there?' Holly asked. From inside she smelled the faint hint of cooking meat, and heard the distant jangle of music. And then she saw the small logo on his jacket – three intersecting circles, their overlapping areas shaded black. She recognised it from the back of the jacket of one of her rescuers.

And she recognised it from home.

'In there,' the man confirmed. 'Welcome to Coldbrook.'

7

In the end, they drove to the Great Smoky Mountains National Park. Tommy knew how much Jayne loved it up there, and the weather gave them a long, dry day of walking and picnicking, talking and being in love. He frequently surprised her with such gestures, and sometimes in his company she went for hours without being reminded of her illness. She'd forget herself under the spell of his kindness. He always waved off any comments, saying, *It's what you do for someone you love*. But she always made certain that he knew how much she appreciated everything he did, and every small part of him, because she never wanted to take him for granted. And the gratitude was for herself as much as for him, a reminder of where she was and how important Tommy was to her well-being. If she didn't thank him, she feared that she would lose her way.

She knew that she was lucky to have Tommy, and at least once each day she experienced a mortal fear of what would happen should that luck desert her.

Walking back towards Tommy's battered old Toyota, holding his hand, Jayne's discomfort was just beginning to grow as the sinking afternoon sun started to lengthen their shadows. The day was already a pleasing memory. Some days lived for ever; she never usually knew that when they were happening, but some time after she would realise that they had been among the best days of her life.

Jayne's mother was still alive, somewhere, and the only time there was true tension between her and Tommy was when he suggested that they should get in touch.

Didn't you see *her?* she'd ask him, never quite shouting, never truly calm. *You have no idea. No concept of what I went through before I met you.* And he'd let it lie because he knew it would do no good. Jayne had made that very clear from the start; she was on her own, two thousand miles from where she'd been born, and her family had died with her brother. He'd been a small-time criminal, dragged into the LA gang culture and found dead at the age of seventeen with a bullet in the back of his skull and his genitals cut off. The coroner hadn't been able to tell whether the mutilation was post-mortem, and Jayne had the impression that no one cared. One less gang-banger, one less headache for the LAPD. And when her mother had received the phone call she'd hung up, drunk another bottle of wine, and told Jayne later that evening when she arrived home from school.

Johnny's dead, hon. Can you fetch your mother another bottle?

Why didn't you call me!?

What good woulda that done?

Johnny!

He knew how it'd end up. I told him often enough. Now get your mother another bottle, hon.

Another bottle, and another, was the way it had been going, and the way it continued from then until Johnny's sad funeral. Three fuckers had shown up an hour after the last mourners had left, when Jayne was still kneeling beside her only brother's grave watering the soil with her tears. They'd sauntered past her and stood beside the grave, then pulled pistols and fired three quick shots as some sort of fucked-up salute. Jayne had stood to run after them, beat some sense into their twisted, drug-addled brains, but her legs had folded beneath her as her muscles cramped, driving wedges of pain into her brain. They'd laughed as they ran away, and she'd woken later with paramedics tending her along with the old lady who'd found her and was fussing around nearby.

Next day, she'd remained at home long enough to pack some clothes and steal a thousand dollars from her mother's back-drawer stash. Then she'd called her school sweetheart Tommy and told him she was leaving LA to live with her cousin in Birmingham, England.

'It's been a lovely day,' she said. 'Thanks.'

'Only did it 'cos I want a blow job tonight.'

'Yeah, right.' Jayne laughed, and the freeing of tension lessened the pains in her neck. *Complete relaxation is the key*, one specialist had told her, while another had said *Exercise as much as you can, gently and often*. Walking in the hills with her love gave her the best of both options.

When Tommy had said he'd come with her, she'd seen a whole new future opening up. They'd got as far as Knoxville, fallen in love with the place, and stayed. On days like today she was living in that future, bright and secure as if she awaited the fate of a normal person, not someone destined to die young. The churu was an insidious beast, kept at bay by a morning massage while it ate away at her from inside.

'No, I mean it,' Tommy said, mock serious. 'I need head. I'll be sitting on the sofa, and you can have a floor cushion so you're comfortable.' He took a small tin from his pocket and extracted a ready-rolled joint. 'Hands free.' He tucked the joint in the corner of his mouth, a poor James Dean. 'Then if you're lucky, baby, I'll return the favour.'

'Nah. *American Idol*'s on tonight.'

The joint tilted groundward. 'A man knows where he stands.'

'Yeah.' Jayne squeezed his hand, and he squeezed back before letting go to light up. She turned away to look down over the hillside towards the car park and the lowlands beyond. The trees cast complex afternoon shadows and in the distance she could just make out the haze of Knoxville. Closer by were several smaller towns they'd driven through on the way here, set in the landscape like diamonds on felt. She caught a whiff of pot and walked a few steps, trying to blink away the memory of Johnny. Usually she could successfully avoid dwelling on the past, even when Tommy's smoke took her back home for a few brief, intense seconds. But today Johnny grinned at her and showed her his latest gang tattoo, a mark he'd got for robbing a drugstore the previous week. There was pride in his smile, and disgust in her voice as she chided him, though now she couldn't even remember the words. Her memories were tainted by the alcohol haze of their mother as she breezed into the room, unaware of either of her children's lives.

'Sorry,' Tommy said. 'I know you don't like it.' He held her arm, having already inhaled most of the joint and stamped it out.

'You know you never need to apologise,' Jayne said, and she meant it. Tommy's need and her own history were different animals, and if they ever met and fought that was her concern, not his.

The view was gorgeous. There were still twenty or more cars in the car park, their owners walking the hillsides or lighting barbecues in the picnic area a quarter of a mile to the north. She could see a few people down by the cars, hanging around the vehicles' open doors as if to put off leaving for as long as possible. And she knew why. Maybe lots of people came to this beauty spot to escape something else, and the process of going back always dampened an otherwise bright day. *Not everyone's sad*, she thought, and as ever that idea shocked her. Was she sad? She liked to think not, but sometimes her friend Ellie would have a glass too much wine and tell her she carried sadness around like a haze. *Not a cloud*, she would say, *not like someone can see, but . . . like heat haze.*

I see you through it and you're distorted. Not the woman you want to be, but the woman you really are. Sad. Jayne would tell her to fuck off, then pour another glass for them both. But these infrequent yet serious statements from Ellie stuck with her, nestling in her subconscious to sabotage moments like now.

'I'm not sad,' Jayne said.

'Well, good.'

'I mean it. I'm not. *We're* not.'

'Hell, no!' Tommy said. She saw the twinkle in his eyes from the pot, the lazy smile that he'd keep for the rest of the journey home, and longer if he smoked some more.

She grabbed Tommy and pulled him close, hugging him tight, tenderness beyond a kiss. 'Take me home and let's see about that sofa.'

'Your wish is my command.'

'As ever.'

They walked down the hillside holding hands, following a rough path that had been worn through the trees by thousands of feet over many years. The churu was biting in now, grating her knees and ankles and setting fires in her hips which would simmer and burn for the rest of the evening, but she was determined not to let it spoil the day.

From somewhere distant, a loud explosion.

'What was that?' Jayne asked.

'Beats me.' Tommy nodded towards the car park, two hundred feet downhill from them. 'They heard it, too.' People were standing still, and some of them were pointing north at the road that wound away from the car park and up towards the more heavily wooded mountains.

Jayne saw where the narrow road passed the car park before it was swallowed behind a screen of trees and a fold in the land. She felt a twinge of unease.

'Backfire,' Jayne said. 'Come on, let's go.'

'What's the matter, babe?' Tommy could hear the strain in her voice, always could. With him she could never feign comfort when she was in pain. 'It startin' in early tonight?'

'It's not that,' she said. A man had walked to the end of the car park and seemed to be on his mobile phone, and he turned to wave back at his wife standing by their car.

'What's he shouting?' Tommy asked.

'Don't know,' Jayne said. 'Maybe there's been a smash?'

'Yeah, must've been.'

They walked on, still holding hands and moving a little faster now, eager to see what had happened even though Jayne didn't really want to.

From behind the fold in the land to the north rose a wisp of smoke, dancing with the breeze. The wisp soon became thicker, and in seconds the smoke was dark and billowing.

'Tommy . . .'

'Yeah. Come on.' They moved faster, although Jayne couldn't see what they could do. The guy with the mobile phone was running for the far end of the car park, and several other people were moving uncertainly in that direction. The emergency services would have been called, and to cause smoke like that a fire must have taken hold quickly. Maybe a fuel tank had gone up. Her heart thudded and, much as she had no wish to see, human nature drew her on. *Everyone loves a train wreck*, Tommy had once said when they were stuck in a traffic queue. A mile and an hour later, they'd passed a crashed car and two people being attended by paramedics.

'Jesus Christ,' Tommy said, 'that guy's leaking claret!'

A man was stumbling along the narrow road towards the car park, emerging from behind the trees, and he seemed to be painted from head to foot in red. From this distance Jayne couldn't be sure, but she thought he was bald and naked from the waist up, the dark red creases that might have been a pattern on a shirt looking more like terrible gashes across his shoulders and stomach.

'Tommy,' she said softly, and he turned to shield her from the sight, holding out his hands. 'No,' she said. 'We've got to go and help. You still got that first-aid kit in the trunk?'

'Yeah.' His eyes were wide with shock, and she could see that he was struggling to hold it together.

'Let's go, then,' she said. 'Looks like that cellphone guy's going to reach him first, and . . .' She trailed off, because the blood-soaked man had fallen to his knees. He pitched forward just at the entrance to the car park, and there was an audible gasp from all observers when his head struck the ground.

The man with the cellphone reached the prone body, and he stood a couple of feet away with his hands held out from his sides. He looked around, as if searching for support, then knelt by the other man's side.

The smell of burning filled the air now, and there was another thump as the unseen vehicle's petrol tank went up. A billow of smoke rose beyond the trees, supported on a ball of flame.

'Someone called the fire department and paramedics?' Tommy shouted. He received a couple of positive responses, then he and Jayne reached the car park and ran to his old Toyota. She grimaced as she ran, the movements grinding pain into her hips and knees, but she was the lucky one here. She was not bleeding.

'Tommy?'

'I can look after him until the paramedics get here,' he said, and she could see that he was shaking. It took three tries for him to slip his key into the lock, and when he glanced back at her she could see the shock in his expression. She nodded. He'd taken a basic first-aid course so he could look after her when she suffered her infrequent churu blackouts. *Not quite comas*, a doctor had told her, and she'd wanted to ask *What the hell do you know?*

The man was standing up. Jayne frowned, already seeing something wrong with the angle of his limbs as they pushed him upright, like a newborn deer just finding its legs, unfamiliar with gravity and light and everything in the world.

'Tommy.' She pointed.

The cellphone guy was still there, standing with the blood-soaked man. He reached out and not-quite-touched him, perhaps afraid of hurting him – he seemed to be covered with wounds, Jayne saw, slashed and holed and torn – or maybe afraid of what this meant. Because the man shouldn't be standing like that. Even from a hundred feet away Jayne could see that the agony had slipped from his face, along with the open-mouthed panic. There was something else there now.

As she tried to identify it, he lurched against the cellphone man, slung one arm around the back of his neck, and bit into his scalp.

'Shit!' someone shouted, and Jayne thought, *Yeah*. A man shouted in shock. A woman screamed. A kid squealed for its mommy.

'Jayne . . .' Tommy said, his hand still on the car door. 'Jayne . . .'

'Someone help him!' Jayne shouted. A car door

slammed and a big guy with a long beard and long grey hair trotted past them. He was carrying a hunting rifle.

Cellphone guy screamed. It was a terrible sound in that tranquil place. The blood-drenched man pushed him away, ripping a chunk from his face and spraying the air with gore. It pattered down on the dry car park, but Jayne saw it painted on the air for ever, hanging there like a still from some horror movie. He chewed and spat, then turned to the car park.

Behind him the cellphone man had collapsed, and Jayne thought, *If I was him I'd be running like hell.*

The blood-soaked man stood silently. And then he ran.

'Get in the car,' Tommy said. He opened the door without taking his stare off the running man.

'No, I'm not—' There were more people running around the bend in the road from the direction of the unseen fire. Jayne counted five, and they were all wrong. Some were stained dark with dried blood. A young girl was wearing a bunny outfit, one leg ripped open. One man seemed to have lost an arm at the elbow, the remnants of clothing and flesh flapping as he ran. The only sound of their progress was the slap, slap, slap of feet on the road surface, and Jayne thought, *They can't* all *have been in the car.*

The guy with the gun stopped and braced himself, lifting the rifle and aiming it at the running, blood-covered man. *I don't want to see anyone shot,* Jayne thought, thinking of Johnny and how they said he'd been found. But the gunshot never came. The man seemed unable to pull the trigger, and the blood-drenched man barrelled into him and knocked him back off his feet. They struggled on the ground, the rifle held sideways between them, and as the attacker's teeth audibly snapped at the big man's face he used the gun to shove him aside.

The long-haired man stood, looking around the car park as if for help. And then behind him the cellphone man got to his feet, and Jayne could see the mess of his chin and throat.

'In the fucking car, now!' Tommy hissed.

'You too!'

'Jayne—'

'The police will be here! You too!'

'Look out!' someone shouted, and the rifle guy spun around. He brought the gun up, and this time Jayne knew he was going to use it. But the blood-covered man took him down again, and moments later the cellphone guy reached them, and together they bit and clawed while the big man screamed like a wounded pig.

'We need to go!' Jayne screamed, eyeing the girl in the bunny outfit as she raced into the far end of the car park. The one-armed man followed, scattering the crowd ahead of him, some diving for their cars, a couple more running in panic with no thought of direction. Jayne started shaking uncontrollably, each shiver prompting stabs of pain from her burning joints. Her vision swayed and swam, darkening briefly, and she thought, *Oh no not now not now.*

A car started somewhere, then another, and she heard the screech of tyres as they sped away. She staggered to the door that Tommy had opened for her and fell in, pressing her head back against the seat. She bit her lip. Her vision cleared a little, and she saw that Tommy had slammed the door. *Tommy, you should be in here with—*

He moved in front of the car and looked along the car park, and a Mazda Miata struck him and flipped him over its hood. He rolled over the windscreen and spun in the air as the vehicle passed beneath him, his head striking first trunk and then the ground as it sped away. *That woman had blood in her ear*, Jayne had time to think, a heart-stopping detail, and then she processed what had happened.

'Tommy!' she screamed. '*Tommy!*'

Someone fired a gun, three times in quick succession.

Jayne cracked the door open and put her right leg out, hanging on to the frame to lift herself up. The fainting spell had passed but she felt so pathetically weak, and now Tommy needed her and there was no way she could let him down. No way. She stood away from the car, and the gun fired again. Across the car park, a Prius had its windscreen shattered by a stray shot.

People screamed and ran. Car engines roared. Someone was on the ground not far away, a young teenage boy, and a man was chewing at one bare leg. The boy screamed and kicked, but even though his other foot struck the man's head and neck and shoulder, the attacker seemed unconcerned. It was the rifle man, Jayne saw. His beard had gone from grey to red. Another gunshot, and Jayne moved around the open door and leaned against the car's wing.

A huge crash came from her right. The Miata had struck a station wagon at the car park's entrance, but she was only concerned for Tommy. Everything else was too much information, and her brain refused to process it. *Keeping it for later*, she thought, and that was fine, because instinct had already told her that this had to be just her and him.

'Tommy,' Jayne said. He was twisting on the ground like a toy winding down.

Another gunshot, and from the corner of her eye Jayne saw a shape fall to the ground.

She started forward just as Tommy pushed himself up onto his hands and knees. Blood flowed from his nose as if from an open tap, and he kept his left hand inches above the ground. *His wrist's broken*, Jayne thought, and she imagined his one-handed massages for the next few weeks.

'Tommy!'

'Fuck . . .' he said, and she thought she'd never heard such a wonderful word. He knelt, then got one foot under himself.

'Quickly!'

'Yeah.'

Another gunshot, and for a second she could not understand what she had seen. Tommy slumped back to the ground – maybe he was ducking to dodge the bullets, making himself a smaller target. But his head had changed shape, and he'd lost part of himself on the gravel. *Got to get that*, Jayne thought, and then cold realisation froze her to the spot. She could not breathe. Tommy didn't even twitch.

A man appeared in front of her, a little guy in shorts and a T-shirt that said *I'm Spartacus*. He was carrying a crying toddler under one arm and in his other hand he held a pistol. He was pointing it at Jayne.

'Tommy?' she said, and the man glanced at Tommy's prone shape.

'Get away from the car!' the man said. He stepped past Tommy and came for her, the gun never wavering. 'Get away from the fucking—'

The running woman struck him and pushed him down, crushing the little boy beneath both of them. The gun discharged and Jayne felt no pain, no punch. The woman was wearing shorts, walking boots and a light jacket, and Jayne remembered seeing her up on the hillside. *Gorgeous day*, she'd said, and as she passed them Jayne had nudged Tommy in the ribs. *But hey, look at that ass*, he'd whispered. *Like a sweet peach.* Now she had what looked like a brutal bite mark on one shoulder, clothing torn away, skin ragged, and she attacked the man like a wild dog.

The boy was screaming, trapped beneath his struggling father and the woman – the *thing* – biting into him.

This is not happening, Jayne thought, but she was a new Jayne once again. The Jayne who'd been walking with her love ten minutes ago had changed into the one seeing a car crash, and its results. And now she was Jayne on her own. Because Tommy was dead, and there was no denying that.

The man's struggles weakened – the woman had bitten clean though his throat. Jayne could not comprehend the blood. His son – if that was who the boy was – was coated in it, still struggling, and the woman shoved the dying man aside as she reached for the child.

'No!' Jayne screamed, in denial at what she was seeing as much as against the woman's obvious intentions. The boy soon stopped screaming.

The woman looked up. *There's nothing in her eyes*, Jayne thought, and she edged back towards the open car door. It was the pain in her joints, the screaming agony in her jarred hips, that gave her the courage to live. It reminded her of her life and everything she had suffered, the trials she went through every day to see another sunrise and eat another meal. And as the woman stood, expressionless and cooing softly, and then came for her, Jayne stood sideways and swung the door wide open. It struck the woman's thighs and sent her staggering back, giving Jayne time to get inside the car and swing the door closed.

They're biting, not eating, she thought.

She tried to slam the door but the woman stuck her arm in the way. Jayne pulled, tugging as hard as she could, before easing the door back a little to slam it again, and again. She heard the crack of bone, but there was still no sound from the woman. She paused, looked up, and the woman grabbed her hand.

Jayne screamed for help. No one heard, or if they did they were too concerned with their own personal dramas. The woman heaved, and Jayne's shoulder burned white-hot with agony as she was lifted towards the space at the top of the open door. *There's a smell*, she thought, realising that the woman no longer smelled like a living person. She smelled like old clothes, damp and stale.

Jayne felt a sick coolness on her forearm, and then hot pain as the woman bit through her skin.

Unable to breathe, she went limp, and as the woman tried to adjust her grip Jayne fell across the seats and kicked out as hard as she could. The swinging door shoved the woman back against the neighbouring car.

Jayne sat up and reached out, slamming the door closed, hitting the locking knob, crying out in victory and pain.

Her arm was bleeding liberally from the bite. *I've got it*, she thought, and then she saw Spartacus and his young son standing up in front of the car. They looked around, faces slack and eyes empty, paying no regard at all to their wounds or each other. Then they saw her through the windscreen.

She heard their faint, haunting call.

The woman who'd bitten her – the woman with a peach ass – pressed her face to the side window, staring in. Her mouth hung open, and her teeth were stained with Jayne's blood.

They'll keep punching until they come through the glass, Jayne thought, but the woman turned and walked away. Spartacus and his son went in different directions, and then they were lost from sight behind the neighbouring cars.

Jayne screamed. She knew that she should remain silent, stay down and out of sight, but she was a different Jayne now, and she was more afraid than she had ever been before. She could see Tommy's body in front of the car, but knew that everything had moved on.

She put her left hand over the bite on her right forearm. The blood was warm and sticky. *They're just biting, passing it on, rabies or something worse.* She waited for whatever was to come, wondering if she'd feel the switch between being her and being one of them, and thought about the zombie films that Tommy had liked so much, and the online discussions he'd entered into, arguing the case for running zombies. *They're hunters*! he'd tell her, and she'd shake her head and mutter something about him being an overgrown kid.

Jayne kept her stare fixed on Tommy's body, ignoring the other movements she saw in her peripheral vision, and plucked her mobile from her jeans pocket. As she tapped in 911, she wondered how the hell she could make whoever answered believe her when she did not yet believe this madness herself.

Her vision darkened and she felt a familiar faint coming on. *Not now not now* . . . But she drifted away, and when she opened her eyes again an unknown length of time had passed. The sky was darker, the mountains above her lit by weakening evening sunlight, and three people were milling around the cars in front of her. All of them were shredded things, though none of the blood looked fresh. She thought they were checking the cars. Her vision swam once more and she rested her arm across her chest, bite on display, as the churu sucked her down again . . .

In dreams there were dead fingers massaging her awake, leaving trails of slick, rotting blood across her hips.

She woke again, jerking upright and crying out as the pain scorched in from her stiff joints. Tears came and blurred her vision, and she wiped her eyes with her arm, forgetting the wound. It was red-raw and still trickling blood, and perhaps that was good. *Cleaning the wound*, she thought, *so that I don't change and start doing what those things were doing.* And then she saw the little girl standing in front of the car.

Jayne gasped and sat up straighter. It was dusk now, maybe an hour since it had happened. Tommy was a shadow on the ground, and there was no sign of the three wandering people she'd seen before. *They must have looked in on me. Maybe one, maybe all three, and did they stand there and* stare *as I slept?*

The little girl wore her hair in a ponytail.

'Poor kid,' Jayne whispered, and her illness dragged her down once more into unconsciousness. Her cousin Jill called her across a stretch of water turned red with blood, reaching out but unable to touch. *I was coming to see you*, she said to Jill, *but I stopped and found peace with Tommy*, and Jill smiled in understanding and waved her urgently across the water. *But I can't, it's dirty, I'm clean, and if I step in I might . . .*

But Jill shook her head. She beckoned to Jayne, and—

—when she woke up her feet were kicking in the footwell, her arms thrashing at the seat, and she was trying to swim. She shouted out again in pain, crying herself fully awake. Her head thumped with the remnants of unconsciousness.

Jayne gasped and took several long, deep breaths. No one and nothing moved around her. Tommy was still there, and the little dead girl had gone. Across the car park lay another body, its face turned away from her. Breathing hard, afraid of another blackout, she searched for her mobile phone. When she found it she dialled 911 again.

Sorry, all our operators are busy with other calls, please stand by.

'What the fuck?' Jayne muttered. She dialled again and got the same message. And again. Then she dialled Ellie's landline and got her answerphone:

'Hey, Ellie here, I've pissed off to my folks in Kentucky. No way I'm hanging around for this shit.'

Jayne cancelled the call, shaking her head and terrified of the falling darkness, dialled 911 one more time – and a woman answered.

'Yeah?'

'I'm . . . something's happened to . . .' Jayne said, and the tears came. 'Tommy.'

'We'll have someone with you soon.' And the woman hung up.

Didn't even ask my name or where I was. Jayne stared at the phone, expecting the woman to ring back, willing help to come and someone to tell her everything was going to be all right. But the phone remained silent.

She started the car and eased forward, pausing beside

Tommy's body. Shadows lurked beneath and around the other abandoned vehicles, cast there by the setting sun. Maybe the infected ones were watching with their empty eyes.

'I'm sorry, Tommy,' Jayne whispered. She tried to remember the last thing she'd heard him say, and the final words she'd said to him.

As she pulled away from the car park she turned on the radio, and soon she realised why all those operators were busy.

8

Jonah had to shoot four more of the afflicted in the head. Sometimes he downed them with the first shot, other times it went wide or struck their chest or neck, and he'd have to nerve himself to shoot again. Each time he pulled the trigger he closed his eyes.

On his laptop he'd worked his way through the facility, opening and closing doors using automatic controls, luring the dead things this way and that until he could lock them away. There were five in the big walk-in fridge in the canteen, three in the services plant room, and two in the gym. The last of the four – those who had surprised him, or who had not gone the way he'd hoped where doors opened or closed – had dashed at him from a bathroom he'd believed to be locked down, and his instinct saved him. He was sure that if he'd had time to think about what was happening, realise what he was doing, then he would have missed. One of them was Ashleigh – she had been an archivist responsible for the storage and duplication of all Coldbrook's records – and he had shot her in the eye.

Jonah dragged each body to the accommodation room nearest to where he'd shot them, and locked them inside.

He'd been keeping a count of each one he'd locked away or put down. He was up to eighteen. With Holly and Vic gone, that left nine people unaccounted for. Some had escaped up the ventilation duct – he knew that for sure – but he had no idea how many. Not nine, he hoped. And yet the fewer that had made it up there, the more remained down here with him.

No one had emerged at the sounds of gunfire and made themselves known. The hope persisted that some were hiding themselves away, and there were still those three closed doors in an accommodation wing. He had passed them by, and perhaps soon he would think about opening them. Perhaps.

Because Jonah thought he might have gone insane. *What if I'm doing this for real?* he'd thought as he stalked corridors and shot down shadows. *What if I've lost my marbles, and picked up a gun, and tomorrow I'll be an item on the news, just another gun massacre that would fade into obscurity for all but those affected?* Madness had been an intriguing idea, and every time he pulled the trigger and opened his eyes again, he'd look carefully for any change in the zombies' faces, any glimpse that there was terror hiding behind the facades he had brought into being. But the empty eyes persisted, and when those afflicted were put down the only change was that the eyes no longer moved.

The change he *did* notice was purely physical – the brains remained wet. While the blood from their non-cranial wounds soon coagulated, tacky and drying, the mess blown from their skulls was still rich with blood. This made no sense if their hearts stopped, but Jonah supposed that blood might sit in the brain for a while, kept fresh and heavy with infection, and the drive to spread the disease lived with it. The infection killed them, and then took over their brains. Could impulses pass along blood-denuded nerves? He thought not, and yet he could see no other way for them to remain moving.

He would not let a supernatural explanation even suggest itself to him. He *could* not. There was a process here, and he had already worked out how to end it. Discovering more was essential.

Thinking through the science of a zombie actually settled his nerves a little. As he considered venturing to his room to retrieve the remaining Penderyn whisky, Jonah switched on the radio.

'. . . *found dead beside the road, and a further five bodies*

*were discovered in the camper van. A police source who
does not wish to be identified said the bodies were "heavily
mutilated about the head". Elsewhere, a Scout troop is
missing in the mountains north-east of Asheville. The
Scouts were due home at midday, but with no communication from them since early morning concern is increasing,
and parents are demanding a search-and-rescue. And in
Bryson City rumours are rife of an army of "shambling
ghosts" seen crossing the hillsides towards the township.
More on these stories—'*

Vic Pearson punched the 'off' button and the car fell
silent. Olivia snored softly in the back seat, and he
wondered when was the last time he'd watched his
daughter sleeping and wondered at her dreams. He hoped
these were still good ones. Soon, he feared, she would
see and know things that might banish childish dreams
for ever.

'Is that all because of what happened?' Lucy asked
from the passenger seat. Vic could not look at her,
because he feared the accusation in her eyes.

'It might be.'

'But have you told anyone? Have you warned them?'

'I told the sheriff.'

'But beyond that?'

The road was long and straight before them, a snake
of headlights and lamp posts, and none of them could

know what they were leaving behind. *He* didn't know, not really. Not yet.

'Jonah will be onto it,' Vic said.

'But it's spreading. Fast. Those shambling ghost things near Bryson City, do you think—'

'Maybe!' Vic said, harsher than he'd intended. Olivia mumbled something in her sleep, words he would never know.

'Don't snap at me, Vic,' Lucy said, intending to castigate him. But her nervous voice betrayed her fear. 'Bryson City . . . that's twenty miles from Danton Rock, maybe more.'

Vic had been thinking the same thing. And the Scout troop north-east of Asheville, that was even further away in the opposite direction. He drove on into the night, but when he closed his eyes he saw the darkness of that ventilation duct and smelled the scorched odour of its lockdown.

'Well, I want to know,' Lucy said softly, and she turned the radio back on.

I let it all out, Vic thought. He needed to tell her. *Everything that's happening is my fault. I let it escape.* But blame was bad enough coming from Jonah, and himself. He was not sure he could bear it from the woman he loved.

Some bland love song breezed into the car, and Lucy turned the dial in her search for more news.

'. . . *the Scout troop, and further reports are coming in of isolated violent incidents across the county. On the outskirts of Maryville a church has been found abandoned with blood splashed across its walls and floor. Police are suggesting vandalism, but eyewitnesses say that there are obvious signs of a struggle. Police in Newport have shot dead a man who was attacking and biting people on the streets. Not sure if that reads right, but . . . And here's . . . . a new item has just been put in front of me, there's a . . . a riot is going on in a suburb of Greenville, South Carolina. There are several fires reported, and the rioting crowd appears to be growing. And reports of . . . again, biting. This is NCRR Radio, more updates on these stories as they . . .*'

'Nothing about Knoxville yet,' Jayne muttered to herself, turning the radio down. 'I might still be okay. I might still make it.' She concentrated on her driving, not too fast, not too slow, not wishing to attract the attention of the law. Her bite was raw and painful, and she had slipped on a denim jacket to cover it up. But she couldn't risk being pulled over in case they checked and saw, and . . .

And what then? She didn't know. Because those fuckers had been zombies: she'd seen the movies and heard Tommy talking about the books he'd read, and she'd watched that guy taken down by the woman and his baby boy bitten, and then stand again as . . .

'As one of them,' she whispered. Tommy had stayed down, unbitten and ignored, because the guy had shot him in the head.

'Tommy,' she said aloud, and still the tears would not come. The fact of his death was firm with her, she had no doubts, yet it had still not hit home properly. The events *surrounding* his death still felt like some kind of mad dream, blood-filled and driven by painkillers and too much wine. She'd wake and tell Tommy about her zombie dream, and he'd laugh and massage her back to life as he did every morning, then go and smoke his joint.

She'd tried 911 four more times as she drove down out of the mountains, only managing to get through once. The guy she'd connected with had taken down the details, waiting patiently as she pulled over and cried as she relayed what had happened up in the car park. Then he'd confirmed that they'd get someone up there 'when they could'. He'd signed off without taking her address or contact number.

Since then she'd driven with the radio on, because word always spread.

She thought about Ellie, her friend who'd already fled Knoxville ahead of these weird news reports. She had always been easily panicked, and seemed to take the world's problems on her shoulders. Every week there was another Armageddon that she knew would be the end of her, from Ebola to swine flu, asteroid strikes to global warming, and for someone with such strength of character Jayne was surprised that Ellie could be so afraid.

'Right to be scared of this shit, Ells,' Jayne said.

And as she ran through a mental list once again – *passport in my desk, couple of hundred bucks stashed in underwear drawer, credit cards, airport a twenty-minute drive from home* – she spared a thought for her mother. It was rare that Jayne thought of her at all. She was a ghost in her past, scar tissue on her memory, and she could barely remember her face. That tie had been severed years ago. There were no more, and it was time to finish the journey she'd begun when she had left LA.

It was dark now, and Tommy was still lying dead in that car park. Mountain animals would be emerging from their hiding places, joining the shadows as they grew from the ground. She should never have left him there at the mercy of carrion creatures.

Gasping a sudden, shuddering sob, she turned up the radio and scanned it to a talk station.

'. . . *seven times, and they jus' tell me "please hold on, we're busy an' try an' call back later", but the guy was* standin' *there, starin' in my window with his* throat *gone and . . .'*

'. . . *ask the Lord for help and forgiveness, sinners, because the time has come to count your sins, stack them against the unbreachable wall of His limitless compassion, and if you don't seize the moment and bow down now the tide of death will sweep over you, and you'll die without Jesus in your heart . . .'*

'. . . they don't die, and if these psycho Rapture dudes realised that they'd be running like the rest of us. They don't die. I saw one hit by a truck and dragged two hundred feet under the wheels, and when the trucker got out and went to check, the roadkill reached up and dragged him down and bit him. They bite. That's what I've heard. I'm telling you, they don't die, and what're the authorities doing about all this? Just what are they . . .?'

'. . . confused right now, but there do seem to be isolated incidents of violence occurring at this time. The situation is under review, and all our resources are committed to investigating the cause of this violence and protecting members of the public from these few individuals who seem intent on . . .'

'. . . and my neighbour called, black guy, and the cop asked if he was white, 'cos if he was white he could help him, and told him there's no brothers when it comes to the end of time, only the Lord and his children. And my neighbour's the best Christian I ever met, and that mother-fucker *asked him if he was fucking* white!'

Jonah turned off the radio and closed his laptop screen, hiding the news site from view. The reports were sketchy, but there was no denying the proliferation of attacks.

He didn't need to hear any more because he knew it was out there in the world, and he was more responsible than that prick Pearson. Vic might have opened the way, but Jonah had welcomed it into the world. *Maybe Bill really did know the risks in what we were doing.* Jonah had read the old man's diaries, witnessed the paranoia he'd been suffering before he died – he thought he was being watched, every minute of the day – but perhaps there was something more. Something he'd never been able to write down.

It didn't really matter any more.

Jonah switched one of the screens to the single inner-core camera. He took a deep breath before looking, because what they had done danced along the fringes even of his understanding. He knew some of it, but not all, and he liked to tell people – financiers, employers, those who sought to question Coldbrook's undertaking – that Coldbrook's core was a sum of the minds and knowledge that had gone in to make it. But he had always known the truth. Bill Coldbrook had made the leaps of intuition to give them this, and then he had killed himself.

Bill's comments about the Core had enthralled Jonah decades ago and they still did now. It sat behind eight feet of reinforced fifty-newton concrete, a foot of layered lead, six inches of steel, nine inches of graphite, and the largest Penning-trap network ever . . . and yet what was inside was a world away.

And Jonah opened his eyes to see.

The glow was both there – and not there. Staggering energies danced within flashes of quark-gluon plasma, countless collisions gave the core a sea of possibilities. It felt as though he was seeing with his own eyes and also remembering the view from someone else's, when the core containment was still being constructed and the core itself remained a dream. It was an incredibly disturbing experience, and the first time he'd ever seen it he'd told Bill that he was seeing inside Schrödinger's box while the experiment was still under way. Bill had laughed, taken him to one side, poured a drink.

What he saw existed in a fold between realities. It was beautiful. It was terrifying. And he shut off the camera, remembering what Holly had said the one and only time she had looked. *It's like seeing into the mind of God.*

'He's having a nightmare right now,' Jonah muttered, and he stared at his list. There were the names of a dozen people, most of whom he had not seen for many years. He hoped they could all help. He flicked on the radio again as he started dialling, keeping it low, a background theme to his culpability.

'. . . *might well be a form of rabies. No one has yet been able to run tests, but from the descriptions that have come in – somewhat glorified and exaggerated, I suspect – it seems that the attacker is possessed by some kind of madness,*

and the victim is quickly infected. I believe one commen-
tator has referred to them as . . . zombies? Well, let me
tell you, science completely precludes . . .'

'We need to stop and rest,' Lucy said.

'I'm fine.'

'You've been driving for hours.'

'Really, I'm fine,' Vic said. 'Just a bit longer.' Lucy had
been scanning the radio, sometimes settling on a station
playing sterile love songs, sometimes finding a news
channel, occasionally encountering religious or talk
shows where the theories were becoming more out-
rageous by the minute. *Zombies*, someone had said, and
she'd snorted and scanned away. And, all the while, Vic
had been absorbing the information and knowing for
sure that it was ten times worse than anyone claimed.

He remembered a few years ago when the terrible
earthquake had struck the Caribbean island of Hispaniola.
Haiti had been devastated, but for a long time the only
firm news coming out of the country had been from
individuals on blogs, independent radio stations and
mobile phones. Confusion had reigned about how
bad the quake had been and how many were affected,
and even fly-bys by the US Coast Guard had given only
a vague idea of the power and severity of the quake. It
had taken almost twenty-four hours for outside agencies
to penetrate to the affected zones, and another two weeks

before the full, terrible human cost had been realised. At the time it had shocked him that, in a world so interconnected through the media and various forms of instant communication, a tragedy such as the quake could have caused such confusion for so long.

That was happening now, in the USA, and it was not a confined incident. But he could still hear that level of shocked confusion in most of the voices he heard, those of some of the newscasters most of all. *How long until the big picture emerges?* he wondered. He did not want to be anywhere near when he found out.

The satphone buzzed. He'd plugged it into the cigarette lighter to charge, and now he plucked it up and checked the screen. *Holly!* But no, of course not. Holly had gone through. Glancing sidelong at Lucy, offering her a weak smile that she did not return, he answered.

'Jonah.'

'Vic. Where are you?'

'Heading north on 75.' He saw no reason to lie.

'How far are you from Cincinnati?'

'Two, maybe three hours. Jonah, are you okay?'

'Do you care?'

'Of course I care!' Vic glanced at Lucy. She was looking at him with something like pity. She signalled to the side of the road and mouthed at him to pull over. He nodded. 'Hang on, I'm driving.' He pulled over and switched off the engine. Olivia stirred in the back seat and then snuggled down again. Lucy leaned back to arrange their daughter's blanket.

'Do you have any idea what's happening?' Jonah asked, and Vic could picture the old bastard's stern expression, his intelligent eyes narrowed to slits beneath the weight of his frown.

'Probably far worse than anyone's guessing,' Vic said. A big truck powered by, rocking their car slightly.

'The radio's bad enough,' Jonah said. 'News is sketchy, and the eyewitness accounts are mostly hysterical. It's spreading, and fast. Some people are almost treating it as a joke! And some of the websites I've glanced at . . . But anyway, that's beside the point. There are people I've spoken to who might be able to help us.'

'Us?' Vic asked. Lucy was looking at him, eyebrows raised, but he held up one hand.

'Don't you want to put this right?' Jonah's voice sounded strained, even through the static of the fluctuating connection.

'You'd ask *me* for help?'

'I'm not asking – I'm demanding. You need to fix this. There are things you know that will be invaluable to the people I'm sending you to, and—'

'Sending me? You're not sending me anywhere.'

'So where are you going?' Jonah asked. Lucy had already asked him that. Vic had not replied, simply shoving the question to one side with a succession of delaying moves: he was tired, let's talk when we stop and eat, don't worry so much . . .

Where exactly *were* they going? If they reached Cincinnati and the chaos spread north, they could drive to Detroit, and head north from there: Canada was a ferry trip away. But after that? He'd only considered it briefly, unable to deal with anything other than getting his family to safety.

'Somewhere . . .' Vic said, and his voice suddenly faltered. 'Somewhere safe.' Lucy reached over and held his hand. She knew when he needed contact, just as she knew when he needed space, and that was another reason why he loved her so much.

'I had a wife,' Jonah said after a pause. 'You know. I've told you. She was beautiful, and I'd have done anything for her. In a way, that's what I still am doing.' He paused, and Vic wondered, *What have you been doing down there?* 'But you also have responsibility, Vic. Don't you understand?'

'Not really. I'm an engineer, not a friggin' genius quantum physicist.'

'The effort will need overseeing. To battle this thing, find a cure, stop it. We have our differences, but you know me and our work here better than anyone. And of the two of us, there's more chance of you staying alive.'

'What's happening down there?'

'Nothing good. Nothing that can be . . . undone.' Jonah

sighed, and Vic heard the rattle of computer keys. *He's only just hanging on.* 'So you'll do it.'

'Yeah,' Vic said. Whatever the truth behind the garbled radio news and witness reports, people were dead right now and they wouldn't be dead if he'd stayed in Coldbrook. He could trace the guilt to earlier than that – to Jonah for okaying the final breach attempt, to Bill Coldbrook for applying his genius to such a project, and back down the line to human curiosity, the search for truth, the quest for a reason – but, however far back he went, the final fault was his.

'I'll tell you everything,' he whispered to Lucy. She nodded slowly, and he knew she realised the gravity of what he had to say. And back into the satphone he said, 'Jonah, I'll do what I can. But on one condition, and this isn't about me and it's non-negotiable: my family stay safe.'

'Of course,' Jonah said.

'I mean it! I'll put myself at risk, but not them.' He looked at Lucy, crying softly in the seat beside him. 'Never them.'

'Never them,' Jonah said. 'And that's why, despite all this, you're not a bad lad.'

Vic coughed, a cross between a laugh and a sob. And the cars and trucks and buses passed them by, most of their drivers probably not even realising that they were going the right way. At the moment the threat was still cloaked in confusion, and perhaps people were always unwilling to accept the worst. But soon, very soon, there would be proper panic.

'The man I'm sending you to is called Marc Dubois,' Jonah said. 'He's a phorologist: studies disease carriers and the spread of epidemics. He's one of the best in the world. He's a good friend, and he's at Cincinnati University. They've got a secure place there. He's preparing it.'

'What sort of place?'

'Somewhere for times like this.'

Jonah gave him Marc's contact details, they finished their conversation, and as Vic disconnected he felt a moment of overwhelming shame. While he'd been running, Jonah had been working, doing his best to devise ways in which this horror could be controlled now that it could no longer be contained.

'So are you going to tell me where we're going?' Lucy asked softly.

'Cincinnati. But first I've got to tell you why this is all my fault.' Vic stared through the windscreen. It had started to rain, and the stream of tail lights looked distorted. His wife held his hand, and he thought of Holly, realising that he had been a student of guilt for quite some time.

'. . . *all but abandoned, though rumour has it there were at least thirty mutilated bodies found around the small town.*

So what happened to the rest of the population of over a thousand inhabitants? Where are they? No one knows. And no one knows why the authorities have labelled reports of "the dead rising" media scaremongering, when it's quite clear from diverse eyewitness accounts that many of these attackers have been shot down, burned, electrocuted, fallen from a great height, or been crushed, only to recover to attack again. And no one knows why at least fifteen churches in Tennessee have reportedly closed their doors to non-believers. Battening down the hatches for the Rapture? You better believe it. Listen out for the sound of Heaven's horns, people. And no one knows quite why that man in Chattanooga decapitated his baby son and three daughters while his wife was at work, or why police used machine guns against rioting civilians in Highland Park. People from Chattanooga, get on that choo-choo first chance you get. And folks are starting to ask why the President has yet to make a statement, why National Guard convoys are driving left and right, unable to find their own assholes, and why towns in Georgia and South Carolina are seeing vigilante gangs shooting people in the streets and burning their bodies. No one knows anything, people. And that's why I'm remaining on air 24/7 from now on, because as soon as Richie Brock knows something, you will too. Remember, my number is—'

Jayne flicked the radio off and checked everything she'd laid out on her bed. Money, passport, purse, overnight bag, clothes. That was it. That was all she wanted to take, because everything else would remind her . . .

She had called her cousin, forgetting that it was late in Britain. *I'm coming to stay with you*, she'd said, and she'd hung up as Jill had mumbled something through her sleepy confusion. At least she knew she was still there.

The bite throbbed. She hated looking at it, because it reminded her again of what she should have become. She should be out there with them now, racing through the streets and looking for someone else to bite. But all she felt was sickness with the pressure of restrained grief, and queasy with pain from the familiar hated fires in her joints.

They probably wouldn't let her on a plane with her medicine.

Maybe all flights had been cancelled.

She wished she had a gun.

Jayne slammed her apartment door. She had a rucksack over one shoulder, a purse over the other, Tommy's key fob in her hand, and a fresh bandage wrapped around her cleaned and sterilised wound.

'. . . *in the head, this is what we've been told by email from someone calling themselves Wendy Coldbrook. "Shoot them in the head – I've done it, and it works." So there you have it, folks. We're being attacked by zombies! Crack out the bourbon, batten down the hatches, and get that*

survival plan you've been working on for fucking years into
action. Whoop whoop! It's Thriller time!'

Jonah sat in silence at last, satisfied that he had at last
been mentioned, but unable to listen to any more radio
reports – confusion, fear, religious tirades, hysteria, ridicule
– and overwhelmed by the mass of information pouring
out onto the Internet. There were a thousand accounts,
many of them undoubtedly made up, but among them
he perceived a few that must be true.

Perhaps some people would heed his advice.

He needed to rest, although he was not yet alone.
There was a sense of something else sharing Coldbrook
with him, perhaps a fellow skulking survivor avoiding
him, maybe other members of the afflicted that he had
not yet found. But in truth it felt like neither of these.
Twice over the past couple of hours he had seen
something that had sparked terrible memories. Once
he had seen a shadow of something inhuman, slipping
around a corner when he approached as if it had been
repulsed by Jonah's own shadow. And when he got to
Control and tried to wedge the door closed – the locking
system destroyed by whatever Satpal had done to it –
he'd looked up into the glass wall, and his reflection had
been wrong. The glass was misted by a strange fog
issuing from the breach, so the image was unclear, but
he had seen swollen eyes and a protruding snout, and

bristles across his scalp holding glinting diamonds of moisture.

My nightmare! A blink, and the image was gone. All the way back to Secondary, he was certain that he was being followed.

Safely locked away again, Jonah breathed in deeply, listening to the sounds of his own body, feeling his weakening heart surging on in his chest. He'd sent Vic to Marc, and through the two of them he could focus all his attempts to find out how to stop this.

It was not going to be easy.

Coldbrook's incredible achievement was tainted for ever.

He stared at the screen offering a view into the breach chamber, thought of poor lost Holly, and wondered what would come next.

Sunday

1

There is a long, high wall surrounding the courtyard. In the courtyard, dozens of people are hustling to load a pile of green boxes into the luggage compartment of a huge bus. The vehicle is battered and filthy. The people appear worried but orderly. All except one woman screaming in French about judgement and sin, and whose loose robes appear to be soiled with her own madness. The others avoid the woman, but some glance at her with impatience, or anger.

From somewhere beyond the wall there comes the dreadful hooting sound that Jonah has heard before, echoed through a thousand mouths. Atop the wall, four men dash back and forth on metal walkways, looking down the other side. They're carrying guns, and Jonah wonders why they are not shooting.

A man and woman are working beneath the bus's raised engine cover. He can hear them talking in hushed, urgent tones, and the people coming back and forth with boxes glance warily their way.

On the wall a pulsing, flexing shadow is silhouetted against the bright sky. Jonah shields his eyes to see better, and he can make out limbs and heads and clawed hands as people start tumbling from the other side.

It's all so hopeless.

More shouts, and the madwoman starts chanting something high and shrill.

There's a gunshot and Jonah thinks, *Fighting back.* But one of the guards kicks up a cloud of dust as he hits the ground, his pistol still clasped in his left hand.

Useless to fight back . . . pointless to resist the tide . . .

It is not his voice.

The trickle of bodies becomes a wave. They are being forced up and over from below, and the size of the pile of corpses necessary to get them over a twelve-foot wall must be unimaginable. *That's the clawing and scraping,* Jonah thinks, *clothes and fingers and teeth grating against the concrete wall.* They flow onto the metal walkway and rain to the ground below, and set against the sky it seems to be one huge, grotesque living mass.

The man and woman working on the engine have pulled pistols from their belts. They dash to where three children cower beside the bus, and whisper words of love to each of them before shooting them in the head. Then they hug each other, and Jonah hears them counting, *un, deux, trois*, before—

—the boat is drifting along the canal, seven people sitting around its cockpit looking shocked and afraid. They are all wet. The vessel seems to be driving itself, and when Jonah looks back he sees the elegant movement of a mechanical flipper shoving at the churned water, giving the craft speed.

Behind the boat and back along the canal, Jonah can see a slick of burning oil reaching from bank to bank. There are shapes writhing in the fire and others emerging from it, swimming under their own power until they sink and the flames on their heads are extinguished with a hiss.

In the boat, a small child slips to the deck and falls still. Her mother attends to her, while the others watch, exhausted.

They are wretched and without hope. Again, the voice is not Jonah's, and it feels like a solid strange weight inside his skull.

The mother breathes a sigh of relief. Her daughter sits up. Jonah wants to shout, because he sees nothing in the little girl's eyes, but he is just as silent here as he was before. The girl's mouth falls open, and—

There are maybe fifty people running across the desert of black ice. Grim-faced men and hard-faced women are arranged around the outside of the group, while at its centre are a dozen children and several very old people. They wear heavy animal pelts, and the adults and a few of the kids carry an incredible amount of equipment on their backs. The old people and very young children carry only their own clothes. Their breath plumes around them, but running keeps them warm, and their pace seems to be steady and comfortable. It takes a moment for Jonah to realise that he is running with them.

They delay the inevitable . . . That stranger's voice, rasping and heavy.

A mile behind them there is a wall of people. They also run, but there is no breath pluming around them, and they carry nothing. Many are naked and pale. Their pursuit creates a distant thunder of thousands of pounding feet, and a humming on the air.

There is no wasted talk within the small group, and also no apparent destination ahead of them. Jonah feels a spike of desperation, but there is a confidence among the people that he cannot deny. *They know where they're going*, he thinks, and then a tall old man stumbles and cries out.

For a moment the group slows, but then one of the women shouts and they run on. She stays behind with the old man, and Jonah, unseen, remains with them.

The man says something to the woman, and even though Jonah cannot understand the words he knows they are soft and loving. She smiles, then reaches behind her shoulder and whips something through the air. As the man's head tilts away from his neck on a fountain of blood, Jonah tries to open his mouth in a silent scream, and—

The shrill ringing of the satphone smothered the sound of thundering feet, and Jonah snapped awake. He'd nodded off while leaning back in a chair, his legs crossed and feet propped on the control desk, and the first thing he saw was the creature sitting on his legs. Silhouetted against the screen display of the breach chamber, it presented the same silhouette as before: spiky scalp, protruding mouth. Its hand was extended, fingers clasped around a blood-red object which waved tendrils like those of a sea anemone.

Those ideas that all struggle is hopeless, those are its *thoughts.*

Still swathed in the residue of sleep Jonah asked, 'Just what the bastard hell are you?'

The shape shifted slightly, and Jonah saw the stains of tattoos across its forearms, old ink smudged by time beneath pale skin. It turned on his outstretched legs to face the other way, and its robe fell open to offer a candid, grotesque view of its genitals. It was a long time since Jonah had seen another man naked, and it added to the shocking surrealism of the moment.

The thing – the man – turned his head towards the viewing screen. Jonah glanced that way, saw the view of Accommodation with the three closed doors, and then he felt the subtle weight lift from his legs. He closed his eyes briefly before looking again.

The strange man had gone. Left him alone. So alone, and the only thing he craved now was company. Jonah looked around Secondary, finding it hard to catch his breath as he tried to comfort himself with the idea that it was a dream. But he could still feel the cold wet kiss of those tendrils against his scalp.

He snapped up the satphone as it trilled again, but when he answered the caller had signed off. *Marc Dubois*, the screen said, but Marc could wait because he was only a voice. Jonah looked at the screen again – those closed doors, hiding things he might want to see, or not – and then ran a check of the route between Secondary and the relevant accommodation wing. No walking things, no shadows. It seemed clear.

Panting, he checked the pistol and stood by the door, staring through the small viewing pane at the silent corridor beyond. He'd dragged the two bodies from out there and locked them in a store cupboard but there were still splashes of brain and dried blood on the floor and walls.

He ignored the mess and ran.

2

I wonder if they feel any different, Jayne thought. *When they change. When they rage. I wonder if they know they've changed*. She glanced at the sleeve of her jacket, beneath which was the bandage, and beneath that the bite, and knew that *she* had not transformed.

Jayne was a frequent student of death. There had been her brother's murder, and her mother's own living demise contained within the murky depths of bottles of cheap wine. And the churu had driven Jayne to consider suicide many times, whether in idle speculation on a cold winter's afternoon when Tommy was out working, or a more serious analysis of the route she could take, and the implications, during those less frequent moments of real despair. Mostly she cast those thoughts aside with a shake of the head, and then went to find something that made her life worth living – the books she enjoyed reading, the food she was adept at cooking, Tommy's unconditional love.

But she often considered what death meant, and she was sad at the thought of everything she was being so easily wiped away.

Now there were these things that seemed to be beyond death. And that changed everything.

Her arm throbbed as she steered the old Toyota into a parking space. The wound had stopped bleeding, but she could still feel the sharp imprints of that woman's teeth, their points piercing her skin and digging down into the meat of her. If Jayne hadn't been lucky, the woman's teeth would have pressed together, scraping across bone and ripping away a chunk of her arm. *And what germs do I have?* she wondered. *What infection did she plant in me, and is it still in me now?* She switched off the car's engine, sat motionless for a while, and decided that thinking about it too much would be the end of her.

She'd been bitten and had survived. Now she must accept it and move on.

The drive through the dark night had been terrifying, and surreal. At one intersection Jayne had seen three cars crashed together and burning, a group of people on the sidewalk shouting and arguing about whose fault it had been. Turning a corner, heading out of town, she'd passed a long straight row of bars and restaurants, and a crowd had spilled onto the streets, bottles and glasses clasped in their hands, singing, living it up. *Tommy's dead!* she'd wanted to shout, but she didn't think they'd have cared. Perhaps many of them didn't yet know about the strange attacks and the even stranger consequences, but she suspected that the ones partying hardest *did* know.

She'd dreaded getting caught in traffic approaching the airport, but there was only a slight hold-up. She'd wondered at that. Had people really not grasped what was happening? But then, she had witnessed things first-hand. Had seen people bitten and shot, run over and killed, only to stand up again and come at her with those empty, animal eyes. Eyes that held the depth of true death. So she supposed that news reports – garbled, confused, and unbelievable as they were – would do little to portray the unbearable truth.

Jayne left the car and locked it, knowing she would never sit in it again. It had been Tommy's secret pride and joy, an old model that had far fewer electrics to go wrong, and which had gone around the clock already. They could have afforded a newer car, but he liked its styling, its look, and he'd said why dump what's not broken? She liked that about Tommy. He never really considered material things to be of any real importance.

A passenger jet roared behind the buildings as it powered along the runway for take-off. At least they were still flying. She'd been worried about that. If this had been an outbreak of Ebola or bubonic plague they'd have shut the airports, seaports and state borders. But apparently it would take a lot longer for the authorities to take action over a zombie outbreak.

Jayne gave a bark of laughter that turned into a cry, and then she walked to the airport building.

The departures terminal was busy. There were businessmen reading newspapers or frowning over their BlackBerries, families huddled together with kids excited and worried adults glancing around, and single travellers, many of whom Jayne could not read. She found herself checking them all for injuries, but all she saw was one man with a fleck of blood on his white collar. *Shaving cut*, she thought, and she had to bite her lip to hold back the hysteria.

The next flight to the UK was in three hours, and she bought one of the last places on it. She used her disabled card to get a comfortable seat, then used it again to be fast-tracked through to the departures lounge. And the whole experience was dreamlike. There were a couple of people crying, and a few who were huddling around the TV in one of the bars, but generally people seemed either unsure of what was happening or appeared not to care.

Jayne spent a few minutes watching the TV, nursing a Jack Daniel's, more because it had been Tommy's favourite drink than because she actually wanted it, and she realised then why everything seemed so unreal. Part of it was the fragmentary nature of the reports – there were clips of distant fires, unfocused telephone-camera imagery of shapes rushing through darkness, and helicopter shots of people moving across hillsides. And part of it was the bizarre nature of what they were seeing. Most of the news broadcasts were confused and unclear: unscripted stories, rushed interviews with traumatised and hysterical members of the public, and a few straight-faced officials denying that the emergency services weren't coping, and assuring viewers that all calls would be dealt with 'within two minutes'.

But scattered among the confused live broadcasts was more telling footage. One brief clip, expertly and probably secretly shot, showed corpses being unloaded from the back of an ambulance. There were so many that they must have been stacked in layers inside, and when Jayne saw the paramedics' face masks she gave another harsh laugh, followed by a sob. But no one looked her way. All gazes in the bar were focused on the screen at that point, as the cameraman panned along the row of corpses. Terrible wounds were revealed, injuries that belonged in a war. And every one of the bodies had head trauma.

'At least someone knows what they're doing,' Jayne said, and two young guys on the table next to her glanced her way with shock written all over their faces. She finished her Jack Daniel's and closed her eyes, feeling the burn.

Human nature meant that it would take a while for all this to sink in.

But it wouldn't take *that* long.

Jayne spent two hours in the departures lounge willing the minutes until take-off away, because once they closed the airport that would be it. She'd be stuck here while they – the famous They, the faceless They – tried to take control of things, and reality would surround her. Once in the air and heading for the UK, the sense of the unreality of everything that had happened would increase. There, for a while, perhaps she would find respite.

Her flight was called and she boarded. She was sitting next to a middle-aged businessman whose constant chatter marked him as a nervous flyer. Her monosyllabic responses soon persuaded him to keep his nervousness to himself, and as they went through the pre-flight checks and safety demonstrations Jayne closed her eyes and could almost believe that none of this had happened. But her arm still throbbed, and Tommy stared at her behind her closed eyes, the expression on his face one of surprise as Spartacus's bullet blew his life away.

They took off, and in the distance Jayne saw a fire blazing somewhere to the north. Fifteen minutes into the flight, an attendant told someone in the seat in front of Jayne that they were the last flight out of Knoxville. From elsewhere she heard someone whisper, 'Morris says they're bombing Atlanta.'

3

They drove through the day, hoping to reach Cincinnati by sunset.

After Vic had told Lucy why and how it was his fault, she'd surprised him by softening a little. He could not be sure how either of them could guarantee it, but their spoken determination to stay together had inspired a measure of strength in him that had been lacking before. Instinct had driven him up and out of Coldbrook, but Lucy's love went some way to driving his guilt back down. He had much to make amends for, but she knew why he had done what he'd done. In her eyes he saw that she understood.

Lucy drove some of the way, but Vic always felt more comfortable driving. And besides, for every mile of their three-hundred-mile journey he was considering road-blocks, state border controls, martial law, public panic, and the rule of chaos. In his pocket he carried his identification card, and in the car door beside his left thigh sat the M1911. If they came across trouble, he wanted to be behind the wheel.

Lucy had spent the first hour of the journey trying to call friends in Danton Rock on her iPhone. Her first couple of calls were answered, and Vic cringed as he heard her telling those at the other end that they should pack and leave immediately. 'Forget the damn school fayre!'

she said to one of them and to another she whispered, 'Something's gone wrong down there and you shouldn't hang around.' But then her third call was cut off unexpectedly, and after that the whole cellphone network seemed to go down. She'd tried a dozen more numbers ten times each, including those of her parents and her brother. It was only as the last call connected and a heavy, loaded silence was the only answer to her desperate pleading that she put the phone down.

She's beginning to understand. This is my fault, Vic thought. But Lucy said nothing more, and she did not try to call Danton Rock again. She said she wanted to save her phone's battery.

They kept the radio on, turned down low so that Olivia couldn't hear it. She was happy playing her Nintendo DS, and the chirpy jingles of the *Keep a Puppy* game provided a surreal theme to the stories they were hearing. As the day wore on and they drew closer to Cincinnati, Lucy moved over in her seat so that she could touch Vic. A hand on his thigh, arm around his shoulders, something that involved physical contact – he took as much comfort from it as she did.

'You can't blame yourself,' she told him as they listened to a report about a huge fire in central Knoxville.

'I can,' he said. Lucy squeezed the back of his neck, and from the back seat Olivia started singing.

The radio reports grew in severity, until one channel

said they were suspending their Sunday music programming to bring all the updates on the developing situation.

'What's a zombie?' Olivia asked.

Lucy flicked the radio off and glanced at Vic.

'Just a silly monster from the movies,' Vic said.

'No such things as monsters, honey,' Lucy said.

They exited the freeway and pulled up outside a rest stop. Olivia whooped and hollered, delighted that they'd reached their holiday destination, and Vic looked at the trucks and motorbikes and dusty cars lining the parking lot, wondering at his child's sense of imagination. Outside the car, stretching the several-hour journey from their limbs, Lucy stood close to Vic and entwined her fingers with his.

'They'll have the TV on in there.'

'Yeah.'

'Olivia will see.'

He bit his lip and watched his beautiful daughter skipping beside the car's hood, singing softly to herself, so vulnerable and dependent.

'It's spreading quickly,' he said.

'Moving as fast as people can run,' Lucy said.

'Faster.' Vic brushed a strand of her hair behind her ear, and she gave him a strained smile. He'd treasure any smile from his wife now as a gift.

'Jonah hasn't called,' she said.

'He'll be busy.' Lucy nodded slowly, rubbing an ache in the back of her neck. 'Holly Wright went through,' Vic said, not sure why he'd blurted that now. Perhaps she had been on his mind, beneath the fear for his family and what was to come. Perhaps leaving her behind was just another facet of his guilt.

'Through the breach?'

'Yeah.'

'Where the thing that started this came from?'

Vic nodded, unable to answer. He felt a weight behind his eyes, and his heart was thumping fast. *Don't let me see that look in your eyes*, he thought, remembering the dream of his sister and Lucy.

They ate, used the toilet, and left the diner as quickly as possible. As Vic drove, Lucy tried once again to call her parents in Los Angeles and her brother in Seattle. But the networks were still overloaded.

As she put the phone down once more, they passed by the sign for Cincinnati.

They met Marc Dubois where Jonah had arranged, in a private staff car park at the university. He was sitting on the hood of his car as they pulled up, and Vic saw him checking out their RAV4. In one hand he carried a satphone, in the other he held a cigarette. He did not smile but leaned in Vic's window, breathing cigarette smoke over him. 'One, two, three,' he said, nodding at each of them without expression, and then he turned away and dialled his phone.

Vic glanced across at Lucy. She raised an eyebrow, then he opened the door and stepped out. His legs and arms were aching, both from the long drive and the escape from Coldbrook that had preceded it. He wished once again that he'd spent more time in that gym.

'Marc Dubois?' Vic asked, though he already knew who he was talking to. *Tall gent,* Jonah had told him. *Should play basketball but he hates sport. Good-looking bastard. Looks like he should be a lady's man, but he'd more likely go for you. Marc is a genius. You'll like him, Vic. Eventually.*

'Jonah,' the man said into the phone. His voice was low, slow and measured. 'They're here. All three.' He nodded a couple of times, then half-turned and looked at Vic over his shoulder. 'So you want me to kill him now, or later?'

Vic tried not to react.

'Okay,' Marc said. 'Speak soon.' He pocketed the phone and sat back gently on the hood of his car. 'He said to kill you later.'

'Doesn't sound like Jonah,' Vic said. 'He's usually one to act on the moment.'

'Seems to think you might be able to help me first.'

'Well . . .' Vic said, trying to size up this man. He gave

nothing away. 'I thought perhaps it was the other way around.'

'You think?' Marc asked. Then after a pause he offered a half-smile. 'Just fucking with you. Here.' He held out his hand and Vic shook it. 'So, let's meet your family.'

Lucy and Olivia were stepping from the car, and when Vic introduced them Marc produced a candy bar for Olivia.

'You want to see some rabbits?' he asked Olivia. She squealed.

'Can I hold one?'

'Oh, honey—' Lucy said, but Marc interrupted.

'Sure you can! One of them is called Olivia, and I'm sure she'll love you.'

'You're just joking!' Olivia said through her laughter.

Marc pulled a face. 'You got me. I'm joking. She's actually called Lady. But I'm not joking when I say she'll love you.'

He looked up at Vic and Lucy, glancing back and forth as if sizing them up.

'Jonah said—' Vic began, and Marc cut him off.

'You okay to drive?' he asked Lucy.

'Sure.'

'Cool. Ride with me, Vic. Need to fill you in on a few things. My place is five miles up into the hills, and I want to get there by nightfall.'

'Why?' Olivia asked.

'Because,' Marc said, leaning in close to the little girl and putting on a spooky voice, '*that's* when the *monsters* come *out!*'

'Monsters? Like zombies?'

Marc stood again, staring down at Olivia from his great height. Then he turned and opened his car door. 'Come on. Light's wasting.'

'Lady rabbit awaits,' Vic said to Lucy, and he kissed his little girl before climbing in beside Marc.

The tall man drove in silence for a while. Vic positioned his wing mirror so that he could keep an eye on Lucy behind them, then he glanced several times at Marc. In profile he presented an intimidating picture – sharp nose, sloping forehead, bald head, lush beard, cigarette smoking in the corner of his mouth. His arms were long, his hands big. He might have been a wrestler or a boxer, rather than what he was. In any other circumstance but this, Vic might have felt comforted by his presence.

'That old Welsh bastard really asked you to kill me?' Vic asked, only half-joking.

Marc turned to look at him, staring for so long that Vic wanted to shout, *Don't forget you're driving!*

'You have a nice family,' Marc said. 'Your daughter is delightful. Your wife's pretty, but sad.'

Vic sighed and looked out of the passenger window.

The RAV4 was following close behind and he wished he was still with them, singing with Olivia and holding Lucy's hand.

Marc reached over into the back seat while still driving, rooting around for something. 'Here. Thought I should show you this.' He dropped an iPad into Vic's lap and Vic winced when the corner dug into his groin.

'What's this?'

'Open it, access the net. I'll give you the website to look at.' Vic did what he was told, then Marc read out a series of numbers and letters forming a website address. After that, a user ID and password.

'What am I looking at?' Vic asked.

'Something you shouldn't be.'

'Whatever Jonah told you—'

'Is true. I've known that man for over forty years. How old are you?'

'Forty,' Vic said.

'Fucking kid. Listen here, Vic. I'm going to do the best I can, and you're going to help me. But what Jonah told me . . . I can't just forget that. Can't forget what a fucking stupid prick you were, wrecking every safeguard built into that place. Can't forget what a selfish *motherfucker* you were, leaving them down there and escaping to save your own damn skin. I'm supposed to be working with you – it's good that I know what a clumsy fucker you are.'

'You don't sound French,' Vic said after a pause. The man intimidated the hell out of him, but he wanted to present some attitude, stand his ground. He was doing enough beating himself up as it was, without taking it from someone else as well.

'Mother was from Quebec.' Marc reached over and tapped the screen. 'Now look. You got some catching up to do.'

Vic looked. The page was laid out in thumbnails, each with a brief description underneath. He clicked on the first, and watched.

Over the next fifteen minutes, while Marc drove and smoked silently and Lucy followed on behind, Vic watched a selection of videos that displayed just how bad things had become. They seemed to have been taken from many sources: hand-held hi-def video cameras; mobile-phone footage; images taken from press sites and news programmes; aerial views, probably from police or military choppers; and several videos that looked as though they'd been taken by a soldier's gun- or helmet-mounted camera.

'What is this site?' Vic asked halfway through. He'd just watched a group of raging, blood-soaked people swept from a roadway by a huge truck with a cattle guard on the front, and then a dozen men machine-gunning them in a ditch. The camera shook as the shooting took place, and turned away when the first of the men lobbed in a grenade.

'Military site a friend of mine gave me access to,' Marc said. 'There's been some rapid response, as you can see. But the scope of this thing is huge. It's spreading like ripples in a pond, except that they're getting bigger and faster. It's hit beyond Charlotte in the east, Atlanta in the south, and there are even reports from Nashville.'

'All in a day,' Vic said.

'Yeah. A day.'

'But we're fighting back, right? The government? The military?'

Marc looked at him, another of those long stares that suggested he'd forgotten that he was driving.

'Sure,' he said. 'But what do they think they're fighting? No one believes in zombies.'

'I don't know—'

'Think about it,' Marc said, cutting him off again. 'You've been listening to the radio. Heard the panic. The religious nuts saying this is the end, God's will, Armageddon. The jokers suggesting that media panic is overblowing everything, it's nothing but a bunch of fucking smacked-up college kids copying each other, japes and jokes on the scale of Orson Welles's *War of the Worlds* radio broadcast. And the official statements tell us less than the radio jocks and the screamed eye-witness accounts recorded by ambulance-chasing reporting teams. Then there're the fucking experts, names pulled off the shelves by radio and TV stations to be talking heads while the news guys go and have their make-up touched up. And none of these fuckers have a clue. Because they don't have an open mind.'

'But the army,' Vic said. 'The government.'

'Yeah, there's been shooting and Chinooks flying around. Who knows, they might have some fancy new crap which they can finally get to try out on some moving targets. You know Bill Hicks?'

'No,' Vic said.

'Pull up G-Twelve!' Marc chuckled, lit another cigarette and inhaled, and Vic went to open a window. But he thought better of it.

'But the spread,' Vic said. 'That's your field, right?'

'Yeah,' Marc said. 'I've never, ever seen anything spreading as fast as this. It's almost word-of-mouth speed, and that's unstoppable by force. So we've got two hopes, and neither of them involves bullets and bombs. First, this thing dies out of its own accord. Whatever the contagion is – and others are working on that – it's come from somewhere else. That place you and Jonah reached. Maybe . . .' He waved his hand, as if to pluck an idea from the air, and chuckled again. 'The ghost of H. G. Wells will save us, and the cold virus will wipe this thing out.' He took another long drag on the cigarette.

'And the other possibility is a cure.'

'Right. And that's where I come in.'

'And me?'

'You?' Marc said, glancing sidelong at Vic. 'Jonah tells me you have a good mind. Sharp. A clear way of lateral thinking. Considering he thinks you're a shit, he talked you up pretty good. So, you're my gofer. I tell you jump, you jump.'

'Great,' Vic said, and he looked down at the iPad again, opening another file. Something was niggling at him. Something he'd seen, but not registered.

'Yeah,' Marc said. He lit a new cigarette from the stub of the old. 'And when it's all over and we've saved the world, *then* I get to kill you.'

4

Jonah stood with the gun in his hand and looked down at his dead friend.

Satpal lay in a sticky puddle of his own blood. Also in the puddle, curled from the moisture, was a photograph of his family back in India. Jonah knew that he visited them at least twice each year, and that they were proud of him.

The first two closed doors on the accommodation corridor had revealed nothing. He'd opened them slowly, carefully, with the gun at the ready, expecting the silence to be shattered with violence. But both rooms were empty, neat and tidy. Whoever had lived in them was dead somewhere else.

Maybe if I'd come down here earlier I could have saved him. Satpal had locked his door from the inside and then cut his wrists with a pocket knife. The wounds looked rough, torn rather than sliced, as if the knife was blunt. It lay close to the photograph.

The blood reflected the ceiling light, and the dead man looked too still. In Coldbrook's sterile environment there were no flies, few insects, and Satpal was destined to rot alone.

Jonah closed the door and locked it again, using his universal key. 'I really am on my own,' he said, leaning his head against the door frame – and then someone walked past the end of the corridor.

Jonah raised the gun and took a few steps back, gasping, his heart stuttering and then racing again. The shadow flitted away, cast by the ceiling lights in the corridor perpendicular to the one he was in. He could tell nothing of the shadow's shape or origin, but he heard no footsteps, no breathing.

There was only one way out from the corridor. Trying to breathe softly and evenly, Jonah started forward. Twenty feet until the junction, fifteen, and still he could neither hear nor see anything. Dried blood smeared the floor, and there was a shoe propped against the wall. It was white and pristine.

He clasped the gun in both hands, waiting for the shadow to flit back again and whatever had cast it to emerge. *Someone else alive*, but it was a vain hope.

This time there was no shadow. The figure walked around the corner and came towards Jonah, his swollen eyes and spiky hair glistening, the protruding mouth gasping out small clouds of moisture, and in his right hand was the organ-like object with a dozen tendrils tasting the air.

Jonah's breath caught in his throat, and he tried to perceive any kind of humanity in this man. But other than his shape, and number of limbs, and gait, there was none.

Jonah's hands shook – this nightmare was so real, the fear he felt so deep and thick, his heart skipping, breath punched from his lungs with shock—

This time I'm not asleep. As the organ-object kissed Jonah's head, his finger squeezed the trigger and—

—the explosion rips through the heart of the ship, erupting from its upper decks and tearing a hole in its hull. Fire and smoke gush out and, as seawater roars into the gap, steam billows in great clouds. They catch the sun and throw rainbows across the terrible scene.

The people with him in the lifeboat cry out in grief and terror. The impact thuds into the small boat, conveyed through the water, and several seams break. Some start bailing, while those sitting on the three cross-braces start to row.

He tries to speak, reaches out to touch, but he is not there. *All to die,* a voice says, and in a spray of water he glimpses that distorted face.

Several people lift long boathooks, because they know what is coming. Jonah sees the shapes swimming towards the boat, scores of them pushing through the violent waves, each face blank, distinguished only by eyes he has seen before, those dead eyes.

No point. They should submit.

The first of the swimmers reaches the boat. A hand curls over the gunwale. Two of her fingers are missing, the wounds grey and bloodless.

Jonah tries to close his eyes, but he sees the first wet body roll into the boat, hears the crunching of her skull as one of the survivors crushes it with their boathook, and then—

—the people finish floating through the air, landing on delicate legs and shrugging light packs from their backs. They stand on the edge of a ravine, the ground beneath them sandy, the sky a startling blue. They wear silver belts heavy with weapons, none of which Jonah recognises. He is stunned at their technology.

They already carry hopelessness in their hearts. That voice, so harsh, it is the thing that haunts.

One of the people is wounded, fine clothing torn and

slick with blood. She sinks slowly to her knees and the others go to help. The scene has the air of post-battle, and he wonders what they have left behind.

Then he sees that they have not gone to help at all. One of them pulls a weapon, and the woman looks up at him sadly, and her eyes remain open as he blasts her in the head—

—the child falls, and lands in the mass of creatures below, and they crowd in and bite like hunting dogs going for a chunk of meat. A man wails but the others ignore him, and Jonah wants to shout, *Can't you understand what he's lost?*

The network of platforms, ladders and bridges hangs from several tall trees. It's an impressive engineering feat, but he does not have the inclination to admire it. Across the platforms there are people shouting, and then he sees why.

The zombies are climbing the uprights, slow and clumsy. Most of them fall or are shot down by marksmen with steam-powered weaponry. But not every zombie falls. For every hundred that do not make it, one manages to crawl onto one of the platforms. The fighting then becomes hand-to-hand, and everyone is involved. Even the children.

Jonah sees a woman hunkered beneath a flexible canopy, a baby at her breast and a long curved knife in her other hand. She is ready to free her child, and herself.

No, he pleads, *please don't, don't make me see.*

The air of this place is filled with their stench, and the aroma speaks of hopelessness.

They all fall in the end.

Jonah closes his eyes—

—the man stepped back and let him go. He had fallen to his knees in the corridor, and for a moment he glanced around expecting to see the burning sea, or the falling dead, or those people floating their way from terror to terror.

Does it really all come to this? he wondered. But, of course, it had – and it would again. Satpal had shown that. A brilliant man, he had seen how things were and had made his choice.

'But not me,' Jonah said. He picked up the gun and fired at his abuser. The man could have killed him at any moment. But he didn't want Jonah dead. He wanted him to see.

'Bastard,' Jonah said. He looked for a gunshot wound in the man's chest, but was not surprised to see none. The man had retreated to the end of the corridor, and stood staring at him, unmoving.

He comes from through there, showing me what happened to his world.

But why?

Jonah was rational and in full control of his faculties,

though events were running away with him, and the idea of madness had seeped away. Yet while he had an answer for the raging things – which required irrational leaps of science – he had no answer for this.

He raised the gun and fired again. The man snorted – his mask emitting skeins of mist or steam – and then he walked calmly out of sight.

'Tell me what you want,' Jonah said after the noise of the gunshot had echoed away. But there was only silence.

5

In some ways, Marc reminded Vic of a younger Jonah, though he looked nothing like him – Jonah was thin and wiry, Marc was heavily built and strong. But there was a grace about him, an inner strength. Perhaps knowing more about the world than most people gave him a peace of mind that many others lacked.

Vic stood in Marc's office doorway and looked inside, and he was amazed. The room was piled high with loose-leaf files, sample jars, DVDs, books, and magazines and newspapers yellowing around their edges. A desk was pressed against the rear wall, and there was a small sofa with a coffee table in front of it, both of which were also homes to boxes of files and papers. Marc was at his desk, working on a laptop. Vic saw the satphone beside him and wondered whether the phone networks were still down.

'You lied about the rabbits,' Vic said.

'Your daughter hates me now?'

'No. She just wanted rabbits.'

'Right.' Marc continued what he was doing, and it was half a minute before he spoke again. 'Come on in.' He still did not look up.

Vic entered and stood awkwardly in front of the loaded sofa, looking around the room and smelling the mustiness of time. 'You work in here?'

'Only when someone releases a plague that threatens the world.'

'Doesn't happen much, then.'

'Threw it together myself – well, paid to have it done. This used to be an old water-pumping station and its offices. A grey concrete block, so no one's interested in it. And, because it's remote from the university, Jonah always called it my bunker.'

'So what's it for?'

'Times when I need somewhere private to work. Lots of personal stuff stored here that I wouldn't want the university to see. And it's a retreat. I wanted to be prepared, just in case something like this ever happened.'

'And it has a helipad on the roof?'

Marc smiled. 'Personal reasons.' He tapped away on his machine for another minute, leaving Vic standing. Then he glanced over his shoulder, nodded at the sofa, and said, 'Just dump all that on the floor.'

Vic cleared the sofa and sat down.

'Your family resting?'

'Yeah.' He'd left Lucy and Olivia in the small room that they'd been assigned. Olivia had fallen fast asleep, and Lucy had said she was going to take a shower and change. Maybe she'd rest, maybe not. Vic had told her that he didn't know how long he was going to be. She hadn't replied.

Marc stood and stretched, then pulled open a drawer in his desk and produced a bottle of Knob Creek and two glasses. Vic couldn't help smiling. So very much like Jonah.

'*This* is being prepared?' Vic asked. He couldn't hold the implied criticism from his voice – he might be guilty, but he had never been meek.

Marc actually looked hurt. 'Did it using my own funds. It isn't the fucking President's White House bunker, but yeah, it's being prepared. There's water and food to last several weeks, a lab and a communications room in the basement – which can be isolated, if needs must. Very secure from the outside. Air conditioning, hermetically sealed doors . . . lots of other stuff.' He waved one hand. 'Don't want to bore you.' He handed Vic a glass, sat beside him on the sofa, and poured.

Vic took a grateful drink and winced as the bourbon burned its way down.

'So what is it you do, exactly?'

'Lots,' Marc said. 'But what's pertinent to our current fucked-up situation is my research into disease vectors.'

'You think this is a bug?'

'Don't you?'

Vic shrugged.

'Just because people are using the word zombie,' Marc said, 'don't go getting all spooked on me. I've spoken with Jonah, and he's seen them first-hand. Killed a few of them himself. The body shuts down. The infection takes over their brain. And once we work out what the infection is, we might have a chance at a cure. Or an inoculation, at least.'

'Body shuts down. Dead.'

'Well . . .' Marc said, and Vic saw the first glimmer of doubt.

'So you produce an inoculation – what about those who are already infected?'

Marc raised his eyebrows. 'Not our priority, sad to say.'

Vic rested his head back against the sofa, changing the subject. 'So who does the chopper on the roof belong to?'

'A friend of mine.'

'You're shitting me.'

'No, really,' Marc said. 'I *do* have friends.'

'I should tell Jonah I'm here,' Vic said. 'Update him. See what he's doing down there. He said he was alone, the only survivor.' *And I worry for him*, Vic wanted to say. But after everything he'd done, that sounded so trite.

'Jonah's a hard motherfucker,' Marc said. 'His father worked in a coal mine, he ever tell you that? Fifty-two years. And every day of Jonah's childhood, his father said he was working down there so Jonah didn't have to do the same thing. His sense of worth comes from that, and his honour, and a lot of his attitude. Then when poor Wendy died . . .' Marc shook his head and poured more bourbon. 'Something on your mind?' he asked.

Vic frowned and looked around the room, trying to grab hold of the thought that had been circling his consciousness for the last half an hour. Marc's perception was sharp and, though they hadn't exactly hit it off, it felt good to be around someone he couldn't hide anything from. It meant that Marc was in control.

'Something's bugging me,' Vic said, closing his eyes and rubbing them.

'Your trip up here? Radio reports? Something you saw on the way?'

'Jesus!' Vic said. He closed his eyes and had it. So *obvious*! 'They were completely still.'

'Huh?'

Vic jumped up and pointed to the computer. 'Those images, that military site. Bring them up again.'

'You saw something I didn't?' Marc said. But he tapped

at the computer and brought up the site, and Vic reached past him and clicked on a film clip taken from a low-flying helicopter. They both watched for a couple of minutes, neither of them commenting, and Vic was starting to think he'd been imagining things. Then he saw it.

He leaned across Marc and hit pause.

'Here,' he said, pointing at one of the zombies in the crowd of afflicted people. 'A woman. She's lost an arm and has abdominal wounds. Run over, maybe. But while all the others are running and doing whatever they can to reach . . .' He pointed below the screen, where a crashed camper van was out of shot. '*She*'s doing something different.'

He hit play again. The woman stood motionless. The only movement was her head, turning left and right as a dozen other zombies raged past her, running as fast as their injuries would allow towards the camper. Some of them fell as the occupants of the crashed vehicle fired, then she too crumpled.

'Didn't see a bullet hit her,' Marc said.

'That's because she wasn't shot. She was watching, that's all. Observing.'

'Why?' Marc asked.

'Don't know. Pacifist zombie?'

'Call Jonah,' Marc said. 'Tell him. I'll patch in on my phone.'

As Vic dialled he thought, *This has only just begun*.

6

Jonah shut and locked the door, though he knew it would do no good. He had been visited before – the dream on the day they made breach, and afterwards. Doors were no barrier.

Bill Coldbrook had killed himself without explanation. Jonah remembered finding the old man hours after it had happened, walking into his room and seeing the stillness that seemed so unreal, and the expression of peace on his face and . . . escape? Perhaps that's what it had been. There had been no note, but the old man's dying expression had said it all.

Not just me, Jonah thought, and the idea was terrible. *That bastard has been here before.*

He wrote down each vision he had been shown. Some might have been of this Earth, though he thought not. He tried not to consider for now the reason *why* he had been shown because that was not something he could discern from a set of notes. But he did not trust his old man's memory. And the visions – they looked more real when written down. More firm.

'What the fuck is going on here?' he muttered, welcoming the sound of his own voice. The silence had become too loaded. He sat in his chair in Secondary, staring at the screen showing the breach and its containment field, and a flicker of blue arced across the screen as the eliminator fried a small creature. Elsewhere, the rest of Coldbrook was still and silent, except for the rooms where he had trapped the afflicted. He flicked past these places slowly, fascinated and horrified.

The assault had left him feeling violated. The man's touch had been uninvited, but more disturbing than the physical intrusion had been the emotional one – those images placed in his mind, not only showing him scenes of horror, but leaving them in his memory. He shivered, and vowed that next time he would fight harder.

The satphone rang, startling him from his thoughts. He snatched it up and took a few deep breaths.

'Vic,' he said.

'Jonah. We've reached Marc, safe and sound. You okay?'

'Fine,' Jonah said.

'All quiet there?'

'All quiet.'

'The breach?' Even over the grumbling connection he could discern Vic's true meaning.

'Nothing,' Jonah said. Vic was silent for a while, but Jonah could hear his breathing. 'Vic, there's no reason to believe that anything bad happened to Holly.'

'Other than she's stepped across into an alternate Earth that might be swarming with zombies.'

'The one that came through was . . . a weak thing,'

Jonah said. 'It walked slowly, not like the ones that have changed here. It looked like an animal.' He thought that through, concentrating on something he'd had no time to dwell on until now.

'But it still caused all this.'

'Yes.'

'And she's there,' Vic said. 'Our ambassador.'

'She'll make a good one.'

'Marc is quite a character,' Vic said.

'Has he beaten your stupid head in yet?'

'I haven't yet,' Marc said, and Jonah smiled. He hadn't realised the three phones were patched in.

'Marc. Good to hear you. Vic might be useful for a while longer yet.'

'Well, maybe he is. Let him tell you.'

'Jonah,' Vic said, 'I've seen something on the footage. Has Marc sent you the passwords to this site?'

'Yes,' Jonah said. 'But I haven't had time to look.'

'One of them doesn't act like all the others. She just stands there, watching. An observer.'

Jonah held his breath and closed his eyes.

'Jonah, you there?'

'This observer – what does it look like?'

'She's lost an arm,' Vic said.

'And her stomach's all fucked up,' Marc added.

'Her face?'

'Well, she looks quite normal there. Expressionless,

but then they're all . . .' Vic trailed off, because he did not need to finish.

'Interesting,' Jonah said. 'Let's see if we can find any more. Meanwhile, Marc, have you any thoughts?'

'Sure. Get me to Coldbrook, let me through the breach, and I'll get a sample of the disease from over there, compare it with however it's spread and mutated in us, and maybe I can come up with something. Piece of cake. In the meantime, things are moving on apace. They've started bombing Atlanta, and it's spreading fast.'

'What have you been doing down there?' Vic asked.

'Just doing my best to survive,' Jonah said. They arranged another call time in two hours, then signed off. Jonah put the phone down and breathed into the silence, and the wall screens flickered off.

He held his breath.

The lights went out as the power failed, and the laptop switched to battery mode, flashing a red-highlighted message:

Net connection terminated.

7

The aircraft was mostly silent, even though it was full, and many people were concentrating on their mobile and laptop screens. Jayne had taken a walk to the bathroom an hour into the flight, and the sight of so many people with their heads tilted down had been unsettling. The night flight passenger compartment was darkened, and the glow from screens and phones had formed islands of light across the cabin. People had been whispering, and one woman was crying. *Bet none of them have seen what I've seen*, Jayne had thought, and in the toilet she too had cried.

An old episode of *Friends* was playing on her seat-back screen, but Jayne saw none of it. *The One Where They're All Eaten By Zombies*, she'd thought as the programme had begun, but she hadn't found it in herself to smile.

The churu had started to settle in her joints and bones, and for the past hour she had been steadily massaging her hips and shoulders. The man beside her hadn't seemed to notice, or if he had he'd not seen any reason to comment. Stranger things were happening. Worse things. She shifted in her seat and groaned as her hips flexed. The man glanced up, then down again at his netbook.

'It's the bites,' he said. They were his first words since the start of the journey.

'Bites,' she repeated. The pain in her arm was a sharp slice down to her bone. It was a different pain from the churu – a wound rather than a blazing ache – and she concentrated on it because it was easier to control.

'Fucked up,' the man muttered, and he started tapping at his computer again.

Jayne looked out of the window; she didn't want to see the computer screen. There was nothing to see outside but she couldn't sleep with this pain, so staring into the darkness was the next best thing. She kept massaging herself – left hip, right hip, left shoulder, right shoulder – and she twisted and flexed her ankles and knees, trying to work blood through her joints. But however much she worked at herself, she knew she'd need help to walk by the time they reached London.

A slow, misty warmth began behind her eyes, and she closed them, trying to will the fainting away. It was never the pain that drove her down into these comas – the worst agonies conspired to keep her awake – but something else to do with the churu. *It's getting inside my head*, she'd said to Tommy, but she had tried denying to herself that the blackouts were getting more frequent, and deeper every time.

It was bad enough having a body she couldn't rely on. The idea of losing her mind . . . she could never live with that. Tommy had known that, too. And they'd never discussed it, because they were both afraid of what she would ask of him.

'Shit,' she slurred, and the mist thickened into a fog.

You okay? she heard from some distance. She tried to nod but that swilled her brain around in her head, her eyes bulged with the pressure, and she squeezed her fingers into her thighs, hoping the pain might bring her around. But she was a slave to pain, not its master, and the voice mumbled something from afar as the darkness pulled her down.

Tommy, slow down, she tries to shout, because he is driving too fast across the mountainside, they are hitting rocks and dips in the ground, and his beloved old Toyota is being shaken apart. Tommy does not answer because he is not driving – the thing that is driving is no one she knows, and nothing alive – and as she opens her mouth to scream, she opens her eyes as well.

On the small screen in front of her, three children played in a garden, spraying a St Bernard with a hose.

Jayne blinked a few times, trying to focus through the pain. She shifted in her seat and cried out, and her heartbeat set whispers echoing in her ears. Her joints burned, but her vision and other senses were rising from the blackout. *How long?* she wondered, and she turned to the man beside her to ask the time.

He was gone. So were the people across the aisle from them, every seat empty. And past the opposite aisle, more empty seats. She turned and looked between the seat uprights, groaning again at the pain in her stiffened shoulders. No one.

Everyone was gone.

Wake up, Jayne, she thought. The guy had dropped his laptop on his seat, and the screen showed a photo of a beautiful woman and two young kids. *Screen saver*, she thought. *How long have I been out?* And if this was still a dream, the woman and kids would have flesh between their teeth.

Her jacket had been sliced off, ragged cuts up the sleeves showing clumsy scissor cuts. Her shirt had been pulled open, her bra sliced in two, and her breasts and stomach were exposed.

'What the hell . . .?' she said, and it was when she grabbed her opened shirt to cover herself that she saw the wound on her arm. The dressing had been ripped back and now hung by one strip of tape. The scabbed bite was exposed, seeping a dribble of thin blood.

It's the bites, the man had said. Jayne pulled her shirt closed, grabbed the seat in front of her and stood, growling her agony between gritted teeth.

The whispers in her ears became startled voices, not her heartbeat at all, and though she heard no words she understood their fear well enough.

They were standing along the aisle, clumped together and staring at her across the heads of empty seats. Terrified.

'I'm . . .' she said, and then a man appeared beside her from the other direction, moving quickly and keeping low. There were grey flecks in his closely cropped hair and his eyes flashed wide and white against his brown skin.

In his hands was a squat pistol.

And he had been paying attention to the news, because it was aimed directly at her head.

Part Two

AMONG THE LIVING

The universe has as many different centres as
there are living beings in it.

Alexander Solzhenitsyn

Monday

1

Holly stared about her in disbelief, the words *'Welcome to Coldbrook'* echoing inside her head. She started to panic, her palms growing damp and her heart racing. Just as shock threatened to overwhelm her there was a brief sting on her neck that spread to burn through her entire being. And then, darkness.

When she woke her whole body felt as though it had been subjected to an intimate, thorough medical examination – she seemed to be naked and her limbs ached.

She was too scared to open her eyes, terrified of what she would see.

Her senses swam. She could smell musty wool and

stale bread, and the unmistakable scent of her own body odour. Her breathing seemed to reverberate, the whole space around her gasping in time with her exhalations. She clenched her fingers, rucking up a rough blanket, and then her arm came painfully to life with a thousand pins and needles. She gave a shuddering sob and tears dribbled into her hair.

At last Holly opened her eyes to see what they had done to her.

The cell was small, a cave more than a structure, with a floor hewn flat and the raised bed she lay on hacked from the wall. Layers of animal skins and holed blankets softened the bed, and she was swathed in a heavy quilt. She wiped at her tears and glanced beneath the covering. She was not naked after all: the dark green smock she wore resembled the clothing worn by her rescuers.

'Rescuers,' she croaked, and wondered how wrong she might be.

Holly sat up, coughing, wishing for a drink. Her eyes felt gritty, her mouth and throat dry, and there was a pressure in her bladder that she was doing her best to ignore. The room contained no toilet area, and the only other fixture was an oil lamp high on one wall. It threw out a surprising amount of light and heat but, when she stood to examine it closer, dizziness hit her.

'Oh shit,' she muttered, leaning back against the rock surface.

One wall of the cell had been built up rather than carved out, heavy concrete blocks cemented together in an even, pleasing pattern. And there was a light switch. She flicked it quickly, but nothing happened. Looking at the ceiling, she saw an empty bulb socket, green with rust.

Welcome to Coldbrook, the tall man had said. But perhaps she'd misheard him, or placed words that she'd wanted to hear in his mouth.

The door was solid wood, its hinges hidden, no handle. There was a locked viewing slot.

Holly hugged herself beneath the quilt, breathing deeply as the nausea receded. Her arm had been pricked a dozen times, leaving small raised scabs. A scrape of skin had been taken from her shin – the edges of the excision were square and neatly cut.

What have they done?

The viewing slot in the door slid open but by the time she'd realised it was already closing again.

The lock clicked, tumblers turned, and Holly backed up to the head of the bed.

The door opened and the man who came in was a walking corpse. The silence was tainted by his soft hooting and he slashed at the air with his hands. The room filled with the stench of old things and forgotten rot. He lurched for her, but she had nowhere else to go. His face was wrinkled leather. His jaw hung down so far that his chin touched his chest, and what teeth remained were black. But his eyes were the blackest.

Holly screamed, cowering against the wall.

The man flipped back, his head jarring forward over the wide metal band around his neck. He sat down heavily, and Holly heard bones crack. The man made no other sound.

Shadows filled the doorway, instructions were shouted, and the zombie was dragged out of the room. They had it restrained on a long collar and stick. Once in the hallway outside, one of the shadows kicked the wasted man over and brought something heavy down onto his head. The crunch was sickening, but in the silence that followed everything felt different.

What the fuck?

Holly slid down the wall to the floor, bringing her knees up to her chest. The tall man who had welcomed her stood at the cell door and provided an answer.

'I apologise for that,' he said. 'We had to check, but you can come out now. The furies never sing to their own.'

'You bastard! You could have just *asked*.'

'You came from somewhere else,' he said. He'd told her his name was Drake Slater, and Holly thought she knew him from somewhere. Stupid, but the idea persisted. He shrugged. 'I couldn't take the risk. We know how the furies work in this world, but in yours . . .' He held out his hands and shrugged.

'How long have I been asleep?'

'Almost a full day.'

'You drugged me.'

He held out his hands again, half answer, half apology. It seemed as though he couldn't stop staring at her.

Holly closed her eyes and drew a deep breath. The food spread before them on the small plastic table in the room that Drake had led her to looked simple and smelled mouth-watering, but Holly had yet to eat. Her thoughts were in turmoil – the reality of her situation threatened to overcome her. And this Earth, this alien place: their food, their water, anything here could kill her.

'We call them zombies,' she said, looking at Drake again. He was dressed in simple clothing, his hair was long and unkempt, yet his eyes sparkled with intelligence. His caution during their conversation was proof of that.

'We used to as well,' he said, 'before they became real.'

'Before?'

He blinked and looked away, unwilling to divulge anything.

'I'm not here to cause harm,' Holly said.

'I know that,' Drake said. 'Now, will you eat with me? You must be hungry.'

'I am,' Holly said. 'What is it?'

'Rabbit, sauté potatoes, mushrooms, spring carrots. Basic but good. In your honour.'

'My honour?' she asked. But she could not smile. She looked at the food. 'Nothing I don't know, I hope.'

Drake put some food on a plate for her and smiled at her hesitation. 'Excuse me,' he said, picking a shred of meat from the plate and eating it.

'So you're not trying to poison me. Thanks. But I have so many questions,' Holly said.

'Us too. Now eat. You need your energy, and you've come—'

'A long way,' she said. And then Holly realised why she thought she recognised this man. He could have been Jonah thirty years ago, thirty pounds lighter, and with a life of struggle already behind him.

Her mind was in a spin.

Holly ate, and the food was wonderful. There was a freshness to it that was usually found only in the best restaurants, or in home-grown food. But after the fifth mouthful she thought of Melinda and had to concentrate so she could swallow without vomiting.

'You've been through something horrific,' Drake said. 'I'll do whatever I can to help.'

'Thank you,' she said. She took a drink of water, then sat back.

'You didn't bring any equipment through with you,' he said.

'I came through in a rush,' Holly said, realising that he knew all this anyway. They must have been watching her from the moment she stepped through the breach.

Drake had guided her to a cave lined with wood panelling and light blue fabric. The ceiling was bare rock, but the furnishings were comfortable and functional. A fire burned in a pit in one corner, smoke rising to a hole in the ceiling. There were light switches here too – and power points, and a phone socket – but they all looked redundant. The basic arrangements seemed incongruous set among this evidence of technology.

There was a bed against one wall, and several curtains hung from wires against the opposite wall, forming what Holly took to be a storage area. She guessed that it was Drake's room – many items were scattered around, some of which she could identify. There were also several pairs of leather shoes beneath the bed, along with a few smaller and more delicate footwear items.

'Your Earth . . .' Drake said. She could sense his eagerness to ask, but she doubted that it exceeded her own.

'What did you do to me?'

Drake sat back again and averted his eyes. 'Our doctor carried out some tests.'

'What kind of tests?'

'She's a female doctor, very gentle,' Drake said, not answering the question.

'You say this is Coldbrook?' Holly asked. 'In the United States?'

'That's an old name for our country, but yes. And you're from Coldbrook, too?'

Holly nodded. She looked at the patch on his jacket again, the three interlocking circles that was so similar to her own Coldbrook symbol.

'We tried to guard the wound you made in the land,' Drake said. 'But one of them must have—'

'One of your furies.'

'They're not *our* furies.'

'So one of them must have what?' Holly asked.

'Gone through. I'm sorry.' He stared at her for a moment, and then picked up some more meat.

'I don't know how bad my world is,' Holly said. Drake would not look at her. 'Do *you* know?'

'No,' he said. He stood and turned, and she knew that he was lying.

'Drake?'

'I need to make arrangements. I'll be back,' he said. 'We can't keep you locked up in here.'

'Drake, what's happening there? Tell me if you know.'

'I don't know,' he said again, but still he would not look at her.

'God help us,' she whispered. And this time Drake did look, freezing where he stood by the heavy wooden doorway, his eyes wide.

'You obviously haven't met the Inquisitor yet, so I'll allow you that.'

'Allow me—?'

'God,' he whispered. Then he slammed and locked the door behind him. He hadn't really answered any of her questions.

There was plenty of food left, but Holly was no longer hungry.

'So what's next?' she asked the silence. 'Bad cop?'

It was Drake who opened her door again half an hour later, and he had two women with him. One of them carried a tall glass of wine, another a bowl of berries, bearing them like gifts.

'This is Moira,' Drake said, and the short, muscled woman who'd accompanied her on the stretcher smiled a greeting.

'Pleased to meet you,' Moira said. It was strange hearing her voice after seeing her communicate with sign language and expressions.

'And you,' Holly said. 'Thanks for helping me.'

Moira nodded but seemed tense, her eyes wide and expectant.

'And I'm Paloma.' The other woman was tall and severe-looking, her coffee skin speckled across her left cheek and neck with what might have been burn scars, or the remains of an old illness. She stepped forward in front of Moira and placed the bowl of berries on the table. 'I hope you liked the rabbit. I caught and cooked it.'

'It was delicious,' Holly said.

Paloma stepped back and Moira came forward, her hand shaking as she placed the wine gently on the table. 'And she's *exactly* like us?'

'As far as I can tell,' Paloma said.

Moira nodded and backed away, and the moment grew ever more surreal.

'You're the doctor?' Holly asked.

'I do my best with what we have,' Paloma said.

'And Paloma is my wife,' Drake said. He remained outside the room, letting the two women go through their routine.

'So, you've established that I'm human,' Holly said. Paloma nodded and Moira stared. 'Why do I still feel like an exhibit?'

Moira laughed and turned away. 'I'm sorry,' she said. 'It's just that I've never seen someone from—'

'We have something to show you,' Drake cut in. Moira raised her eyebrows – annoyed rather than chastened by Drake's interruption, Holly thought – and Paloma smiled for the first time.

'So I'm not a prisoner any more?'

'You never were.'

Holly stood, taking a sip of the wine and swallowing a handful of berries. They could be drugged, or poisonous, but the women could have harmed her in either way without the subterfuge. So she accepted their gifts and sat back down.

Drake shifted uncomfortably, Moira looked back at him, and Paloma simply stared at Holly.

'Tell me one thing before I come with you,' she said.

'Of course,' Drake said, and there was a vulnerability in his voice she'd never detected before.

'What's beyond the hills?' Holly asked. 'What else is out there?'

'The rest of our world,' he said. '*Our* Earth.'

Holly nodded, her heart thudding as she remembered the way that zombie – that fury – had come through the breach. Staggering, slow, weathered away.

'It ended,' Paloma said. 'Before I was born. The furies' threat lessens as they age, but they left little behind.'

Holly felt sick. It was a truth that she had expected, but to hear it spoken was still a shock.

'And you fight them with just bows and arrows?'

'Silence is our best defence when we're out in the open,' Drake said. 'That's why we use . . .' He signed, clicking his fingers, and smiled at whatever he had said. 'And why we find it safer using bows and crossbows – anything louder would be foolish. Destroy what's left of their brains and they become still. Properly dead. An arrow or a bolt usually does it. But decapitation makes sure.'

'Are you the only ones still fully human?' Holly asked, barely able to speak because the answer might be so awful.

'There are isolated islands of survivors,' Moira said. 'A few communities here and there. Wanderers. The older ones tell us what it was like before, and there are books.'

'So we *do* mourn what should have been,' Paloma said, as if to know that was important.

'I'll tell you the rest while we walk,' Drake said.

'Where are we going?'

'Down into Coldbrook. You don't think we spend our lives living in caves, do you?' He smiled that confident smile again, and Holly had to remind herself that she was the stranger here, she was the visitor.

Gaia was another world, and yet it was very much like the Earth that Holly knew. They spoke English here, and she craved to know the extent of the similarities. Had they known Mozart and Metallica, Shakespeare and Stephen King? Was there Britain and Australia, or had their history evolved away from her world's long enough ago for such things to be vastly different?

Everything Jonah had believed was true, and he didn't yet know. He might even have died without knowing.

As they left the small room and headed along a corridor lit by oil lamps, Drake started talking.

'There's a whole history to tell you. I'm keen to know of the differences between our worlds, when our Earth and yours . . . parted ways. That should be easy to pin down date-wise, but the actual cause . . .' He shook his head, but when she glanced at him Holly saw an excitement that reminded her so much of Jonah. 'But first and for your own safety, you need to know about the world you've come to. Our Earth is a dead world. It died forty years ago with the Fury plague, in nineteen seventy-two. It spread quickly. Spanned the globe. And less than six weeks later, all was lost.'

'Forty years!' Holly gasped. 'None of you can be—'

'There are a few here old enough to remember,' Paloma said from where she and Moira followed behind. 'Though most of them try to forget.'

'So what are you still doing down here?' Holly asked.

'Same as you. What else is Coldbrook *ever* for?'

'What do you mean?'

But Drake walked on ahead in silence. *He keeps thinking he's said too much*, Holly thought.

The corridor was long, curving down to the right, and the walls were made of smooth blockwork. There was a wire tray just below the ceiling that contained a spaghetti of wires of all colours.

'You still have electricity?'

'Only for what's important.'

'What happened after the plague?' Holly asked, because she sensed that was all he felt happy talking about for now. And besides, knowledge of the plague on

257

this side of the breach could perhaps help her when she returned to her own world.

If *I return*. The idea was harsh, but it had to be considered. These people were being pleasant enough for now, if cautious. But if they wanted to keep her here for some reason, there was no telling how forceful they might become.

'With few left alive to spread the plague, the furies' numbers went down. They ground to a halt slowly, faded, and now it's rare for them to hunt for new victims. If you go too close, though, and they smell you . . . then they rise.'

'They're still alive after so long?'

'Nowhere near alive. But though their bodies wither, their heads remain full of whatever drives them.'

'And you don't know what that is?'

Drake didn't answer, but carried on talking as if he had not heard Holly's question. 'The surviving communities of humans live in the hills, the deserts, at the icy poles, on islands. Wherever the furies aren't too prevalent.'

'There seem to be some around here,' Holly said.

'Yes,' Drake agreed. 'But we're special. Most people are living their days as best they can, others have embarked upon . . .' He motioned her and the others through a door into a wide lobby area.

'Upon what?'

'There are extermination squads in Italy,' Paloma said.

'Well, that's good!' Holly said. 'Surely wiping out the furies is best for everyone?'

'They're not exterminating furies,' Moira said.

'Oh.'

'This way,' Drake said, nodding towards a door set in the lobby's far wall. There were more oil lamps here, and the ceiling had collapsed in one corner, letting in a landslide of heavy rock and soil.

'So you never made a breach?' Holly asked. And if that were true – and they had never found their way into the multiverse – then the Fury plague must have originated in this world somewhere. Another thought that led to a thousand more questions.

'We did,' Drake said. 'But not like you. And that's what I have to show you. It'll answer so much more, but it won't be pleasant.'

Paloma produced a small cloth pouch from her pocket and waved it towards Holly. 'I have this if it all becomes too much.'

'What is that?'

'It'll calm you.'

'No, thank you,' Holly said. She had no idea what they were going to show her but Paloma's offer of some herbal drug troubled her.

'I'll take her from here,' Drake said.

Paloma nodded and turned away, but Moira shifted from foot to foot.

'Can I not stay? I took down the fury that nearly killed her. And she's *special*.'

Drake seemed uncertain, but Holly nodded.

'I don't mind,' she said. She hoped that Moira might be a little more open, if she had the chance to talk with her alone. The source of the plague was a mystery still, and the Inquisitor that Drake had mentioned, and . . .

And a million other things, she thought. *Jonah should have been here, not me*. She knew that he and Drake would have had so much to talk about.

'One thing,' Holly asked. 'Are you the lead scientist in Coldbrook?'

'I'm the one they look up to.'

'They?'

'There are about forty of us here, adults and a few children. Let me show you what I'm taking you to and then after that we can talk some more. But it will clear up questions that I really don't feel qualified to answer.'

'Your accent,' she said.

'My father came from Wales.'

She gasped. 'Jonah Jones?'

Drake stared at her. 'His name was Richard Slater. His middle name was Jonah.'

Holly frowned, trying to make sense of what this might mean, if anything. Drake's similarity to Jonah had unnerved her. But perhaps it meant nothing.

'There's too much to understand,' he said softly,

squeezing her arm. She realised it was the first time he'd touched her, and she suddenly felt safer than she had before, more protected. There were still so many unknowns. This . . .' He opened the door and indicated the short corridor beyond, a stairwell at its end. 'This will help you begin to understand.'

Drake went first and Holly followed, with Moira behind her. They descended the staircase and passed through a series of doors. The bland interiors reminded her of a gloomy version of the Coldbrook she had known for so long. That thought brought no comfort. As Drake opened a door set in a smooth concrete-walled corridor, she saw what he wanted her to see.

But it was only as the mass of zombies came at her that real understanding began.

2

He follows Charlotte through downtown Boston, and from the beginning he knows that this dream is different. His troubled, dead sister arrives at their parents' house and knocks at the door, and Vic senses the change as the door swings open. His mother is there with the family heirloom grasped in her grey hands, one of her eyes missing, and a swathe of her scalp ripped off. Charlotte thanks her, and their mother closes the door on her own blank expression.

The dream progresses. Vic tries to shout out to these

dead fools who give gifts that will guarantee the death of his sister. But, as ever, he has no voice.

He can only follow.

Vic knows what is coming, and that just makes it more terrible. At last she reaches the large house. The toys in the garden are rusted now, the flower beds overgrown.

Charlotte rings the bell.

Lucy answers the door. 'Charlotte! You're looking well. Death becomes—'

And Charlotte goes at her, dead fingers clasping, ragged teeth biting, and as Lucy giggles at the mess of her own face Vic hears his daughter's singing from inside the house.

Vic woke up with a gasp and everything came back to him at once. Lucy was staring at him, her head pressed into the pillow. There was a tear nestled on the bridge of her nose, and as he watched it ran down across her face.

'She's dreaming,' Lucy said, and Vic heard his daughter mumbling to herself. He could not discern the words, but Olivia's voice was unhappy. She was not crying but pleading.

'She'll be okay,' Vic said. Such a hollow platitude.

'I didn't hear you come in.'

'Didn't want to wake you.' Vic looked at his watch and rubbed his hands across his face. 'Four hours. I only wanted to crash out for an hour.'

'What happened with Marc?'

'We spoke to Jonah.'

'He's okay?'

Vic frowned. 'I think so. Alive, at least. But . . .'

'He's an old man.'

'Only in years.' Vic smiled.

'And no news from Holly?'

Holly, Vic thought, and blinked at a sudden intense memory of loving her in the shower. 'Nothing yet,' he said.

'Hey.' Lucy touched his cheek and turned him to face her. 'We're here, and we're all okay together. That's good enough for now.'

He kissed her and held her against his body.

'You should go back to Marc,' she said. 'Lots to do.' She sat up and ran her fingers through her hair. Olivia had settled, breathing softly in the cot at the foot of their own bed. The room was barely big enough for the three of them.

'What're you going to do?' he asked, and Lucy nodded at the laptop on the table beside the bed.

'Catch up. Try and call my folks. Email them, IM, Facebook.' Her voice was filled with dread, and Vic thought he should stay. But seeing the disaster together could not lessen its impact.

'Okay. Not as if there's far to look if you want me.'

Lucy smiled up at him as he dressed, and he bent down to kiss her again. Her breath was stale and her shoulders tense.

'Be back soon,' she said, and Vic nodded.

Marc was in his communications room, talking with another tall man. The room was small, square, and each wall was lined with benching. There were laptops and telephones, and on one wall a blank screen promised much. There were also radios and satellite communication equipment. It was as basic as Vic had already come to expect of the bunker – the walls were bare, the furniture functional – but the equipment was top drawer. Cigarette smoke hazed the air.

'Vic,' Marc said as soon as he entered. 'I was going to wake you. There's bad news, and fucking terrible news. Which do you want first?'

Vic shook his head. How could he answer that?

'Well, we've lost touch with Jonah.'

'No,' Vic said. He glanced from Marc to the other man, and felt his stomach drop. 'Nothing at all?'

'Email's out, satphone gets nothing. He's no longer online.'

'Could be a power fault in Coldbrook,' Vic said.

'With luck that's all it is,' Marc agreed. The alternative was too grim to voice.

'So if that has happened, what're his chances?' the other man said. Vic stared at him, then glanced at Marc.

'Vic, meet my partner Gary Volk.'

'You're English?' Vic asked.

'Only until they ask me to pay my taxes,' Gary said.

'Jonah will be cut off down there,' Vic said. 'If the main power's gone, backup should kick in. But there's no saying what damage has been done to Coldbrook. He'll have plenty of air and supplies, and there are torch stocks in every room. But without power he won't be able to get out. Ever.'

'But the core?' Marc asked.

'Balanced, and self-sustaining. It doesn't need any outside power source.'

'So why not run Coldbrook from the core?' Gary asked.

'Because you don't use antimatter to run your food blender,' Vic said.

Gary raised his eyebrows, then smiled. 'Forgive me. I'm just a musician.' His smile was disarming, his eyes filled with a constant glimmer.

'Gary owns the chopper that you saw,' Marc said.

Vic stepped forward and held out his hand. Gary shook it without hesitation and Vic was relieved. He was sure that Marc must have told him what he'd done.

'So what's been happening?' Vic asked.

'You missed the President's address,' Marc said. He nodded at an open laptop on the benching. Its screen saver was a butterfly shedding sparkling dust as it flapped its wings. It was simply beautiful.

'And what a joke that was,' Gary said.

'Want to see it?' Marc asked.

Vic blinked, uncertain, because yes, he did. Gary

snorted, and Marc tapped a few keys. When the clip started, he moved the slider along until it was a couple of minutes in.

'This is the interesting bit,' Marc said, and he hit play.

The President flickered as the clip began, his face shimmering, and Vic remembered the hope they had all felt when he had taken office, and the belief that he might alter their broken country. Now he had something else to say. And though he clung to hope, Vic could see shadows in the man's eyes.

'. . . to combat the spread of the infection, while our scientists strive to understand it and create a means of treating it. And I would say to the press and the media that they are *not* helping matters with sensationalised reports, and that they could provide a valuable service to the country by helping, rather than criticising and hindering, official efforts to take control of the situation. They can begin helping by broadcasting this important announcement, and making sure it is spread as far as possible: There is now an immunity register published online, and I would urge anyone who suspects that they, or anyone they know, are immune from the infection to enter their details in the register. Links to the register can be found on the front pages of YouTube, Facebook, Twitter, other social networking sites, and all major search engines and email providers.' He took a pause, and just for a moment – perhaps the space of a blink, but Vic knew he had not imagined it – the President's lip quivered. But he was too strong to reveal his tears. 'This is *not* a plague of zombies,' he said. 'It is a terrible disease, and soon we shall find a cure. Thank you.' The President turned to leave, and as the assembled journalists started shouting Marc cancelled the clip.

'Immunity register?' Vic asked.

Marc clicked on a bookmarked website. 'As quickly as new names go up, older entries are being marked red.' He pointed at the red-blocked screen. 'Discounted. The pattern's pretty fucking consistent.'

Vic blinked at the screen, then turned away. 'They're taking steps,' he said.

'But it doesn't help us,' Marc said. 'Here.' He tapped a few keys and a map of the USA filled the screen. It was blank, a simple outline with fainter lines indicating state boundaries. There was a colour-coded key down the left-hand side, and a line of editing icons across the top. 'This is a program I've been working on for a while. It can plot disease vectors, reported outbreaks, confirmed outbreaks, and lots of other stuff.'

'Such as?'

'Pretty much anything you want. Code input differently and it'll bring up a different map. Convert it into graphs, or hard-data listings. So we can plot incidences of immunity, designated safe areas . . . anything there's data on. I've set it to follow all the online news channels.

Uses word-recognition software to plot reported out-breaks. And it follows more reliable sites to plot confirmed outbreaks.'

'What other sites?'

'A variety,' Marc said. 'Military, Homeland Security. Stuff I shouldn't have access to. I set up an automatic renewal on a search engine, repeating searches every ten seconds, and then word recognition again on the blogs it brings up.'

'What words did you use?'

'Zombie. Do you think we need any other?'

'Zombie,' Vic said, staring at the screen. 'So how does this help us?'

'It doesn't,' Marc said. 'Not in the slightest.' He sat back and pointed at the keyboard. 'Hit enter.'

'What am I seeing?'

'Rate and extent of spread.'

Vic hit enter and sat back. A clock at the screen's top right started at 00:00, and progressed half an hour every ten seconds. And in a little over eight minutes, he saw what he had done.

The outbreak centred on Coldbrook, in the southern arm of the Appalachians. To begin with the spread was slow, and the red dot barely changed for the first two hours. At hours three to five it snaked from that area a little, several distinct lines of red bleeding outward along roads. And once the roads were lit red, the spread happened faster. At hour six it flooded Greenville in the south, at hour eight Knoxville to the north. And then the spread increased, the red smudge bleeding outwards as if it was a schematic of the land's greatest wound. Highways fed the spread, and the landscapes around them were soon flooded as well. At hour fifteen, Atlanta, Charlotte, Louisville and Nashville were within its grasp.

'Got a cousin in Nashville,' Gary said. 'Top bloke. Barman.'

'This just marks distinct outbreaks,' Marc said. 'Once they reach a certain concentration, the program fills in the surroundings.'

Vic waited a further couple of minutes until the program ended, frozen in time over twenty hours from when he had got out of Coldbrook. Then he sat back and held his hands to his face.

'The military?'

'As you'd expect,' Marc said. 'National Emergency, the Guard called up, doing everything in their power, blah-di-fucking blah. Offered my services, they just said they had their own people. But they don't have what we have – Jonah, and Coldbrook.'

'Had,' Vic said.

'He'll get back online. He has to.'

'Haven't they sent anyone to Coldbrook?' Vic asked, realising that he should have asked Jonah.

'I asked,' Marc said. 'They told me that information

was classified. So I made a call, spoke to a guy I know. The term he used was clusterfuck.'

'And you've missed all the political shouting,' Gary said. 'National, international. Thanks to the Internet, the whole world's watching this in real-time. All flights from the States turned back, north and south borders closed.' He laughed out loud, a shocking sound. 'Lot of good that will do! Like closing the borders to flies.'

'What are these?' Vic asked. Initially he'd believed that the scattered red dots elsewhere across the country might have been a fault on the laptop screen, or perhaps reports of false sightings. But the more he looked at them, the more they seemed to blink like red eyes.

'Isolated outbreaks,' Marc said. 'Something like this doesn't just spread evenly.'

'But Jacksonville? Dallas?'

'People run,' Gary said. 'Christ knows I would.'

'I did,' Vic said softly.

'And that's why the spread can never be stopped physically,' Marc said. 'Gary's fly comment is pretty good, but still not accurate. There's film all over the Internet of these things being shot, but short of building a five-thousand-mile-long wall to contain the whole area . . .' He raised his hands despairingly. 'There are planes, trains, cars, helicopters, boats. Those infected don't show intelligence – certainly no more than a rudimentary memory, and perhaps a basic ability to learn through repetition.

But they could be trapped in a hold or a car's trunk. Or maybe the infection can survive for a time in spilled blood.'

'Holy fuck,' Vic said.

'That's just what Marc's been saying,' Gary said.

'I've been busy while you were resting.' Marc dropped a leather notebook in Vic's lap, folded open at a page filled with names. 'Jonah and I . . . we've been friends since you were shitting your diapers. Don't agree on everything, that's for sure. He's a stubborn old fuck.'

'You know him well,' Vic muttered.

'But one thing we've always agreed on is that there's no politics or religion in science. No boundaries. Secrecy benefits states, but shared knowledge is the way forward for mankind. He's already spoken to some of these people, but not all. He didn't get through the list before . . .' He shrugged.

'Spoken why?' Vic asked.

'For help. There are scientists around the world working on this, and I've already established a direct line with some of them.'

Vic started reading the names on the list. Some had a tick beside them, a few were crossed out. He recognised a few from conversations with Jonah over the years – and he knew a couple more by reputation. Others he had never heard of, and there were a few names he could not even pronounce.

'Robert Nichols, professor of cellular immunology,' Vic read. 'Lucy-Anne Francis, physical cosmologist. Kazuki Yoshida, thanatologist. Caspian Morhaim, microbiologist.'

'You know so many interesting people,' Gary said.

'And a musician can say that?' Vic asked. He felt a brief, vivid flood of optimism, fed partly by Marc's actions and the knowledge of the people they already had on their side, ready to work as hard as they could until this was over. But perhaps it was also inspired by knowing . that Marc was now in control.

'So what's the bad news?' Vic asked.

'That was it,' Gary said. 'For the fucking terrible news, you'll have to follow me.'

'Where to?' Vic went cold, because the two men had suddenly grown grimmer than ever. The smoky air in the room felt heavy, loaded.

'The roof,' Gary said. 'I saw the first fire to the south half an hour ago.'

They climbed to the wide roof together and stood at the parapet. It was dawn. To the east the horizon was smeared deep pink and orange, reminding Vic of Marc's disease-spread program. And to the south, Cincinnati was already awake.

There were three spires of smoke, each arcing gently to the west and spreading into a high haze. Two of them were several miles away, their sources hidden by folds in the land and buildings in the city, but Vic could see the glimmer of fire at the base of the third column. It was perhaps two miles away.

'That's a new one,' Gary said. 'Closer.'

'Bengals' stadium ablaze,' Marc said. 'You know . . . everyone runs.'

'What do you mean?' Vic asked, but then he realised what Marc was getting at.

'They run to survive, or they run to spread the disease. Those fuckers' main aim isn't to eat fucking brains, or whatever it is they do in the movies. They spread the disease, as quickly and widely as possible. This is no passive contagion.'

'Hush,' Gary said. They listened, and to begin with all Vic could hear was a gentle breeze blowing dust across the rooftop. Behind them the helicopter's tied rotors groaned a little, as if the machine was keen to fly. And then, in the distance, a sound like bubblewrap being popped.

'Gunfire,' Vic said.

'You sure?'

'Yeah.' He scanned the landscape over the rooftops down the slight slope from them, trying to look away from the fires to see what was happening elsewhere.

It was Gary who saw the helicopters. 'There. Two o'clock. See them? Hovering over those warehouses.'

Vic saw. He made out three of them, and saw the distant flashes of their guns. Apaches, maybe. A few seconds later, that bubblewrap popping came again. It was too far away to see what they were firing at.

A flash reached them from the other direction, and he saw a bloom of flame and smoke rising from behind a line of buildings to the south-east. A few moments later the explosion sounded as distant thunder, followed by several more in quick succession.

When the breeze lifted, the rattle of small-arms fire reached them and Vic wondered whether the army was down there in the streets and parks, the city centre and the outlying areas where tens of thousands lived. Cars were streaming from the city now. The main roads were mostly hidden from view but where they were visible he could see that they were jammed, the vehicles crawling no faster than someone could run.

The sound of shooting grew louder. The military helicopters prowled above Cincinnati.

'Why aren't there more?' Vic asked. 'More helicopters, more soldiers?'

'Confusion,' Gary said. 'You should hear some of the shite from politicians on the TV. Some think it's a terrorist attack and are calling for an air strike on the Middle East. Don't believe a word of it – talk about Holocaust denial. And there're more than a few who think it's God's handiwork.'

Vic waited another five minutes on the roof, watching the chaos advance across the city towards them. Sirens wailed. There were more fires erupting now and the flames were spreading fast. When he saw the first people fleeing the city on foot he went back down. With every step he descended he knew that many people were dying at that moment. And right then he needed his family like never before.

3

'We're turning around,' Jayne said.

'Yeah.'

'Is it because of me?'

Sean Nott tapped the gun on the back of the seat, his lips pressed together. She'd already realised that he said a lot with his face. 'I'll go find out,' he said.

Jayne went to stand, but winced in pain and settled in the seat again. She'd told him about the churu, and what it did to her joints, and how she'd had it her whole life, but she wasn't sure he believed her. The fact that he hadn't blown her brains out was a good sign. But he was just one, and the others were many. And the others wanted her dead.

'I won't go all the way forward,' he said. 'Just far enough to speak to them.'

'You saved my life,' Jayne said, and Sean smiled

uncertainly. She knew that he'd originally worked his way through the plane to kill her.

She watched him go and took another sip of orange juice. He'd handed her a sweatshirt, then they'd retreated to the back of the aircraft where the small kitchen and several toilets huddled at the rear of the economy seating area. The other passengers had watched them go, and Jayne was certain it was only Sean's gun that meant she was still alive. *Sky marshal!* he'd shouted as he dragged her along the aisle, her body exposed, the bite attracting frantic attention. *Sky marshal! Stay back!*

She's got a bite!

She's talking, not biting.

A fucking zombie bite on her arm, man!

And if she turns I'm the one with the gun, so—

Gonna kill us all—

Don't give a—

Asshole.

She'd cried and whimpered, from pain more than from fear, and for those first few minutes she'd talked constantly, not wishing to give Sean a moment's doubt. She bit her lips until they bled, trying to hold back another churu blackout. He'd sat her in the last row of seats and stood across the aisle, watching her – and watching the other passengers where they'd retreated past the central toilets into the next compartment. He'd shouted updates to them – *She's fine, she's talking, not a bite at all* – but their only reply had been to scream back at him. There were sensible people among the passengers, she knew that. Compassionate, caring people. But right now even those wanted her dead.

Sean was working his way along the aisle, and she could see moonlight sweeping across the seats as the aircraft continued its turn. *We're going back,* she thought, and a chill went through her.

'What's happening?' Sean asked. The curtain twitched and a face peered out. The woman looked past Sean to Jayne, and Jayne tried to smile. The woman's face remained blank.

'They're turning us back,' she said. 'She still . . .?'

'She's fine.'

'We should put her in the hold!' someone shouted from beyond the curtain.

'She's unwell,' Sean said.

'You said she was—'

'It's an old illness! Something genetic, something called churu.'

'I've never heard of it.'

'So she's fragile, and she might freeze down there.'

'And?' The shouter appeared beside the woman, drawing the curtain back to face Sean. The marshal had paused halfway along the compartment, and there were still ten paces between them. But for a moment, Jayne was sure the man was about to charge.

'She *must* be immune,' Sean said. 'Have any of you heard anything about people being bitten and treated in hospitals? Anyone else immune?'

The woman shook her head gently, looking past Sean again. 'The President made a speech,' she said. 'He said they're doing everything in their power to help, and they won't rest until—'

'Anything significant?' Sean asked.

'Immunity register,' the woman said.

'They're saying *no one's* immune!' the man said, and then another woman pushed through, a stewardess who had served Jayne's supper an hour after take-off. Her presence seemed to calm the man and woman, and they relaxed a little.

'It's spreading fast,' the stewardess told Sean. 'There's martial law across five states. I've got a friend who works in the NYPD and they're getting ready to isolate Manhattan. And, from everything I've seen on YouTube and the news channels, it infects you in minutes.'

'Any cases of bites not turning anyone?' Sean asked.

'Hey,' the stewardess said, her smile forced, 'that'd be *good* news. You think the media would want any of that right now?'

Sean glanced back at Jayne, and she saw the man tense as if ready to make a grab for the gun. She opened her eyes wider, nodded past Sean, and he turned back quickly. The tension relaxed as quickly as it had built.

'Why are we going back?' Sean asked. The aircraft had completed its turn – the moonlight was shining through different windows now.

The stewardess seemed uncomfortable, and Jayne realised that none of the other passengers knew either.

'So why?' the man prompted.

'They won't let us land,' she said. 'UK air-traffic control says they're scrambling the RAF to turn back any North American flights.'

'And they threatened to shoot us down if we don't comply?' Sean said. The stewardess didn't answer, which was answer enough.

Sean started backing along the aisle, but the stewardess stayed where she was, watching them go and giving Jayne a half-smile.

'A deep bite?' she asked.

'Yes,' Jayne said, joining the conversation for the first time.

'It drew blood?'

Jayne nodded.

'And you're sure the person who bit you was . . .?'

'I'm sure,' Jayne said. 'Then I shut myself in a car. She . . . *it* looked in. Then left.' More pain flared through her hips, and she pulled herself upright, groaning at the effort.

'There's food and drink back there,' the stewasdess said. 'Look in compartment six. Some nice salads.'

'Thanks,' Sean said. 'Will you tell us when we're close?'

'About three hours.' She glanced back over her shoulder, then lowered her voice. 'I think some of them might come for her before then.'

Sean nodded his thanks, and he and Jayne watched the stewardess disappear behind the curtain again.

'If they come?' Jayne asked.

'No one's going to walk into a bullet,' he said.

'You'd really shoot them?'

She saw doubt and fear in what she'd previously thought were the eyes of a strong guy. She guessed Sean was around fifty, stocky and fit, and he had scars – two parallel wounds on his left cheek, pale against his dark skin. She might ask about them, given time.

''S long as *they* think I will, we'll be okay.'

'I might be immune,' she said. 'What if I am?'

'How rare is that disease of yours?'

Jayne nodded slowly as understanding dawned, and Sean sat in the seat across from her, leaning out so that he could see along the aisle.

'Fuck,' he said softly.

4

Jonah knew that this was action for the sake of it. But sitting in Secondary in the dark with nothing to do would drive him mad, so coming back down to Control was at least something to occupy his mind. *Nothing will have changed*, he thought. He slid the gun into his waistband and pulled back the chairs he'd propped beneath the door's handle. As he opened the door, something whispered behind him.

Jonah whirled around and shone his torch back along the corridor. The wall was smeared with dried blood, black in the artificial light. Nothing moved.

'Is that you?' he said. Nothing answered. 'Bastard!'

He was talking to shadows.

He tugged the door open and stepped inside Control. It was cooler than the rest of Coldbrook. The air held a hint of something alien to this place – flowing water, soil, healthy plants. He breathed in and held his breath: the scents of another world were startling. Previously the containment field had kept the two worlds separate, but Holly had switched it off to go through. *Holly is through there*, he thought, staring at the breach. It glowed gently in the torchlight.

Moths fluttered in the light, creatures from elsewhere. Their presence took his breath away.

He'd thought seriously about going through, but not yet. He could not abandon his world while there still might be a chance for it. So he stood just inside the door and aimed the torch around the room, switching to wide beam so that shadows could not hide for too long. A few flies buzzed in the light. The moths spiralled in confusion, dusting the beam. The withered creature still lay where it had fallen.

And that was when the dark started talking at last.

'It hurts when you pass through.'

Jonah gasped and pressed himself against the glass wall. He shone the torch this way and that, tracking its beam with the gun.

'But pain purifies.' The voice was low and wet. 'It purges the old. Emphasises the new. The pain is necessary. There is so much more to come.'

Jonah swung left, and when he turned back the man stood in front of him, several paces away and different from before. He still held the pulsing red organ, its tendrils stirring as the light hit them, but his other hand had removed part of his mask to speak. His newly exposed lips were as pale as dead fish, the flesh around his mouth smooth and speckled with moisture. He pressed the mask back across his mouth and Jonah heard a pained inhalation. Steam hazed the air. Then the man removed it again to speak some more.

'I am the Inquisitor, and you will be prepared and instructed.' His teeth were rotted, black and cracked, and a faint mist seemed to issue from his throat.

Jonah raised the gun and aimed, but the man merely pressed his mask back against his mouth. He had yet to expose his eyes. Jonah flicked the torch this way and that, trying to get its light to penetrate the goggles. They glittered wet and dark.

Jonah lowered the gun, backed to the doorway and slipped through, never taking his gaze from the man. He followed.

'This world is dead,' the Inquisitor said. 'You are honoured, because for you it is the beginning.'

'This world is *not* dead!' Jonah said, surprised at the forcefulness in his voice.

The intruder breathed in heavily once again, hissing softly as he exhaled.

Jonah flipped the torch around to check the corridor, and when he turned back the man had gone. A light mist hung in the air where he had been.

'Where are you?' Jonah whispered. 'Inquisitor. Bastard.' Control was silent, the corridor behind him whispering once again with scratching echoes of the dead.

Jonah stacked the chairs against the door, slid down the wall and nursed the torch. He remained there for some time, because that place was as safe as any.

5

The zombies surged by, and none of them had eyes for Holly. They were hideous. Many appeared unharmed and unchanged, apart from the blankness in their eyes and the sense of terrible purpose in their actions. Some had been wounded, and the injuries were many and varied – bullet holes, knife wounds, scrapes and gouges, burns, crush injuries, impact marks. Some were naked, some were in their nightclothes, others wore uniforms, suits, or casual clothing. The one thing that united them, other than the empty eyes, was the blood.

It was smeared across their mouths and jaws, their chins and throats and chests. These creatures had been biting, and they were seeking more.

Holly started backward, but Moira held her still.

'Be calm,' Moira said.

The zombies flickered from view, only to be replaced by more, and Holly realised that she was looking at a projection. The room was large and dim, the atmosphere heavy with moisture, and there were things in there that she could not comprehend.

The projection point of view shifted, turning to follow the path that the zombies were taking. The image splashed with something wet, and when it cleared she saw a long straight street, lined on each side with tall buildings. One of the buildings was on fire – people at the higher windows were shouting and waving. Their voices must have been desperate, but she could hear nothing. This was a vision only, and for that she was glad.

The street was jammed with zombies, and they were

being cut down by gunfire from further along the street. Many of them stood up again and carried on running, or hobbling, or crawling if their legs or hips or spines had been destroyed. Many more – those shot in the head – stayed down.

The view suddenly shifted as whatever was observing this chaos climbed on top of an overturned car. And from higher up the sight was even more astounding.

The street was barricaded with a line of tanks parked side by side next to a Dunkin' Donuts. Their big turret guns pointed along the street, but it was their machine guns that were doing the damage, raking left and right and making the air in front of them shimmer with heat and smoke. The silhouette of a helicopter gunship came quickly into view above them as it passed over the barricade and opened fire.

They were zombies, yet the devastation wrought upon their bodies was shocking. Holly wanted to turn away but found that she could not. She was riveted. She had the sense that she would have to see this eventually so she might as well go through with it *now*, see it all *now*.

The helicopter hovered over the street and its guns swivelled on their mountings. Glass shattered, raining down from the tall buildings, bodies were ripped apart, and then the helicopter turned towards her point of view, and Holly whined a little, trying to edge back.

'It's not happening here,' Moira whispered in her ear.

The image flashed yellow, and then white, and then it became a pattern of falling snow on the air. Beyond the faded image, panting slightly where she lay on a clear fluid bed, a woman grasped at the air as if to hold the last drifting flakes.

'What the fuck was that?' Holly said.

'Take a breath, Holly,' Drake said. 'And look around. This is the heart of our Coldbrook.'

Holly looked closer. The woman wore a simple robe similar to a hospital gown and lay on a large flexible bed that was moulded perfectly to her body. Above her, where the image had seemed to be projected onto the air, hung a framework of clear loose pipes. They looked like unobstructed flows of water, but Holly guessed they were held in place and shape by whatever forces contained the clear bed. Leading up from the framework into the ceiling were thicker pipes, dark and solid. Small sparks flared and died along them, leaving the surfaces and performing tight orbits before fading away. She stretched up to get a better look, but Moira touched her on the shoulder.

'Don't get too close.'

'Is she the one who . . .?' the prone woman asked.

'Her name's Holly,' Drake said.

'That was my world,' Holly said softly, pointing to where a vague haze still hung in the air. 'So she was there, seeing it? My world?'

'I'm so sorry, Holly,' the woman said, and she averted her eyes as if ashamed.

'What is all this?' Holly asked.

'Our version of what you called a breach,' Drake said. 'There's more to see. Gayle?' Drake asked.

'About seventy miles north-west of here,' the woman said softly.

'That all came from what happened in Coldbrook?' Holly asked. But no one answered, because they knew she was coming to terms with what she'd just seen.

'We can show you more,' Drake said, nodding towards the rest of the room. Heavy curtains hung as dividers, but beyond Gayle – the woman still lying meekly in front of her – Holly could now make out variations in the room's lighting, and colours beyond those curtains.

'More?' she said. And though what she had seen was terrible, she nodded and followed Drake.

Spread throughout the large room were men, women, and some children, perhaps a dozen in total. Half of them were twitching in their fluid beds while images played in the air above them. The projection's outer extremes would flex and bend, pipes leading up into the ceiling sparking and whipping from some unseen influence, and the sleepers were connected to the screens with more of those fluid connections, watery snakes squirming through the air. The remaining people lay in deep slumbers. They all looked exhausted, and Holly wondered briefly whether they were here against their wills. But Gayle had apologised to her, and she'd heard a level of admiration in Drake's voice. Maybe these were the only people in Gaia's Coldbrook who were able to do this. And whatever these devices were, they showed her how her own world was dying. Though the images were silent, she could imagine every scream of pain and roar of destruction.

She saw a field, crops trampled by hundreds of running people. In the distance she could just make out the first regular shapes of buildings, the only taller structure a church spire. They were running towards a small town.

Rushing through an indoor market, stalls crashing and crushed, jewellery and paintings, books and pots, sculptures and other craft items trampled into the floor, as sellers and customers alike were caught and bitten.

And then she saw the High Museum of Art in Atlanta. One of her favourite buildings, now it had bodies scattered on the lawns, windows smashed, and smears of blood across its light brown façade. People were rushing from the main entrance, and she knew what they all were.

It was then that Holly realised that these sights were viewed through a zombie's eyes. Somehow, the people lying around her were seeing the downfall of her Earth through the eyes of monsters.

'How does this work?' she asked. 'Where is your breach generator? I don't understand.'

'You walk into our world from another, and *you* don't understand?' Drake said.

'But these things . . . this technology.'

'Quantum bridges. I've read my father's notes, and he handed down most of his knowledge. Once they learned how to stabilise micro-black holes in the lab they could draw through gravity lines. You thought we were backward?'

'No, no,' Holly said. But perhaps she had in the beginning, just a little. She'd seen bows and arrows, basic clothing, and people living in holes in the ground.

'Come with me,' Drake said. 'It's best not to talk too much in the casting room. It's tiring work, and sometimes to watch it can be . . .' He shrugged.

'Draining,' Moira said.

Holly nodded, feeling a surge of anger. But that faded quickly, replaced with a hollow hopelessness and a feeling of guilt that she was the one who'd escaped.

'Please,' Drake said, holding out his hand in invitation. 'We'll tell you what happened here. As much as we can, at least.'

'As much as you can.'

'We don't know everything. It was before most of us were born.'

Holly shook her head. All the parts made sense, but

together the big picture was a blur, a confused reflection of what she had seen happening on those strange screens. *It all started here*, she thought. *That first zombie came from here.*

And for Earth to become like Gaia was now the best she could hope for.

'No one from here has ever travelled to an alternate Earth.' Drake had just prised a door open and they stood in a ruined room, the concrete walls crumbled with damp, metal reinforcements rusted and protruding like rotten teeth. A series of glass pipes were strung horizontally across one wall, many of them holed and smashed. Furniture was simple and functional. The room was lit by several hanging oil lamps, though electrical wires protruded from holes in the ceiling.

'So I guess I'm quite a surprise,' Holly said. Neither Drake nor Moira answered, and she marked that as something to investigate further.

'Coldbrook is all much like this, fallen into ruin,' Drake said. 'The black hole is supported deep beneath us, fed by artificial light. It doesn't need any maintenance, though the containment is checked every few weeks. But to maintain the rest of the facility, so deep underground, seemed pointless.'

'Even though you still have furies?'

'You've seen them. After forty years, they're

slow-moving. Not really a threat unless you get too close. We maintain the areas we need, and that's all.'

As they walked on, Holly remembered Melinda holding out her arms to welcome the stumbling figure and falling beneath it as the fury bit into her. 'That's how it happened,' she said. 'Someone got too close.'

They passed a glass wall and Holly experienced a pang of recognition. But beyond the wall was something very different from Control. A large room held several metal columns upon which sat the remains of glass spheres, five feet across and smashed.

'What's that?' Holly asked.

'My father said it was a broadcasting station,' Drake said. 'I used to play in there when I was a kid, until the spheres got smashed.'

But Holly was barely listening, because another possibility was niggling at her.

'You were watching our world before we formed the breach,' she said.

'Yes,' Drake said.

'How long before?'

'It's complicated,' Drake said, cutting Moira off as she started to speak.

'Try me. I'm a scientist. Couldn't you have *warned* us?'

'No.'

'Why?' They were in a wide corridor now. Plaster had fallen from the walls. Holly kicked out and sent a chunk of it across the floor. It struck the opposite wall and exploded in a shower of damp fragments. Drake stepped back, and Moira slipped a hand into her pocket. 'Do you have some sort of *Star*-fucking-*Trek* non-involvement policy?' Holly was starting to shout now, unable to stop the rage, sad and pointless though it felt. 'Why in God's name didn't you—'

Moira gasped. Drake shook his head.

'Because we couldn't,' he said. 'We can *view* through to your world, but not go through physically, never interact. You saw Gayle and the others – we call them casters. And yes, they were seeing through furies' eyes. But they have no control over their host, other than their intrusion making it calm and observant. It's remote viewing.'

'How long have you been watching?' Holly asked again, still shouting, stepping forward with her arm raised. Moira had taken something from her pocket.

'Your world?' Drake said. 'Almost thirty years.'

'Thirty years?' Holly said, stepping towards Drake. 'Thirty fucking—' A sting in her neck, hands catching her and easing her down, and her last thought before unconsciousness was, *They sent it through themselves . . .*

6

Vic Pearson watched his wife and daughter sleeping, and when Olivia woke up he stayed with her and they talked.

'Mommy said I can't watch TV.' Bleary-eyed from sleep, Olivia was still as sharp as a button. With her mother asleep in the big bed, she was now working on her father. But there was no joy there.

'It's broken, honey,' Vic said.

'It wasn't broke after you left to talk to the men. Mommy was watching it, and it made her cry so she turned it off. I heard shouting.'

'The TV set's OK,' he said, 'but the place they send the signals from is broken.'

'Huh,' Olivia said, looking suspiciously at him. 'You're lying.'

'Olivia!' But he couldn't get angry with her.

'They send those pictures from all over, not just one place. Davey in school told me. His dad's an astronaut and he sees everything.'

'That's how Davey knows everything, then,' Vic said, nodding wisely.

'I guess,' Olivia said. 'I need to pee.'

'Go ahead, honey.'

Olivia stood up from her creaking camp bed and crossed to the small en suite bathroom. She turned on the light and left the door open a crack, glancing through it at Vic as she so often did at home. He forced a smile and she smiled back.

Some of the national channels were still broadcasting normal programmes – he'd scanned through to see

Seasame Street, an endless loop of *Frasier*, and a daytime soap he couldn't identify – but most local channels were filled with the news. One bulletin showed a towering pall of flames and smoke rising above Chicago airport, where three passenger jets had collided. Vic didn't want Olivia seeing the truth.

He sighed, and Lucy stirred. He leaned down and kissed her, smelling her stale breath and confusion.

'Oh, Christ,' his wife said as she remembered. She raised herself on her elbows, then glanced across at the bathroom. 'She okay?'

'Yeah. Wants to watch TV. I won't let her, and we left her DVDs at home.'

Lucy sat up and hugged her legs to her chest. Vic wanted to lean in to her, but he wasn't sure that would be welcome right now.

'What's left of home?' Lucy asked.

'I don't know.'

'Our friends,' Lucy said. 'Mark, Sarah, Steve, Peter? What about them, Vic? Are they all dead? And our house? I locked the doors but do you think . . .?'

'Home is wherever we are,' Vic said, eager to snap his wife out of this.

Lucy looked at the bathroom door again. Water was running in there, and Olivia was humming a tune that Vic could not identify. *Coldbrook is your home*, Lucy had

told him, sometimes angry, sometimes just acknowledging what they both knew.

'But if Jonah wants you to do something, go somewhere?'

'Then I'll take you with me.'

'And if it's dangerous?'

Vic blinked, hating the vulnerability in his strong wife's
eyes.

'What?' she asked.

'I think it'll be dangerous everywhere.' His gaze turned
to the bathroom door and he saw Olivia through the
gap, singing to herself in the mirror and fluffing up her
sleep-flattened hair. *Bad hair day!* he'd say to her sometimes. If only that was all they had to worry about now.

He thought of his daughter dead, and hooting that
dreadful call.

'Has it reached here?' Lucy asked. Vic nodded, and
she seemed to strengthen. She'd always been scared of
possibilities – Olivia being hurt, Vic getting ill – but was
more capable than him at handling certainties.

'Mommy,' Olivia said, leaving the bathroom and turning
off the light behind her. 'Are we going to die?'

'We're not going to die because Daddy's friends are
here to help us,' Lucy said. 'There are some poorly people
out there who need helping, but once they're all better
we'll be able to go back home. Okay?'

'Will we catch what they have?'

'No,' Vic said.

'Because we're behind the fence?'

'Yes.'

'Oh. Okay.' Olivia jumped on the bed, and Vic leaned over and tickled her, and Lucy bent forward and started tickling her daughter as well. The little girl squealed with delight and squirmed from the bed, picking up a drawing pad and flopping down on her own bed.

The phone by the bed rang. Vic snapped it up. 'Developments,' Marc said. 'Communications room, now.'

'This is now?' Vic asked, staring in disbelief at the laptop screen.

'Constantly updating,' Marc said. 'Margins of error, but . . .' He waved a hand.

It doesn't matter, Vic thought. *Whatever margin of error you apply to this . . . it doesn't matter.*

He knew well enough that the contagion had reached Cincinnati, but the extent of spread elsewhere was shocking. The red smudge on the screen had turned into a widening, deepening stain on the map of the USA. The solid red mass covered much of Georgia, Alabama, Tennessee, North and South Carolina, Kentucky, Indiana and Ohio, with tendrils stretching into neighbouring states three hundred miles or more from Coldbrook. But beyond this were those other spots of infection, satellite stains that were spreading as quickly as the original, flickering on the screen with the promise of fresh growth.

From New Orleans in the south to Philadelphia and New York in the east, to Detroit in the north, and even as far afield as San Francisco and Seattle in the west, the infection now spanned the country.

'Shit,' Vic muttered. 'Aircraft, you think?'

'Yeah,' Marc said. 'Public and private aircraft, zombie stuck in the cargo hold. And don't discount the speed of spread along roads. Drive for ten hours straight with your foot down, and you can get from Atlanta to Dallas. One car or truck doing that with one of those fuckers trapped on board . . .'

'So what the hell do we do now?' Vic asked. A feeling of unreality descended, distancing him from events. If he thought about this too much, he'd go insane. It was not a conscious defence, but right then he welcomed whatever instinct was striving to protect him. He looked up at Marc, and at Gary where he sat with his feet propped against a desk across the room.

'I did consider getting back to Coldbrook,' Marc said. 'The first disease vector came through there, which might help me examine the disease source. And if it meant me going through the breach to find out more . . .' He shrugged.

'Coldbrook's locked down,' Vic said.

'You got out, you can get us back in,' Gary said.

'But still no contact from Jonah?'

'No. But we can't assume that he's dead.'

Back to Coldbrook. Vic had done everything in his power to flee that place, and in doing so . . . He closed his eyes and shook his head, that sense of distance buffering him once more against the truth. It would have got out anyway, he was sure. Something like this couldn't be confined.

'But now . . .' Marc said. 'Now, I don't know if it's even worth trying. Just . . . don't know.'

'Not worth *trying?*' Vic asked. 'What the hell are you talking about?'

Gary strode across the room and leaned on his shoulder, tapping at the keyboard. 'As we said, there have been developments.'

Vic looked away from Marc and back at the screen. *He's scared.* It was the first time he'd really seen that in him.

There was a new screen open on the laptop. It displayed a world map. There were red dots outside the USA.

'You're fucking kidding,' Vic said.

Mexico.

'It was easy to expand the program to include foreign media,' Marc said.

Cuba, Haiti.

'But this could be a glitch? Are these confirmed?'

Guatemala, Belize, Costa Rica.

'Not as definite as our own map,' Marc said. 'I've got no tap into any foreign military, for a start.'

Canada, Alaska, Greenland, Iceland.

'This is just so shit,' Gary said.

As Vic watched the screen, Lima grew its own red spot.

Feeling aimless and hopeless, Vic returned to their small room. Lucy had turned the small TV away from her daughter's bed – Olivia lay there with her headphones on, playing on her Nintendo DS – and lay across the blankets with the remote control in one hand, ready to click it off the minute Olivia came to see. *She knows I lied about the TV being broken*, Vic thought, and he felt a sudden surge of love for his daughter.

'Seen this?' Lucy asked without turning to him. A man was being interviewed in a smart studio in Washington. He wore a suit and tie, and beneath his name on the screen was written *Government Spokesperson*. She had the sound turned down too quietly to hear but Vic could guess what the man was saying: *Stay calm, help is coming, we're working on the problem, and soon . . .*

'Then there's this.' She flicked to another news channel, this one cable. The live report was coming from Atlanta, the reporter apparently on top of a high building somewhere, and behind her the city was burning. All semblance of impartial reporting was gone. This woman was terrified, and shocked.

As Lucy nudged up the volume, the woman's voice

299

faded in. '. . . toll is catastrophic, the number of infected beyond counting. What you can see behind me is the result of aerial bombardment, and further north there are many people trapped in their homes, a few of them broadcasting by radio. The military won't comment, and—'

Lucy turned the TV off. Olivia glanced up at her, smiled at Vic, then went back to her DS screen.

'It's the end, isn't it?' his wife asked. Vic sat beside her on the bed.

Vic thought of lying, but Lucy was too sharp for that. And he had already lied too much. 'It might be. It's beyond our shores now. Marc says there's no way to stop the spread, and the only hope lies in a cure.'

'They shouldn't show that stuff on TV.'

'I think we're beyond niceties,' Vic said. 'But we're safe here.'

'How do you figure that?' Lucy kept her voice low, but he could see the tension in her face.

'They can't get in.'

'And how much food do we have? How much water?'

'Lucy—'

'Enough water for a year, Vic?'

'Mommy,' Olivia said. She'd dropped the DS and pulled out her headphones, and she glanced back and forth between Vic and Lucy. 'Mommy, why do we need so much water?'

Lucy's face crumpled, but she did not move.

'Please,' Vic whispered as he moved past her, sweeping their daughter into his arms and pressing her head to his chest, wishing she could unhear and Lucy could unsay, and wishing with every atom in his body that he could undo.

7

Before they saw land beneath them, the other passengers made two attempts to get at Jayne. The first time Sean ushered her back into one of the toilets and closed the door, and she heard the shouting and screaming, threats and promises, and then the loud gunshot that silenced them all. A few moments later Sean opened the door and brought her out, never taking his attention from the aisle and the next compartment, curtained off once again. Jayne emerged expecting to see a body on the floor, but Sean had pointed his gun into the kitchen area. He'd fired into one of the food trolleys.

The second time, two men rushed them, hunkered down behind another food trolley. Sean crouched down in a shooting stance, but then the trolley caught a chair's arm and jarred to a halt, and the men had been thwarted. They retreated back along the aisle, one of them dabbing a bloodied nose.

And now they were over the USA again, and their worries were starting all over again.

'Why Baltimore?' Sean asked. The stewardess had come to talk, informing them where they were and that they'd been instructed to land.

'Closest airport. We'll be flying on fuel fumes when we land.' The woman's stare kept flickering to Jayne, and Jayne offered her a smile. She'd taken some horse-strength painkillers and now the churu aches were more manageable.

'Why can't they just leave us be?' Jayne asked. 'Not as if I've tried to eat any of them.'

'Most of them are scared,' the stewardess said. 'But there are a few who want to feel that they're doing something.'

'By killing an innocent woman?' Sean asked.

'I'm sorry,' the stewardess said. 'We'll be landing in twenty minutes.' She turned and walked back along the aisle.

Sean told Jayne not to strap herself in. He stood in the aisle beside her, gun in one hand, the other holding onto the seat in front of her. He no longer kept a watch on her. The man was tired.

'So what happened to you?' she asked.

'What do you mean?'

'I mean your . . .' *Family*, she wanted to say. But she hardly knew him, and what right did she have to know? 'Your story.'

'Right,' he said, glancing down at her. 'Yeah. Well, been

working the airlines since 9/11, the pay's good, get to travel. My wife moved to France ten years ago with my daughter, and I only see them once or twice a year.' He was staring along the aisle again, and his voice was flat and emotionless. Everything tied up inside. Jayne knew how that felt.

'At least they're safe,' she said. 'You should call them, now we're close to land.'

'If I hadn't left my phone up there.' He nodded along the aisle.

'Oh, sorry.'

They were silent for a while, feeling the strange lifting sensation as the aircraft lost altitude in preparation for landing.

'What should we do when we're on the ground?' Jayne asked at last.

'I've been thinking on that,' Sean said. 'Mostly up to now I've just been acting for the moment. Keeping you safe.' He looked at her, and she wondered how old his daughter was. 'And, if you'll let me, I'd like to continue doing that after we land.'

Jayne smiled.

'So once we land, we need to slip away and—'

The shouting was sudden, and shocking. Some people were speaking, others simply crying out in despair, and Sean knelt beside Jayne and levelled his gun along the aisle. *He looks terrified*, she thought. It had been her own pain, the threat to her own life, that had obsessed her since she'd woken half-stripped and exposed from her churu blackout. But here was Sean, protecting her because he knew it was right. And she could smell his fear, sense the tension in his body as he aimed the gun.

'What?' Jayne said. 'What is it?'

'Dunno,' Sean said. He was glancing left and right, sweating. 'When I say, get back into the rest room. You good to move?'

The curtain whipped aside and she held her breath, readying for the gunshot. But it was the stewardess, holding on to the seats as she hurried along the aisle to them.

'Far enough,' Sean said, sounding almost apologetic.

'What's happening?' Jayne asked.

'We've got to land in Baltimore, like I told you,' the stewardess said.

'And?' Sean asked.

'Baltimore's burning, and the airport's been overrun.'

'Oh, Jesus,' Sean whispered.

The stewardess stood there for a while, saying nothing, staring at Jayne. She'd helped them, and perhaps she felt some investment in her. *Or maybe she's just thinking about what's about to happen.*

'I live in . . .' the woman said. Then her face crumpled and she ran back along the cabin.

'We need to get ready,' Sean said. He tucked the gun into his shoulder holster and went to the kitchen behind them. Jayne tried to turn in her seat, but the pain in her hips screamed out. She leaned back and sensed their descent.

Baltimore's burning.

'Out of the frying pan . . .' she muttered as Sean sat next to her and handed her a bag.

One of the terminal buildings was on fire. Others looked untouched, but there were people on the concrete surrounding various parked aircraft. Some of them swarmed around a mobile staircase beside a 757, clambering up the stairs, falling from the top, rising to climb again. The thought of what might be happening inside the aircraft's cabin was horrible, but Jayne could not turn away.

The crowd's attention turned to their own jet.

'Hope the pilot's got enough sense not to taxi back there,' Sean said. The plane touched down, they bounced, jolted left and right, and Jayne wondered whether the vagaries of fate would allow her to die in a plane wreck. But then the wheels hit the runway again and they were down. The aircraft's jets roared in reverse thrust and Sean pressed an arm across the front of her shoulders to keep her back in her seat. She winced at the tensions in her body, and the pains they aggravated.

'Soon as we slow to turn—' Sean said, and the aircraft

veered so sharply to the left that Jayne was sure the wing tip would skim the ground and they'd be flipped.

Screams from the cabin in front of them, hidden by swishing curtains. The continuing roar of the engines. And Jayne saw shapes below them, passing beneath the wing and the fuselage, and the smears of several people crushed across the concrete.

'He's dodging them,' she said, and Sean uttered a short, sharp laugh.

The aircraft straightened, and as it slowed they felt several shuddering impacts. Jayne closed her eyes and saw Tommy struck by a bullet, and she was glad that he'd died so clean.

As the engines powered back and the plane drifted to the right, Sean jumped from his seat and went to the rear exit door on the starboard side. 'Are they *all* . . .?' he asked, amazed.

'All infected,' Jayne said. 'I can see blood.'

Sean stood back and seemed to gather his thoughts. Then he went through the kitchen to the opposite door. 'Here!' he called.

Jayne was already out of her seat, wincing against the pain but finding movement relatively easy. Sean was removing a locking bar from the emergency-door handle.

'When I open this, the chute inflates and forms a slide. You'll have seen it in the movies. I'll go down first, and you wait until I signal that it's safe. Got it?'

'Yeah.'

He pulled his gun, looked at it, tucked it back in the holster. 'Can you tie the bag to your belt?'

Jayne did. It contained bottled water, a tin opener broken so that the blade was exposed, and a penknife. Not much of a survival kit.

'Oh shit,' she whispered. Sean smiled at her and nodded. 'Why are you doing this for me?' she asked.

He held the door handle, breathing heavily, glancing outside, judging when to pull. 'My daughter's about your age,' he said. 'Which sounds fucking trite, I know. Sad middle-aged motherfucker who couldn't keep his family together.'

'No, not trite,' she said.

'And because you're special. Bitten, but still well. And this . . .' He pointed at the window, what lay beyond.

Saving his daughter by saving me, Jayne thought. And she smiled at the man, because he was honest.

The plane stopped.

'Okay,' he said. 'One . . . two . . .'

From the front of the plane came a heavy *clunk!* and the hiss of air as one of the aircraft's other escape chutes was released. Someone shouted, and Sean and Jayne pressed their faces to the door's window.

They saw the first few people tumble from the end of the inflated chute, stand up and then look around in panic. Seconds later, shapes darted from beneath the aircraft and fell on them.

'Oh, Jesus!' Sean said. He hadn't seen this before.

'I can't do this,' Jayne said, 'I can't, I can't . . .'

'We can't stay here,' he said. 'They might climb the chute.'

'Okay,' Jayne said, taking a deep breath. 'Sean, I've seen them before. They're fast. Their main aim is to spread whatever it is they have. They're not like . . . you know, "real" zombies. Don't eat your brains, shit like that.'

Passengers scrambled on the chute, struggling to halt their slide after seeing what had happened to those who'd reached the ground. But it was to no avail. And by the time they reached the bottom, some of their bloodied fellow passengers were standing to welcome them.

'Right,' Sean said, his voice and hands shaking. He took a couple of deep breaths. 'We wait until those things start climbing the front chute, and when enough of them are distracted, I'll pull the handle and we go through this exit. And I've got an idea of *where* we can go.'

'You do?'

'Yeah.' And he smiled. There was some measure of control in him again, as if his blood was up and he was now riding the situation. Once again, Jayne promised herself to ask about his scars.

They leaned down to watch from the window. Passengers had stopped sliding down to their doom, and the zombies were beginning to climb the chute. There was screaming from further along the aircraft, and the sound of something ripping and hissing as they tried to dislodge the chute. But even as it deflated and shrank, the bloodied people still clawed their way upward. Some hung on tightly and stayed still while others used them for hand and footholds. A woman fell away, shoved from the aircraft doorway out of Jayne's view, and her head cracked against the runway concrete.

'Be lucky like that another fifty times,' Sean muttered.

The curtain was ripped from its rail and the remaining passengers backed along the aisle, forgetting all about Jayne now that the true infection was among them.

'The gun!' someone shouted. 'The marshal's at the back of the plane!'

'You could hold them off,' Jayne said, and Sean hesitated, his hand still on the door handle.

'He's in!' someone shrieked.

'Jayne,' Sean said. He turned the handle and stepped back. The door's bolts blew and it fell outward, the chute inflating in seconds and before she could say anything Sean had dropped onto his behind and slid down.

Instinct took over and Jayne did the same. If she'd waited a few more seconds she might have been trampled by the panicked passengers, or pulled back from the doorway so that others could escape. Because this was pure panic – screaming, raving, spitting panic.

She slid down the chute and heard the first gunshot.

'Hand!' Sean said, holding out his left hand. She took it. 'Can you run?'

'Yes.'

He fired again, and a woman wearing a stewardess's uniform flipped back and down. For a blink, Jayne thought it was their stewardess, but this one was Asian, her tights ripped and her legs pale.

They ran directly away from the aircraft. There were shouts behind them, and Sean turned and fired again. Jayne could not help glancing back.

Three shapes were rushing at them from around the plane's forward exit, where the collapsed chute was still alive with zombies crawling and scrambling upward into the interior. Jayne hoped that the runners were escaped passengers, but then she saw the fresh blood across their mouths and chins.

Sean paused and let go of her hand, and dropped them all with one shot each to the head.

'Don't slow down,' he said, grabbing her hand again.

Someone had opened the rear door on the opposite side of the aircraft, and that chute too was now down. Several people had made it away and were running. They were being chased – the uninfected were easy to identify because they looked back over their shoulders in sheer terror. One of the men was holding an old woman's hand and attempting to pull her along. The woman fell, and he knelt by her side, hugging her to his chest and refusing to let go. As the first of the pursuers reached the pair, Jayne looked away.

There's love, she thought. *Unselfish, unconditional. I've had love like that.* The idea filled her with a brief, irrational sense of elation, and she squeezed Sean's hand. He squeezed back.

They crossed a grass verge and headed onto another runway. This one was empty, and beyond it lay several wide taxiing routes where two large aircraft were parked. One of them had a mobile staircase against its side, and the door was open.

Limbs aching, joints screaming at her to slow down, stop, rest, Jayne looked behind her again.

'Sean, three more!'

'We'll outrun them.'

'They'll see where we've gone – what if they can communicate?'

'Run on.' He let go of her hand and Jayne ran on, but then turned and slowed, walking backwards so that she could watch.

Sean shot a woman, used two more bullets to down a teenager wearing a Ramones T-shirt and a lipless grin, and when he fired at the last man his gun clicked on empty. He cursed, ducked, and drove his shoulder into the man's midriff, standing and using the zombie's momentum to propel him up and over. The zombie landed on his back with a dull thud, and before he could stand again Sean was stomping on his head, crushing it.

Jayne ran towards the aircraft, swallowing down bile. Her vision swam. Smoke stung her throat and nose, and her eyes were watering. There was a bus parked a hundred feet from the plane's left wing, and she kept a wary eye on it.

'Let me go first!' Sean said from behind her. She slowed, he overtook her and grabbed her hand again, and then they were at the foot of the stairs. Panting, he slammed a fresh magazine into his gun and started up the staircase. 'Wait halfway up. Stay ready to run back down.'

Jayne nodded and sat on a stair, watching him climb and then looking back the way they had come. She hoped there had been more escapees, but she could see none. Scores of frantic figures were gathered around the plane's exits, climbing the deflated chutes, falling back as those trapped inside struck them with feet or chairs or metal food canisters. A food trolley was shoved from one door, taking several clinging attackers with it. The forward door had been pulled shut again, and she wondered what was happening inside right now. She could see movement through the windows but could make no sense of it. *Fighting to the last.*

'Jayne,' Sean called from above. 'Come on.'

She climbed the last few stairs and entered the aircraft,

standing beside the marshal where he kept his gun at the ready.

'Got to shut this door.' As he did that, Jayne stumbled towards the front and sank into a seat, starting to giggle when she realised this was the first time she'd ever been in First Class. She picked up some cutlery from a seat tray – real stainless steel, not the plastic stuff she was used to – and giggled some more. And when Sean appeared and raised an eyebrow she showed him the knife, and laughed so much that it nearly made her sick.

Sean checked the aircraft three more times before declaring it clear.

They sat together, drinking orange juice and eating cold chicken curry, and then Jayne raided the First Class kitchen and found the drinks store. They cracked open a bottle of wine. They said little, because they could still hear the sounds of chaos from outside. Looking across to the aircraft they had abandoned, they saw that both starboard doors had been closed, and now and then they could make out vague movement inside. 'Survivors,' Sean said, but Jayne could only imagine the alternative – that they'd somehow locked all the doors without realising that the contagion was inside, and now it was an aircraft filled with zombies.

Sean tried his cellphone constantly but he could find no signal.

Their aircraft had been stocked and prepped for flight. The seats were neat and tidy, kitchen lockers filled with ready-meals waiting to be warmed, and Sean said the fuel tanks were probably full.

'Don't suppose you know how to fly a 757?' he asked.

They'd finished one bottle of wine and started on a second before Jayne asked him to finish his story.

Sean looked at the gun on the small folding table he'd brought out of his seat. He rubbed his glass back and forth across his lip, then drained the red wine in one swig.

'Does it matter any more?' he asked.

'Sure. You saved me. It matters to me.'

'But why'd you want to know?'

Jayne shrugged, because there was no clear answer to that. 'My granny told me never to trust a man with scars.'

Sean touched his cheek. 'I was a cop in New York,' he said at last. 'I saw the towers come down, felt pretty hopeless. I'd put my years in, so I handed in my notice to become a sky marshal. Felt like that was taking action. Stupid, maybe.'

'Not stupid,' Jayne said. 'So is that how you got . . .?' She touched her own cheek.

Sean snorted softly. 'Last week on the job, some drunk in a Greenwich Village bar took a swing at me. Still holding his glass.'

Jayne couldn't think of anything to say to that. Shitty luck, pure and simple.

Sean glanced around for the wine bottle, poured some more, and then paused. In the distance an aircraft's jets roared.

All the time they'd been hidden away no other aircraft had landed. *Last one out of Knoxville, last one back to Hell*, Jayne had quipped. They had seen fires in the distance, watched blood-covered people rushing across the airfield, and there had been a series of explosions from the main terminal.

Now came a sound more familiar to airports.

'Jesus!' Sean said, darting to the window. 'Pilot must have survived.'

It was the aircraft they'd come in on. It taxied away from them, one emergency chute still hanging deflated from a rear door. Its big wheels passed over one of the prone shapes beneath it.

'Maybe he locked himself in the cockpit,' Jayne said.

'Or the survivors have had a vote. Not much to stay here for.'

'Didn't the stewardess say they were flying on fuel fumes?'

'Yeah,' Sean said.

They watched, standing side by side. Five minutes after firing up its engines, the plane powered along the runway and lifted off. It climbed quickly, tilting its wings and catching the rays of the sinking sun as it headed north.

'Canada?' Jayne said.

'Maybe.'

They moved to the other side of their aircraft to see the escaping one climb away. It was little more than a diamond in the sky, reflecting the tired yellow of late-afternoon sunlight, while Sean went to find another drink.

And Jayne could not breathe as she watched the aircraft die, a falling star, barely visible as it plummeted into the hazy distance. She did not see the impact, and she turned away as Sean returned and asked her what was wrong. She told him.

'Fumes,' he said.

They opened another bottle of wine.

8

Every minute I've been out of it, Holly thought as she came around. *Every minute, every second, it's getting worse*. The scenes that she had seen in the casting room flashed before her again and again, and before she opened her eyes she saw a parade of dead children and bloodied, blank faces.

Drake Slater was sitting beside her as she surfaced. The fainting fit pulled away quickly, her senses returned, and she realised that she'd received a far lower dose of whatever had knocked her out than she had last time.

'Nice way of greeting a visitor,' she muttered.

'Sorry,' Drake said, not sounding like he meant it. 'We've grown used to looking after each other.'

'And you drugged me because I was losing my temper?' Holly sat up on a cot bed. The room around her was sparse and functional She ran a hand through her knotted hair, wishing for a brush, some shampoo. She was beginning to understand why the people here wore their hair short or in tight braids.

'Moira heard you say "God".'

'Oh?' She'd already clocked their aversion to the G-word.

'We're people of science. But that doesn't mean we don't fear the Inquisitor.'

Holly remained silent, hoping that he would continue. And he did.

'I'm as convinced as I'll ever be that you're telling the truth, so . . . I suppose that now it's safe to tell you. There are those who believe that because some of us survived, the Inquisitor will return one day.' He smiled, with little humour in his expression. 'It's the opposite of the old Jesus legend.'

'This Inquisitor – it's a legend?'

Drake shrugged. He seemed suddenly nervous again, evasive. So Holly tried another tack.

'You cast God aside so easily?'

'Easily?' Drake asked. 'Not easily at all, as far as I'm

aware. When I was a child God was a comfort to many, though not all. Much like in your world, I suspect. My father was a true believer but, since the Furies, God has been down there with them. And any mention now is an offence.' He shrugged, at the same time trying to smile.

'Just because this happened doesn't mean that He doesn't exist,' Holly said.

'Perhaps in your world. But keep it to yourself. There are people here who'd attack you if they heard that, and some who might even kill you.'

'I don't understand.' Holly shivered.

'We believe the End was God's fault,' Drake said. Holly snorted, but he continued. 'That's what most of us believe. It's what the Coldbrook journals tell us – that the Inquisitor was a servant of God, and it came through to ensure that the Fury plague took our whole world. It oversaw our demise, and then took Coldbrook's chief with it. To another new world. A new Inquisitor to continue spreading the disease.'

'The Inquisitor sounds like a ghost.'

'Most people believe in it.'

'And what do *you* think?'

'I think God was as much to blame for the Furies as he was for a hundred wars through history.'

'But that was forty years ago. You're maybe forty yourself? I haven't seen anyone here old enough to remember.'

'There are a few. But blame is handed down through the generations. And there is proof.'

Holly leaned back against the wall, saddened, and convinced more than ever that Drake was only telling her parts of the story.

'I'd like to know . . .' Drake said, but he trailed off as if he was unsure.

'Know what?'

'Where we parted,' he said. 'Where our Earths became different possibilities.'

Holly smiled. 'You're talking Jonah's language now.'

'We seemed to be far ahead of you,' Drake mused. 'Our technology a long way further on than yours. Perhaps that's why the Furies hit us first.'

'You don't seem *that* far ahead,' Holly said defensively. But then she thought of the casting room, the incredible technology of the mini-black hole, and wondered just how much Gaia had lost.

'You're aware of the many-worlds interpretation?'

'Jonah's tried explaining it to me. An infinite number of universes, created at every possible quantum event? Everything that could have happened in our history but didn't has happened in some other universe. Or something.'

'Every decision, every event, creates another possible universe,' Drake said.

'Much more eloquent than me.'

'So which decision or event separates our Earths?'

'How can we ever tell?' Holly asked.

'It could be something as small as someone turning left instead of right,' Drake said. He stared at her, his piercing eyes filled with his sense of wonder. *Jonah would love him*, Holly thought.

'You had Beethoven?' she asked. 'Mozart? Brahms?'

Drake nodded. 'Shakespeare, Dickens, Melville.'

'The First World War?' she asked. 'Hitler? Nagasaki?'

'Churchill, Stalin, Roosevelt and Truman.'

'The Swinging Sixties?'

'I've read about that,' Drake said, and Holly could see that he did not understand. How different his forty years must have been here, compared to her thirty-seven years on Earth. So different that she could not count the ways.

'Kennedy?' she asked. 'Led Zeppelin? The Beatles?'

'"Lucy in the Sky",' Drake said. 'This could take for ever.' He shook his head, smiling, and his sense of wonder was more visible than ever.

'Jonah would so love to meet you.'

'And I him.' Drake stared at her, more intensely than ever, and for so long that Holly felt the true impact of the distance between them. Then he smiled again, and held her hand.

'I have more to show you.'

'I'm not sure that I want to see it.'

'You have to,' he said.

'Why?'

'Because others here at Coldbrook insist upon it,' he said. 'This plague was no accident.'

'And you have no cure,' she said. 'In all these years, has nothing been found?'

'There have been attempts,' Drake said. 'But no cure. I've been looking for one all my life. Even Mannan . . .' He trailed off, clenching his hands as if realising his mistake.

'So many secrets,' Holly said. 'What or who is Mannan?'

Drake shook his head slowly. 'In your world, are there still wars?'

'Wouldn't be Earth if that wasn't the case,' Holly said.

'That's the one thing the furies stopped, at least. There are no more wars, because the whole world's fragmented and regressed. From here, we sometimes deal with a dozen other communities, some of them quite large. But there is always some risk from the furies. One community gets too close to another, too tied in, and they'll both go down if the plague catches them out. So isolation is the key to survival.'

'That excuses secrets?'

'From you, yes. Of course. You're not just from another settlement or continent.'

'Hopeless,' Holly said.

'Hope is what keeps some of us alive,' Drake said, and the sudden passion in his voice was contagious. 'Much of the world has given up, winding down as much as the furies have. But we still have reason to believe.'

'In a cure?' she asked. 'Something unproven and seemingly beyond your reach? Surely you need proof to believe.' She didn't mean to mock him but she was tired and scared, and she didn't care about Drake's disquiet. She grasped at her own faith, and it gave her comfort in this strange place, with these strange people.

'Perhaps,' Drake said softly. 'The Inquisitor, have you seen—?'

Someone passed by the open door – a young boy bearing a tray of food and a steaming bowl. Drake glanced over his shoulder, then nudged the door closed.

'I'm so tired,' Holly said, leaning back against the wall. She let her eyelids droop and willed her muscles to relax, slumping down, feigning sleepiness when in fact she felt more awake than she had since arriving here through the breach. She wanted to be with Vic and Jonah, she wanted to know that her friends and family were still well, but most of all she wanted to be alone. And then she could decide what to do.

'I want us to be friends,' Drake said.

'We are . . .' she said, her voice slurring. *Leave me*, she thought. She lowered her head with every breath, and Drake came to her, easing her down onto the cot. His hands lingered on her shoulders, but she kept her eyes closed. *He's touching someone from another world*, she thought, realising only moments later that she felt the same.

Holly breathed deeply, concentrating on the fluid movement of the darkness behind her eyelids and wondering whether that was the true space between universes. Even when Drake left the room and closed the door she kept her eyes closed. She prayed into the uniform darkness, silent prayers that banished the gnawing loneliness inside her. She had never been embarrassed by her beliefs, even though there were many among her friends and colleagues who claimed not to understand them. Even that lovely old Welshman was a staunch atheist, and they'd had many long discussions about how she could maintain such faith while remaining a scientist. *Just because most things demand proof doesn't mean that there's something that never will*, she'd say, and Jonah would shake his head and take another sip of his whisky.

She opened her eyes to silence. The room was empty, the oil lamp still alight on a small table beside the door. *There's something deeper*, she thought. This Coldbrook was similar to her own in name only, and she knew she had barely touched its surface. She had to get a grip on the place.

Holly stood up and rubbed her eyes. The door was locked. She knelt and examined the lock, then carefully unscrewed the oil-flow control knob on the lamp. She plucked the pin out, and the flame increased in intensity. Kneeling at the lock again, she remembered those old days at university when she was tasked with small engineering problems. *It's as important to know how to take things apart as it is to know how to put them together*, her lecturer had said. It took her a minute to strip the lock, and a minute more to roll the tumblers and slip back the bolt.

The corridor outside was clear, its wall lamps providing low-level lighting. The floor sloped down to the left, so she went that way, conscious that the air was growing cooler and the lighting fainter. It wasn't far to the first stairwell and Holly did not hesitate. She went down.

A trickle of water ran along the lower corridor that she soon reached. The floor sloped here as well, and the water seemed to have been flowing for a long time – it had worn a channel at the junction of wall and floor, and she could see mineral deposits below its clear surface. She followed the slope, then paused at an intersection with another, darker corridor. Its wall held only one oil lamp, and beyond this oasis of light the darkness was deeper than ever.

Holly smelled food. Warm, spiced, perhaps a soup. And she remembered the steaming bowl passing the doorway: Drake's reaction had been cagey – he'd nudged the door closed.

'There's someone down here,' she whispered. As she edged forward, a crack of light appeared under a door in the wall to her left. She heard singing coming from inside.

The voice was low and rumbling, the tune nothing that she had heard before. She wasn't sure whether it was words or just notes, but the song seemed to settle in her stomach and vibrate there. She paused for a few seconds, then walked on. Why keep someone locked away down here?

Or *were* they hidden?

Approaching the doorway – seeing the light spilling into the corridor, and sensing the warmth and illumination beyond – Holly thought that perhaps she should have fled at the first chance she'd had. They had saved her life after she'd come through the breach, but everything she'd seen and heard since then had made her more and more uncertain.

She nudged the door open enough to see inside, and gasped. The square room was much larger than she had expected. It was well lit with at least six oil lamps fixed to the walls. The half of the room closest to the door was a living area, with several huge floor cushions bearing the impressions of frequent use, a selection of threadbare rugs covering the floor, and a couple of low, wide tables bearing books and candles. The wall to her right was lined with shelves, bearing books and pictures and other objects that she could not quite make out.

There was a distinct dividing line across the room marked by waist-high cabinets, and beyond that was a sleeping area and a table and chairs. The bed was wide and round, scattered with crumpled sheets and blankets, and several pillows that were propped against the side wall. The formal seating area comprised a table and six metal chairs. The walls were lined with dozens of movie posters – *Psycho*, *Once Upon A Time In The West*, *The Graduate*, *Peeping Tom* – with barely a space showing between them. Some of them seemed to have been drawn upon with elaborate markings, others appeared to have been vandalised with a knife. They were all pre-1972.

The room looked very lived-in. Cared for, but well used, and shockingly normal in many ways. There was one door leading from the back left corner of the room and it hung open, light and steam spilling out from behind it. A man was washing there, and singing while he washed.

Drake was keeping this from me, Holly thought, and that was reason enough for her to stay. She entered the room and pushed the door closed behind her. Crossing the room, dodging books on the floor and several empty cloudy glass bottles with chipped necks, she approached the postered wall. The posters were all old, with tears and worn edges, and many of them had yellowed over time. One was smudged beyond recognition, as though it had been soaked and dried again, the names and the shout-line blurred. Another was stained a rusty red. Blood? But she saw names that she recognised, and familiar faces.

'Hello,' a voice said.

Holly jumped and took a few steps back. The singing had stopped.

'I said, hello,' the short man said.

'H-hello.'

'You must be the next one.' He was standing in the doorway, steam drifting and swirling around him, a heavy towel tied around his waist. In his right hand he held a smaller towel that he was using to rub and dab at his wet hair. His left hand was missing.

'Next one?' Holly said. *Why call me that?* She glanced at him and then looked away again.

'You can look, you know,' he said. He walked into the room and sat on the edge of the circular bed, whose base appeared to be made from chairs with their backs removed.

She glanced at his back and saw a constellation of scars.

'Would you like some soup?' He pointed towards the table, where several bowls sat stacked beside a steaming container, and wine bottles caught the light. 'A drink?'

'Y–yes, please. Thank you.'

'Pour some for me, too.' He draped the towel over his head and continued to rub, tilting his head to the left so that he could use his stump as well.

Holly walked to the table and kept her back to the scarred man. She sniffed a bottle and poured, the ruby fluid splashing into the glasses. She heard him humming as he dried himself. *God help me look at this man with kind eyes*, she thought, turning around with a glass in each hand.

He threw the small towel onto the bed, then unknotted the towel around his waist and dropped it. Unabashed at his nakedness, he walked past Holly and opened one of the low cabinets that divided the room. Trying not to look, but unable not to, she saw more scars on his right leg, and noticed that a chunk of flesh had been taken from his right buttock, his hip, and his lower back. His shoulder blades were slashed with dark red welts, old and rough. He might have been fifty or sixty – she could not be sure.

He turned back to her as he shook out a pair of trousers. His genitals were intact, but his face was not. She looked from one to the other, and then he grinned.

'It's good wine,' he said, nodding at the bottles. 'They grow vines up in the mountains, use water lenses to concentrate the weak sunlight. A huge amount of effort for such little gain, but that's what I love about it so much.' He seemed to drift away for a beat, staring past her with his one good eye, unaware of his nakedness. 'But then, you probably know that.'

'Yes,' she said, unsure why. She watched him slip into

his trousers and button them with one hand, an easy fluid movement that he'd obviously performed many times before. And she knew then that all his old wounds were bites. Some were obvious, like the chunks taken from his hip and buttock, and the garish purple wounds on his legs. Others – the torn cheek and eye, the rash of bubbled flesh across his throat – were not so obvious, but she still thought she could see teeth punctures and track marks. Bites. Many terrible, brutal bites.

'Your name is . . .' she said, trailing off as he stared at her with frank fascination.

'I'm Mannan,' he said, a flicker of doubt furrowing his forehead.

'Yes,' Holly said, stepping forward and handing him a glass. He nodded, tipped his glass against hers, and took a small sip.

'Please,' he said, pointing at her glass with the stump of his left arm. Healed puncture wounds, skilful surgery, skin folded and stitched. 'Drink.'

She drank, and it was gorgeous, with a rich fruity depth.

'This time comes around so quickly,' Mannan said, draining his glass. 'I won't pretend I don't enjoy it, or that I'm sorry they keep trying. Even though it's hopeless. Never works.' He held his glass out to her, requesting a refill. 'I won't pretend it doesn't make me happy.'

Holly filled his glass again. Her heart was thumping

now, because something was so wrong here. *No cure,* Drake had told her, and yet here was a man clothed in bites, a man whose naked parading of his scars had seemed without deliberate design.

'Your scars,' she said, looking at him more closely now that he was partially covered. She saw now that some wounds were old – scar tissue forming a hard, ridged landscape of pain – and some more pink, recent. He raised his left arm, and at first she thought he was pointing at something away from them, a map or something else on the far wall. But then he performed a slow circle, arms raised so that she could view each terrible, ugly wound.

'A yearly test,' he said. 'I wear them with pride. They're evidence of my uniqueness.'

'You're immune,' she said. Drake had kept this from her, a hidden man clothed in fury bites and living a pampered life below ground. And as she thought perhaps she could ask why, Mannan's expression changed.

'Where are you from?' he asked. 'You don't know of me?'

'And you haven't heard everything about me,' she said, realising that she must be a secret as well. Whatever 'next one' meant, it was nothing to do with her.

Mannan threw down his glass. Holly jumped, taking a few steps back until her thighs hit the table. He didn't take his one-eyed stare from her face, and Holly dared not look away. She could see danger in him as well as pain: her pulse thrummed in her ears, her vision blurred.

'Last year,' he said, touching the indentation in his left hip. 'The year before.' He held up his stump. 'They lost control of the fury then, and by the time they smashed its skull it had chewed so hard that my bones fractured and crumbled.' He touched the stump to the ruined cheek and eye socket. 'Five years ago. Casey was holding the collar rod, she tripped, it took off part of my face and then turned on her. Drake was holding a dressing to my face, but I had one good eye left. I saw her fall, saw the life go from her eyes. And she stood again, and they fired an arrow through her head. Casey.' He touched other scars one by one, but no longer relayed their history. Perhaps he was paying homage to Casey as the most important.

They bite him every year, Holly thought, trying to discern his intent. But his ruined face was unreadable, scar tissue having hardened it against the subtleties of expression. *He's immune, and they test him every year.*

'I'm not from your world,' she said. 'I came through a breach from somewhere else. A parallel Earth. Another universe.'

'Whatever,' he said, his one eye glittering. He grinned again, started singing once more, a wordless tune. Then he cut off his song. 'One thing I ask, and I ask it of everyone, only when they get down here, though, not so Drake could hear, if Drake knew he wouldn't approve, so don't—'

'No,' she said, trying to sound strong but hearing only fear in her voice.

'Don't interrupt.' He moved quickly, pinning her back against the table. 'The one thing I ask is . . . when I'm inside you, I like to be bitten.'

She shoved him back, pushing away from the table and heaving with all her strength. Mannan stumbled back against the bed, laughing, touching his scars again, one after the other and perhaps in the order of their annual origins, and as he came at her once more Holly realised that he was down here because he was mad.

She darted to the left, heading for the gap in the room divider, but he was quick, and lithe for his age. He rolled across the bed and jumped over the divider, kicked a floor cushion, tripped her. By the time she'd gained her feet he was at the door. He shoved it closed.

'Let me out,' she said.

'You knew what you were doing, coming down here,' Mannan said. 'They *told* you what you were doing, and what would happen, and that you need my child. So don't be afraid. I might be scarred up here . . .' He indicated his scars again, that sequence of touches that might have become some kind of personal prayer. 'But I'm not scarred *here*.' He unbuttoned his trousers and wriggled until they dropped. His erection sprang up, and he closed his hand around it, stroking.

Holly thought of Vic and Jonah and the others at

Coldbrook, and she felt certain that they were dead. If they were still alive, how could this be happening to her? How could she be so alone and so threatened, here in the depths of another Coldbrook?

'I told you, I'm not from here,' she said. Her voice shook.

Mannan came forward, a monster from the mind of Goya.

Holly looked at his erection and smiled. He chuckled back at her – and she kicked him between his legs as hard as she could. He gasped in shock, then screamed louder in agony, and for a crazy moment she wanted to stay and apologise. But he grabbed for her foot, and when she took one step away from him she found it easier to take another.

'One more scar, fucker,' she said. Then she ran.

9

'I am the Inquisitor,' the voice said, 'and you will be the same.'

Jonah opened his eyes and looked around his room. Nothing.

'See what we have done,' the man said. Jonah tried to sit up, but there was a pressure on his shoulders, pushing him back down. That flailing red organ was pressing against his head once more. The Inquisitor was standing behind his bed, upside down in his vision and even more grotesque.

He sees people on a beach and drowning in the emerald sea, trying to escape the deadly tide from inland.

'A living history of the greatest Inquisition,' the man said, lifting the orb away momentarily. Jonah gasped as he was pulled from the dream, glimpsing once again that smudged tattoo on the Inquisitor's arm. He felt around on the bed for his gun, his finger brushed cold metal, and—

He looks across the countryside at a farm, where cattle lie dead and bloated in untended fields and winged things swoop in to chew on them, carrion creatures almost the size of the cattle themselves, their auburn and white fur glimmering with wet blood.

'And your world now needs you to write its final book.' The Inquisitor was beside the bed now, sticky wet mask held inches from his face. He pressed forward with the thing in his other hand one more time. Jonah lifted the gun. The Inquisitor moved swiftly, knocking the weapon back onto the bed, and Jonah felt those tendrils kissing his temple again, wondering if he was already dead . . .

Eight people rush across red sands, eight hundred follow, and it is the living who will lose this race . . .

Men and women with pronounced brows, wide faces, and more hair than anyone he has ever seen pursue the uninfected past a high bamboo wall . . .

Thousands of dead bob in the ocean, clawing at the hull of a ship drifting in their midst . . .

Biting, screaming, dying, rising, he saw it all, realising that much of what he was seeing was not from this world but another.

And he had the dreadful sense of another mind existing alongside his own, believing that this all constituted a great cleansing.

When the Inquisitor finally left him and Jonah sat up, he raised the gun and lifted it towards his head, remembering his father's face and the strength he had given his son. 'I *am* being strong,' he said, but something knocked the gun aside. He tried again, and it happened once more. There was nothing in the room with him. The muscles in his arm flexed, the skin was depressed as though squeezed by fingers, and for all the world he would have loved to believe it was Wendy insisting that he remain alive.

But he knew that was a lie.

10

It was three hours before Sean was able to use the phone. Jayne had watched him trying again and again, had seen the subdued fear behind his eyes, but she hadn't been able to bring herself to ask.

Outside the aircraft, fires raged in the airport terminal.

The two of them kept away from the windows, afraid of being seen.

'They're aimless,' Jayne had said, watching one man stagger crablike across the wide concrete runway. His head rested on his left shoulder, and one leg was turned so that the foot faced backwards.

'Only when there's no one to bite,' Sean had replied.

Jayne tried not to think about what would happen if they were discovered. The door was securely closed, and the only other way up to the aircraft cabin was to climb the wheel structures. *We're an island*, she thought, imagining them surrounded by a sea of quiet, patient zombies. Perhaps they would gather and wait, a hundred of them or a thousand, or ten thousand when everyone else had been infected. Their purpose would not be complete until everyone was like them, and they would stare up at the aircraft windows, looking for signs of movement there and at the plane's doors, standing through darkness and light, rain and sun, until something happened.

'We're trapped here,' she said.

Sean's face lit up.

'Reception!' he said suddenly, walking away from Jayne as he tapped in a number, then standing with his back to her and the phone held against his ear. He dialled again, stood listening. And again.

'Sean.'

'Maybe she's out,' he said.

'What time is it over there?'

Sean glanced at his watch. 'Six hours ahead. Early morning.'

'They'll be in bed.'

'She keeps her phone with her all the time. You know how girls are.' He came back and sat beside her again, looking at the phone as if willing her to call back. But it remained silent.

'Maybe her phone's off.' Jayne could think of nothing else to say. There could be a hundred reasons why his daughter was not answering, but only one that really mattered.

'France?' he said. 'Could it really have reached *France*?'

'I can't see how.'

Sean stared at her for a long moment and neither of them spoke. Then he stood and went to a window again, careful not to get too close as he looked outside.

'I've got to tell someone about you,' he said.

'What about that immunity register?'

Sean shook his head, held up his cellphone. 'Online. I'm still a dinosaur, no smartphone for me. I can call and text people on this, that's about it.'

'How about . . . what's it called? Centers for Disease Control. I read about it in that Stephen King book.'

'Never read him,' Sean said, turning around. 'I'm more of a thriller guy.'

'Well . . .' Jayne said, no knowing what to say.

'Wait a minute,' Sean said. 'There *is* someone I can call. Just hope I still have the damn number.'

'Who is it?'

Sean sat beside her again and placed a hand on her leg. His palm was hot, his hand heavy, and Jayne closed her own hand around his.

'Old school buddy,' Sean said. 'Moved to the UK, became a doctor. Always was a clever bastard.' He searched for a moment, then gave a yelp of joy and put the phone to his ear.

'Leigh? Sean. Yeah, man, I'm fine. Can you fuckin' believe it?' He paused, nodding, and Jayne heard the distant whisper of a voice she did not know. 'Well, listen to this,' Sean continued. 'Got something else you're never gonna believe, and I need your advice on how to handle it.'

And he told his old school buddy about Jayne.

Leigh Keene hung up the phone and sat up in bed.

'What is it?' his wife asked. She'd started awake when the phone rang, and already sounded sleepy again. He had no idea how she could sleep with all that was happening in America.

'Old school friend in the States,' Leigh said. 'I've got to go downstairs.'

''kay,' she said. She sighed softly, already asleep. *I hope you can stay so peaceful*, Leigh thought, and his heart ached with worry for her and their baby son who was asleep in the next room. Leigh was a paediatric consultant at a big London hospital – loved kids, always had – and he could barely breathe because of his fear of what was happening.

Downstairs, he sat at his desk and flicked on the wall-mounted TV. He blinked in shock. 'Jesus. South America.' He tapped the desktop nervously, then dialled a number on his BlackBerry.

Four thousand miles away in Toronto, a woman dabbed at her mouth and excused herself from the table. She walked outside the restaurant as she answered her phone, pulling a cigarette from her pocket at the same time. It had been a weird night, marked with an almost manic need to indulge. It had reminded her of a movie she'd seen about what everyone did for their last night on Earth. It was fucking terrifying, but the atmosphere dragged her on.

She paused as she saw the name on the display. Pressed connect. 'Leigh?'

'Emma! Emma, thank Christ, I thought you weren't going to pick up.'

'I'm at a restaurant.' It was raining. She stood under a canopy with other banished smokers and lit up.

'Good,' Leigh said. 'Good. I thought . . . I don't know what.'

'I'm not munching on brains yet,' she said, and a couple

of her smoking companions glanced her way. Emma
glared back; she'd never been shy.

'I know this is out of the blue, and we haven't spoken
for a long time, but—'

'It's been four years,' she said.

'Yeah. Sometimes feels like yesterday. Listen, are you
safe? Do you have a plan?'

'I'm fine,' Emma said. 'Leigh, I'd love to think this is
all because you're concerned about me, but I can't believe
that.'

'I've always cared,' he said.

She wondered where he was now, where his new wife
and child were, and she was jealous all over again. 'Yeah,'
she said.

'Emma . . . I have some information about someone
important. And you're the only person I could think of
who might know what to do.'

Emma closed her eyes.

Emma called her cousin – Tim Love, a cop – and told
him about the immune girl in burning Baltimore. Before
he headed out with his unit to Bethleham, where he
would have his infected brains blown out by a bullet
from Lieutenant Susco's pistol, Love called a friend of
his in the Baltimore PD. His friend called four people
and ordered that they prepare for a rescue mission to
Baltimore Airport, and one of those people – a corrupt

Sergeant called Waits who was buried up to his ass in the city's main drugs-distribution ring – called his mistress in New York to say goodbye. And he told her where he was going, and why.

The mistress was married to Nathan King, a writer and boozer. A troubled man, King had many acquaintances but only a handful of true friends. And one of those friends was an eccentric gay scientist the size of a grizzly bear, called Marc Dubois.

King called Marc, and told him what his wife had heard.

11

'I knew she was getting it in the ass from someone, but a fucking cop?'

Marc glanced at Vic and Gary. He'd switched the phone to loudspeaker as soon as King had told him the news.

'What?' Vic whispered, holding up his hands. Marc had gone white but something about his manner indicated excitement. Over the past few hours Vic had seen enough terrible sights with Marc to know how the man reacted to bad news. This was something different.

'Say it again,' Marc said. 'I've got some people here who need to hear it.'

'I said I knew the bitch was—'

'Fuck it, Nathan, I don't give a shit about who's drilling

your wife!' Marc said. 'The reason you called me. Me, of all people. The *reason*, Nathan.'

King told them what he'd heard. Vic listened to the rest of the conversation in a confused state, and not because he couldn't hear the words. It was his heart. It had become a rock in his chest, a solid weight that he didn't dare call hope. *Immune!* The online register had become a joke, with thousands of entries and thousands more red-lined 'discredited' markers. If this was true, the woman trapped in an aircraft at Baltimore airport – bitten, still alive, still *human* – might just be the most important person on the planet.

'Vic?' Marc said, and Vic realised the tall man had been talking to him.

'Sorry. I . . . Yeah.'

'I said, we should trust this. Her name's Jayne Woodhams, and she's not on the register. Doesn't matter how it got to us, and I can't imagine how King heard about it. He's a drunken pseudo-philosopher, not a scientist. But . . .'

'Immune.' It was all Vic could say.

'So what do we do?' Gary asked. He was leaning back against a desk and wearing a big cowboy hat.

'Someone has to get her and keep her safe,' Vic said. 'There's that place in Atlanta, the disease place. Get her there.'

'You've seen what's happening in Atlanta!' Marc said.

'Have you heard from them?' Gary asked.

'No,' Marc said, shaking his head. 'I know a dozen people at the CDC. Can't reach any of them. The phones just ring.'

'So where else?' Vic asked.

'You know where else,' Marc said. 'I told you, I'm the best disease expert in the northern hemisphere.'

'I thought you were boasting,' Vic said, but he was thinking of Lucy and Olivia, and how safe they might be in that sparsely furnished room.

'Here,' Gary said.

'Yes,' Marc said. 'We've got to fly to Baltimore and bring her back.'

It was Marc's idea that Lucy and Olivia should go with them. Vic's sense of relief when the phorologist suggested that they should stay together was immense – there was no way he'd ever have left them behind, but the thought of confronting Marc over that had troubled him.

Olivia knew that everything was wrong. She grasped her rag doll Scruffy in her left hand, and its hair was wet and stringy from where she'd been chewing. But how could he explain so that she would understand when he didn't understand himself?

'Where are we going?' Olivia asked.

'You ever been to Baltimore, honey?' Gary asked.

'Uhhh . . .' Olivia glanced up at Vic, then shook her head.

'Well, we're going to visit a lady there.'

'What's her name?'

'Jayne,' Gary said.

'But can we fly in the dark?'

'My helicopter is special. It's called an Agusta 109 – very nice, *very* expensive – and it has computers and electronic gizmos and other magic stuff, all there to tell us whether it's safe to fly, and whether there's anyone else close by.'

'Magic.' Olivia looked at Gary and giggled uncertainly.

Marc entered the room, a heavy bag over one shoulder, and when Vic offered to take it Marc shook his head. 'Not now,' he said quietly.

Gary made a pantomime of putting on his cowboy hat and leaving the room, then turned back and knelt so that he was on Olivia's level. 'Say, honey, you want to come and sit in the pilot's seat?'

'Yeah!' the girl said.

'Is it safe?' Lucy asked.

'It's fine,' Marc said. 'I've just been up there to check.'

Olivia and Gary left, and Marc placed the bag on a desk. The desk's legs creaked, and Vic saw the sheen of sweat across the man's forehead. He knew what he was carrying.

'I hate guns,' Lucy said, moving to Vic's side so that their arms pressed together.

'And I hate zombies,' Marc said, hefting the bag again. 'Shall we?'

Olivia was sitting in the helicopter wearing the pilot's helmet, its dark visor down, while Gary sat next to her, running through a pre-flight check. Vic saw her through the windshield and felt an intense gratitude. How Gary had managed to get her across the roof and into the machine without her seeing or hearing any of the chaos below, Vic did not know. But he would have to thank the man later.

From the roof, everything they saw of Cincinnati meant death. Fires consumed the city, screams gave the fires voice, and the stink of cooking flesh added an extra dimension of nightmare to the screams. At least one of the city centre's distant skyscrapers was ablaze, and a series of mysterious explosions thumped in the far distance.

Once on board and strapped in, Gary gave them all a brief rundown of what to do if they had to perform an emergency landing on land or in water. It felt like a pointless exercise, but Vic saw that Lucy was paying strict attention, and he had something else to thank the pilot for. They had wrapped the rifles in heavy coats, not wanting Olivia to see them.

But as they took off from the building and headed east across the city's northern extremes, it became impossible to hide anything. Olivia sat between Lucy and Vic, each of them holding her hand, but her helmeted head turned left and right as she looked from the aircraft's large door windows. They left Cincinnati behind, and as they flew over farmsteads, towns and cities, some areas had fallen into darkness, blocks of shadow surrounded by illuminated streets and buildings. And there were the fires, frequent conflagrations ranging from single house fires to a huge, advancing wall of flame that looked like a boiling rip in the land.

'Is that a volcano?' Olivia asked, shouting above the sound of the motor.

'It's a fire, honey,' Vic said.

'It's very big.'

An hour out of Cincinnati, Gary shouted something unintelligible and the helicopter shook, rocked and dipped, accompanied by a terrific noise. Vic leaned across and hugged Olivia and Lucy towards him, an instinctive embrace. But Gary quickly brought them under control, and they could all hear his rapid breathing in their headphones.

'What the fuck was that?' Marc shouted.

'Fighter jet,' Gary said. 'Barely saw it.'

'I'm scared!' Olivia said. 'And Marc swore.'

Marc nudged Gary, then touched his headphones. Gary nodded and flicked a switch.

'Okay, guys, here's the news. I can't raise Baltimore airport at all. I've spoken to two en routes – they're the centres that control air traffic – and neither of them were interested.'

'Not *interested*?' Vic asked.

'One woman . . . I've never heard a controller sounding like that. It wasn't even panic, it was more like resignation. She said the military has so much stuff up that it's proving impossible for them to function.'

'Meaning what?' Marc asked.

'Daddy?' Olivia said, and Vic squeezed her knee.

'Just grown-up stuff,' he said.

'It means we're flying on our own,' Gary said. 'That's no bad thing normally, but the way things are I won't know what we're flying into.'

'Like that jet,' Lucy said.

'Like that jet,' Marc echoed.

They fell silent. Olivia still held Vic's hand, her grip hot and clammy with fear. Vic watched the dark sky beyond the windows, noticed that the moon was low and yellow, and wondered whether they would even see anything that might come to smash them to atoms.

America passed beneath them, burning.

Tuesday

1

If Wendy had come back to him as one of those things, Jonah would have understood. It would hardly have been a surprise – he'd seen them kill, he had shot some himself, and the images of their grinding teeth and rupturing skulls were imprinted for ever on his mind. His waking nightmares made him terrified to sleep. And if she had returned as the Inquisitor, he would have understood that as well. The Inquisitor was in his mind now, and sometimes Jonah believed that thing was steering his every action, subconsciously or not.

But Wendy came back as herself.

I'd never let you put that gun to your head, she said,

sitting at the foot of his bed. Jonah knew that she was not real, yet he welcomed her here with him, reaching out and not quite touching. She seemed unaware of his distress, or his need for contact. She looked vaguely disapproving, as she had on those few occasions when he'd returned home after having drunk too much.

'But I don't know what else to do,' he said.

There is always another way. You told me that when I was so ill, and I wanted to talk about—

'No!' Jonah said. He had never entertained the thought of helping her on her way, had never permitted her to talk about it. Many times since then he had felt the guilt of that, and had dreamed about the agony he might have saved her from.

You're not in that much pain, Wendy said, scolding. *So don't you* dare *let yourself consider that* now, *Jonah Jones. There is always another way.*

Jonah blinked and Wendy disappeared.

Got to get away, he thought. The gun sat on his bedside table, solid evidence of his despair. But he would not betray Wendy with such thoughts again, and even now they felt distant and alien to him, the remnants of a dream rather than of any real desire to end his own life.

How could he? After all this, after what they had done, how could he ever consider taking the easy way out?

Jonah stood and slipped the gun into his belt. He felt watched at every moment – turned quickly, saw shadows at the periphery of his vision, heard breathing identical to his own – but there was no reason to believe that the Inquisitor was *always* there. Jonah had to believe that he was not.

What the Inquisitor was, why he was here, what he wanted of him . . . these were questions whose import-ance were secondary to Jonah's survival. He could remain here and accept what this thing was doing to him, or he could leave. The choice was stark – and simple.

Jonah left his small room, carrying the heavy flashlight that illuminated the whole corridor ahead of him. He headed away from Control to begin with, slipping into the canteen area where the smell of food starting to rot was already evident. He could hear movement – scratching, shuffling, the gentle caress of material against metal – and he wondered how those creatures he'd locked in the walk-in refrigerator could know that he was here. Entering the huge pantry, he selected some dried food. Tins would be too heavy, and he'd be able to add water to the sachets.

Where am I going? he wondered, but though the voice was his own he tried to ignore it for now. One thing at a time. 'Jesus, I could do with a shower before I go,' he said aloud, and he actually giggled. It felt good – but it sounded desperate.

There were canvas bags beneath the canteen counter, used to collect plastic and tins for recycling on the surface. One would be enough. He dropped the sachets inside, added a few small bottles of water, then returned to the common room and lifted the small bar's flap. He'd all but finished the Penderyn whisky and the next best thing was a bottle of Jameson's. Sighing, unscrewing the top, taking a long swig. As it burned its way down he remembered that thing's image.

'Fuck off,' Jonah said. 'Just fuck off!' The sounds of movement from the canteen became more frantic, as did their calling. If he left those afflicted in the walk-in fridge for ever, would they always move? The thought was horrific, but he had seen that wrinkled, shrivelled creature that had come through and killed Melinda, and he recognised its age. In ten years or a hundred, whether or not he remained down here, others might venture down to discover where it had all begun, and they might hear the movement of creatures trapped behind the doors he had locked . . .

'If there's anyone left,' he muttered. Since the power had gone out, he'd had no way of following what was happening on the surface. He was delaying what needed to be done, and he knew why – he faced a terrible dilemma.

He could go back through the garage, move the Hummer, and climb up through the ventilation shaft.

Follow in Vic's footsteps, retracing the route this terrible contagion had taken.

Or he could go through the breach.

Jonah smiled. He took another drink, then screwed the lid on and placed the bottle in the canvas bag. There was no decision to be made. He was a scientist, after all. And perhaps the next couple of hours would see him and Holly reunited, and the culmination of his lifetime's dreams manifest around him.

Jonah knew that he could do nothing more here.

The Inquisitor was waiting for him twenty metres from Control. Jonah dropped the bag and heard the clunk of glass hitting concrete. *Don't break*, he thought and fire throbbed in his head. He kept hold of the flashlight and shone it directly at the man who turned, beckoned him to follow, and then disappeared into a perpendicular corridor.

Picking up the bag, Jonah smelled the stench of spilled whisky. The bag leaked. Good Irish dripped across the floor, the sachets of dried food were swollen from the fluid, and Jonah felt a terrible sinking feeling in his gut when he realised how unprepared he really was.

'Oh, bollocks to it all,' he said. The gun heavy and useless in his belt, Jonah held on to the wall and swung around into the side corridor, home to a plant room and three storage rooms. It was barely twenty feet long, and at its end stood something that brought Jonah up short, winding him. He tried to breathe, but it was as though the air was gone from Coldbrook. He tried to rationalise what he was seeing, make sense of it, and though the true meaning was clear he could not yet accept it. It would take the Inquisitor and its deft touch to make him accept.

It would take surgery.

It was not a table, or a chair, but something in between. Hanging on hooks suspended from shadows were the elements of Jonah's new face-to-be: bulbous eyes; a snout; a bristled film to cover his own scalp.

'It is required that you accept,' the Inquisitor said.

'No,' Jonah said.

'You will never die.'

Jonah managed to laugh, because the Inquisitor spoke as if he was offering something attractive.

'Fuck *off*!' Jonah could not help looking at those other objects, wondering what they were. He guessed that they belonged inside him.

2

As Holly ran she thought of the horribly scarred man and what his presence might mean. And she wondered just what these people were, to experiment on their one true hope like that – having him bitten by a fury each year to confirm that his immunity persisted. It was monstrous and inhumane, and it chilled her to the core.

They're the survivors, she thought, but even that was not quite right. Their parents had been the survivors, if their Fury plague really had been forty years ago. Drake and Moira were the survivors' children, and this was the only world they knew. But that did not excuse them.

She followed the stairs back up to the room where she had been pretending to sleep, and inside she tipped a chair onto its side and heaved at one of the legs. She exerted an even pressure, wanting to break it slowly rather than smash it. She could not afford to be caught and making too much noise could attract unwelcome attention. The leg creaked, she strained harder, and finally it gave with a brief snap. About fifteen inches long, it was easy enough to carry.

The thought of striking anyone with it was horrible. But Holly took a few deep breaths and hefted the impromptu club in one hand. *I need Vic*, she thought. *I need Jonah. I need home.*

And, for the first time, the importance of Mannan's immunity to her own world struck her like a bullet.

Someone was approaching.

Holly propped the damaged chair against the wall, fell onto the cot, and curled around the leg with her back to the door. She consciously regulated her breathing, all too aware of the thudding of her heart but unable to slow it. The footsteps paused and she heard the creak of unoiled hinges. She feigned a comfortable sigh. The person passed by and continued along the corridor . . .

And the smell of food reached her.

They were taking more food down to Mannan.

She stood and moved to the door, and as soon as she heard the first footfall from the stairwell she dashed up the corridor. Fear drove her on and made silence impossible; her breathing was ragged, her footsteps clumsy and panicked.

She reached a place she recognised and saw the strange light emanating from the casting room's side corridor. It hazed the air, flowing and ebbing as the images within played across those bizarre screens. She marched past the wide doorway, not slowing down, not risking a glance inside, trying to exude confidence and a sense that she belonged here. Once past the room she listened for raised voices but heard none. The casters were viewing her world's apocalypse in stoic silence.

When voices mumbled from rooms, she passed them by. Reasoning that stealth and caution would make her more noticeable than brashness, she strode along corridors past other open doorways and found herself eventually in the upper caves where she had first woken in this Coldbrook.

She paused at the entrance to a wide communal space. Across this roughly circular area was a curtained opening, behind which she suspected the door to the outside might lie. Either side of the opening were heavy shutters, planks of wood secured together with metal bands and suspended from thick metal hinges fixed into the stonework. And beyond these shutters, on either side, were racks of crossbows and bows, but no guns.

A man was sitting in the middle of the room, leaning back in a chair and reading a yellowed book. There was a low table beside him, on which lay a crossbow, a crumb-strewn plate, an oil lamp, and a horn-shaped object with a bulb at its narrow end.

Did they really still guard against the furies, after so long? Or was he there to keep on eye on her? Holly didn't know, and she did not give herself time to dwell on it. The longer she waited to think things through, the closer she came to being caught. There was really only one way out, and she had to take it.

Stay, they're safe, Drake is a good man, they're the descendants of survivors, and in this world this place is Coldbrook! The words were those of her own timidity, trying to make her stay. But while she listened to them all she could see was Mannan stroking himself as he came for her, and those bite-scars that made him, ironically, less than human.

As she strode across the cave's rough wooden floor, the man lowered his book and started to turn around.

Holly swung her club hard, wincing, closing her eyes

at the last instant and aiming for a point behind his ear. The impact jarred through her hands and up her arms, and her own cry was almost as loud as the man's. He shouted again, with pain and shock combined. Holly stepped back.

The man was still standing, one hand grasping his ear. Blood seeped between his fingers, and he worked his jaw as if he was trying to say something. But no words emerged. His eyes became unfocused, and as Holly raised the chair leg again he sank slowly back against the table, his free hand reaching around to slow his fall.

'Sorry,' Holly said. 'I'm sorry.' She shoved him away from the table and he sprawled across the floor, groaning softly and with his right hand still pressed to his head. She snatched up his crossbow and ran for the heavy curtain.

Beyond it was a short, narrow corridor, with several heavy wooden doors set in its wall. It was lit with a string of electric lights – the first she had seen other than those in the casting room – and at its end was a heavy metal door.

Oh fuck oh shit it's locked and I'm trapped and he'll get to me before the others and beat me and—

But when she grabbed the handle and turned it she heard tumblers roll inside the lock mechanism. It was only bolted. Pulling back three bolts, she tugged the door open and smelled a rush of fresh air, only noticing at the last moment that there was a periscope viewing device set in an alcove beside the door.

Should have checked, Holly thought. But she was rushing headlong now, and to pause would be to lose momentum. If there were furies out here, she would have to fight her way past them, outrun them, or shoot them in the head with the crossbow. She glanced at the weapon and realised that she had little idea how to work it. But she could not leave it behind.

Holly shoved the door closed behind her, and realised that it was night outside. The moon was almost full, a silvery smear against the dusty sky. And, for the life of her, she had no idea which direction to take from here.

The breeze whispered through stiff bushes and it was as if the laws of acoustics were different here. Holly's footfalls kicked up that scent of almost-heather and the darkness hid the differences between here and her own world from sight. Made them even more threatening.

She ran along the shallow valley floor, trying to keep to shadows where she could, even though the moon's illumination was weak. *They're not clouds*, she thought, glancing up every few seconds at the smear of moonlight. It looked as if the moon had been crushed and smeared across the heavens, and she wondered how heavy the dust layers high in the atmosphere must be to give that effect. Plants still grew and people still lived, and she'd seen that the sun still found its way through. It was just another disturbing difference that made this place somewhere she should not be.

After a few minutes Holly paused and listened for any sounds of pursuit. Surely they'd know by now that she had escaped? When she thought she'd gone far enough she turned up the hillside, heading through sparse tree cover for the ridge. She'd always had a good sense of direction, and she had a positive feeling about where she was heading. She could not remember in detail every part of her journey on the stretcher, but this somehow felt right. She paused and turned every couple of minutes, trying to locate a view she might have seen before.

On the ridge she tried to find her bearings. Another ridge across the valley cut a recognisable line against the faint moonlight, spiked here and there with more trees than she was used to, yet it was a place that she knew from her own world. And closer, the slope she was about to take down from this hilltop swept towards the valley floor in a familiar bowl shape, home to a narrow creek and a chattering stream, slopes clothed with trees. She had come climbing here once with Melinda, searching for old birds' nests, and both of them had been in awe of the wilderness around them.

The wilderness closed in on her now, though, and awe was tainted with fear.

She moved down from the hilltop into another dip in the landscape and crossed a stream, lifting the hem of her shapeless dress and gasping at the water's coldness. On the opposite bank she paused, and thought she heard footsteps.

Holly inhaled sharply and held her breath. She looked around, but could see no one, nothing. *Animal*, she thought, but that brought no comfort at all. *It could be anything*.

'What the hell do you think you're doing, Holly?' she whispered, but nothing replied, nothing ran at her.

She continued across an open area of hillside, noticing a dense woodland that began thirty metres down the slope from her. She was certain she remembered this from her journey here, but back then it had not felt so threatening. Now she sensed things among the trees, things that smelled like old stale clothes thrown out.

Just spooked, she thought. And as she tried convincing herself of that, she saw them.

Several figures came out of the shadows, little more than shadows themselves. It took only moments to see what they were, and Holly cried out in fear, firing the bolt already loaded into the crossbow. It whispered uselessly away into the darkness. They shuffled uphill towards her, and she was glad that the poor light hid their features.

She sprinted to put distance between herself and the

stumbling furies. She didn't know whether they could run, had no idea if they could track her by her scent. She knew nothing about them and her fear was like a cold rock in her stomach. She had a growing certainty that she was going to die in this older, deader world.

Seeing the furies made her more aware of shadows across the hillside where there should be none, movement that might or might not be plants shifting in the breeze. She paused for a moment and tried to reload the crossbow – there was a rack of six bolts on its underside – but dropped the bolt and cried out as her finger caught in the mechanism. She picked up the bolt and ran on.

It was difficult for Holly to admit that she was lost. Everywhere she saw views that she *might* have seen when they'd brought her here. But when she followed a gurgling stream in the hope that it might be the one running past the breach, and found herself among ruins, she could no longer deny the truth.

At first she was not quite sure what she was seeing. The mounds were uneven, the plant growth thick. But then she saw an obvious wall on her left, its upper few feet camouflaged with a few lone ivy tendrils, its blocks square and even.

Holly tried to place where she was in relation to her own world – if the hillside had been similar to that location on her Earth, then these ruins should not be here.

But she and Drake had failed to pinpoint precisely where the two worlds' realities had parted and become differing possibilities, and this could be anywhere.

She moved on, because she still sensed the worst dangers were creeping up on her from behind.

It must once have been a small town at least, because the deeper in she went, the more regularly spaced the ruins became. There were house-sized buildings with roofs stripped away and few walls remaining upright, larger structures with sparse steel ribs stark against the sky, and a set of sharp curves that froze her to the spot. Rusted, one of them missing its upper portion, their shape and design seemed unmistakable, and she had always known them as the Golden Arches.

'McDonald's?' she whispered, almost laughing. 'Fucking McDonald's!' But Holly could not pause to wonder. All around her there was movement in the shadows.

She plunged ahead, following what had once been a road. Now was just a clearer pathway between ruins, turning slowly to the left and heading uphill to the shoulder of a narrow valley. For a moment it seemed familiar, and she was struck with a peculiar sense of déjà vu, a disconcerting feeling that she was not doing any of this of her own volition. She had walked this way before.

Holly tripped, staggered forward, found her balance, and then tripped again. She dropped the crossbow and put out her hands, cushioning her fall against a wall. She gasped and breathed deeply a few times, trying to calm her galloping heart. And then whatever was moving made itself heard.

Nails against stone, bone against brick. And the ground around her feet shifted.

Fuck fuck fuck – she pushed herself upright and snatched up the crossbow. Something bumped against her shoe. She staggered back a few steps and watched a figure rising, arms splayed against the wall, bony fingers clawing at the ivy-covered brickwork.

Holly knew that she should run but something held her there. A sick fascination at the sight before her. A terror at the old, dry smell released to the moonlight. A sense of unreality at what she saw standing, because now there was more than one. The ivy-clad wall seemed to shiver as the plant stalks were tugged and ripped by many hands, and the shadowy heap along its base resolved itself into terrible shapes. They pushed themselves up through a covering of trailing plants, and their stale stench was mixed with the tang of turned earth. They must have been there for a very long time.

They sense me, Holly thought. And at last that gave her the impetus to run. The old dead town around her rustled as undead things shifted. She clasped the crossbow nervously, conscious that it had only six bolts. Flight, not fight, was her only hope.

As she fled the ruined settlement her lungs burned and her legs ached, but she could never stop running. Every backward glance revealed that she was being followed. She sensed other shadows stirring around her: a wet shape rising from a cold stream here; three small figures crawling from the space beneath a fallen tree there. And while none of them appeared to move quickly, their direction was relentless – up, and towards her.

Holly ran uphill, and as she began to believe that she'd taken entirely the wrong direction and was lost in this place that she had named Gaia she passed a pile of fallen masonry that looked familiar. The first time she'd been here she had been traumatised by her journey through the breach, her senses mangled by memory, the sweat of fear slick on her cool skin and the sight of the blood-drenched Melinda still imprinted on her mind's eye. Now she looked around and realised the extent of the ruins she had stumbled across. What she had taken to be rock formations were actually leaning walls, clothed in creeping plants, and the stark angles of a bare tree were in fact rusted ribs from a building's corroded metal roof. Allowing herself a moment's pause, Holly approached the slumped building where she had rested once before and recognised the place where she had sat. Looking closer at the *Exit* sign carved in stone, she wondered briefly who had once walked beneath it.

The breach lay downhill from here, in the next valley.

The infection was already loose in her Coldbrook, and she had to weigh that knowledge against the risk of leading the pursuing furies through.

In the end, her survival instinct won out.

Down in the valley, the site of the breach was sheltered from the wash of moonlight by the hillside. Yet there was a glow down there, nestled in the shadows like a smudge on her sight. But to the left and right Holly's night vision picked out a worrying detail – two silhouettes, upright, motionless against the breach's impossible light.

The idea of being almost home drove her on.

As she made her way down the hillside, she made sure that the crossbow was ready.

Every sense alert, her breath shallow and fast, blood pumping with adrenalin, Holly moved as fast as she dared down to the valley floor. She followed the stream, pausing to glance around after every few steps. *I'm going to shoot someone through the head*, she thought, but they were no longer 'someone'. These were little more than remnants, Godless and a travesty against nature. Once they might have had a life, but their stories had come to an end before she was born in a universe far away.

Approaching the breach, she caught a whiff of something terribly familiar. She gasped in surprise, a sense of unreality washing over her yet again. The scent of mulled wine brought a rush of memories. She blinked them away and advanced, the crossbow held ready before her.

The voices were low and relaxed, chatter between people who knew each other well. There were maybe six distinct voices, men and women, and none of them sounded afraid.

Why aren't they scared? Holly wondered, and the weight of the threat behind her spurred her on. She moved forward, and when she heard the first sign of surprise in their voices she spoke up.

'I'm no fury!' she said.

'Step forward!' someone responded.

Holly held the crossbow up, swinging it left and right as she moved into the eerie glow. There were still two of them standing in front of the breach, aiming their own weapons towards her, and several more were gathered around a steaming pot to her left.

'It's the visitor,' she heard one of them whisper, and she could not hesitate. She had no idea if this world's humans could communicate across large distances, if this group knew of her escape, or whether they'd been told to stop her at all costs. She did not know anything, except that her own world was a few small steps away. And she so wanted to be there, even after everything she had been shown in the casting room.

'Out of my way,' Holly said, circling around them and approaching the breach.

'We can't let you through,' one of them said. He stood his ground, but she could feel nervousness radiating from him in waves.

'You're not "letting" me through,' Holly said, 'I'm insisting on it. And there are furies behind me, maybe hundreds of them, and—'

'Hundreds?' another of them asked. A woman, she seemed less intimidated by Holly, and more in control. She'd be the one to watch.

'They rose from the ruins,' Holly said.

'You went into the *ruins?*' a man gasped.

'I . . .' Holly began. But they were whispering, and their fear was palpable. Holly glanced up and back at the hilltop, relieved to see it was still an unmoving silhouette against the strange sky.

'They track you,' the woman said.

'Then come through with me.' Holly lowered the crossbow, feeling vaguely stupid aiming it at another human being. She could never kill anyone human, she realised, and if they restrained her by force she would have to accept that. She desperately needed to get through, but she could not take human life to do so.

'Through?'

'There.' Holly nodded at the breach, nestled thirty metres behind them at the foot of the hill like a haze of mist catching moonlight.

'Travel through there has been forbidden,' the woman said.

'But you won't stop me,' Holly said. She caught a look between the two guards and their companions, a quick glance that spoke volumes. The woman guard started signalling with the fingers of one hand. 'No,' Holly said, and she raised the crossbow again. 'I have to get home.'

'We have orders.'

'There's no more time.' Holly took one last look behind her. Dawn was already penetrating the dusty atmosphere, lighting up the hillsides, and she could see movement up there now.

Another series of finger signals but Holly was no longer concerned with their stand-off. They were all out of time.

Lowering the crossbow for the second time, she ran between the guards towards the breach beyond them.

3

The nights, Jayne realised, were always going to be the worst. Tired, terrified, and vaguely hungover, Jayne stirred from a dream-filled sleep and took a couple of seconds to remember what had happened. She'd once enjoyed these brief moments before the stab of pain, these seconds of reconstruction, when her waking mind would bring together the disparate strands of her life and identity to remind her who she was.

Today it took her two whole heartbeats to remember that Tommy was dead.

'They're still out there,' a man's voice said.

Jayne kept her eyes closed for a moment longer, examining the ache in her head as a way of trying to bypass the heavy, hot pains in her limbs and hips. She pretended, in those few moments before reality smashed its way through, that *this* was her dream – this place, this time, with these diseased, dead people wandering the airport as they searched for anyone they had missed. And it might have worked for longer than a second if Sean had not persisted.

'Jayne? You awake? You okay? I said they're still there.' His voice became muffled, and she knew he had turned again to one of the aircraft's dulled, scratched windows. 'Some have gone, I think. Or maybe they're just waiting somewhere out of sight. But lots of them are just . . . wandering. Like cattle.'

Jayne opened her eyes at last and grimaced at the familiar pain. Soon she would have to start massaging her limbs and joints, give herself the gift of movement.

'How long have I been asleep?'

'Couple hours,' Sean said.

'What's happened?'

He shrugged, his back still turned towards her. She could see the window misting and clearing as he breathed, and she wanted to tell him to get back. But it was dark inside the cabin, and outside there was flickering, dreadful light.

'Terminal's still burning. Hour ago, a big passenger

jet overflew the airport, real low, then headed north. A few minutes after that an F16 went back and forth a few times.'

Jayne sat up slowly, wincing against the pain in her stiff limbs and joints. As she started massaging, the determination in Sean's voice gave her a boost.

'Did you speak to your daughter?'

He shook his head. 'Nothing.'

'Did your friend call back?' she asked.

'Leigh? Yeah.' Sean paused.

'And?'

'And he said he'd put a call in, and entered you on the immunity register. Help should be on its way.'

'*Should* be?'

Sean turned around at last, retreating from the window, and for a moment Jayne saw the glimmer of distant fires reflected against his skin.

'Shouldn't we be calling the police, or something?' she asked. 'Or . . . I don't know, the army? Scientists?'

'I've been thinking about this,' Sean said, shaking his head, 'and—'

From outside they heard the whoop of a police siren. Eyes wide, Sean glanced from Jayne to the window and back again.

'Help?' she asked.

'Maybe. But we have to be careful.' He was still nursing the gun in his hand, and she wondered whether he'd closed his eyes even for a moment while she had been asleep. She felt very selfish. She had rested, mourning a love she knew was dead, and all the while Sean had watched over her, not knowing what had happened to his daughter.

Jayne pushed herself upright and staggered across the aisle to the far seats. Sean grabbed her hand and eased her down, and they looked out of two adjoining windows. In the distance, past a series of boarding gates where several aircraft were parked, a blue light flashed three times. A siren whooped again, followed by three more flashes.

'What are they doing?' she asked.

'Looking for survivors, maybe?'

'Or looking for us?'

Below them, several shapes emerged from beneath the plane's fuselage and headed across the wide span of concrete. One man walked quickly, almost with authority, but the splash of dried blood down the back of his white shirt was stark and black. The others followed at a slower pace, a couple of them hindered by the wounds that had changed them.

'Hiding beneath us,' Jayne said.

'Sneaky bastards.'

'Sneaky? You think they *can* sneak?'

Sean gave her a sidelong look and shrugged.

'We should signal them,' she said. 'But we should warn—'

'I doubt they need warning.' He tensed for a moment, thinking. He chuckled. 'Wish I could drive this thing.'

'Wish I could *fly* this thing.'

Sean nodded, still distracted. 'Cabin lights,' he said at last.

'I'm sure there's a master switch, but where?'

'Maybe it doesn't matter.' Sean reached for the overhead control panels, pushed buttons, and the weak reading lights flicked on.

'Might as well light a match,' Jayne said, watching from the window. She could make out two vehicles, one a police car and the other a larger truck. In the flickering light of the burning concourse, they looked white.

Sean walked back and forth along the cabin, flicking on the lights.

Something exploded in the blazing terminal, sending a column of fire and rolling black smoke skyward. Gouts of flame arced comet-like from the blast, and as they rained down they too started exploding in brief, incredibly bright bursts.

'Gas canisters,' Jayne said. 'The cop car's moving back.' She heard Sean's footsteps as he raced to switch on more lights and suddenly she felt incredibly exposed here in this contained space. The glare of the explosions and the subdued lighting behind her combined to blur her vision, and outside there could be any number of grim faces turning her way. *They'll see us now*, she thought.

Whether or not those cops are here for us – whether or not they see us – the zombies will know we're here. This might have been their one safe place, but now it was compromised.

'I think we have to get out,' she said when Sean crouched by her side.

'Come on, come on,' he said, willing the cops to see them.

The two vehicles were reversing away from the burning terminal and away from them, moving slowly but obviously under control. There was a flash from the truck's passenger window that might have been a gunshot. And then the police cruiser stopped.

'Come *on*,' Sean said again. The cruiser's blue lights flashed a few times, and he reached up and flicked two reading lights off and on.

'They won't see that,' Jayne said, but then she grinned. They *had* seen it, because they'd been watching for it. And now they were powering across the airport, skirting around the burning main building, and as the police car veered around a staggering figure she closed her eyes just before the truck ran it down.

'Jesus Christ,' she breathed, and Sean squeezed her hand.

'Come on. Back door on the starboard side.'

'I'm scared,' she said, thinking of a car journey through what was happening out there. Here they had drunk wine and talked, and she had slept. Out there, carnage and chaos ruled.

'We could never have stayed here for long,' Sean said. He looked older than he had before, his eyes heavier and darker because of his fear for his daughter. *France?* he'd said, amazed, and Jayne still could not believe that the infection had travelled so far so quickly.

'I know.' She nodded, and started rubbing her shoulders with both hands.

'I'll open the door.' He walked slowly, glancing back as she followed. Jayne felt protected, but she also knew that she was providing Sean with a distraction, and a cause.

The blast of warm air when Sean opened the door was shocking. He stood back slightly, gun raised, then edged forward slowly.

'They there?' Jayne asked. She had to raise her voice against the roaring fires, and she realised how close they were. And the fact that they were in an aircraft that probably contained tens of thousands of gallons of fuel hit home.

Sean waved her over with one hand, then shoved the gun in his belt and held out his other hand palm out.

Jayne joined him at the door, wincing against the incredible wave of heat radiating from the conflagration. It stretched her skin and dried her eyes, and when she gasped her lungs burned.

The police cruiser was parked thirty feet away. The truck stopped thirty feet behind that, its bodywork scratched and bumped. There was a swathe of dried blood across one wing and up the door. Its windows were darkened, and she felt someone – something – staring at her.

The cruiser was similarly battered, and the driver's window had been smashed. Even before the door opened she saw the size of the man in there, and as he got out of the car and looked up at them, Jayne felt an unaccountable rush of optimism. The cop must have been six and a half feet tall. With someone like him coming for her . . .

She closed her eyes and sighed, wondering how she could be so foolish. Maybe because she had always needed someone to help her look after herself. Was that a weakness? She hoped not.

'You the girl got bit?' the big man shouted up at them. He disregarded Sean and stared right at her.

Jayne raised her arm and pulled up her sleeve, displaying the bandage.

The man leaned back into the cruiser and grabbed a shotgun. He held it casually, as if he was used to it. He was sweating visibly through his uniform.

'Who're you?' Sean asked.

'Sergeant Waits, Baltimore PD. You?'

'Sean Nott. I'm a sky marshal.'

'Right.' Waits glanced around every few seconds.

'There are lots of them round,' Sean went on, 'so be careful.'

'Careful. Right.' Waits looked back at the blacked-out truck behind them, and Jayne wondered what might be inside.

'Did Leigh call you?' Sean asked.

'Leigh?' The big man shifted the shotgun to the other hand, moving forward and leaning against the truck's damaged hood. The blood did not seem to concern him.

'About us.' Sean touched Jayne's shoulder, and she could feel his hand shaking. 'About Jayne.'

'Don't know no Leigh. Just know a girl's got bit, hasn't turned. Been plenty of claims on the register, but none confirmed so far.'

'Where will you take us?' Jayne asked.

'Back to the station.' Waits looked around again, and gave a vague signal to the truck. 'From there, don't know yet. How long you been up there?'

'Several hours,' Sean said.

'It's fucked as hell out here,' Waits said. 'We been through some stuff. But the station's tight, and it'll be a damn sight safer than—'

They all heard the sound at the same time – the thumping of feet against metal. Jayne knew instantly what it was, and even as Sean gasped and Waits turned she shouted, 'Bus!'

The vehicle was between the fire and the aircraft, where it had stood silent and unthreatening since they had closed the aircraft doors. Now she could see movement inside, silhouetted against the flames.

A man appeared on the bottom step wearing a bus driver's hat, and when he stepped forward it was like releasing a stopper from a bottle. They flowed out behind him, rushing towards the police vehicles as fast as their various injuries would allow. For many of them, their wounds did not slow them at all.

Waits rested his elbows on the cruiser's roof, aimed the shotgun, and fired. The resulting mayhem was so sudden that Jayne did not even see if anyone fell, and then Sean was grabbing her arm and pulling her inside the aircraft, reaching for the door handle and tugging it closed.

Something struck the aircraft with a loud, hollow *thunk!* and she realised that the shooting had begun in earnest.

'The window!' Sean said, pulling the door closed and engaging the locking lever.

'Window?'

'We might need to move fast, so we have to know what's happening.'

Jayne tried to move quickly, but her joints screamed and the churu threw grit into her eyes, clouding her vision and disturbing her balance. She staggered along the aisle and fell sideways across a row of seats. She could hear gunfire outside, the *pop pop* of individual shots and a heavier, more sustained burst of machine-gun fire. She bit her lip and her vision cleared, and she felt a terrible, unreasonable shame at being such a burden.

'It's okay,' Sean said softly. He was beside her on the seat, helping her upright and then leaning across her to look outside.

'I don't believe this,' Jayne said. Tears burned in her eyes.

'It's not over yet,' Sean said. But she could tell that the words belied his belief. So she pushed him away, and leaned forward to see from the window herself.

And it *was* all over, because Waits was already down and smothered with raging, thrashing people, and the cruiser's other door was open and a uniformed woman was being dragged out, and she was shooting people in the head – three, four – before a young boy bit into her arm and she dropped the gun. And as automatic gunfire raked the cruiser from the truck's lowered windows the monsters turned that way, rushing forward and being cut down, walking across those who fell to press themselves against the truck's side, forcing those inside to withdraw their weapons and close the windows. The zombies – there must have been fifty by then, perhaps more, and others were rushing from all directions to join in

— swarmed around and over the truck, punching and stamping and head-butting until windows smashed and gunfire erupted again.

As Jayne saw Waits standing, different from how he had been before, she pulled back from the window.

'He saw me,' she gasped.

The gunfire ceased. Someone screamed, the sound distant and muffled.

'They can't get in,' Sean said. He was passing the gun from one hand to the other, as if he was trying to find a way to hold it without his nervous sweat making it slick.

'But he knows we're here,' Jayne said.

Sean blinked at her and shrugged. But there was nothing he could say.

From outside there came that familiar, terrible call. Jayne looked again. They stood motionless now, following Waits's stare, and before she pulled away from the window again Jayne was aware of every single one of them looking up at her. And she knew that they would wait.

4

This time the dream staggers rather than flows, shifting from one scene to the next like a damaged film missing random frames. And Charlotte stalks the suburbs of Vic's guilt.

379

This is my dream I can change it I can make it better.

Charlotte chuckles. The dream flickers, and then they are outside the strange place that always feels like home. Vic tries to run, but he is on his hands and knees, his fingertips melting into the hot road. Charlotte knocks on the door and Lucy answers.

No, he tries to say. Charlotte turns to laugh at him or show him her dead eyes, but it is not Charlotte at all – it is Holly standing there dead before him and mocking his remorse.

'Holly!' he shouts, shocked that he had found his voice at last. 'No, *Holly!*'

Her mouth falls open and she—

—Vic snapped awake, Olivia crying beside him, and Marc looked back at him from the cockpit.

Shit shit shit, he thought, blinking quickly but not really wanting to close his eyes again. He was afraid that she would still be waiting there behind them.

He looked over Olivia's head at Lucy, and his wife was just turning away. 'Lucy?' She didn't hear him, and though he took a deep breath he did not speak again. He remembered the end of his dream and what he'd been shouting, and wondered whether he had scared them all with his yelling out of Holly's name.

Even though the light was weak and the helicopter shook, he could not mistake Lucy's expression when she'd turned away from him – the heavy eyes, her sadly etched mouth. So Vic hugged his daughter, accepting her innocent, uncomplicated love and wishing his could be like that.

He looked from the window and saw a landscape fired by a red-palette dawn. *Red sky in the morning* . . . he thought, and Olivia snuggled into his embrace. He remembered Holly, not as she had been in his dream but as he had known her at the height of their affair. Never demanding, never intrusive, their few tentative conversations about being together properly had always been initiated by him, and she had never forced the issue. In her silence he had read the truth – she had wanted it more than anything.

But he'd never truly considered leaving Lucy, and when she had fallen pregnant his and Holly's relationship had stopped without either of them needing to say anything. He could remember each intimate detail, every sigh and position from the last time they had made love, but he had no idea whether either of them had known it was going to be the last time.

Gary was flying quite low, and as the minutes ticked by it became easier to see the truth of what had happened below them. It also became harder for Vic to reach out to Lucy and try to explain. Her expression as she'd turned away should have prompted him to reassure her, but it had scared him too much. So he looked at the ruin outside and wondered how it could have spread so quickly.

The rolling landscape was speckled with individual homes and groups of buildings, and every few minutes they passed over larger townships. Fires were burning, many small, a few large, probing up at them with smoky fingers – accidents, people protecting their homes, authorities burning bodies on pyres that got out of hand. Some of the smoke was grey and light, some heavy and dark and thick, and he had no desire to understand the difference.

'Daddy?' Olivia shouted against the helicopter's roar. She was fidgeting against him again. Vic gazed down at her. Lucy was looking at him now and something in her expression seemed to have relaxed.

'I need to pee,' Olivia said.

Vic nodded, and smiled at Lucy. She didn't smile back, but the mistrust had gone from her eyes. Perhaps she'd thought it away, or maybe she'd simply discarded it because of everything else that was happening.

Vic slipped on his headset and asked, 'Gary, where are we?'

'Baltimore's close. Airport in about thirty minutes.'

'Sorry, I slept,' Vic said.

'Need the rest,' Marc said, turning and looking over the facing seats at the family. 'Don't worry, honey, you can pee soon.' He smiled at Olivia and touched his microphone. Lucy got the message and took off Olivia's headset.

'What?' Lucy asked.

'Everything's buggered,' Gary said. 'Air-traffic control's working so hard to avoid collisions that, they don't have time to answer anything incoming. And since we're approaching a bloody massive airport I'd like to know what's happening there.'

'I guess we can just assume it's batshit,' Marc said. 'I don't think Baltimore airport's going to be fucking around with passport control right now.'

'I'm feeding radio just to my headset, ' Gary said. 'I haven't even told you this . . .' He reached across and held Marc's hand, clasping it tightly. 'Two passenger jets collided above Washington. Three more above Chicago airport, and I've heard of at least four others going down. And there are rumours about military jets shooting down anything that ventures out over the Atlantic.'

'Our air force is shooting down passenger planes?' Lucy asked, shocked.

'I didn't say *our* military,' Gary said. They fell quiet at that, and Vic reached across to touch Lucy. For a moment she seemed to stiffen, but then she squeezed his hand.

Vic soon grew tired of looking down and seeing what was becoming of the world, so he looked to the skies instead. That was not much better. In the space of the half-hour it took them to reach Baltimore airport, they saw several smaller helicopters, three fast jets, and at least a dozen military helicopters, some of them Chinooks with vehicles slung beneath them. Their bellies were probably full of soldiers. Most of the army's choppers seemed to be flying north.

'Attack or retreat?' Marc said, and no one risked a response.

Olivia's desperation grew intense, and in the end Lucy fluffed up a blanket and sheltered her while she peed into that. The smell filled the cabin. No one commented, and Vic felt an intense gratitude to the other two men for that.

'Airport's close,' Gary said, his voice quieter than before. 'Better come see.'

Vic and Lucy crouched forward, and Olivia went with them, holding their hands. She felt cold to Vic, and he tried to remember the last time they'd eaten or had a drink.

The sun was a pale smudge on the horizon directly ahead of them, veiled by the massive spread of smoke that stained the eastern sky. It reached high into the air, and thousands of feet above them the spreading cloud was smeared with a dirty sunrise. At the base of the column of smoke was the glow of distant flames.

'That's the airport?' Lucy asked.

'Yeah,' Gary said. He flicked a switch and spoke into his microphone, the words inaudible to the others. Vic tried to read his expression from the side but it was inscrutable.

'She must be dead,' Lucy said.

'No,' Marc said.

'How can you know?'

'I can't,' he said, never once looking away from the smoke and flames. 'But if there's even a remote chance that she isn't, then it's our duty to search for her.'

'And put my daughter at risk?' Lucy asked. Vic felt a swell of pride.

'Absolutely.' Marc turned around and smiled at the little girl who was unaware of their conversation. 'Absolutely. This woman could save a billion other kids.'

Lucy snorted and looked away. *He's right*, Vic thought. *It's gone so far so quickly, and if she* is *dead then maybe* everyone *is dead*.

'Honey, we've come all this way,' Vic said. He meant from Cincinnati, but when Lucy smiled he thought back to the very first time he had set eyes on her, when he had fallen for that smile.

'I'll go in upwind, from the south,' Gary said. 'But it's still going to be bad. I'll do a flyover. You all need to be looking, because I'm going in low and all my attention will be focused on not hitting anything.'

'What are we looking for?' Lucy asked.

'Anyone alive.' Marc had produced a gun from his bag and placed it casually across his lap. Vic saw Olivia's eyes straying that way. They went wide.

'Where's *your* gun, Daddy?' she asked.

He thought of every way he could answer that: how to protect her, to shield her. But he realised that he was still thinking safe thoughts, from a time when safety was a very different thing. Baseball matches were cancelled, Oprah was not on air, and the schools were closed today.

'It's here,' he said, pulling the M1911 from his belt. 'And Daddy uses this to make sure that no one ever, ever hurts you.'

Olivia nodded, her eyes still wide.

Gary flew them in at about five hundred feet, curving across the southern part of the airport and keeping away from the blazing terminal buildings. Small explosions were erupting in there all the time, terrible flowers of flame and smoke, and the eastern concourse was also ablaze. Several large airliners burned fiercely in islands of fire and wrecked fuselages. Vic hoped they had been empty when they'd exploded but realised that it probably didn't matter.

'If they were trapped in a plane they might have left by now,' Vic said. 'Who'd want to stay here?'

'Someone who had to,' Lucy said. 'Gary, swing around again, take a wider sweep further from the fires.'

Vic raised his eyebrows at Lucy, surprised at her sudden involvement. She offered him a nervous smile, resting a protective hand on Olivia's leg.

'Further from fire sounds good to me.' The helicopter banked and curved around to the south.

'What did you see?' Vic asked. But Lucy was frowning, shaking her head.

'Something that didn't register,' she said. 'But it's bugging me.'

The stench of smoke already filled the cabin. Olivia coughed. She seemed more scared than before, and Vic guessed it was to do with the sudden flurry of activity. Until now the little girl had been sitting with her parents on a long helicopter ride, and maybe it had even been exciting for her. Now there was smoke and fire, and a burning airport.

'It's okay,' Vic said, pressing his mouth to her ear.

'There,' Lucy said. 'That plane down there, close to the grass verge. Furthest one. See it? Do you see?'

'I see it,' Marc said. 'But what am I looking at'

'Not the plane,' Vic said, understanding at once. 'Gary, take us lower.'

'Oh, shit,' the pilot whispered. He had seen it as well.

They hovered two hundred feet away, maybe a hundred feet off the ground, and countless eyes turned their way.

'Must be a thousand of them down there,' Vic said.

They surrounded the aircraft, most of them motionless, a few sitting or lying down because of the damage done to their bodies. They all turned their heads to watch the helicopter, and some were now walking their way, a few of them running.

Though they were well off the ground Gary took them a little higher.

Vic saw a couple of battered police vehicles and noticed that one of those running at them was a big man wearing a torn uniform. His face had gone, replaced with a dark mask of dried blood.

Olivia had pressed her face against Vic's side and he held one hand to the side of her head, just in case she peeked. He wished someone would screen his eyes from the view as well.

'They're just waiting there,' Lucy said.

'Maybe they've got nowhere else to go,' Gary suggested.

'Or maybe they know that someone's alive in there,' Marc said. 'Look!' He pointed, and Vic saw the faint flicker of a weak light being turned on and off inside the plane. 'Gary, any way we can signal them?' Marc asked, and Gary swung the helicopter left and right three times.

'Okay,' Lucy said. 'So.'

Many of the shapes were below them now, looking but not reaching up, aware in some animal way that they could not touch the helicopter yet knowing that there were people inside. Vic could see their faces, devoid of emotion. He could see the dried blood. They were dead but walking, and they wanted to bite his family.

'Fuck them,' Vic said, his voice shaking. 'Fuck them all. We put down and shoot them, and then get to the plane and—'

'How many bullets do you think we have?' Marc asked him, a note of sarcasm in his voice.

Gary lifted them a little higher and swung in a circle around the besieged jet. The zombies watched.

'What if we land a few hundred feet away?' Vic said. 'Sit there, wait for them to come at us. Then take off and land back here.'

'No,' Marc said. 'We can't assume that whoever's inside will know what we're doing. We don't know if they're hurt. And if it *is* the girl we're after and she *has* been bitten . . .'

'Are we just going to let her on board?' Lucy asked. 'Without checking?'

'No,' Vic said. 'No way.' He stared at Marc when the tall man looked back. He squeezed Olivia tighter.

'Fine,' Marc said. 'Gary, got a rope or a ladder in this thing?'

'Yeah.'

Vic swallowed hard. *What the fuck?* But something had to be done. His legs ached from inaction, and his heart throbbed with the need to make amends. To Lucy and his daughter, for deeds unspoken; and to everyone else. *I'd be dead if I'd stayed in Coldbrook*, he thought, but 'if' was no defence.

'Where is it?' Vic asked.

Vic sat in the helicopter's open doorway, gripping the door's handle with both hands while Gary manoeuvred closer and lower. Beneath them the hordes were stirring, some of them now even reaching up, unlike before, as though to snatch the helicopter from the sky.

'This is as low as I go,' Gary said in his earpiece, and Vic took a look down. They were hovering above the aircraft's wide wing, and either side of the wing he could see what awaited him if he slipped and fell. The zombies' hands, clawed and ready to rip and tear. Their open mouths, showing expression only with the bloodied teeth they contained. Marc was strapped safely into the seat beside him, ready to lean from the doorway and give him covering fire with his rifle. *Shoot me if I fall*, he wanted to say, but Lucy still had her headpiece on, sitting behind him in the cabin and shielding Olivia from the roaring, smoke-laden wind.

'Won't be long,' he said instead, and he and Marc locked stares. Marc nodded once. Maybe he already knew what his responsibilities were.

Vic kicked the coiled rope ladder from the door. It unfurled and landed on the wing, much of it still rolled up. He looked at the aircraft again, and at the faces watching from the window of the emergency door leading onto the wing. They looked as nervous as he felt.

He turned around onto his belly and eased himself out of the door. As his feet found the ladder Lucy's words surprised him, soft as a breeze in this storm.

'Come back to us.'

'Put the coffee on,' he said, but he could not look at his wife and child again. Not until he was back.

Vic started to climb down. When he was a kid he'd had a tree house in his grandparents' garden. Something straight out of *Huckleberry Finn*, his grandfather had claimed, but Vic had always seen himself as Calvin and the tall childhood friend he hadn't thought about in thirty years had been Hobbes. 'If you could see me now,' he said, and he wondered what had become of Hobbes and where he was. As kids, they had both negotiated the rope ladder up to the tree house with ease, and his grandfather had said that such a thing was like riding a bike. All about balance and confidence. But they hadn't had a buffeting wind to contend with, nor a motor roaring so loud that the noise felt like a physical impact. And if they'd fallen there'd only have been cuts and bruises, and fallen leaves clinging to their clothes.

Hand over hand, ever cautious, Vic descended from rung to rung. He glanced down when he thought he was almost there, to find he was only halfway down.

'Bloody cold out here,' he said, and he heard Marc laugh in his ear. But no one else replied. This action was all down to Vic, and keeping his concentration tightly focused was paramount. There could be no distractions.

A gust of wind set him swaying. He clung on tight and closed his eyes, stomach lurching as he felt himself swinging through the air. He looked up again and saw Marc looking into the cabin, then back down at him.

'Sorry!' Gary said. 'The fire's whipping up a windstorm. Don't want to hurry you, but—'

'Yeah,' Vic said. As he started down again Marc's voice crackled through his earpiece.

'Fuck, fuck, fuck. Vic, you got trouble.'

'What?'

'Down. Look down.'

Vic looked down. The drifting helicopter had dragged the rest of the ladder from the wing, and now it was unfurled all the way to the ground. And the things were already trying to climb up it.

The first one was the tall cop, his face bitten off, teeth bared because he had no lips.

'Hold on!' Gary said. 'I'll swing around and—'

'No time,' Vic said softly. 'Can't risk them catching me. They're not worried about dying.'

'Oh, Vic,' Lucy said, but he did not reply, did not even want to give voice to his despair. He had seconds, and every one of them had to count.

He glanced up. Marc leaned out of the doorway, aiming the rifle down.

'Vic, I can't see past you.'

'I've got it. Gary, hold that fucker still!' He turned sideways to the ladder and threaded his left arm and right leg through, bending his elbow and grabbing a rung above him, pulling his knee around the rope, and tugging the gun from his belt with his right hand. It slipped in his palm, and he cried out as it almost fell from his grasp.

'Fuck!'

The faceless cop was a dozen rungs below him and scrambling up the rope ladder, hands and feet missing every third or fourth rung, one eye gone, the other blood-shot and burst, and Vic had no idea how he could see or sense anything.

He clasped the gun tightly, aimed down at the cop's bloody face and pulled the trigger. Nothing happened.

'Safety!' Marc screamed in his ear, and Vic flipped the safety lever with his thumb and pulled the trigger again.

The cop's head flipped back and bits of it spattered down across the white wing below them. He held on for a few seconds, a woman in a bright floral dress tearing at his feet and trousers in her frenzy to get past him. Then he fell back into empty air and took her with him. They both struck the leading edge of the massive wing and spun into the manic crowd below.

The rest of the ladder was clear.

'Fucking hell,' Marc said. 'Lucy, he's fine. Fucking hell.'

'Couldn't put it better myself,' Vic said. He hung there for a moment, not daring to move in case his thundering heart shook him from the ladder. He didn't deserve to fall after marksmanship like that.

Thirty seconds later he was on the wing, pulling the ladder back up before more of the zombies could climb it. And twenty feet away the emergency door in the fuselage swung open. He crouched down and aimed the gun, and the man who emerged held up his hands, displaying his own gun tucked into his belt.

'You the sky marshal?' Vic shouted.

'Yeah. But who the hell are you?'

'Wyatt Earp.' The woman who emerged after the man grinned, glancing up at the hovering helicopter. 'Wyatt Earp, that's who he is. Come to restore justice to Zombie Town.'

'Gotta admit, that was some shooting,' the sky marshal said.

Vic started shaking. He sat down heavily on the wing before enjoying the contact as the man and woman shook his hand and helped him up. He told them to go first because he had to pull himself together before climbing again. The two men watched the woman's slow climb, and Vic was aware enough to notice the bandage on her arm.

'She was really bitten?' he asked.

'She was,' the other man said. 'Seconds away from getting her brains bashed out by the passengers.'

'And what happened to them?'

The man heard him but didn't answer. Neither did his expression change. He watched as the woman reached the top of the ladder and was helped into the helicopter before he spoke again.

'That's some girl,' he said. 'That really is some girl.'

We'll see, Vic thought. Then he pointed at the ladder, pleased that his hand was no longer shaking. 'After you.'

5

They would have tried reaching Jonah by now. If his calls had made waves, then Coldbrook's surface enclosures would be swarming with military, and they would have worked their way down to him with cutting equipment or explosives.

So it was obvious that there was no one. He was alone down here with no knowledge of what was happening in the world above, and with the Inquisitor getting ready to turn him into one of his own. Ridiculous, and yet Jonah could not rationalise his way out of this understanding. He was being harried by something he could not explain.

Control and the breach chamber were still barricaded with the furniture he had put back outside the compromised door. He started pulling it away, aware all the time of the weight of the gun in his belt. It seemed to do no good against the Inquisitor, but Jonah himself was still human flesh and blood. Alive or dead, he intended to stay that way.

The Inquisitor was behind him, out of sight, somewhere in the darkened facility. He shone his heavy torch back along the corridor, but saw nothing. That only filled him with dread.

You'll live for ever, the Inquisitor had said, and Jonah couldn't think of anything worse. These many years without Wendy had been bad enough; eternity without her was unthinkable.

He pulled the last chair away, peered into the room and shone his torch around. Shadows stretched and shifted from behind the many control desks and terminals. Jonah entered Control and almost went to look at the corpse from the other Earth. But he did not have the luxury of time.

'So there it is,' he said, standing a dozen steps from the breach as he had so many times since its formation. It was night through there now, and what little of the landscape he could see was heavily shadowed. His heart was thudding, skipping a beat every now and then as it so often did nowadays. He held his hand to his chest. *That bastard wanted to open me up.*

Holly had punched off the eradicator so that she could escape through, but Jonah had no idea whether it had been set on a time delay. And with power off there was no way to find out. The core, and therefore the breach and its associated containment and eradicator, was self-sustaining, but now impossible to assess.

Something scraped against the floor. He wasn't sure where the sound had come from or what had caused it, but he held his breath and listened for more. Nothing.

'Time to get out of here,' Jonah muttered, drawing the gun from his waistband. He was nowhere near prepared but he could stay no longer.

He strode towards the breach, the threat of being killed by the eradicator a remote concern because he would feel nothing. His body would close down, his mind following soon after, and perhaps he would die thinking of Wendy and everything they had not had time to do together.

As he was about to enter, hair standing on end and body tingling all over, he saw a shadow moving towards him. He raised the gun, heavy and comforting in his hand. *Perhaps I'm seeing myself*, he thought, because he had no idea what crossing between this world and another might do.

Then the tip of a metal-and-wood device was pointing at him, a shape emerged behind it, and Holly said, 'You can put can the gun down, Jonah.'

'Holly!' he gasped. She stood in the space between two Earths, edging forward, the crossbow pointing at his face. Behind her, only darkness.

'Jonah?'

He kept his gun trained on her, but he had almost forgotten about it in his surprise.

'Holly, I . . .'

She came forward from the breach, and Jonah could see that so much about her had changed. She was sweating, panting hard, grubby, wearing long shapeless clothes. And her eyes were wide and determined.

'Gun, Jonah.'

'Oh.' He lowered the pistol and smiled, and then Holly's eyes went wide.

'I'm not one of—' he said – and she fired.

HollyshotmeHollyshotme! The bolt flew past the side of his head and he felt a brief draught as it whispered by. Then he heard an impact behind him and a startled exhalation, and as he spun around Holly was shouting, 'What the *fuck* was that?'

'What?' Jonah felt a momentary queasiness, and the world tilted around him. Holly did not come to help him and he had to lean over and rest his hands on his knees. There was nothing moving in Control apart from a trace of mist.

'That *thing*.'

'There's nothing—'

'Weird guy behind you. Gone now.' Her voice trembled a little, and at first he thought it was from fear. 'Not one of them?'

'The Inquisitor?' Jonah asked, realising that Holly was afraid she'd shot someone else. '*You* saw it?' But his rush of elation was quickly tempered by Holly's expression.

'Inquisitor.' Holly blinked a few times, shock settling across her face. 'Jesus help us. The Inquisitor? *That's* what you called it?'

'It's what it calls itself.'

'Oh, Jonah, we have so much to talk about.'

'Through there,' he said, pointing behind her.

'No.' She was loading a fresh bolt into the crossbow.

'Yes!' They *had* to leave here, because the freak had revealed himself to both of them.

'No, Jonah. No way. They're close.' She looked behind her and, though he could see no shadows moving through there, Jonah could see that her fear was very real.

'Who?'

She pointed her crossbow at the first fury that had come through and started all this. 'Like that,' she said. 'Hundreds.'

'Oh.' Jonah stepped closer to her. She smelled strange, but she was still his Holly.

'Is there *anywhere* safe?' she asked softly.

'I don't think so.'

Holly's face fell. She leaned against Jonah, hugging him tight.

'Oh, Jonah, what have we done?'

He had a thousand questions for her – about the crossbow, her clothes, the smell, her knowledge, the things through there, what she had seen, what she had heard . . . But one most of all.

'The Inquisitor,' he said.

'Drake mentioned it.'

'Drake?'

Holly pulled back, and her slight smile shocked him. 'In a way, he's their version of you.'

Jonah froze. 'Holly . . .'

There were figures moving behind her, through the breach. The darkness throbbed and shifted, a pulsing riot of shadow that was drawing closer.

'Might be the guards,' Holly said, but there was doubt in her voice.

'Guards?'

Holly concentrated, peering through the breach, turning her head slightly left and right. She lifted the crossbow again, and it seemed such an unconscious gesture that Jonah wondered how much she had changed. When she'd gone through she had been a scientist, now . . . now she looked like someone out of *Mad Max 2: The Road Warrior*.

'No,' she said. 'Not the guards. Don't know how time changes when . . .' She grabbed Jonah's arm and started for the door. 'We have to get out of Control and lock it up, tight.' She looked around the large room, and he knew what she was searching for.

'It'll come again,' he said. 'But . . . you hit it, and it went?'

'I'm sure the bolt got it in the shoulder,' Holly said. She shook her head, frowned. 'Maybe it was a caster.'

'Caster?'

'Furies that don't move, just observe. They watch through them.'

'You know about them?'

'Oh, yeah. Come on. Out of here, then we've got some catching-up to do.'

The breach was moving now, and through the hole between the two worlds Jonah could see limbs and shuffling bodies.

'Power's off all over?' Holly asked.

'And communications.'

'You're alone down here?'

Jonah didn't answer that, and the image of the Inquisitor rose up again.

Holly grabbed Jonah's arm and pulled him up the stepped ramp. They closed Control's doors and set about piling the furniture against them again. They gathered more items from the storeroom close to the staircase – several cots to prop against the corridor's opposite wall, filing cabinets, and more chairs.

'This won't hold for ever,' Holly said.

They were coming through. In the weak bluish light of Control's emergency lighting, they looked like strange plants with the power of movement – ragged limbs, wild hair, sunken skin like bark worn down by decades of sun and darkness, heat and frost. Their eyes were dark cavities in their dead faces. There seemed to be no purpose in their movement other than simply to keep going. Jonah could see no expressions on their faces, apart from those placed there by injury or deformity. How old these things were he could not tell, but he sensed an age to them that stripped away any shred of humanity that even a dead thing might possess. They were no longer meaningfully human, though in shape and build they resembled roughly what they might once have been. These were *other*.

'My fault. I woke them.' Holly held Jonah's arm again, giving and receiving comfort. He could barely tell her how good it was to feel her warmth.

One of the zombies that had come through was different from the others. He wore clothes similar to Holly's, and the weak light reflected from the fresh gaping wound in the side of his face. Jonah could see the man's teeth. He could also see the slackness of his face, any expression fallen away in death.

'Oh, God!' Holly said, burying her face against Jonah's chest.

Without speaking, he picked up Holly's crossbow and guided her away from Control.

'Secondary?' she asked softly.

'For now. I've locked some of them away. Shot a few.' Jonah expected some reaction, but Holly didn't even glance at him. 'Vic got away.'

'Away?'

'He ran. I think some of the infected followed him.'

Holly paused, cautious, as she asked, 'You don't know what's happening outside?'

'A little. I know it got out. But since the power went down . . .' Jonah shrugged.

'It's spread,' she said. 'Jonah, it's spread a lot. I've seen it. Images from the casters. I walked through from our world to theirs, but they *cast* through. Send their consciousness through, somehow, and take control of furies, see through their eyes.'

'*You*'ve seen this?'

Holly nodded.

They reached Secondary. Even though he knew otherwise, Jonah felt safer when they'd closed and locked the door. He retrieved more torches from the emergency store and placed them around the room.

'Vic grabbed his family and went north,' Jonah said.

'Why?'

And he told Holly everything. About what he'd been forced to do down here, and about Vic, and the Inquisitor, though he had trouble explaining what he could not comprehend.

'But what happened to you?' he asked. 'What's through there?'

'There's *nothing* through there,' she said. 'Gaia . . .' She barked a bitter laugh. 'Great name Melinda came up with there. Gaia had its apocalypse forty years ago.'

'Forty years . . .' Jonah said, and the shock was profound. *This has all happened before.*

'There are survivors,' Holly said. 'I emerged close to *their* Coldbrook and met Drake. He told me a little.'

'But the thing that came through,' Jonah said. 'All those things in Control. Forty years old?'

'They call them furies.'

'Furies. Good name.'

'But there's hope!' Holly said.

'Hope?' he blurted, feeling the attention of something unknowable focused on the back of his neck. He glanced around, but there was nothing to see. When he looked back Holly had her eyes closed.

'There's hope hidden in the deep basements of their Coldbrook,' she said. 'His name's Mannan, and he's immune to the furies' bite.'

'Immune,' Jonah said. He breathed in the word and let it settle. In his mind's eye he saw that Inquisitor monster watching him, waiting.

6

Jonah poured a drink while Holly fired up a laptop. As she accessed the CCTV log to see what had happened moments before the power outage, she recalled the Gaia survivors projecting images of her own world's destruction onto fluid screens. Her own technology suddenly seemed inferior; the program froze for a few seconds, screen flickering. She felt disassociated from what she was doing, as if she had left a part of herself back through the breach, and she realised that no one knew what effect passing through might have.

'Maybe I've doomed myself,' she muttered.

'I think we've all done that,' Jonah said. He placed a glass containing warm orange juice beside her.

'I always said you should have let me show you how to use these things,' Holly said.

'I can use computers.'

'Sure. But you don't understand them.' She sat back and viewed the screen, tapping the mouse button to advance the log instant by instant.

'That's what you're paid for.' Jonah sipped his own juice and stared at his glass, and she knew that he was thinking the same as her.

'So, the Inquisitor,' she said, failing to sound casual.

'What did your Drake tell you?' Jonah asked.

She shrugged. 'Not much. Just that it was there too.'

'He haunts me,' Jonah said, and then he stretched back in his chair and closed his eyes. Holly glanced sidelong at him and saw an old man made older by this disaster. Then she concentrated on scanning systems until she found what she was looking for.

'Well, seems I'm owed overtime. And a bonus. Because I can tell you why the power went off.'

'Can you fix it?'

'Maybe.' She froze the screen and turned the laptop to him.

Jonah leaned on her shoulder and glanced at the screen. 'What am I looking at?'

'Schematic. Look.' Holly pointed at the routings indicated, and the red-boxed area that showed where the problem was. 'There's a duct around the core. Carries cables from the ancillary generator to feed Coldbrook's life-supports and energy requirements. And it's fucked.'

'So what fucked it?'

'Dunno.'

'Can you *un*fuck it?'

Holly laughed, unused to hearing Jonah swearing so harshly.

'What?'

'You. Trying to sound American. "Unfuck." Would they know that word in your Welsh valleys?'

'Unfuck the problem, Miss Wright. That's an order.'

'It's Ms I'm a modern American lady.' She tapped a few more keys and memorised the location of the fault, trying pointlessly to access some of the webcams that had been set up in the duct. Their playback logs had been damaged. Power surge, she guessed. She tried some other routes, working hard, concentrating, and if it hadn't been for the darkness that was all she could access she might have believed for a moment that nothing was wrong.

'Jonah,' she said. 'I know where the problem is, and I might be able to fix it. But I'll need a gun, just in case. And . . .' She looked up, briefly blinded against the darkened room by the computer screen's glow. For a second she thought there was something standing behind Jonah. But it was only his shadow.

'And?' he asked.

'Will you be all right?'

He didn't answer right away. The silence made Holly uncomfortable, because it was Jonah betraying weakness and fear. However badly things had gone wrong, she wanted him to be her rock.

'To be honest, I thought I'd come with you.'

And Holly was happy with that.

They headed for the narrow staircase that led down to the maintenance levels surrounding the core. Each of them carried a heavy torch, and Holly had stopped by an equipment room to collect a tool belt. She'd also accepted a gun from Jonah and tucked it into her waistband.

They'd passed the gym door from behind which came a steady, insistent scratching. *Two in there*, Jonah had whispered.

'Here,' Holly said when they reached their destination. 'You been in here since?'

'No.'

The door to the small plant room was closed. It housed two large electrical distribution boards and an access walkway into the secure housing around the core. If she'd read the diagnostic information correctly, the problem had occurred somewhere between the plant room and the core.

'Right.' Holly hefted the gun, feeling awkward. She hadn't fired a gun in years. 'Maybe I should take that.' She nodded at the crossbow that Jonah had brought with him.

'Confined space?' he said, raising one eyebrow.

Holly opened the door while Jonah stood back, his gun and torch aimed. She prepared herself for a surge of activity – movement, shouting, gunshots. But after a few moments her old boss sighed quietly and nodded.

'Don't nod off while I'm in there,' she said. 'I know what you old guys are like.' She turned away from his glare, smiling as she entered the small room. The tool belt was heavy around her waist, and she held the gun in her right hand, pointing the way.

She swept the torch's beam around the room. It was as she remembered it – it seemed to have been left untouched by what had happened. She gave the distribution boards a cursory glance and saw no immediate problems. The space was narrow, and she had to turn sidelong to squeeze past the boards and into the narrow passageway beyond.

The walls here were bare concrete, lined with cables and wire ducts, old routes marked out by pocked holes. Her belt scraped one wall, and a shower of grit and dust fell softly to the metal gangway. She shone the torch down into darkness.

'Okay in there?' Jonah called. His voice was muffled, even though he was only about twelve feet away.

'Yeah. Nearly there.'

She shone the torch along the gangway and moved on. When she reached the end it split and curved left and right around the outer extremes of the core-containment wall. A deep darkness dropped below to where the core's base was cast into rock. It was to the left that she hoped the problem lay.

She spotted them from several feet away. At first she thought it was a pile of old clothing, perhaps left there by the maintenance crews. But then she saw that the dim shape was more than a heap of discarded clothes.

'Anything?' Jonah called, and she could barely hear him. The gap she had crossed swallowed his voice.

'Won't be long,' she said, and, as her own voice echoed away above and below, shadows around the shape moved.

But it was only the shifting torchlight. Holly stepped forward and saw two people who'd been fried by the massive electrical current that had passed through them both. One – she thought it was a man – was holding a long metal pole. The other corpse was beyond identification, and it had its arms wrapped around its burned chest, face buried against its stomach. Clothes had burned. Flesh and hair had burned as well, and she wondered how the fire had not spread further.

One had been attacking, one defending. The final defence had been suicide.

Though the power was out, Holly still stayed a couple of steps away, examining the mess of scorched flesh and material and trying to see where one body ended and the other began. It was grotesque. She felt sick and unsettled, shining her torch across motionless bodies.

She stamped her foot and made some noise. No movement. The brain could be destroyed in more ways than one, but she still had to be careful.

Undoing her tool belt, she took out a telescopic wooden pointer and started nudging at the bodies. The pointer sank in and she cringed in disgust – the disturbance seemed to release the smell. It rose around her and she tried breathing through her mouth, but then she could taste the greasy reality of death.

Gotta get this done as quickly as possible. She fixed a voltmeter to the end of the pointer and started testing the bodies and the equipment they had melted into for any signs of power. There were none.

Holly got to work.

She had to scrape cooked flesh away from the damaged control panel. Some of it crumbled away and that was fine, but some was still moist. It stank. She gagged in the confined space, determined not to vomit because that would only add to the reek. She tried not to identify what she was seeing, but sometimes the fingernails were obvious, and she had to crack a jawbone to prise teeth from around a thick cable.

She worked at the damage, and every now and then she heard Jonah calling her name. 'Almost done,' she said several times, and she lost track of time as she worked. The toolkit carried some spares, but in other areas she had to steal fittings from boards and equipment which she knew were non-essential. Six feet from here was a TV and audio distribution panel, and she didn't think that she and Jonah would be watching reruns of *Lost* again any time soon.

The first time she heard the scraping she thought she'd dropped and trodden on one of her tools. Immersed as she was in the repair work, she did not check. The second time, she knew that she had not moved at all.

'Hear something,' Jonah shouted.

Holly looked down. The corpses were moving. The part grabbing for her was identifiable only by its watch, and even then it was barely recognisable as a hand.

She grabbed for her gun and dropped it. It bounced, flipped between the gangway's safety rails, and she heard its impact down in the dark a few seconds later.

'Jonah!'

'. . . to check . . .' she heard, his voice further away than ever.

'Jonah!'

The thing shifted for her, rising up. As a hand grasped her belt and pulled her down, Holly tried to scream.

7

Jonah didn't want to leave but the noises drew him away.

It wasn't until Holly had returned through the breach that he had acknowledged his ownership of this place. Being here on his own had been bad enough, but now that Holly had seen what had become of Coldbrook he was suddenly more protective of the facility. It was a part of him that had been hurt.

Holly was working hard to repair the power, and simply waiting out in the corridor felt far too passive. She was safe. She would succeed.

And that noise . . .

As Jonah hurried along the corridor curving around the core he tried to analyse the sound. It was a distant whisper, yet he knew it would be loud close-up. Scratching and whipping, like twigs or branches scraping against a window.

At the foot of the narrow stairs he suddenly knew where the noise was coming from, and realised that he should have known from the beginning. He glanced back the way he'd come, listening for Holly. All was quiet. So he passed the staircase and continued along to Control, afraid that the Inquisitor would be waiting for him around every bend.

Even before he approached Control's glass wall, he could see the frenetic movement within. Strange torchlight was flickering and fading as something moved across the large room.

He moved to the glass and looked in. Something ricocheted from the wall, leaving a wide, starred impact mark. *An arrow!* Jonah jerked back.

Sweet Jesus.

The conflict raged in silence behind the glass. A fury turned towards him and climbed across one of the work-stations, knocking a broken computer screen to the floor, sprawling out of sight and then standing again. It came for him, striking the window and rebounding, then bashing at the glass with knotted fists. Bits of it broke away. It was very, very old, and this close he could see that its eyes were shrivelled and dry.

Several shadows stood or squatted just within the breach, firing bolts and arrows into the mass of zombies. Jonah checked the furniture that he and Holly had piled outside the doors. It seemed secure. But he was shaken, and as he backed away along the corridor everything inside him screamed at him to wait. Soon they would be through, and he wanted to be there for that moment.

He wanted to see those people from another Earth. But he had a responsibility to Holly, and even more so to Coldbrook.

Furies fell, and the air in Control filled with the dust of ages.

8

Holly brought the screwdriver down again and again, each impact juddering through her hand and wrist and arm. In the wild torchlight bits spattered across her thighs and stomach, and she screamed to rid herself of the sickening noise, and retched to purge the terrible slick taste of the dead flesh. Now that it moved, it was easier to discern which body part was dead and which was not within this merged mass, because the fury had not begun to rot.

It fell away from her, its burned hands slipping down her body. The face was shattered from twenty impacts from the screwdriver, thirty, more. She kept striking until all movement ceased.

'Jonah,' she croaked, unable to shout. 'Jonah.' But she no longer needed Jonah. She stopped stabbing. The screwdriver felt like an extension of her hand, and she was unsure she'd ever be able to rid herself of its feel.

Holly turned away from what she had done.

'Few switches blown,' she said. Her hoarse voice was

surprisingly loud in the dark space. She kept the torch beam on the tangled bodies, and now neither of them moved. Each time she breathed she tasted death. 'I can take them from other boards. Clean it down. Make sure there's no . . . stuff still causing shorts.'

Talking to herself made it easier. She set to work again, slipping the screwdriver into her pocket first and wiping her hands on her trousers.

She cleaned the damaged board, bypassing a melted area, replacing wires with temporary cold-set solder, moving switches, cannibalising the distribution board that served the entertainment system.

Holly closed her eyes after a few minutes and took a deep breath, then carried on.

When she'd finished she stepped back, looking down at the corpses.

I got it all over my hands.

She flicked a lever switch on the board and heard the hum of power.

Under my nails, in the creases of my skin, and maybe I cut myself with the screwdriver.

From the plant room she saw a faint glow of light, and knew that her repair had worked, for now.

Jonah should be shouting but he's not there, or if he is he's waiting for me with his mouth open, his eyes empty.

'Jonah?' she said. She made her way back through to the plant room.

Jonah was not waiting there.

Outside, the corridor lights were on again, and she heard that low background hum of Coldbrook that until now she hadn't realised had been absent. *The hum of life*, she thought, and she had never welcomed the thudding of her heart so much.

If she became a fury, would it cease?

Next to the plant room was a small closet-type door, and behind it she found stacks of cleaning equipment and products. The bleach was in a large industrial bottle, unbranded and strong, and Holly poured it over her hands, rubbing them together and crying as the fumes got into her eyes. She gagged, pouring more bleach because maybe the first splash hadn't got right down into her nails, or into those wounds she could not see. It burned. It hurt.

When arms closed around her from behind she almost screamed, but then she smelled Jonah's familiar breath and allowed herself to collapse against him.

'Hey, hey,' he said, taking the screwdriver from her hand. She hadn't even realised that she'd drawn it from her pocket.

'Jonah,' she gasped.

'You did it.'

'There was one of those . . . one of them . . .'

'Come on,' he said, and he was as strong as ever. 'Hurry.'

'What?'

'I think your friends are coming to find you.'

'Drake?'

'I'm a little disappointed, truth be told. It means I don't get to go through and find him.'

With Coldbrook lit up and alive around them once more, Jonah led her towards Control.

As they reached the window, Holly saw Drake and the people he had brought through the breach with him. Most of them were gathered by the doorway. They were all heavily armed, and several of them patrolled the room, stabbing fallen furies through the head.

Drake and Jonah gazed at each other, and Holly knew that this was the true meeting of worlds.

Wednesday

1

From the moment they left Baltimore, Vic knew without asking that the helicopter was over-burdened. Gary concentrated on flying, and for the next hour Vic saw the pilot glancing nervously at readings on the display panel that Vic could not see, and probably would not have understood if he had seen them. It would do no good mentioning it to anyone else. Things were bad enough already, and Lucy had always been a nervous flyer.

There was plenty of air traffic. Most of it was military – Chinooks, heavy transports, and fast jets that screamed across the sky. But there were also private flights, mostly helicopters. Once they saw a distant speck in the sky spinning earthward, and watched as it struck the ground and bloomed into flame.

'Marc, I just want to check out the map,' Vic said. He opened Marc's laptop and casually angled it away from Olivia and Lucy.

Marc paused for only a moment before he realised what Vic meant. 'Click on US-map-red,' he said, without turning around.

'Right.'

'For the world map, it's world-map-red.'

Vic opened the map of North America first. The clock in the screen's corner refreshed and started skipping forward from zero. In seconds it had passed Day One, and the spread of red dots merged and flowed like spilled paint. He tried to keep his face neutral, tried to keep the screen turned away from Olivia and Lucy's line of vision. But his wife leaned over their daughter's head and tilted the screen her way.

As the counter hit Day Four and clicked over a few more hours, the spread was extensive. The entire eastern seaboard was solid red, and to the west there were concentrations of colour, mainly centred around cities and the coastal regions. Looking at the screen chilled him, and when Lucy turned away without even acknowledging him he grew colder still.

'What about France?' Sean asked, leaning across and

tapping Vic's knee. He had realised what Vic was looking at. Beside him Jayne stirred, also waiting for the reply.

Vic closed the window and opened the world-map-red file. It took longer for this program to load, and with the timer starting from zero again the spread of red was slower, and less detailed. The spots spread across the map like measles. North America had the greatest concentration, South America was speckled more heavily to the north, and Alaska and Russia were also infected. Europe sprouted its first spots in Britain and Spain, and they spread quickly to the south and east, appearing all across northern Europe before heading towards the Middle East. Africa developed its own blemishes. The old Eastern Bloc countries succumbed. It looked as though a child had flicked its paintbrush at the screen before taking a breath and then concentrating on colouring in certain areas more fully.

Sean clicked off his safety belt and leaned over the open screen, looking at the mass of red slowly filling out France and Britain. He remained motionless for a few seconds, then quietly sat back down and refastened his belt.

Jayne whispered something in his ear and he nodded, unable to look at her. 'And England?' Vic heard her say. Sean's hard expression did not change. Vic saw their sadness and grief, and he closed the laptop and switched it off, unable to look any more.

His heart was racing and he felt sick, and even though he heard Marc's voice hissing from the headphones around his neck, and the man was turned around in his seat, Vic could not move his hands to slip them on again. Marc saw his expression and stopped talking, and Vic was glad he did not have a mirror. His face, he knew, told it all.

Panic gripped him, and he considered what the fall would feel like. He could open the door and fall out sideways, sure that Sean would leap across and close the door before anyone else was endangered.

But his family were here.

Just before he thought he might go mad and start screaming, Lucy took his hand. He could not bear to look at her, in case that uncertainty was still in her eyes. But he took comfort from the contact, and allowed himself to calm down.

They flew on, the silence between them heavier than before, weighted with knowledge and consequence.

Half an hour later Olivia started prodding him and said that his pocket was beeping. Vic pulled out the satphone. There was a message waiting, and the name on the screen was the last he'd expected to see.

'What?' Lucy asked.

'Jonah.' He read the message. It was from just before they'd lost contact with the Welshman. He must have sent it but it had failed to transmit, and now for some reason it had come through late. Vic sighed, because it could mean nothing. Perhaps he was about to read the old man's final message.

And look after that family of yours, you bastard, the message read. Vic smiled and showed it to Lucy. She pointed at the phone.

'What?'

'Next to Jonah's name.'

And Vic slapped his forehead because he had been so stupid. The small green square meant that Jonah was available, the line between them live, and that *must* mean something good.

'Marc!' Vic said, slinging on his headset. 'I think I might be in touch with Jonah.' He called Jonah's speed-dial and held the phone to his ear. Somewhere in Coldbrook a satphone might be ringing, and Vic could not help imagining what might be hearing that noise, the things passing it by.

And he could not help thinking of Jonah as one of *them.* Much as he and the old man had never really been friends, the idea of such an ignominious end for Jonah broke Vic's heart.

The phone was answered.

'Vic?'

'Holly?' he gasped, feeling a surge of emotion. 'Jesus, *Holly!*'

'Vic! You're okay, you and Olivia and Lucy?'

'We're fine, all fine. We're flying from Baltimore back to—'

'What are you doing there?'

'Long story. But you! Jonah said you went through. Did you? What happened? And where is he?'

'Right here with me,' Holly said. She sounded close enough to touch, and an unbidden image flashed across Vic's mind – Holly naked in his small room down in Coldbrook, smiling contentedly, skin flushed and hair awry. He blinked hard and looked at Lucy, mouthing *Jonah's okay*. She nodded and smiled.

'I haven't been able to reach him,' he said. 'I thought he was—'

'What's it like out there, Vic?' Holly asked. He wasn't sure how to answer. Wasn't sure he *wanted* to.

'It's bad,' he said. Across from him, Jayne averted her eyes and Sean looked out of the helicopter window. Dawn had smeared itself across the landscape, and the sun was trying to break through clouds of smoke heavy in the air. Somewhere to the south of them, a city burned. 'And it's spreading.'

'How far?'

'Everywhere,' he said.

'Washington? New York? What about south, how far south?'

'Everywhere, Holly. South America. Europe. It's . . .'

He heard her repeating this information, and even below the helicopter's thudding rotors he heard Jonah's voice.

'Pass it over,' Jonah said in the background, then he was on the line. 'Vic. It's good to hear you. But Europe?'

'We think so.'

'Where are you now?'

'We're airborne from Baltimore back to Cincinnati.'

'Is Baltimore okay? What the hell were you doing there?'

'No, it's fucked,' Vic said. Marc was leaning back over the seats with his hand held out, gesturing with his fingers: *Pass the phone.* 'Jonah, Marc wants to talk,' Vic said. 'But you're okay down there?'

'Yes,' Jonah said, but everything about the tone of his voice said *No!* 'Sitting here right now with my other.'

'Your what?' Vic said, confused.

'From over there. My opposite, from through the breach. It's seriously fucked there, too.'

'Oh, Jesus.' Vic stared at Jayne where she leaned against Sean. Her eyes were drooping, and her skin looked incredibly pale. It wasn't just the early-morning light. 'Jonah, we went to Baltimore to get someone who's immune.'

'Immune?' Jonah said. Behind his voice Vic heard others, a babble of excitement. One was Holly's; he didn't recognise anyone else's.

'Here. Marc.' Vic passed him the phone and sat back down.

'Are we going to see Uncle Jonah?' Olivia asked, and Vic shook his head, stroking her chin when she pouted in disappointment.

Marc talked briefly into the phone, then snapped it shut.

'That was quick,' Lucy said.

'Yeah.'

'So who was that?' Sean asked.

'Friends of ours,' Vic said. He didn't think explaining would be for the best. *We made a hole into another reality and the zombie plague came through and I let it out and now it's spread everywhere and . . .*

'Glad they're safe,' Sean said.

'Me too.'

Marc was talking to Gary, headphones pulled back so they could communicate directly. Gary was shaking his head slowly, tapping a couple of dials on the control display before him. Marc became more animated, glancing back into the cabin. He was looking at where Jayne and Sean sat with their backs to him, and Vic knew what was being discussed even before Marc addressed them.

'Change of plan,' Marc said.

'We're going to Coldbrook,' Vic said. 'Good idea.'

'Hope so.' Marc gave him a piercing glare, then turned around again.

'Why are we going back there?' Lucy asked. 'I don't want to go back. I don't want to *see*.'

'Not Danton Rock,' Vic said. 'Straight to Coldbrook.' He didn't want to see what had become of their home town either.

He realised that Marc had kept his satphone, but he couldn't really blame him.

Gary turned the helicopter and the angle of sunlight across the cabin changed. *Back to Coldbrook. Scene of the crime.*

Lucy leaned in and rested her head on his shoulder, and Vic found himself looking at Sean. They exchanged a smile. It did nothing to fill Vic's hollow heart.

2

We're the different sides of the same coin, Jonah thought, but even that idea felt wrong. As he watched Drake sitting upright at Coldbrook's library table, nervous and proud, gaze constantly flickering to the wall of books that gave the room depth and warmth, the truth was much more miraculous. They were more than like-minded.

'It's not the best,' Jonah said. 'I smashed my last bottle of Irish. This is a nasty blended make. Cheap. Harsh. But we'll just have to make do.' He poured two fingers into each of the four glasses, and felt everyone's stare upon him.

'Jameson's was my father's favourite,' Drake said. 'But

I've never tried it. Someone from our Coldbrook once found a bottle of Knob Creek.' He took the glass that Jonah offered him, smiling his thanks. 'For days after I couldn't see straight.'

'That's some rough stuff,' Jonah agreed, lifting his own glass. Holly took her drink, still shaken. She was sitting very close to Jonah, and he could feel the fear coming off her in waves. Beside Drake was a woman who'd introduced herself as Moira. *A lovely Welsh name*, Jonah had said, but the woman had not reacted.

'We should drink a toast,' Jonah said. Drake and Moira startled him by standing, and he and Holly followed suit.

Drake stared unflinchingly at Jonah. There was an ease between them that was almost friendship. It felt good, but Jonah could not yet bring himself to trust it, not after what Holly had told him. Everything was so strange.

'Five days ago I drank to success,' Jonah said.

'Huh. Well, then, how about to survival?' Holly raised her glass to Drake. 'You've managed it for forty years. We've only just begun.' Before anyone else could echo her toast she drank the whisky, grimacing slightly as she sat down and placed the glass on the table.

'Survival,' Jonah said, and Drake and Moira agreed. They drank, Jonah refilled everyone's glass, and they made themselves comfortable again.

Fourteen other people had shot their way through the

breach with Drake. They had not lost one person to the furies. Two of them had collapsed in Control, and one was still unconscious. The effect of the breach, Drake had said, and Jonah had noted Holly nodding in understanding. *I'll feel that soon*, he'd thought. Because there was one thing he was determined to do, furies or no furies, Inquisitor or no Inquisitor. And that was to see Earth as it was in another universe. He'd spent so much of his life seeking it, and despite everything he could not deny himself that experience.

Holly had yet to make a full inventory of the damage done to their control room, but Jonah didn't want any buttons pushed in case processes started or ended accidentally. The breach itself was stable, linked directly through the core, but there were a hundred other accidents waiting to happen.

Three other Gaians were in the library with them, delightedly perusing the walls of books. Jonah had already realised that their ragged appearance belied their intelligence.

'I'm sorry about the man I hit,' Holly said. 'And the breach guards . . .'

Jonah noted Moira's expression hardening, but Drake nodded. 'And we apologise for Mannan,' he said.

Holly waved a hand, dismissing something she had yet to tell Jonah about. She poured more whisky and sipped, sighing and sinking into her chair.

'So, welcome to our Earth,' Jonah said.

'Take me to your leader,' Drake said.

'If only I could.' Jonah's smile became heavy. 'After Coldbrook's power went down, I lost track of what was happening up above. But Holly's filled me in. She said you're able to see through the eyes of the furies?'

'Our casting technology, yes.'

'You built a window, we made a door,' Holly said.

'You're still one step ahead of me,' said Jonah. 'I'm the only person in the room who's still a one-world horse.'

'We must change that,' Drake said.

'This casting . . . how do you do it? Is there temporal dislocation? How does the targeting work?'

'I can tell you,' Drake said. 'But I'm sure you'd rather see for yourself, wouldn't you?'

'Probably not,' Holly said. 'It was . . . horrible.'

'We've come from a dead world to see your world dying,' Drake said.

Jonah felt a spark of anger. 'We're not finished yet. There's hope.'

'Hope?' Moira mocked.

'Holly tells me that you have someone immune to the disease. I assume you've been studying him?'

'For a long time,' Drake said.

'And they test him,' Holly said. 'They let him get bitten again and again. *Chunks* have been taken out of him.'

Drake and Moira shifted uncomfortably, but Drake recovered quickly. 'You can't judge us. I won't allow it.'

'Allow?' Holly scoffed. 'He tried to—'

'And I apologised for that,' Drake said.

'That was a mistake, Holly,' Moira said. 'You're precious to us. We'd have suggested that more subtly.'

'Suggested what?' Jonah asked.

'They try to reproduce Mannan's immunity,' Holly said. 'And when I found him, he thought I was there to . . .' She pressed her lips tightly together. 'To be *impregnated*.'

'He was still curled in a ball last time I saw him,' Moira said, her eyes sparkling. 'You certainly know how to look after yourself.'

Drake leaned forward suddenly and grasped Holly's hand.

'I was born into a place you can't understand. Everything I know of my Earth before the End is from books, or recordings, or knowledge and stories handed down from my father. It's not even a memory for me. And though some of us are resigned, I've *never* been able to let go of hope. Mannan is an oddity that none of us has ever been able to figure out, and that's a frustration and a complication.'

'Where did he come from?' Jonah asked.

'Forty years ago, in the midst of our epidemic, my father heard about him,' Drake said. 'Mannan was barely a teenager at the time. He was bitten in Illinois, survived, and my father did everything he could to get him to Coldbrook. There's quite a legend built around it. Many died in their efforts to save Mannan, and for a time – well, my father remembered it as a time of hope . . .' Drake trailed off, not needing to say what had happened afterwards. No cure, no inoculation.

'And he's the only one?' Jonah asked.

'Who knows?' Moira asked. 'Could be others on other continents. But we don't travel. People came from France six years ago,' she said, shrugging. 'Three years before that, a group travelled up from South America. They brought news, but none of it good. So there *are* travellers, but not many. And their life expectancy is short. Knowledge is dying.'

'But you have your casters,' Jonah said.

'Between veils,' Drake said. 'But not across oceans. That would be like you using your breach to travel to the next town – impractical and, so we found, impossible.'

'How do they work?' Jonah asked.

'Our casting engines create mini-black holes, we stabilise them, and the casters move across the resulting Einstein-Rosen bridge.'

'How do you deal with the Hawking radiation?'

'Hawking?'

Jonah frowned. 'No Hawking? Well . . . the overflow radiation.'

'Oh. We feed it back via a second black hole within the first.'

'Neat,' Jonah said. 'But only their consciousness goes through?'

'Of course,' Drake said. 'They want to come back.'

'Jonah, the processes don't *matter!*' Holly said. 'It's sharing our knowledge of the furies that's important.'

'Mannan,' Jonah said.

'Yes,' Drake said, pouring them all another drink. 'We've tested his blood, transplanted his DNA, examined every part of him again and again. Brain scans, cell cultures. We regularly try to impregnate volunteers, but we fear he's infertile. That could be bad luck, or something to do with his immunity.'

'I want to meet him,' Jonah said.

'You're a doctor?' Drake asked.

'No, but I know one. Marc Dubois, the best.'

They drank. The air between Jonah and Drake was loaded, with positive potential rather than with tension.

'I know something about your world,' Jonah said softly. 'More than Holly told me. I've been *shown* more.'

Moira's eyes went wide, but Drake only nodded.

'We thought so,' he said. 'We believed it was Holly to begin with, *hoped* it was, because she's so strong.' Jonah sensed Holly absorbing the compliment, and he hoped she was buoyed by it. 'But then she mentioned you, and I knew.'

'The Inquisitor,' Jonah said. 'I thought perhaps I was going mad.'

'Are you keeping a diary?' Drake asked.

'No. Never been much of a diarist.'

'Why do you ask?' Holly said.

'Because the woman whom the Inquisitor took from our world kept a diary before she went. We've gleaned much from that.'

Jonah looked past Drake at the other visitors poring over books, holding them like newborns as they turned the pages carefully. Perhaps they really were the most precious of things – their power could not be cut off, and their batteries would never run out.

'He showed me things,' Jonah said. 'Holly, the morning we breached he showed me the death of the world we had just found our way to. I didn't know it then, but now . . .' He glanced from Drake to Moira. 'It's tragic.'

'What did you see?' Moira asked.

'People dying. Being herded into trucks. An American flag with too few stars. Burning fields, black glass deserts. Stranger things, but all to do with the disease those furies are spreading, I guess. And the Inquisitor told me—'

'"It is required that you accept",' Drake said.

'From your woman's diary?' Jonah asked.

Drake nodded, glanced at the bottle, and Holly poured some more.

'But it's not all our world,' he said softly.

'What?' Holly gasped.

'What it showed Jonah. Those sights. They weren't all views of Gaia.'

'But . . . how can you know?' Holly asked.

'Your casters,' Jonah said, a dreadful realisation striking home. He felt weak, numb. 'Not just our world, Drake. How many others do you watch?'

Drake drained his whisky again, and his expression changed. Jonah had recognised his excitement at being there, and seen his own intelligence echoed in the man's eyes. But now there was something else – something like fear.

'Many. We don't cast so much now. The energy levels required are massive, and our matter fields have been failing for years.'

'But we've been watching your world, and it gave us hope,' Moira said.

'Not hope enough to stop something coming through,' Jonah said.

'And that guilt is on me,' Drake said. 'I should have posted more guards. Been more careful.'

'But what of all the other Earths you've seen?' Holly asked.

'Over the past decade, I'd say that one in a hundred we've cast to is uninfected,' Moira said.

There was a stunned silence.

'I assumed it *started* in Gaia forty years ago,' Holly said softly. 'So how was your world infected?'

'A breach, similar to your own but more violent. It caused a quake. It was thought that our casting attracted that Earth's attention, but I don't know. Now we believe there are endless people like you and us across the multiverse, striving to explore, looking to travel. And chance dictates that such undertakings will cross paths, here and there.'

'As we did with you,' Jonah said.

Drake nodded.

'This breach into your world,' Jonah said. 'Something came through.'

'We knew what it was. We'd been casting for ten years by then. The breach was half a mile from Coldbrook, and the army guarded it. It all went military very quickly.'

'We should have guarded our Coldbrook better,' Holly said, but Drake shook his head.

'It would have made no difference. The breach remained static for almost a year. My father and his team experimented, sending in drones, animals. But it was solid, like a mirror. Everything I've read and the memory casts I've viewed . . . everyone thought it was benign. They built a structure to encase it, and closed it off from view. And then the fury came through. Chaos found a way.'

'It's still there?' Holly asked. 'Their breach?'

'Sealed up.' Drake nodded.

'And you never tried to go through?' Jonah asked.

'No,' Drake said. 'My father saw no point.'

'So the Inquisitor,' Jonah said, trying to take it all in, trying to absorb the end of everything when Coldbrook was always meant to be the beginning of something wonderful. 'He spreads the plague?'

'No, no,' Drake replied. 'There's not one Inquisitor, but many. They *oversee* the spread, record it, and recruit a new Inquisitor for every world killed.'

'And that means we now have a chance to fight back,' Moira said.

'But how do you *know* all this is true?' Holly asked.

Drake sighed. 'It's largely conjecture. But maybe now we'll have the chance to test.' For the first time he looked away from Jonah as he spoke. To Jonah, that didn't bode well.

'The woman,' Jonah said. 'The diaries.'

'Her name was Kathryn Coldbrook,' Drake said. 'My father worked with her fifty years ago, just after she and her organisation had performed the first casting through the veils. The casters became very famous.' He snorted. 'I have her biography. Our world was open to wonder back then, so my father told me. Receptive to it.'

'Not cynical,' Holly said.

'Well, I think we'd barely be human without healthy cynicism,' Drake said. 'I don't think Kathryn was a very nice woman. Father told me she was an unpleasant genius – single-minded, arrogant, and didn't suffer fools gladly.'

Holly glanced at Jonah, one corner of her mouth turned up. He raised an eyebrow.

'But she was brilliant,' Drake continued. 'My father worshipped her memory, and he must have read her diary a hundred times. The experiments, the celebration when they made their first cast. The Inquisitor visiting her. That came over as a madness, of course, but now we know better.'

'She's viewed as a monster now,' Moira said. Jonah was taken aback by such a comment, and surprised at some of their almost mystical phraseology – veils, monsters.

'That's not her fault,' Drake said. 'Understand, this is all gleaned from her diaries, with plenty of guesswork thrown in. But my father always said Kathryn had a unique mind. He said she was able to embrace the imagination in her scientific studies. She was even . . .' He frowned.

'She had *faith*,' Moira sneered, as if the word tasted foul. Jonah thought that he would have to ask about that.

'Maybe that made it easier for the bastard thing to take her,' Drake said. 'I've always wondered. Though she was a woman of science, she was also a slave to mysticism.'

'So what the hell *is* that thing haunting me?' Jonah said.

'Someone who perhaps has a sense of humour. Your world had the Spanish Inquisition?'

Jonah nodded.

'We believe that they are Inquisitors of the multiverse, from a version of Earth so thoroughly obsessed by and convinced of their own exclusive holiness that they cannot allow any other.'

'Cannot allow?' Jonah said.

'Maybe they found the fury disease in one reality, grasped its potential, and encouraged its spread,' Drake continued. 'Or maybe they conceived and released it themselves. Nurtured it from world to world to destroy everyone not of their Earth.'

'That's . . .' Holly shook her head.

'Genocide,' Jonah said.

'Billions killed across the multiverse,' Drake said. 'Trillions. Beyond counting. Infected, and waiting to rise again to attack those not infected. Every Earth explores, and when they break through to what they think will be somewhere similar they find furies.'

'And there aren't many worlds still holding out,' Moira said.

'Yours is!' Jonah said. 'Forty years you've been surviving, and—'

'You can hardly call it surviving,' Drake said, his composure slipping. 'It's barely existing.'

'You said we might be able to fight back,' Holly said. 'What did you mean? How can you defeat something that's already won?'

'Kathyrn Coldbrook's diaries,' Drake said. 'She sensed something observing her even before she and my father succeeded with their first casting. In later entries she reveals her belief that her Inquisitor guided her towards success, though not quite the success he intended. And following our eventual infection he courted her, preying on her guilt with nightmare images that she noted in her diary. Some of which you might recognise, Jonah, were you to read it.'

'I don't think I want to.'

'The last few pages are very confused. Painful to read. So much self-doubt as she denied what she was seeing, what the Inquisitor was doing to her. As he was *luring* her. It's as if she was trying to keep hold of herself, but also being torn in other ways. And one day . . . she vanished.'

Silence descended, and Jonah glanced at the other three people around the table. Drake and Moira displayed a sadness that seemed to fit their hard faces well: a familiar emotion. Holly was staring down at her hands.

'Bill Coldbrook died,' Jonah said. 'I took over his work.'

'And have you ever felt watched?' Drake said, leaning forward again.

'Yes,' Jonah said. 'And so did Bill. I think that made him paranoid and drove him to suicide.'

'And now an Inquisitor is after Jonah,' Holly said.

'They take you,' Drake said. 'That's what Kathryn seemed to imply. Across secret bridges and through unknown wormholes those bastards have created with technology that must be so similar to yours, or ours. They take you back and *convert* you. And then you go out as one of them and oversee the destruction of another Earth.'

'This was meant to be so special,' Jonah said.

'Countless Earths think that.'

'So those things helped us to make the breach?' Holly asked. She sounded hurt, and Jonah felt the same. He thought back to Bill before his suicide, what he had accomplished, the breakthroughs he had made, and Jonah tried to see where the tipping point had been. It had still taken them ten years after Bill died to complete the project, and there had been several failed attempts. But they could never have succeeded without Bill's radical, groundbreaking work as their foundation. And somewhere in that foundation had been a rock cast by something alien.

'It's pure evil,' Jonah said.

'So you have to *fight* it!' Holly said. 'It might not be over.'

Holly felt a rush of hope. Drake had shown her views of her own blighted world in the casting room, and Vic had confirmed those images in their short conversation.

But now they had a chance – a challenge – and they had to grasp it and make it work.

And Vic was coming back.

'We need access to Mannan,' Jonah said.

Moira and Drake leaned in close to each other, whispered something that no one else could hear: urgent, serious. Then Drake stood and shook his head.

'Not here,' he said. 'We can't bring him here.'

'We don't need to.' Jonah stood as well, walked around the table and stood in front of the man from another world.

He held out his hand.

After a moment's hesitation Drake took it, and smiled. 'That's something I thought I'd never do,' he said. 'Shaking hands is so . . . mannered. It's something we only ever see in memory casts.'

Holly found Drake compelling, almost hypnotic. He carried himself well, and had a natural grace and intelligence. But she realised now that there was something else – he was completely out of place here, no matter how relaxed he seemed.

'You must go through,' Holly said. 'You *have* to, Jonah. I'll stay here and wait for Vic and the others. I can check the systems, make sure the repair holds, run some diagnostics on the core. And I'll try and figure out how to get them down here when they arrive.'

'Perhaps Moira can stay with you?' Drake suggested.

'She services our casting-field generators. I'm sure she'd be fascinated with your technology.'

'Yes!' Moira said.

'Of course,' Holly said. 'She saved my life. I owe her a tour, at least.'

'I'll leave this with you,' Jonah said, placing his satphone on the table. 'Marc thinks they're three or four hours out.' He waved her over and they embraced. 'Get them in safe and sound. The girl's precious. She might be priceless.'

3

Jayne felt the churu settling into her joints and bones, seizing them, a shadow in her mind that was grinning in anticipation at her having to move again. Worse, they were now all talking about her. Sean had tried slipping off her headphones, thinking she was asleep. But she'd slapped his hand away, felt his chest moving as he laughed softly, realising more and more how strong she was. Or, at least, how strong she wanted to be. Leaning against him was the only thing that made her feel remotely safe, and she sensed their mutual respect growing. She knew what he had seen of France on the guy's laptop screen. And he was still trying to protect her.

'Because Jonah said they have someone immune on

their side, too,' Marc said. 'That's why we need to get to Coldbrook.'

'So what happens when we get there?' Sean asked.

Marc was silent for a while and Jayne lifted her head to look back, grimacing against the pain. Marc had turned in his seat and was looking down at her, tapping one finger against his headphones.

'Fuck you all!' Jayne said. 'You talk about me, I'm gonna hear it. You have no idea what the fuck I've been through, and who I've seen die, and thanks for rescuing us and everything, but you are *not* gonna talk about me as if I'm not here. Or as if I'm a . . . a fucking *animal*, to be experimented on.'

'Oh, hey,' Marc said, and even through the electronic crackle she could hear the shame in his voice. 'I meant nothing, Jayne.'

'I got a question,' Sean said. 'What the fuck is going on? And that's just for starters. To follow that one up, what the fuck is a "breach"? And who is on the other side? Is this a war?'

'The man said "fuck",' the little girl said, opening her eyes, and Jayne couldn't hold back a laugh. Her mother quickly plucked the headphones from her daughter's ears and hugged her.

'Vic, you want to give them the quick version?' Marc said.

'Well . . .' Vic said, and he glanced nervously between

Jayne and Sean. She tried to sit up straighter, then actually cried out in pain as her hips flared in agony, and growled against the fire searing through her veins.

Vic's wife let out a startled cry.

'Hey, no, I was like this long before I was bitten,' Jayne said, remembering the passengers on the plane – their fear, their pack mentality. This was a much smaller aircraft, with nowhere to run. 'I have a disease called churu. It's not contagious, and—'

'Churu?' Marc said. 'You have *that*?'

'Since birth. It sucks.'

'I'll bet,' he said, thoughtful. 'Tell them, Vic. Then Jayne and I need to talk.'

'Zombies are a disease, and I'm the cure, is that it?' she asked, only half joking. Nobody laughed.

'Well, here's the idiot's guide,' Vic said. 'Coldbrook is a big experimental complex built beneath the Appalachians.'

'Very James Bond,' Sean said.

'My boss Jonah Jones has been there since it began over twenty years ago, and he's been running it for ten, trying to create a path between this world and another. Across the multiverse. Find an alternate Earth.'

'I take it back,' Sean said. 'It's *Stargate*.'

'It's neither,' Vic said defensively. 'It's the most important scientific experiment for decades. It's SETI, with proper funding. It's the Large Hadron Collider, five steps on.'

'Then why haven't I heard of it?' Sean asked.

'You read the scientific journals regularly?' Vic asked, raising an eyebrow.

'It went wrong?' Jayne asked.

'No,' Vic said. 'It went right. More right than we ever really hoped. Jonah's the genius, I'm just an engineer and the science is sometimes beyond me. But the concept of what we were doing set my imagination on fire. And, a week ago, we did it. We formed a breach across the multiverse, between this Earth and another.'

'This came through,' Sean said.

'And it spread.'

'Were there no safeguards?' Jayne asked, amazed, terrified. 'I mean . . . when they first brought back rocks and stuff from the moon, you know? They kept it all locked away. Isolated.'

'There were safeguards,' Vic said. He glanced at his wife and daughter, and his wife looked down into her lap. 'I made a mistake – and it's out because of me.'

Jayne closed her eyes and the first thing she saw was Tommy's head changing shape as the bullet hit him.

'So now . . .' Sean said, and his voice sounded hollow.

'Now we have to try and stop it,' Marc said. 'It's spreading incredibly quickly.'

'How come?' Sean asked. His voice was softer now. Angry. Jayne felt his heart racing.

'It's no normal disease,' Marc said. 'That's a given,

but this fucker is different from anything I can think of. Think of a common cold, spread by airborne particles and contact contagion – rub your nose, open a door, next person who touches the handle can pick it up. Now move that one step on – everyone with the cold does everything they can to spread it. That's this disease. It's active, not passive. It doesn't sit there and wait to be spread, it spreads itself. And infection is instant.' He fell silent, and Jayne could almost hear him thinking.

'Except with me,' Jayne said.

'Yeah,' Marc said. 'Except with you. So tell me about your churu.'

'You sound as if you know it.'

'I'm a phorologist, but before I specialised I did my thesis on rare conditions like yours.'

Jayne told him. About how she'd had the condition ever since she could remember, and when she was a child it had been an inconvenience more than anything – sore feet when she ran too much, aching limbs in the mornings. About how when she hit puberty it grew a hundred times worse, and ever since then she'd lived with the joint pains, the headaches and intermittent churu comas, the daily massages. She said more than she'd told Sean during the hours when they'd been stranded on the jet but held back the tears, because she had defeated self-pity years ago.

'It can't be a coincidence,' Marc said. 'So far there's no confirmation of anyone else surviving a bite, *anywhere*. If you're bitten, and the skin breaks, that's it.'

'What does that mean?' Jayne asked. 'That you can make a cure from my blood?'

'A cure?' Marc shrugged, averting his gaze. 'It takes years to develop vaccines. But we don't have years, or even weeks. We have days.'

'I see,' Jayne said. 'So I'll be experimented upon.'

'Never without your permission,' Marc said, and she could hear the strength in his voice. He was the man in charge here and she was glad for that. He sounded like someone she could trust.

'It'll cost you,' she said, wincing when she tried to smile. 'I like good beer. Imported, preferably British ale.'

Marc chuckled, and the others smiled. It seemed to light up the cabin brighter than daylight ever could.

4

'We believe the Inquisitors favour the geniuses, and the depressives,' Drake said.

'How can you be so sure?'

The tall man smiled, but the expression did not reach his eyes. 'Years of study and guesswork. Kathryn Coldbrook disappeared from sight. I believe that, to accept such a fate, the victim must be without hope.'

'That's why it shows me the fates of worlds,' Jonah said, understanding at last.

He felt the immensity of time, space, and reality, and recognised his own size and worth among it all. He was a short-lived animal in the ever-evolving, ever-expanding actuality of the multiverse, a speck of sand on a world where time had reduced *everything* to sand. He had always done his best. But however much he had done, and however much he still had left to do, he was nothing compared to this.

Nothing, in the face of the truth before him now. Here was a pathway from one universe to another, and it existed not because of him and his work but because all realities combined had sought it – and allowed it.

He could not even claim to have found the way. It was always meant to be.

'Oh, fuck my old boots,' Jonah muttered.

He and Drake walked forward and entered the breach together.

Jonah tried to breathe, but he found no air.

He walked and his senses worked, but he felt removed from his body – a consciousness hitching a ride in something mindless and soulless. It was a shocking sensation, because for a moment that might have stretched into years he saw himself as a fury, an automaton without thought or feeling. Then Wendy was with him, changing his mind, telling him that he was wrong and that he was an animal, a beautiful, genius animal with a precious mind and memories that were always, always his. He remembered her saying that on his fortieth birthday when they had picnicked together at the top of the Sugarloaf mountain in South Wales, watching families gasping and sweating as they completed their climb, and dogs panting, and Wendy had poured him another glass of wine. He walked on and his father came through the front door, his skin blue from impacted coal dust, his eyes red and his face lined with years of hard graft. He ruffled Jonah's hair and never once looked back to check that his son was following him into their small back garden, because he always followed. Jonah's mother brought his father a huge mug of tea and sat with him for a while, and neither of them spoke. That had been the day when four of his friends had died down the mine.

More memories flowed together like a dream, senseless and yet meaning everything to Jonah. His grandmother told him to do 'a good lot' when he went to school – her way of saying *work hard* – and he'd spent his whole life trying to do a good lot. He hoped that she would have been proud. His friend Bill Coldbrook raced over the edge of a ridge on his mountain bike, screaming with glee as he rocketed out of control downhill, his long hair swishing behind him, and Jonah could only follow, aghast at the flippant way in which Coldbrook put his genius mind in danger. It was only as they reached the valley floor that he realised that genius could stagnate – and how to keep it alive.

He would have gasped if he'd had any breath, and as he was drawn on he felt a tug coming from behind him, a gravity exerted on every atom of his body and tying him to every other part of his universe. *This is where it's all wrong.* The wrench gave way and he felt the pull of the new world, and realised that what they had done should never have been allowed. Matter cannot be created or destroyed. There were consequences to removing himself from one universe and entering another. The look in Drake's eye, a startled bird taking flight from the other side of a small stream – these were immediate effects of his arrival in this new place. And he could breathe again. But perhaps his intrusion would echo on. Maybe, in a billion years, stars would twist into the bellies of black holes because of him and galaxies would collide. He was the butterfly, and the multiverse his hurricane.

Jonah went to his knees and drove his fingers deep into the soil of this whole new world.

Drake had released his hand at some point, though Jonah felt as if someone was still grasping him. He looked at his right hand, pressed to the damp grass, fingers curled into the soil, and he felt the warm presence of another.

'Jonah, stand up,' Drake said. 'I've got so much to show you.'

Jonah stood, and several people who were standing around him took three steps back. To begin with he thought they were scared, but they were smiling softly, and one of them – a short woman, with dyed purple clothing – nodded a greeting.

'It's beautiful,' he said. He breathed in and smelled heather and the subtle perfume of unfamiliar flowers, and beyond the gurgle of the stream all he could hear was the soft whisper of a breeze through the shallow valley. The sky was a startling red, and he glanced at his watch to see how long past dawn it must be. But the watch's hands had stopped.

'Just past noon,' Drake said.

Jonah turned and saw a pile of beheaded furies' bodies stacked a hundred feet away from the breach. A couple of people were piling wood around the heap's base, preparing a bonfire. There were plants close to the stream that seemed to be propped on three stems instead of one. They looked alien and elegant. He looked up.

'The sky,' Jonah said.

'Dust,' Drake said. 'Final solution. They nuked New York first, then Washington, then the West Coast.' He shrugged, stretching. 'Europe, too.'

'Bombs against that?' Jonah asked, looking at the stacked bodies once again.

'Nothing else had worked,' Drake said. 'I'm not sure I can blame them.'

'What about fallout?'

'Levels can still be high, if the wind's in the wrong direction. But the bombing was quite limited. They soon realised it was useless.'

Drake signalled to one of the guards with a series of bizarre finger gestures. Jonah was just about to ask about the sign language when Drake held a finger to his lips.

'From here to the facility, we move in complete silence,' he said softly. 'They can scent us but they home in on sound as well.'

They set off and as Jonah walked he looked at a sky made beautiful by the dust of destruction.

In Coldbrook they took him down to stare at something monstrous.

'This isn't what you said you were going to show me.'

'Yet it's something I thought you should see.'

They had walked across Gaia's strange yet familiar land-scape, and though Jonah itched with questions he had obeyed Drake's instruction to remain silent, observing with an intense excitement the variety of flora and fauna, and the distant hills hiding valleys that might contain anything.

Now, in the depths of Drake's Coldbrook, he looked at something that did not belong in this – or any other – world.

'Kathryn Coldbrook ordered it retained,' Drake said. 'My father said she believed some cure could be created from the thing that came through and infected our world. The first vector. Then she disappeared, and everything died, and it's been here ever since.'

'And you've been experimenting on it?' Jonah asked, horrified.

'Not for decades,' Drake said. 'The few efforts we can still make, we concentrate on Mannan.'

It was chained to a wall, a manacle around each wrist and ankle. They were tightened around bones, not skin and flesh. There was another restraint around its neck, screwed securely around its spine. Dried skin and flesh hung around the rusty iron like some sort of grotesque plant growth. Three sets of iron gates and a scratched glass screen locked it in, but somehow it could still sense them standing just inside the large cell's door.

'How can you live here with this in the same place?'

'Most people have forgotten about it. And . . . we keep others.'

'But not like this?'

'No, not like this.' Drake sounded almost respectful. 'This one is unique.'

Locked away for forty years, infected on another Earth before that, whoever it had once been was long since gone. But the physical aspect of its heritage was still visible.

And it was not quite human.

It had a heavy brow, and what little hair remained was long and black. Its face projected forward, like an ape's. The arms were long and the hands large. It looked mummified – skin tight and shiny across some bones, but hanging loose across its stomach and chest – and its eyes were shrunken and deep.

It jerked forward when it sensed their presence, drawing in its legs and arms where it sat like a dying spider. The chains clanked and dust fell from them; they had not moved for some time. Even though it was badly desiccated, Jonah could see signs of mutilation from those early experiments. An opening had been cut into its skull, and he saw the shadowy insides – the brain was still wet. The flesh had been scoured from one forearm. There were holes in its chest, one of which he was sure he could see through.

'Horrible,' he said.

'I just see pathetic,' Drake said. 'It's a dried-up old thing, victim of the Inquisitor's kind.'

'Then why not put it down?'

'You talk as if it's a suffering animal,' Drake said, surprised. 'It's nothing like that. It was dead before it came through and doomed my world. Why put down something that's already dead?'

Jonah looked at his counterpart and saw a strong, determined man. But Drake was also someone who had been living in the aftermath all his life, scratching and surviving amid the rubble of his dead civilisation. If he was harsh, it was because that was all he had.

'In our world, they were Neanderthals,' Jonah said, turning his back on the horrible thing.

'Ours also,' Drake agreed. 'It seems that they didn't die out on every Earth. Another reason why the Inquisitors have to be defeated, and destroyed. They'll kill anything that isn't them. It's worse than genocide. Not the extermination of a people, but an entire species. A reality. And if they finally succeed—'

'They'll never succeed.'

'Why not?' Drake asked.

'Because the multiverse is infinite.'

'Then they'll commit infinite evil, and cause infinite pain, because they can never stop. Infinite Earths that might never breach without their help will be exposed to . . .' Drake nodded at the wretched animate corpse.

'There must be a way,' Jonah said. 'With that bastard stalking me.' He looked around, away from the trapped dead thing and back out into the narrow tunnel beyond. He hadn't seen the Inquisitor since coming through, but that didn't mean it wasn't there. Sometimes when he blinked it was watching him, standing behind the operating table with the objects it wanted to graft onto Jonah. Just waiting for him to accept his fate.

'There might be,' Drake said, his voice sad once again, hesitant.

'How? You think you have a way?'

'First, I can show you more of what is out there. You want to see?'

'No,' Jonah said. 'But I must.'

'My wife, Paloma,' Drake said, introducing Jonah to a tall, thin woman. 'She's our doctor. She will work with Marc when he arrives.'

'Pleased to meet you,' Jonah said, extending his hand. Paloma glanced at it and smiled uncertainly. Drake went to her side and hugged her, then whispered something in her ear. Her eyes went wide and she averted her gaze from Jonah, trying to appear less shocked than she was.

'Something I should know?' Jonah asked. Drake was guiding him here, choosing what he should hear and know, and that was a level of control no one had ever had over Jonah. He bristled, but also felt something like a child. They might be survivors barely scraping an existence, but something about Drake's world was far ahead of Jonah's.

'I'm telling her about Jayne,' Drake said, not looking at Jonah.

'Good,' Jonah said. 'Hopefully she and Marc—'

'Yes,' Drake said. 'So, casting library. This way.' And he left the room, expecting Jonah to follow. Paloma remained looking at the floor, and Jonah walked closer to her than he had to, hoping that she would glance up. But she did not. *Dead man walking*, he thought, not sure where the words had come from.

He followed Drake. They passed through a series of doors, and then Drake paused at a doorway, put his finger to his lips and nodded inside. 'Casting room,' he whispered as Jonah drew close. 'This will upset you.'

And how right Drake was. For a second Jonah was amazed at the technology behind what he was seeing, and a hundred questions occurred to him all at once. But then he realised what was being displayed on the screens hanging above the prone people, and such petty queries fled.

He saw his world in flames and turmoil. Burning cities, rivers of bodies, masses of humanity no longer human.

'Enough,' Jonah said, turning away. He met Drake's gaze. What he'd just seen was more terrible than the visions shown him by the Inquisitor, because this was *his* Earth.

'I'm sorry,' Drake said.

Jonah was going to reply, and then he saw a shape moving along the corridor., dragging a familiar shadow. *It can't be. I'm a universe away!* But the Inquisitor was there, those horrible objects dangling from its hand. They swung like heavy wet organs removed from another body. They dripped.

One of the Inquisitor's shoulders was bleeding, the blood looking surprisingly fresh against the old, dusty robes. *Holly shot him with her crossbow*, Jonah thought, and that gave him a brief burst of confidence. 'I do not accept,' he said hoarsely, and the Inquisitor faded away.

'It was here?' Drake said softly, his tone full of wonder and dread. He grabbed Jonah's arm and pulled him away from the casting room, back along the corridor to a narrow doorway. 'We don't have long.'

'Why the rush?'

'Because the Inquisitor won't wait for ever for you to accept. Kathryn's diaries said as much. *It's dancing with me when I don't want to be its partner. And yet this game must have an end.* She found her end, Jonah. And unless we hurry, you'll find yours as well.'

'You have a plan to deny him?'

'Trust me. We're like brothers. You're your Earth's me, do you not see that? Don't you feel it?'

Jonah nodded, and made the decision to trust this man. He had little choice, and behind Drake's apparent arrogance was a self-confidence that Jonah had to respect. Any genius had an ego; he only hoped that Drake's was justified.

They entered a new room and Drake flicked on several lights. 'We have to destroy them. You see that?'

'I'm keen to hear your plan. But what's this?' The room held four wardrobe-sized objects that seemed to shimmer with power. They dripped with condensation.

'Our casting-field generators,' Drake said. 'Just let me get this ready and I'll tell you my plan.' He went to a cupboard and took out some objects. Jonah heard various clicks and clunks as he sorted them.

A network of clear cables rose from each generator into the ceiling, pulsing with gentle blue sparks. Jonah thought of the core back in his Coldbrook, how huge and unknowable it was, and the idea of what might be inside these units made him shiver.

'Amazing,' Jonah said.

'It's all amazing,' Drake said, his back still turned to Jonah. 'So you see why we have to win? All those Earths, gone. All that wonder, knowledge and industry, hope and ambition. All that art. You understand why we have to fight?'

'Of course,' Jonah said.

'Good, Jonah. Good.' Drake turned, lifted a small crossbow, and shot Jonah in the heart.

5

Vic follows his sister through the ruined streets, and Jayne is staring at him from every window, every open door. There are cars slewed across the roads, resting on deflated tyres and with their windows slicked with something wet and mossy on the inside. A few have burned, and their stark black skeletons are now home to weeds that wave in the breeze.

As Charlotte approaches the door in the house that he always knows but never should, a noise thuds in from all around.

'What?' a disembodied voice asks.

Charlotte knocks on the door and it swings open beneath her fist, letting out a wafting shadow that quickly grows and shelters the sun from view, and his dead sister turns to him, with her perfect skin and lifeless eyes.

'We've been leaking fuel,' Charlotte says, 'and the gauge is fucked. We're running on fumes.'

Vic's eyes snapped open and he gasped. The shadow fled. 'Daddy?' he heard in the distance, and Olivia was tapping his arm. He lifted his right headphone and leaned down. 'I'm scared,' she said.

'Okay, sweetie. Hang on.'

'How the hell are we leaking fuel?' Marc shouted.

'I don't know!' Gary said. 'Ricochet back at the airport. Gremlins.'

'How far are we from Coldbrook?' Vic asked, feeling a little like a kid sitting there in the back: *Are we nearly there yet?*

Nobody answered for a few seconds. Sean was awake and alert, but silent. For the first time Vic noticed that he'd tucked his pistol into his waistband, shifting it from the holster at the small of his back. More comfortable, probably. Jayne seemed to be asleep.

'Hundred miles,' Gary said. 'But we're going down now.'

'Crashing?' Sean asked. He'd braced his leg in front of Jayne's, and her eyes were still closed.

'Controlled descent,' Gary said.

Lucy hugged Olivia between herself and Vic, the little girl picking up on the panic filling the cabin even though she could no longer comprehend what most of them were saying. Vic looked at Jayne and she was staring at him from beneath half-lowered eyelids. Sean tried to protect her without squeezing her too tightly.

'We'll be okay,' Vic said, leaning across to Lucy and forgetting that everyone could hear.

'I love you,' she said in response. It took his breath away.

Vic nodded, because saying it back would have sounded as empty as he still felt.

'Going down in the mountains,' Gary said.

Sean caught Vic's eye, and they both understood the dangers that would soon be stalking them.

Gary swore. The aircraft's motor started coughing, shaking the whole fuselage. As their controlled descent changed into something that was under little real control, Vic held his family and thought of Holly and what she might have witnessed. And the simple truth was that he wanted to see her again. The idea felt like a betrayal when he had his wife's head resting against his, their daughter crying between them. But he could not shut her from his mind.

'Now!' Gary said, and that was their only warning. They struck the ground violently, the floor punching up so hard that Vic thought his ankles had fractured. Jayne's eyes snapped fully open and she stared at him. The helicopter bounced, tipped to the left, and then rolled up and over its nose as the rotors slashed at the ground.

The fuselage ruptured. Someone screamed. As Vic squeezed his eyes shut and held on to his family, his life, something warm splashed across his face.

6

'So what did you feel when you came through?' Moira asked. The question surprised Holly. It was the first time that the other woman had spoken in ten minutes, and the silence between them had become heavy.

'I . . .' Holly shook her head, glancing away from the laptop screen at last. Moira was watching her intently. Her, not the screen showing scenes of chaos and horror. For a while, Holly had believed that the silence was the result of a shock felt by both of them. *Was she watching me all the time?* 'It was strange.'

'I'm just wondering if it's the breach that does that, or crossing the veils,' Moira said.

'What's the difference?'

'The veils are just . . . there,' Moira said. 'Natural divisions. The multiverse has them because that's the way it is, the way it developed. But the breach is unnatural. Man-made. You've messed with physics, assaulted the solidity of the veils and, by punching a hole in the multiverse, maybe you've caused injury.'

'How can you even guess at that?' Holly asked, interested and even a little offended. 'You were born after everything went wrong. You weren't part of the experiment.'

'Everyone at our Coldbrook has learned about the science of the End. We've had to, so that we can continue living there. Kathryn Coldbrook's books and diaries are still there, and there's a whole library of memory casts from before.'

'So you're blaming *us*? Saying that we should have never done it?'

'You can see the results,' Moira said, nodding at the screen.

Holly looked again. It was a YouTube video clip from London, and it showed the South Bank ablaze, bodies swimming into each other as they were swept down the Thames, and smoke rising from some sort of firefight on Tower Bridge. The film had been taken from inside the Tower of London where, according to the voice-over, thousands of people had taken refuge. Holly had never been to London.

'You don't seem moved by this,' Holly said. She hit another website, where a French reporter was filming herself standing at the head of a street somewhere in Toulouse. Smoke rose in the distance, and people streamed past her, their flight fuelled by terror.

'I've seen it all before,' Moira said.

'This is my world,' Holly said. She felt numb, bitter, scared.

'Yes,' Moira said, 'and you see why we have to do something.'

'Do what?'

'Whatever we can.' Moira closed the laptop cover gently, leaning in closer to Holly. The warm aroma of whisky hung on her breath.

'I'm concerned only with survival,' Holly said. 'And with trying to stop this before it gets worse.'

'There's a bigger picture,' Moira said. Anger simmered beneath her calm, gentle voice. '*Much* bigger.'

'Really?' Holly said. 'Then God help us.'

Moira froze. 'You dare mention *Him*?'

Holly stood and went to the back of Secondary, where she'd dropped two toolkits before checking over the computer systems. She picked one of them up. The Internet had drawn her in, compelled by the need to know, but now she felt was chilled by a fear of something closer. *We don't know these people at all*, she thought.

'Jonah's already gone,' Moira said.

'What do you mean?' Holly spun around to confront her. The woman was standing closer, frowning uncertainly as if she regretted what she'd said. She held both hands behind her back. Holly stared, but Moira gave nothing away.

'What have you done?' Holly asked, advancing on her. Moira backed up against the desk. The screens on the wall behind her showed a silent, unkempt Coldbrook, and Holly had a brief but startling thought: *I wish nothing had changed*. If they'd never succeeded with the breach the original team would still be down here together, working, debating, arguing. And Vic would still be here, his gentle flirting with Holly a constant thrill for both of them. Any flirting could become a match to touch-paper, and she had always lived in hope.

'Holly, I need you to sit down.' Moira nodded at one of the chairs, then brought her left hand around from behind her back. She held a rough-handled knife.

'What?' Holly asked. 'Are you *threatening* me?'

'Not a threat.' The other woman brought her right hand around, holding a tight coil of thin, strong twine. 'Sit down, Holly. Please. It's only for a while, just to ensure you don't try to—'

Holly snatched at the twine. Moira pulled it away,

and while doing so she lifted the knife in her other hand, its gleaming point catching the light from the viewing screens.

'Please don't fight!' Moira said, uncertainty in her voice for the first time.

Holly lowered the tool bag slightly, swinging it by the handle and bringing it around swiftly towards Moira's head while stepping to the left and reaching for the twine again. Moira leaned back but the bag struck her across the left cheek with a metallic *clunk*, and she grunted. Holly felt something punch against her stomach.

She gasped and dropped the heavy bag. It struck her right foot, and for a moment that pain was dominant. Then she felt a warm flush across her hip, and the chill wash of real agony. And blood.

Part Three

THE SOUND OF WHITE NOISE

Death is nothing to us, since when we are, death has not come, and when death has come, we are not.

Epicurus

Thursday

1

Jonah's head thrummed and the world swayed: someone was doing something to him, and he thought, *He's back.*

Jonah wondered whether the Inquisitor had ever left. That first time had been before the plague came through, and perhaps Jonah was back there now, waking from a nightmare of the End of Days and succumbing to whatever had struck him down in his sleep. The dreams had been realistic – a culmination of his secret fears and concerns over what they were doing down in Coldbrook.

But it was not the Inquisitor kneeling above him. Drake was sweating as he manipulated something on Jonah's chest.

Behind him were the casting-field generators, the network of suspended pipes glowing and sparking slightly. *How does that work?* Jonah thought – and then he remembered Drake and the crossbow.

He drew a deep breath and the pain seared through him.

'I'm almost done,' Drake said. He knew that Jonah was awake, but he hadn't even glanced at his face. 'Keep still, or you'll kill us all.'

'Almost done . . . what?' Jonah breathed. But Drake ignored him.

Jonah closed his eyes again and tried to remember: the heat and humidity of the generator room; Drake's insistence that something had to be done, something had to stop the Inquisitors' crusade.

And then the man's sad expression as he'd shot him in the chest.

My heart! Jonah thought, and though he still felt the familiar thuds of heartbeats and heard the whisper of blood through his ears, they seemed different. Strained – like a car that had burned off all its oil and was grinding its engine parts.

'What have you done?' he said.

'I've made a trade,' Drake said. He sighed and leaned back from where Jonah lay on the floor. He was looking him in the eye at last.

'A trade?' Jonah asked.

'I'm sorry, Jonah. I've taken hope from you and given it to everyone else.'

'And how have you done that?'

'Don't you know yet? Haven't you worked out the only way?' Drake was sweating, tense.

'You've turned me into a weapon,' Jonah said, beginning to understand.

'I've been waiting for someone like you for years, Jonah! A final hope. I believe the Inquisitor will take you back to its own Earth to initiate you into its ways.'

Jonah touched his chest. 'And when I'm there, I release the plague that you've implanted in me.'

'You've seen it flitting in and out, ghostlike. I think what they do is part casting, part breach, but they travel with impunity and without fear of infection. To beat them, we have to get past that. Take the fight to their world.'

'It won't know what you're doing?'

'It's not all-seeing, Jonah. Not everywhere all the time,'

'You don't know any of this for sure.'

Drake shrugged. 'Isn't all science a matter of best guess?'

'No,' Jonah said. 'But . . . that doesn't mean you're wrong.' He tried to sit up, but Drake laid a strong hand on his chest.

'Not yet,' Drake said, hesitant. 'So . . . you'll go? You'll help?'

'Have you left me with any choice?' Jonah asked. He felt a sickening weight in his stomach, and was surprised to discover it was the fear of death. He'd never thought he would be afraid, not after seeing Wendy die, witnessing her grace and dignity. But now there was so much still undone.

'No choice.'

'You've made me a prophet of blood and fear.'

'It's what *our* Coldbrook has been about for years. All our tests on Mannan and we've never moved one step closer to a cure. But we *have* tested this controlled plague-delivery system on him, and over the years we've perfected it. We've watched, and waited, and planned for the arrival of someone like you. Someone courted by an Inquisitor. And, Jonah, you're doomed anyway. Why not save the multiverse before you die?'

Jonah laughed. It hurt, but feeling pain was to be alive. 'You make it sound so noble!' he said.

'Isn't it? You've seen only a fraction of the castings. Most places we look, we see death and pain, and those furies waiting for any hint of life to return. We need a cure, yes, but part of that must be taking the fight to them.'

'Help me up,' Jonah said at last. 'You know what, Drake? I'm an old man. I've got a dodgy ticker, which I'm surprised is still ticking after whatever the hell you've done to it. If you'd only asked, I'd probably have gone anyway.'

'I had to make sure,' Drake said softly. Jonah could see the obsession there. Perhaps part of it was revenge, but mostly it was a desire to make things right. Drake had been born after his world's worst suffering, but he had witnessed that of so many others.

'But I want to travel,' Jonah said. 'Through the breach where the disease entered your world.'

'Why?' Drake asked, surprised.

'Because I want to see. Take it as . . . a dying man's wish. And the Inquisitor will follow me.'

Frowning, Drake nodded.

'So how does all this work?' Jonah said, touching his bare chest. As Drake began to explain, Jonah watched the shadows.

The Gaians of Coldbrook looked at Jonah as if he was some kind of Messiah, an irony that did not escape him. *I've come to save everything*, he could have said, and the crazy bastards might even have bowed down before him.

As he and Drake walked, Jonah thought about those he was leaving behind, Holly most of all. A precious friend, almost a daughter. She deserved an explanation and a goodbye, but he could give her neither. That made him sad. Soon he would exist only in Holly's memories, as Wendy did in his own.

They approached the final door that Jonah knew led to the outside, and he grabbed Drake's arm. The other man turned quickly, startled, ready for an attack. Jonah smiled and held up his hands.

'You've already killed me, Drake,' he said. 'I just want to say something.'

'Say it quickly,' Drake said. He was looking behind Jonah, nervous and unsettled, and Jonah knew what he was looking for. *He'll be here soon*, he thought, *but not just yet. The Inquisitor needs me on my own.* Because Jonah had plans beyond those that Drake had made for him.

'I'll do my best to carry this through, even though you took the choice from me. But you have to promise to help my friends. They'll need access to Mannan and they might need protection. And they'll do their best to come up with a vaccine.'

'Of course,' Drake said. 'A cure is something I can never give up on.'

'Holly will make sure –' Jonah began. Then a look that chilled him crossed Drake's face.

Jonah shoved him against the door. Drake grunted, wincing when his head was bashed back against the metal. 'What have you done to Holly?'

'Stopped her following you through. I didn't want her involved, seeing what I had to do to you.'

'Stopped her how?'

'Moira stayed behind to tie her up.'

Jonah sighed, missing Holly even more. 'Tell her . . . tell her you asked me, and I agreed to all this,' he said.

Drake nodded, and Jonah felt the respect between them growing again. Drake was a scientist and a ruthless man, ready to compromise his own morals for the greater good. Was that reprehensible or admirable? Jonah couldn't decide. He didn't have forty years of living as a survivor to influence his choices.

Drake opened the door, and cool night air sighed in.

Eight men and women came out with them into the darkness, and they walked silently towards the head of the valley. Though none of them spoke, Jonah could sense the respect they held for him. A few glanced his way now and then, as if to imprint him on their memories. Perhaps they'd tell their children and grandchildren of how they had seen the man carrying the Inquisitors' doom in his heart.

After an hour walking through the night, he saw the bulky angles of a building on a shoulder between two mountains, several hundred feet below the ridge line and on the moonward side. It reminded Jonah of a coal mine on a hillside back home.

'Jonah,' Drake whispered, 'is it following?'

'I have no idea,' Jonah said. 'You said yourself, it's not all-seeing.'

Drake glanced at him, worried.

Jonah smiled. 'Yes, Drake. It's following. Has been for a few minutes.'

They moved off again, climbing the ridge until they were level with the large structure, then cutting across the hillside. Shale slopes whispered in the darkness as they dislodged stones, and shapes scattered to hide in shadows as they approached.

Jonah slipped his fingers inside his shirt and fingered the small wound on his chest. It was two inches below his left nipple and towards the centre of his chest, and it felt more like a boil than an entry wound. Its head was smooth and warm to the touch, and hard – when he pressed it the nodule sank into his loose old-man's skin but hurt only a little. If he took a deep breath, he could feel the small charge inside surrounded by fury blood. Before they parted company Drake would give him the trigger.

He felt curiously detached from the thing in his chest. It was not a part of him. If anything, it was a part of Drake's desires and destiny, not his own.

At a silent signal the eight people spread out across the slope, four above and four below the point where they had stopped.

'I'll take you from here,' Drake said. 'There are traps.'

Jonah felt stares on him as he and Drake walked towards the building, but no one spoke. Perhaps they were so used to moving silently when they were outside that they could not bring themselves to say anything.

The last time Jonah glanced back, the people had merged into the shadows.

It took another few minutes to reach the structure and as they drew near Jonah could make out the haphazard nature of its construction.

'They started building quickly around the breach. Then later, after The End when the survivors made their home in Coldbrook, they decided that further protection was needed. Walls and traps. Safeguards. It's become something of a ritual for us to build some more onto this every three years.' Drake pulled an object from his shoulder bag and handed it to Jonah.

'And this will be the trigger,' Jonah said.

'Might feel strange to you.' Drake placed it in Jonah's hand. 'Squeeze hard, and the pod beside your heart will burst.' Warm, the size of a peanut, flexible, still Jonah sensed a solid centre to the item. He nodded and placed it carefully in his jacket pocket.

Drake led him inside. Jonah had no sense of leaving anything behind, perhaps because everything he had was already a world away.

They passed through a series of doors – most of them locked – passageways and arches, working their way deep into a labyrinth of concrete and rock. Drake took a route that was clear only to himself, and here and there he held up a hand and went about making their way safe. Some traps were basic: tripwires firing spring blades and primed crossbows; false floors above deep, spiked pits; hidden triggers that anything unaware could activate and which would bring spikes or blades or crushing rocks down upon them. Other traps were more mysterious to Jonah: slow-flowing waterfalls that Drake had to divert, their effect unknown; openings haloed by weak light, the air within sparking softly. Jonah wanted to ask about every single one, his scientist's mind alert. But there was no time for investigation.

As they went deeper, they came across the first trap that had been triggered.

'From here, it might not be safe,' Drake said. He aimed his light into a pit. Jonah looked and saw an old scarecrow-like thing down there. It was impaled on several long, thin spikes, and now it squirmed at their presence, clicking in its throat. Its face jutted out, leathery skin stretched over a bony forehead. Drake fired his crossbow and stilled it.

'Here,' Drake said. He delved into his bag and handed Jonah his pistol. 'I'll guide you to the breach, and protect you. Beyond there you might need this.'

'How far?' Jonah asked, still looking into the pit.

'Three traps.'

A shadow closed on Jonah and pulled back again. His Inquisitor, letting him know it was there. He sensed no alarm radiating from it, no fear that Jonah was running away. He guessed that it could follow him to the ends of the Earths.

They went on, and each of the other three traps held the remains of a Neanderthal fury. Two were dead, their heads ruined. The third was pinned against a wooden frame that had sprung from the wall and been pushed back by those that had come after. It lifted its head at they approached and Drake destroyed it.

Jonah was amazed once more at the fury's decayed state. It was over forty years dead, yet it had still had the ability to move and the will to spread its disease. He experienced a moment of panic that made his heart flutter and caused him to lean against the passage wall.

They walked on and soon passed through a final doorway in a thick stone wall. The wooden door had been pulled to one side, its top hinge pulled away from the crumbling rock.

'I'll reset them all on the way back out,' Drake said.

'I know,' Jonah said. *And I'll be committed to this*. But he hadn't for a second thought about turning around. This might have been forced upon him, but, though he could never believe in fate or destiny, his mind was set.

'This is it,' Drake said, and for the first time Jonah heard a weakness in his voice. Awe did that, perhaps. And maybe fear.

The breach was in front of them, set into the original hillside like a black diamond. Light did not escape it: it neither shone nor glowed. It was simply a blackness in the shadows thrown by Drake's torch.

Jonah held out his hand to Drake, and they shook.

'They'll write poems about you,' Drake said.

'Poems? Christ. I'm Welsh. Give me a good song any day.'

Drake laughed sadly, not quite understanding. 'Good luck, Jonah.'

Without another word Jonah passed through, and his greatest journey began.

2

Jayne surfaced slowly from the churu coma, her senses coming alive as her pain grew. She felt as if she'd been torn apart and thrust back together again. The roar of the helicopter's motor had stopped, replaced now with screaming and other, more terrible sounds. Something dripped. Someone cried, and it sounded like a little girl.

Jayne opened her eyes, and even that hurt. Groaning out loud, she lifted her hands and checked her body for wounds.

There was blood on the back of her head, but she didn't think that it was hers.

'Sean?' she said, glancing to her left. Sean was gone. His safety straps were cut, and his absence seemed unnatural.

She closed her eyes, trying to process what she'd seen just across from her. Then she looked again.

The guy, Vic, was dead. Head flung back, from the chest up he was red. His mouth hung open, and blood dripped from between his teeth. His little girl was standing with her back to him, less than three feet from Jayne, tugging at her mother's safety straps.

'Hey,' Jayne said.

The girl staggered a little, kicking something on the floor, letting out a wretched cry.

Someone screamed again, and the wrecked helicopter seemed to shake.

The woman – Lucy, Jayne remembered, the name coming to her even though she wasn't sure they'd even been introduced – was whimpering as she wrestled with her straps.

'Hey,' Jayne said again. The woman looked up, her eyes wide. Her face was misted with blood, but it didn't seem to be her own. She blinked a few times, glanced above and behind Jayne, and started moaning.

The little girl stood back and kicked the thing on the floor again. She froze, crying, and then a sharp metal snap signalled Lucy's freedom. She snatched up her daughter and pressed her face against her chest before jumping through the hole where the cabin door had previously hung.

Jayne looked down at the thing on the floor and realised it was a head. *Not Sean, not Sean*, she realised, because this dead person was white. The head was smashed and the only reason Jayne managed to keep from screaming was that it was looking away from her. *At least he's safe now*, she thought, and then she did scream.

The dead man opposite her lifted his head and looked at her.

'No!' she shouted. 'No, he's one of them, no, help me, *help* me!'

From somewhere behind her came more anguished screaming, and then she recognised Marc's voice calling Gary's name again and again.

Sean appeared in the doorway, streaks of vomit across his chin and down his chest. He climbed in, shielding Vic from Jayne's view, and—

'Get your gun out!' she shrieked. He held her, leaning in and ignoring the vomit as he pressed close, whispering into her ear that it was all right, she was alive, *alive*!

'He's not one of them,' he said. He half turned. 'Vic! Vic!'

'Yeah,' Vic said somehow. Jayne struggled against her straps, pushing against Sean to move him aside so she could see. She'd heard Vic talking, but she had to see.

Vic's eyes were a startling white against the blood and other stuff coating his face. He spat, retched.

'No more puke,' Sean said. He put one hand on Vic's chest and brought a knife around, and for a moment Jayne thought he was going to put the man out of his misery.

Sean sawed and hacked at the restraining straps.

'Your family,' he said, and Jayne saw Vic stumble from the wrecked aircraft and fall to the ground outside.

'Sean? I saw his head. I saw Gary's *head*.'

Sean glanced down and then came for her, putting himself between her and what she didn't want to see again. Behind her, Marc's shouting had ceased, and now she could hear him whispering. She didn't want to hear what he was saying.

'Got to cut you out,' he said. 'I'll carry you as best I can, but you can't—'

'Marc,' Jayne said.

Sean glanced behind her. 'Saying his goodbyes,' he said, and he went to work on her straps. His eyes were wide, and she wondered what he had seen.

'There,' Sean said as the straps fell away from Jayne. She slid a little to the right, not realising until then that they'd come to rest at a tilt. He did not apologise as he slung her arm around his neck and lifted.

Jayne half turned as she stood, and she strained to see over her seat into the pilot's cabin. Lights were still on across the control panels, the windscreen and its framing had vanished, and she could see Marc in silhouette, hugging his lover's headless corpse. Stunned, speechless, she let Sean help her from the helicopter and down to the ground.

They'd crashed fifty metres from a road that skirted

a large lake and had taken down several small trees in the process. Debris lay scattered across the rocky slope, and there were several deep gouges where the chopper's rotors had struck and dug into the ground. Vic sat on a splintered tree, hands resting on his knees as he stared at the ground between his feet. His wife knelt next to him, and their daughter stood in front of them and hugged them both.

'Mummy, Daddy,' she said, over and over. 'Mummy, Daddy.' Jayne was pleased that the family was still together and when Sean eased her arm from around his neck she would not let him go.

'Thank you,' she said.

'Can't believe we survived that,' he said, looking at the crashed helicopter and shaking his head. 'How the *fuck* did we survive that?'

'Mummy, Daddy,' Olivia said again, 'there's a man.'

'He looks . . .' Lucy said, and she pointed, saying no more.

Along the road from where they'd come down, just past a marked parking area, two cars and a station wagon were parked on the grassy verge. A naked man had emerged from the shelter of the vehicles, crossed the road, and now he was running towards them, weaving through the trees growing across the slope.

'Everyone together!' Sean said. He pulled Jayne so that she stood behind the family.

'Hide your girl,' Jayne said. Lucy nodded, pulling Olivia down so that she sat huddled against her chest.

'I . . . I got this,' Vic said, standing and pulling the pistol from his belt. *He looks just like one of them*, Jayne thought. Blood shone in his hair, and his face and throat were speckled with stuff that she didn't even want to think about. He'd tried to wipe it off but had succeeded only in smearing it more thoroughly over himself.

'Just keep your eyes open for others,' Sean said. He walked forward to meet the man running at them, and Jayne knew that she should look away. This was something she'd seen before and had no wish to see again, but looking the other way made her feel vulnerable. She'd always been someone who was happier to face danger rather than turn her back.

She glanced back at the helicopter and saw Marc dropping from the cockpit's doorway. He landed softly, rifle in one hand, blood smearing the other. She didn't know how to act so she smiled at him. He seemed not to notice.

Sean waited until the man was a hundred metres away before he gave him two chances. 'Stop or I'll shoot you in the head!' The man did not pause. 'Say something!' The man said nothing. Sean fired when he was twenty metres away and put him down with one shot.

Jayne breathed a sigh of relief, and then Marc was with them, standing shoulder to shoulder with Sean.

'Good shot,' Marc said.

'Thanks. You okay?'

'No.' His voice was flat, cold. 'Anyone else hurt?'

'Bumps and bruises,' Sean said.

Marc looked back at them, and he only glanced at Vic before his eyes settled on Jayne. *He doesn't want to see his lover's blood*, Jayne thought, and she felt an affinity with this man. They had both seen the people they loved violently killed.

'Look! A little girl!' Olivia sounded so excited, as if she was looking forward to having a playmate.

'Down to the lake,' Sean said. 'Marc, you want me to . . .?' He held out his hand for the rifle, and Marc handed it over without a word.

They started down the slope, Lucy carrying her daughter, and behind them Sean shouted the same two warnings he had given the man. But Jayne could already visualise the ragged mess of the girl's neck and chest. And soon her pretty pale face would be wiped away.

3

Vic stripped and washed in the lake, barely aware of his nakedness in front of the others, concerned only with cleaning the blood from his skin and hair. He submerged himself several times, and beneath the water the world seemed so much further away. The last time he went under he considered staying there, so he didn't duck down again.

Marc stood up on the road, keeping watch. Sean was closer to the lake but he too turned in slow circles, keeping watch on the landscape, Marc's rifle now in his hands. Vic's pistol lay on the bank beside his wet clothing. The satphone was there as well, its volume turned up – he'd tried calling Holly and Jonah, but there'd been no answer. He tried not to think about that too much.

He'd washed the blood from his clothes as well as he could but the stains remained. He'd be cold and wet when he got dressed again, but he did not care. All he cared about was close by: the woman and the child who were watching him. Lucy was concerned, Olivia scared.

Jayne sat with her back against a smooth boulder, gently massaging her knees and hips, hardly seeming to notice her own tears.

Vic rubbed his hands together just beneath the surface of the cold water, and felt that they could have belonged to someone else.

A hundred miles, Gary had said as they were going down. On any normal day, it would take three or four hours in a car. But today it was a much greater distance. The irony did not escape Vic: the infection he had released had spread so quickly because modern communications had made the world so small, and as a result the world had become so much larger again.

He waded from the lake, feet slipping on slick stones beneath the surface, and for a moment he was a boy in Colorado again, swimming with his friends and building campfires to cook hot dogs and burgers.

Olivia, scared though she was, giggled at the sight of her naked, shivering father.

'We need to check the cars,' Marc said from up on the road.

'But those things,' Jayne said.

'If there were more they'd have come. They're driven. I see no intelligence in the fuckers.'

'I'll come with you,' Sean said.

'No. Stay here.' Marc looked down the slope at Vic. 'You okay now? You ready to use your gun if you need to?'

'I'm fine,' Vic said. *I was covered with his lover's brains.* Not all of his shivering was due to the cold.

'I'll shout when it's clear.' Marc started along the road towards the three vehicles, the pistol grasped in his hand.

Vic struggled to pull on his sodden clothes.

'You're shaking, Daddy,' Olivia said. She was so sweet, innocent, beautiful, that he wanted to pick her up and run with her until they reached somewhere safer than anywhere else.

'You think Marc's okay?' Sean asked. He'd come down the slope to stand between Jayne and Vic's family. The rifle looked heavy in his hand but he seemed hardly aware of it.

'I don't know,' Vic said truthfully.

'Well . . .' Sean said. 'Jayne's the important one here. She's our reason for keeping going.'

'He just saw his partner decapitated,' Jayne said, struggling to her feet. Sean went to help her.

'What's that mean?' Olivia asked. 'And where's that tall man Gary?'

Not so tall now, Vic thought, shocking himself by uttering a sharp laugh. He tried to turn it into a cough, but the others knew. Sean smiled. But it was a sad expression that conveyed understanding. *Are we all going fucking mad?* Vic thought. Then they heard a motor.

The station wagon swung in a half-circle around the other two cars and came their way. The offside wing was smashed and the bonnet crumpled, but the engine sounded fine to Vic. When Marc parked and slipped into neutral he gunned it.

As the engine's roar echoed into the hills, he leaned from the driver's seat. 'Got a GPS. Couple of guns. Come on. Fuck, I can't wait to see that mad old fucking Welshman again.'

They gathered their things and climbed into the vehicle. Sean flicked on the radio as Marc drove, scanning across the frequencies. Some stations were playing music on a loop. Here and there they found someone still broadcasting, ranting, crying, occasionally issuing instructions from a government that otherwise seemed conspicuously absent.

Elsewhere, all they heard was the sound of white noise.

4

Holly pressed her hand to her wound. She had never felt so hopeless. She sat in Secondary and scanned Coldbrook on the cameras that were still working; there was no sign that Moira was still there. And why should she have been? She'd stayed behind for long enough to put Holly out of action, then fled back through the breach to her own wretched world.

Holly had never found it in herself to trust Drake fully and at the time she'd put it down to the distance between their lives. Now she wished she had trusted herself. Because Jonah was dead, and she herself might well be dying. The dressing she'd found in Secondary's first-aid box was already soaked through, and blood was pooling on the concave stool she was sitting on. Her behind was wet from it. Her vision was growing fuzzy. *I'm losing too much*, she thought, and decided to look at last.

Holly had always been terrible with blood, especially her own. Now she could smell it on the air. She groaned and the sound came from very far away.

But there was too much left to do for her to die. If she bled to death, Vic and the others might never make it inside alive. She had to make Coldbrook safe. Warn them, at least. Find out what route Vic had taken to escape, whether he'd left it open and if it was now a way for the furies to get in.

So she bit her lip and looked, dropping the sodden bandage and examining the wound. The knife had slid in just above her hip, perhaps skimming across her pelvic bone. She had no idea how deep it had gone, but the blood was still flowing freely. It was a neat incision.

'Not too bad,' she said, but she couldn't know that for sure. She rummaged in the first-aid box and found another dressing. Pressing it hard against the wound, she tried to remember everything she knew about dealing with injuries like this. It all came down to one thing – she needed a hospital.

'Shit outta luck,' Holly whispered. On a wall screen in front of her a pale shape moved along a corridor.

She held her breath. Looked again. Two people she used to know were wandering aimlessly, covered in dried blood. On her way out, Moira had taken the time to open some doors.

'No,' she said. 'Oh, you bitch.' She glimpsed the satphone on the floor by the door. She'd thought it was safe in her pocket but it must have dropped out during her tussle with Moira. All she had to do now was reach it.

It took a couple of minutes to slip from the blood-drenched chair and move across to the phone. The wound hurt like fuckery, but Holly reached the door without fainting. She leaned against the wall and slid down it slowly, dropping to the floor and crying out as the wound flexed. Blood pulsed over her hand. *Got to keep still for a while, let the bleeding ease.*

She dialled Vic, suddenly desperate to hear his voice, to hear *any* voice. From the corner of her eye she glimpsed movement on the screens again, but this time she didn't look. The idea of seeing this blasphemous mockery of death made her feel sick – she might be dead soon herself. But she had plenty of fight in her yet, and a powerful rage against Drake and Moira. And if Jonah—

'Jonah!' Vic's voice said. 'Jesus Christ, where the fuck have you been?'

'Don't blaspheme,' Holly said, smiling despite herself.

'Holly . . .' Vic said. She could hear background noise, wondered how close they were. They should have arrived by now, surely?

'They tell me Jonah's dead,' Holly said.

'What?'

'He went through with Drake. They left a woman with me to fix up Coldbrook. She's called Moira. And she told me they're using Jonah to hit back at the Inquisitors.'

'The what? Holly, I don't know what you're—'

'Moira left, and she let furies out on her way. It's not safe down here any more, Vic. They're loose in Coldbrook, and I'm not sure I can . . .' She sobbed.

'How many are there?' he asked.

'I don't know. Two, at least.'

'We crashed,' Vic said, lowering his voice. 'Pilot died, but the rest of us are okay. We've picked up a car and we're driving to you through the mountains.'

'How far away?'

'Hundred miles. Bit less.'

'Right,' Holly said. *Right, a hundred miles, a few hours barring any hold-ups.* 'Okay. Can you get back into Coldbrook the same way you got out?'

'I think that's for you to tell me.'

'You still have the immune girl, and Jonah's friend?' she asked.

'Yeah,' Vic said. 'But he says it won't be—'

'Don't tell me he can't do it, Vic,' Holly cut in. 'We've got a chance to stop the infection, and that's all that matters. You hear that? Close the breach, save the world. The girl and Marc, they're *all* that matters. Now tell me how you got out, and I'll do my best to get you back inside.'

'What about the zombies that the woman let out down there?'

'Yeah. Well.' Holly looked at the open cabinet from which she'd grabbed the first-aid box. There was still a pistol and a shotgun in there. 'You'll have to leave that with me.'

They talked, and planned, then Holly stood and ripped

off her loose Gaian dress. She tied it tightly around her waist. She used scissors from the first-aid kit to cut off one of her trouser legs, folded it, and packed it hard against her wound, tightening the dress some more. It was temporary, but she only needed it to last until she could find some proper clothing and a bigger bandage.

Then she'd get Vic and the others into Coldbrook, and whatever happened after that would not be in her hands.

5

Jonah stepped between worlds, and from the first moment it was clear that this breach was different. It felt *stranger*. The flood of memories assaulted him, and he'd been braced for them, but these memories were also different, though it took him a while to realise why. He saw Wendy sitting by a river reading a book, constantly brushing the hair from her eyes. Then she was walking through a small valley town in Wales, a few years older, her hair now gathered in a functional ponytail and her hands gripping heavy shopping bags. He smiled at her and she smiled back absent-mindedly, soon looking away. Then she was in a car, sitting at traffic lights and tapping one finger on the wheel. She stared into the distance, and she was in the car alone. When she glanced his way it was a quick look, something inconsequential, and

Jonah wanted to reach for her . . . but these were not his memories. He was seeing the love of his life, but through strangers' eyes.

The pull of Gaia grasped him as he walked forward, stretching his skin, tugging his hair, and he thought he was trapped in a particular moment, ripped apart and smudged across this veil between realities. And then he staggered forward into another Earth, and the first breath he took cleared every vision from his memory.

He'd emerged into a high-ceilinged, cathedral-like building. Bright moonlight came through a ragged hole in the roof high above him, reflected from what seemed to be broken hanging mirrors and chandeliers. The structure rose and curved inward to enclose him like a giant shell, its extravagantly painted ceiling faded with dust and time. The breach was resting within a circular stone wall. He climbed a small set of steps and mounted the wall, and the true size and grandness of the place struck him.

He'd been in some of the largest and most beautiful cathedrals in Britain – York Minster, Lincoln, St David's – but this place was easily three times their size and it took his breath away. Birds flew in its upper reaches. Plants sprouted from ledges and cracks in the walls. Three-storey-high windows had been smashed, and where any glass remained it was heavily obscured by dust or mould. He was afraid to move, in case the echoes of his footsteps came back at him. He took in a breath, and let it out again in a slow, amazed exhalation.

Then he noticed the statues. They stood in alcoves at floor level all around the building. Many were hidden by shadow, but where moonlight touched some their features were evident. He had seen their likeness before, deep in Gaia's Coldbrook where that wretched creature was kept.

Jonah descended the steps from the breach's containment wall, passing tangles of technology – round containers, wires, and a scatter of circuits spilled across the floor – and sensed movement in the distance. His heart thudded, and he pulled the pistol from his belt and flicked off the safety catch. He still felt vaguely foolish holding a gun.

After a pause he moved on – and then he saw the Inquisitor. It was standing among a spread of chairs and desks, apparently set around the breach at random. Many of them were broken now, or perhaps rotted down into disrepair, and the Inquisitor seemed unaware. It was concerned with nothing but him.

Jonah put his hand in his pocket and held the soft round object. Then he turned and ran.

He was surprised to find that the building's door was made of heavy wood with metal crosspieces, just like a church door at home. For these people, perhaps their breach had been a god, encased in a building of devotion and worship.

'It is required that you accept.' The Inquisitor's voice echoed, but Jonah didn't even turn around.

'Fuck you!' he shouted. Outside, a shadow rose within a mass of brambles. Not the Inquisitor. Jonah paused, lifted his gun and fired. The shape fell out of sight.

Moonlight revealed the landscape to him. Low-lying buildings dotted the surroundings like stone igloos, their curved roofs reaching down to the ground, and tall poles rose high above them. They supported complex frameworks of wire and mesh, and he thought they must be aerials. They might have looked like Neanderthals, but the people who had lived here had been at least as advanced as him.

Jonah wanted to stay to discover more, explore the remnants of this Earth's art and culture, their amazing architecture, the sad story of their demise. But another shadow was coming at him now, long-armed and heavy-shouldered, shambling, and he waited until it was close enough before putting a bullet through its forehead.

Something tugged him onward, and the building behind forced him away. His skin tingled. Perhaps the Inquisitor was exerting some repelling influence on him . . . but he thought not.

He thought it might be another breach.

Sad at everything he was missing here, Jonah started to run. 'Not yet, you bastard!' he shouted again, wondering how long it had been since words were last spoken here.

Other worlds beckoned.

6

The car stank of unwashed bodies – and fear. No one seemed to care. They wound the windows down and breathed in the fresh mountain air, and Vic didn't understand how the views could still be so beautiful. Wasn't the world stained now? Wasn't it tainted? It took him a while to realise this was not the case at all. *Humanity* was stained and tainted. The world was doing just fine.

Jayne was sitting behind Sean, leaning against the door and groaning in pain. Whatever weird disease made her immune – and she'd shown him her bite, wet and infected but not deadly to her – he wasn't sure it was anything better. She was a pretty girl aged by her disease, face drawn and eyes pale with the knowledge of pain. She'd told them about the boyfriend she'd lost.

They passed people both living and dead, most of them still walking. The living would be at the side of the road, waving them down for help, shouting, begging. But everyone in the car knew they could not stop. They had no more room in the vehicle. Many people carried guns, and several times Vic heard shots behind them when they passed by, and once something struck the vehicle's wheel arch like a sledgehammer.

There were many dead wandering this part of the Appalachians. They sometimes saw them on the slopes, sad pale shapes moving aimlessly until they saw the car, even though sometimes they might be a mile away. Others had remained close to the road. Marc called a warning whenever the station wagon was about to hit someone, and usually there was time to cover Olivia's eyes. Usually, but not always. His daughter had stopped crying, and Vic hated what that might mean.

An hour into the journey, and maybe halfway there, they saw a roadblock on top of a ridge. Marc stopped the vehicle.

'No way to go overland,' Marc said.

'Sure it's a roadblock?' Sean asked.

'The road's blocked,' Marc said, his words slow with sarcasm.

'Yeah, but is it intentional?' Vic said.

Marc tapped his fingers against the wheel. 'Why bother blocking the road? Zombies don't drive.'

'We could go back,' Lucy said. 'Find another way around. Somewhere safer.'

'Nowhere's safe,' Jayne said. Vic had thought she was asleep – her eyes were still closed.

As Marc edged them forward again Vic let go of Lucy's hand and pulled the M1911 from his belt.

'Let's not look too threatening,' Sean said. He lowered his window and leaned his arm outside, casual, cool. 'Vic, keep your piece handy. But out of sight. Marc?'

'I'm just the driver.' In the mirror, Vic was amazed to see Jonah's old friend smile.

They rolled to a stop fifty feet from the roadblock. A couple of big trucks had been parked nose-to-nose across the road, and whoever had done it had chosen the place carefully. Rocks on one side and a ditch on the other made passing impossible.

A man emerged from behind the truck on the left: short, long hair, a gun in his hand. There was movement in the ditch to their right, and Vic saw three faces peering up at them.

'You got any food?' the man called.

'I'm hungry,' Olivia said, reminded of her rumbling stomach.

'Nothing,' Sean shouted back. 'What're you doing hanging around—?'

'My family's hungry,' the man said. 'Can't go to the towns. Can't go to houses. They're *everywhere*. And I can't call anyone, the goddamn phones don't work. And we're starving. So . . .' He lifted the gun and aimed it at the car. 'So get out, hands up. And—'

'We don't have any food,' Sean said.

'Thomas!' a woman said. Vic tried to see past Sean and Marc but he wasn't sure where the voice had come from.

'Thomas,' the woman repeated. Sean opened his door and slipped out, lifting his gun and pointing it at Thomas's face.

'Oh Jesus,' Lucy whispered.

Vic wanted to get out but he was trapped between his wife and daughter on one side and Jayne on the other. He reached past Jayne for the door handle, and Marc hissed like an animal.

'Stay inside!'

The two men pointed guns at each other. In the ditch, the three faces stared, terrified.

'We're not infected,' Sean said. 'And we have someone very important with us. Someone who might be able to help stop all this. We're going to somewhere in the mountains, an underground bunker called Coldbrook, where it'll be safe. There'll be food and water and shelter for you and your family.'

Thomas held the gun as if it was hot, and Vic thought he'd probably never fired it before. It took only a few seconds for him to lower it, and from somewhere behind the trucks the woman called out a third time, startled and scared: 'Thomas?'

'Good,' Sean said. He kept his gun raised and stepped forward, and for a second Vic thought he was going to shoot the man in the face. Then he'd kill his wife and kids and steal whatever they had, because survival was the only law now.

But Sean paused again. 'One of those yours?' he asked, nodding at the trucks.

'Both.'

Sean nodded and lowered his gun. 'Bring the one with the most fuel. Follow us.' He clapped the man on the shoulder, then returned to the station wagon.

'Jesus Christ,' Vic muttered as Sean slammed his door closed again.

'Nope,' Sean said, 'just some dude who doesn't know shit about safety catches.'

They headed off with Thomas and his family following on behind.

Marc got out next time and talked to the people they saw, a group of three teenaged boys walking along the road and, amazingly, still alive. They carried automatic weapons and when he returned to the station wagon Marc said that the boys had been using them against the zombies. They joined Thomas and his family, sitting in the truck's bed.

A car, eight bikers from a gang called Unblessed, a bus with several adults and twenty kids, more walkers. They found some of them stationary, parked on or just off the road and waiting for something that would never come – or fearing something that would. They passed others going in the opposite direction and flagged them down; some stopped, some stepped on the gas.

And Vic began to feel that this was something good. Once inside Coldbrook they'd be somewhere easy to defend, and from there Marc could start his development of a vaccine or cure. With luck the food and water would last.

As they advanced towards Coldbrook and the convoy grew they saw more and more movement in the hills. Several times they passed zombies stationary by the roadside, and with the vehicle's windows down they could hear their haunting calls. They did not stop.

They moved south-west, parallel to Route 81 but sticking to minor roads. There was a general agreement that to hit the highways would be a bad idea. And, as the afternoon wore on, Vic gained a sense of their wider surroundings and the stories unfolding around them. The people they picked up either lived close by or had fled to the mountains from surrounding cities and towns, believing that the wilds might be safer. Most of them told tales that proved this was not the case. Many had lost family – brothers, parents, wives, children – and they wore the haunted, often hopeless expressions of refugees.

Vic knew that the zombies could not follow on foot, but the larger the convoy of survivors grew, the more he came to fear that news of their existence was being broadcast. The few times they stopped, he climbed from the car and heard a gentle hooting in the distance. It might have been a breeze in the hills.

But he thought not.

7

Holly checked every CCTV camera that was still working at least three times, until she knew that she could wait no longer. A strange, heavy numbness had spread around her side, and she wondered whether she was bleeding internally. She balanced the danger of making her way to the garage against staying put, and opened the door.

She was fairly certain that there were at least three furies loose in Coldbrook's corridors.

Are the keys still in the Hummer? Are there more furies loose in the garage area? Can they smell my blood? Will I pass out before I can even get there? There were so many variables and unknowns that Holly tried to thrust them from her mind, and concentrate only on what she knew: she had a job to do.

She worked her way slowly from Secondary, down the staircase, and towards the common room and garage beyond. Vic and the others could easily get down into Coldbrook, but that single parked vehicle crushed against the door was a problem. And a bleeding Holly offered the only chance that it could be moved. The weight of responsibility pressed down on her even as the pain spread and numbed her, and she felt a strange dislocation from her body.

A figure shambled around a corner ahead of her. One side of his face was black with dried blood. On seeing her he ran, uttering that mournful noise, alerting any other furies in earshot.

Holly leaned against the wall and raised her pistol. She fired and the bullet punched the fury in the chest. He jarred to a halt, and in that moment when he was motionless she aimed again and shot him in the face. He went down, rolled onto his side with his face against the wall, then grew still.

Her hearing dulled, breathing hard, Holly forced herself on. She kept the gun aimed at the motionless fury, not knowing whether they could feign death, not knowing even now whether they had the will to deceive. She realised that she must have known him when he'd been alive, but she didn't think too hard about that. He had died almost a week ago, and now she had put him out of his misery.

A wave of dizziness caused her to slump towards the floor. She railed against it, bit her tongue, pressed the hot gun barrel against her cheek. But the numbness seemed to spread from her wounded hip and up through her chest and neck, distancing her senses and luring her towards darkness.

And though she knew that peaceful eternity was waiting for her in Heaven, now she wanted only life.

'Fuck it!' she shouted, clearing her senses with an outburst of rage. In the distance, from a direction distorted by echoes, she heard first one short hoot, and then another, both of them drawing closer.

It didn't matter. She had the gun, and there was only one possible outcome. *If Vic and the others can't get down here, they might die. If they die, any chance at a cure is gone. If there's no cure, my Earth dies just like all those others.* The future depended on whether she could reach a Hummer, start it, and drive it a few feet.

It was so ridiculous that she might have laughed.

Left arm pressed across her stomach, her hand clasping the temporary dressing tighter to her right side, Holly started along the corridor again. She knew the complex well, not only the passageways and rooms but those spaces between and behind them where cable routes and plant rooms linked the facility together.

That was how she would beat the furies. Two left, but with her senses fading in and out she could not risk simply charging ahead blind. She had to balance speed with caution.

As she moved, something bothered her. A mistake. An idea that she had left herself open to danger. But she did not dwell too heavily on it, because that would divert her concentration.

Coldbrook was abandoned and run-down, and all but silent. There were only her footsteps, shuffled sounds whispering along a corridor stained with dried blood, scattered with items discarded in panic, the walls pocked with bullet holes here and there. And then there were the bodies.

They stank. The smell filled her nose. She tried breathing through her mouth, but that made it worse.

Pausing at the door of the common room, Holly held her breath and listened.

No footsteps. Nothing moved. Coldbrook's lighting hummed softly, and deeper down was the constant presence of the core, a sensation more than a noise, betraying itself through the fabric of the place as it had ever since it had first been initiated many years ago.

As she reached for the door, her satphone rang.

'Shit!' Startled, she pulled her hand from her wound to go for the phone. Blood had dried against her hand and she ripped part of the padded trouser leg and tied dress away. The pain stabbed through her, and she dropped the gun.

Something banged against the other side of the door. It struck again and again, the lever handle flipping down and up, down and up. The fury was struggling to open the door, some fragmentary memory telling it what to do. Holly stooped for the gun, and then pitched forward as a fainting spell washed over her. *Oh fuck, not like this*, she thought, and as the door creaked open behind her she realised she had lost.

'Fuck fuck fuck!' she shouted – pure rage, pure hopelessness, the most defined and lucid moment of her life so close to its end.

The door banged against the wall. Footsteps. She rolled towards the sound and screamed, but the thing stayed silent. The fury tripped over her and struck the ground head first, thrashing like a landed fish for a few seconds as Holly scrambled aside, kicking against it, pushing against the floor until she sat against the wall and the gun was by her side. She grabbed it up and held it in both hands, and then the fury turned to face her.

Sugg. Their chef. A calm, quiet man, he'd spent most of his spare time birdwatching in the mountains above them. Now he looked relatively untouched apart from a terrible bite on his left hand. But Holly knew there was nothing at all human about him, and she shot him in the neck. He fell back, lifted himself again, and she fired into his head. This time he lay still.

Panting as she tried to retain consciousness, Holly realised that the satphone was still ringing in her pocket. 'Oh Vic, for fuck's sake,' she breathed. As she plucked out the phone she heard several sets of running footsteps.

Moira must have released more than three furies.

Holly propped the phone between her knees and aimed along the corridor, back the way she had come. *How many bullets?*

The first person around the corner was Drake. He paused, took in the situation, then ran on. Moira came behind him, then several more Gaians. They were armed, sweating, grim-faced, and Holly thought they had been in a fight.

She did not lower the gun.

'Take one more fucking step,' she said, voice husky with threat.

Drake raised his crossbow and fired in one fluid movement. From behind him three more bolts blurred along the corridor.

Holly did not even have time to close her eyes before the projectiles struck home.

The fury staggered three more steps through the doorway, bolts protruding from her throat and face. Her mouth worked, and a high keening emerged, something like the strange hooting Holly had heard before. The woman who had been Sam – Coldbrook's accountant, who had famously arrived at their last Halloween bash dressed as Carrie, complete with a drenching of fake blood – fell close enough for Holly to touch.

'Any more?' Drake asked.

Holly sat back against the wall and looked at him from under drooping eyelids. 'Ask Moira,' she said. And then they came close and she blacked out, allowing unconsciousness to claim her now that, perhaps, she was safe.

*   *   *

When Holly came to, Drake's wife Paloma was kneeling beside her, tending her wound, frowning in concentration.

Holly hissed in pain and Paloma glanced up, obviously surprised that she was conscious.

'Sorry,' the tall woman said.

'Right.' Holly looked down at the gun in her hand. The phone between her knees had stopped ringing. She wondered if she was dreaming this, living a moment that never was as she sank deeper towards death.

'Do I need to take your weapon?' Drake asked. He was standing beyond Holly's feet, between her and the huddled shapes of two dead furies.

'Yeah. Probably. Fucker.'

Paloma grunted, something noncommittal and impatient.

'I have to . . . apologise,' Drake said. He squatted in front of her, coming down to her level. 'Moira was meant to tie you up, that's all. When she came back to me she was mortified that—'

'That she thought she'd killed me?'

'Moira is in awe of you. And a little scared of you.' Drake shrugged. 'We all are.'

His wife unfolded a paper sachet and spread something on the knife wound, and Holly screeched at the sudden shattering pain. Paloma held her hand and squeezed softly, and then the pain faded as quickly as it had arrived.

'It'll settle soon,' Paloma said. 'The wound isn't too deep, and I don't think it's damaged anything important.'

'Other than me,' Holly said.

Paloma's smile was lopsided. 'You know what I mean.'

Holly nodded her thanks and the woman stood, backed away, gave Drake room to move in closer. A couple more of his people stood further along the corridor, their backs turned. Holly could no longer see Moira.

'Well, I suppose I should blow your head off first,' Holly said. 'You're their boss, after all. What have you done to Jonah?'

Drake blinked uncomfortably but did not reply.

'Is he dead?' Holly asked.

'No. Yes. Maybe. I don't know yet. But it doesn't matter, he's—'

'Doesn't *matter?*'

'He's lost to us, Holly. And he's a brave man.' Then Drake told her where Jonah had gone, and why.

'*This* world is his priority!' Holly said, stunned. But even as she spoke she wondered at the truth of that. Since his wife's death Jonah had spent his life striving to reach the multiverse, *beyond* this world. His priorities went farther.

'He's a complex man,' Drake said, and in his voice she heard him saying, *As am I.* 'By doing what he can to stop those bastards – something I've craved my whole life – Jonah might save everything.'

'Or he might destroy the last place that's protected from this plague,' Holly said.

Drake inclined his head. 'Perhaps. But they're the last world worth saving.'

'You can arbitrarily decide that?'

'Yes, I can.'

Holly shook her head.

'Holly,' Drake said. 'Jonah demanded that I come back. His parting wish – his *demand* – was that I should help you and your friends in your vain search for a vaccine.'

'You think it's in vain.'

'You've seen Mannan. We've discovered nothing.'

'But you're not us.' Holly went to stand, and Drake and Paloma tried to help her. She waved them away. Tucking the gun in her belt and grabbing the phone, she pushed herself up the wall, fighting weakness more than pain. She'd lost blood. But she still had her determination.

She looked down at herself. Bloodied trousers, bra on display, dress tied around her waist. 'While I'm doing this, maybe you can find me some clothes,' she said to Paloma. Then she headed into the common room, and Drake followed.

Moira was there, examining coffee machines and juice dispensers on the counter. The short woman glanced her way, but Holly did not acknowledge her presence.

In the garage there were two bodies lying beside the Hummer, and its windows were smashed. Jonah had fought to block the doorway when the plague had already spread, and it was with that realisation that Holly felt the first stab of sorrow. *I'll never see him again,* she thought, and she remembered him laughing, talking about things she barely understood and drinking his precious whisky. A complex man, Drake had called him. He didn't know the half of it.

The keys were still in the vehicle. Holly drove it ten feet from the doorway, wondering whether she was changing anything. Perhaps the fates of whole universes hung on what she was doing right then. Or perhaps nothing mattered at all.

'That'll need guarding,' she said, pointing at the door as she walked back towards the common room. Drake nodded.

Moira was standing by one of the easy chairs where Holly had once sat and talked with her friends and colleagues. She had the look of a cowed dog seeking attention.

Pausing before her, Holly said, 'Right, then.'

From the garage, soft hooting.

And then came the screams.

8

All the time Jonah ran, he expected the Inquisitor to appear in front of him and trip him, stun him, carve him up and implant those grotesqueries that would make him one of its own. But he was starting to think that he was precious to the Inquisitor. He was his world's chosen one — his reality's human who would become one of their wretched missionaries — and so perhaps he now held the highest card. He had to submit to his fate in order for the Inquisitor to operate . . . because the being had no wish to harm him.

It would have been funny if it were not so perverse.

So he slowed to a walk, always conscious of the gentle tug drawing him forward, the stronger force pushing him from behind. If he veered aside from the invisible path the sensation would tell him, and he could easily correct his course. He had always been one to take his own route through life, but things were different now. He felt the spike of the alien object nestled against his heart, and the warm flexible globule in his pocket. In many ways he no longer belonged to himself.

Jonah absorbed the experience and relished every sight and sound, though many of them were bad. This world had once been wondrous. It was dead now, haunted by shadows, inhabited by slow-moving things that were easy to outrun. His heart thudded, stumbling frequently, palpitations taking his breath away. He considered the irony of dying now of a heart attack, and thought of the science that the Inquisitors must have to enable them to change him so thoroughly. *You will never die*, he had been told. If that was the literal truth, then the knowledge and technologies involved were incredible.

And I'm going to kill them all, he thought. But he couldn't let any craving for understanding distract him now. It was all so tragic.

He allowed himself to be steered, passing those strange shell-like structures, until he found the breach that must have broken through into *this* world. It rested in a natural dip in the land, and a stream flowed directly into it. Jonah did not even break his step.

The pull that Jonah felt was subtle, the repelling pressure from the world he left huge. Memories struck him as soon as he entered. In many of them, Wendy seemed to exist in other people's snapshots – walking in the background of a holiday photo, passing a group of people playing frisbee in a park, sitting five tables away in a restaurant as romance blossomed between a couple she would never recall seeing. His heart warmed at the sight of her, and yet the memory of her seemed more remote than ever. And as he emerged into raging snow, he already felt cold and distant.

Jonah had always loved the snow. When he'd been a child it had been something that transformed the South Wales valleys into a kids' playground, and as an adult it had always reminded him of those times, giving him a glimpse and a memory of home. But emerging into this other Earth, the shock of dislocation was almost enough to stop his ailing heart and kill him.

He gasped and sat down hard. Flakes settled in his thinning hair and clung to his stubble, dancing in front of his eyes, landing on his tongue. When they melted there they tasted of distances he could never imagine. *I'm leaving a part of myself everywhere I go,* he thought, and it was a strangely comforting idea for someone so rooted in science and reason. Much of this new world might well resemble the one he had left behind, but an understanding was slowly dawning – the more breaches he found and fled through, the further away he was from home.

Then he lifted his head and really looked, and wonder overcame his trauma for a time.

This dark breach was set atop a pedestal in a wide room. The roof was holed in several places, the whole structure charred and warped as if by some huge fire, and the snow swirled through the gaps. Surrounding the breach was a circle of solid desks, half buried by snow but their purpose obvious and thus reminiscent of Coldbrook. Some were barely damaged, others had been melted into grotesque shapes by the fire that must have ruined this place long ago.

The little stream passed around Jonah's feet and added its contributions of ice to the frozen sculptures that hung from the pedestal.

There were five other pedestals, leading off from his in

a broad curve around the room. Two of them were empty, but the other three supported obsidian globes, depthless black orbs that swallowed the snow and gave back nothing.

'Bloody hell,' Jonah muttered into the gusting snow.

Breathing hard, he stepped forward and almost slipped on ice. Carefully, he descended from the pedestal: three steps to the floor, where the snow came up to his shins. He glanced back at the breach he had come through, ready to bring his gun to bear against any threat that presented itself. None of the furies from that world followed him, and neither did the Inquisitor.

There was no movement around him apart from the falling snow. Whatever had befallen this world had occurred long ago, or if it was still going on it was happening else-where. The massive holes in the roof seemed to have been punched in, not out, and he imagined the people of this Earth lobbing artillery shells at their Coldbrook facility from a distance in a vain attempt to close the breaches they had made, shut them off from the terrors pouring through. But by then it had already been too late.

Something rose across the room. It crackled and snapped as it pulled itself from the ground, frozen there, a sticklike figure made into a snowman. Jonah took a few steps towards it and put a bullet into its head. The snow was splashed red. All those years the fury had lain there dead, and its brains were still wet. Jonah wondered at its dreadful dreams.

He turned a full circle, taking in the whole huge room, intrigued by notions of the possible technologies hidden beneath the white blanket. But he did not have time to explore. That was not why he was there.

The Inquisitor stood at the end of the room in an open doorway. The space behind him was shaded and free of snow: a corridor, perhaps, leading deeper into this Earth's Coldbrook.

Jonah backed away towards one of the other breaches. The Inquisitor advanced, matching him step for step. The wound on its shoulder had ceased bleeding, the blood by now a stiff black carapace. He hoped that the wound might even have left a scar.

I'm not running, he thought, because it was obvious that this was something that could not be escaped. So what was he doing? He felt the awfulness of the distances he had come.

'Accept,' the Inquisitor said.

'No,' Jonah replied, and he dashed at the next breach. He didn't even pause for breath before walking through, though he did have time to think *I wonder where all the others go?*

9

'It doesn't mean there's anything wrong,' Lucy said. 'Maybe she's just busy.'

'Yeah.' Vic had been trying to contact Holly and the phone rang and rang. Every time he blinked he saw Holly as one of those things, only now she was grinning with his dead sister's grin.

'What's wrong, Daddy?' Olivia asked.

'Nothing,' he said, smiling at his daughter. 'You and Mommy are here, so everything's fine.' Lucy half-smiled and looked away, out of her side window at the wild mountainsides passing by.

Sean had taken over the driving, and Marc sat in the passenger seat with his laptop open. On the dashboard in front of him was the notebook with the handwritten list of names. There were at least eight people crossed off. Others had ticks beside them, and a few more had yet to be contacted.

'Those names you've crossed off—' Vic began, but Marc did not let him finish.

'Dead.'

The silence in the vehicle was sombre. Beside Vic, Jayne shifted, groaning softly.

'Just because you can't contact them—'

'This one,' Marc said, voice loud and firm. 'Radomyr Golovnya. Lives in Kiev. The Russians have used some unknown weapon along their western borders, and Ukraine and Belarus have been affected. So Radomyr, a brilliant physician, a man I once argued with for six hours about the common cold, is dead.'

He struck the pad with his pen, indicating another name. 'Rob Nichols. Quiet guy, too humble for my liking – I mean, he was a fucking genius. He lived in Wales, he and Jonah went to the same school but at different times. And I can't reach him, and I know he's dead, because I've seen what's become of Cardiff.'

'Phone lines and networks—' Vic began, but Marc cut him off again, needing to name his dead friends to vent his rage and grief.

'Kagiso, she told me that her name means "peace". Johannesburg. It's just . . . gone. They nuked it. Kagiso was the best paediatric-disease researcher I've ever met. Beautiful woman.' He shook his head and touched another crossed-out name. 'Caspian Morhaim, micro-biologist. Kicked out of seven universities, four ex-wives, seven kids at the last count. Completely fucking insane. Knows more about hot viruses than anyone. He once told me, "Ebola is my bitch." Spends half his life in BSL-4 labs, then for kicks he bungee jumps and free-dives, just to clear his head. He worked in Galveston, University of Texas. And Texas is fucked.'

Marc touched other names and shook his head again. The car remained silent for a while, all of them waiting for him to go on. But now the silence became a respectful goodbye to the dead they all knew.

He's thinking of them still walking, Vic thought. He closed his eyes and could only picture Holly.

'But there are others? You'll get the help you need?' Sean asked. They were climbing the side of a mountain, the road zigzagging through a heavily forested area. The truck and school bus followed, along with several more vehicles that had joined the column. Some of the Unblessed gang had taken to roaring ahead to clear the way, and often they'd leave a corpse or four by the roadside. Other times, the rest of the survivors would catch up to find the bikers shooting at shapes that were pushing their way through the undergrowth. No one thought that target practice was a bad idea.

One of the bikers was a huge man with incredible facial hair. Each time Olivia stared at him from the station wagon window he performed a clumsy dance for her that ended in a pirouette. Vic treasured the sound of his daughter's chuckling and realised that he had not made her laugh since this nightmare had begun.

'Help,' Marc said. He turned in his seat to look at Vic and his family, and at Jayne leaning against the door. 'Yeah,' he said, 'I've got help. Some people are emailing me as much data as they can. A few are on the move like us, trying to survive. But they've said that they'll send me information, opinions, theories, guesswork as long as they can. They're making it their prime aim.' He shook his head. 'Some I believe, some I don't. Prime aim . . . that's got to be family, hasn't it?' He glanced at Vic. 'Hasn't it?'

Vic nodded.

'But do any of you have any idea what I have to do?' Marc asked. 'Any concept of how difficult it is to analyse a new disease and create a vaccine? Give me ten years and I might have an idea of what we're dealing with here.'

'Are you saying you can't do it?' Lucy asked. 'Because we've come all this way with you, back to where we *started*.'

'We came because Jonah told us to,' Marc said, 'and now Jonah's gone.'

They rounded a bend and the road levelled out across the mountain's wide summit. To their left, nestled in a valley, glinted a gorgeous lake, surrounded by wooded slopes and seeming peaceful and calm.

'I'll need volunteers,' Marc said. 'Eventually, if I think I can pin down why Jayne's immune, and create some sort of vaccine, I'll have to test it on someone. They'll have to allow me to infect them. I'll make mistakes.'

They soon reached a crossroads and Vic directed Sean to make a left turn, taking them down around the lake and up the other side of the valley. Over the next ridge lay Danton Rock, and in the valley beyond that was Coldbrook.

'We should stop when we find somewhere clear,' Vic said to Sean.

'Sure thing.'

'Good,' Jayne said. 'I need to stretch my legs before Mister Cheerful here starts cutting me up.'

Marc laughed. Jayne grinned. And Vic felt excluded from their contact, an outsider in a car filled with fellow survivors. He thought of trying to call Holly again but Lucy was sitting beside him, warm and quiet. He'd done everything to get his family back – and he would do anything to keep them.

The huge biker's name was Chaney. He came from San Francisco, claimed to be descended from Jack London, and said he was a lawyer. He and the rest of his Unblessed were bike enthusiasts from all kinds of backgrounds and jobs, weekend warriors rather than a hardcore gang. They'd been up here touring the Appalachians when the outbreak began. There had been almost twenty of them back then.

'Why didn't you try for home?' Vic asked Chaney.

''Cos I'm clever,' Chaney said. 'Decided to wait it out where there aren't many people.'

Vic didn't ask where a casual gang of bikers had found and learned to use so many weapons.

They got everyone together, and Vic told them that Coldbrook was a government seed vault, a storage facility buried deep in the mountains and designed to withstand catastrophes ranging from nuclear war to climate change to meteor strike.

'And there's room for all of us down there?' Chaney asked. There were over fifty survivors in the convoy now, in a collection of cars, trucks and motorbikes, as well as the bus filled with kids. Vic thought of Coldbrook jammed with all these people.

'Yeah,' he said. 'For a while. There are labs and admin offices down there, and sleeping quarters. There's an air vent leading to the surface – easy way in, in case it's locked down.'

'And what're you?' Chaney asked. The big man was smiling, Vic thought, though the extravagant beard all but hid his mouth.

'Plant scientist,' Vic said. 'Er . . . fungi.'

'Pomologist,' Chaney said.

'Yeah. That's me.'

Chaney nodded. 'So we get down into your Coldbrook seed vault, then find a cure for a disease that turns everyone into zombies.'

'That's it,' Vic said. He nodded at Marc. 'Marc and I were at . . . university together. He's an expert in epidemics.' He stared at Chaney. 'A phorologist. And he's in contact with a lot of his associates around the world. And with Jayne he thinks we might have a chance.'

'Shouldn't this all be . . . I dunno, the government?'

'What government?' Sean asked.

'The Centers for Disease Control in Atlanta is gone,' Marc said. 'And the fact is that Jayne's here with us, not anywhere else. How that got to be is a story for when we're tucked away safe and sound, but—'

Five gunshots rang out.

'Three of 'em were coming up through the trees!' a man shouted from the edge of the clearing.

'Keep your eyes peeled!' Chaney called. From away in the distance came that low calling.

'Vic,' Sean prompted.

So Vic told them all about Danton Rock, and how the only road to Coldbrook passed through that town. Never for a moment did it feel as though he was talking about his home.

'So let's roll,' Marc said.

They returned to their vehicles, and as Vic and Lucy helped Olivia back into the car, Vic felt someone standing behind him.

'Ma'am, could I speak with your husband?' Chaney asked.

'Only if you promise to dance for my daughter again,' she said, smiling.

'Well, now,' Chaney said, and Vic was amazed to see a blush on his cheeks, 'I'm afraid true art can't be produced to order. But I'll see what I can rustle up later.'

Chaney walked a few steps to the side and Vic followed him.

'Okay, so it's not a seed vault,' Vic said.

'No fuckin' shit. I don't give a damn what it is, so long

as what you told us is true. First, that it's safe. And second, that your guy there might be able to come up with a cure.'

'Both true,' Vic said.

''Cos me and my guys have done okay staying in the hills away from other people.'

'Really?' Vic asked. 'You're doing okay?'

Chaney blinked a few times, but never looked away from Vic. 'You got something heavy on your shoulders, man,' he said.

'Tell me about it.' Vic smiled and held out his hand, and Chaney gripped and shook it.

Back in the station wagon, Marc was already working on his laptop again, and Sean was strapping on his seat belt. 'Everyone belt up,' he said. 'Gonna be driving fast, and not stopping for anything.'

Vic breathed in the mountain air and heard that haunting call somewhere in the distance. They were about to drive through Danton Rock, where they would see people that he and his family knew.

He checked the M1911, then pulled the satphone from his pocket.

10

At the first scream Moira's eyes widened and she darted past Holly, pulling free the crossbow slung around her shoulder, loading it as she ran. Holly had time to notice how gracefully she performed these actions. And as she burst through into the garage once again, Holly realised how foolish they had all been. She'd nodded to the door that the Hummer had been holding shut and had told Drake it needed guarding. But that had been wrong.

It had needed *checking*.

There were six zombies, three of them wearing the familiar dark blue outfits of Coldbrook's surface security staff, two in army fatigues, the other one naked and burned. All of them were fast. By the time Holly had reached the garage doorway, two of them were down. One lay still, the other waved her hands in front of her face trying to grab the end of the arrow that stuck out from there. The female zombie kept striking the feathered flight, swinging her head left and right in the process, making no sound.

Drake was twenty feet from where Holly stood, close to the Hummer's front end, reloading his crossbow. He glanced in her direction, then raised the weapon and fired at the burned fury. The bolt ricocheted from its shoulder and clattered against the wall, and the blackened thing darted for him.

Holly pulled her gun and aimed, but Drake was in her field of fire.

Moira ran, slid across the polished concrete floor, and

tripped the running fury. She rolled aside before it could leap at her.

Holly pushed herself from the doorway, groaning at the pain of the slow fire in her side. She aimed at the fallen fury and was about to fire when another of Drake's people shot it from across the garage. It rolled three times and then lay still, dark fluid leaking from its head.

'Watch the doorway!' Drake shouted. Holly paused, thinking he was talking to her, but he was waving at his people. 'Don't let any of them in. Don't let them through!'

'Over there!' someone shouted. 'Down. Get down!' The thrum of a crossbow. The thud of a bolt's impact. The impact of a body falling to the floor. All of this was at the other end of the garage beyond the Hummer and the 4x4s, and Holly stumbled sideways to get a clear view of what was happening, her pistol held in both hands. Behind her, three Gaians were guarding the doorway, one facing into the common room just in case any furies had slipped through without them noticing.

Good, Holly thought. *More cautious now*.

And then she saw a fury kneeling on a woman beside one of the 4x4s, darting his head to bite at her thrashing hands. She was not screaming. She bucked and tried to roll, knocking his face aside each time he snapped at her, trying to shake him but unable to do so. From somewhere out of sight an arrow embedded itself in his shoulder, but he barely paused.

The Gaians were used to furies worn down by forty years – deadly if they could get close enough but slow and withered. Not new furies like these, heavy and strong. Fast.

The dead soldier grabbed both of the woman's hands and leaned down into her face.

'No!' Holly shouted, and she ran past the Hummer, joined by another Gaian nocking an arrow as he ran. As Holly neared the thrashing pair and aimed at the fury, the man's arrow slammed into the Gaian woman's head, slamming it to one side, spilling blood. The fury sat back and turned to Holly.

Holly gasped, looking at the woman's legs kicking slowly as if she was swimming down into darkness.

'Shoot it!' the man said.

The fury stood and turned towards Holly, and she shot it in the face. It went down and she turned away, trying to see who or what was groaning in such a horrible fashion until she realised it was her.

Paloma dragged herself from beneath the Hummer and walked around the other side, towards where Holly had last seen Drake. There was blood staining the Gaian doctor's neck and shoulders, and her scalp was shredded across the back of her head.

'Drake!' Holly shouted as she ran. Each step drove pain up into her side, and she thought of the Gaian leader's wife tending the wound. 'Drake!'

Two of the three people guarding the doorway into the rest of the facility were raising their weapons, but they were too far away and they would not be fast enough.

'Paloma?' Holly heard Drake's voice as she rounded the Hummer's rear end, her pistol raised.

Drake held his unloaded crossbow in his hand, and as Paloma staggered to within five steps of her husband his expression changed from relief to horror.

Holly took careful aim at the back of Paloma's head and pulled the trigger.

The satphone was ringing. Holly could not answer. She could not look at the man whose wife she had shot. *Wherever* she looked, all she could see was the woman's head blown apart and the shower of blood and brains that had obscured her view of Drake.

She tried to pluck the phone from her pocket, but her fingers refused to obey her commands. The ringing ceased.

'Holly!' Drake said again, and this time he grabbed her face between his hands and lifted it so he could look into her eyes. She wanted to close them. But knew that she would have to face him soon.

I'm sorry, she tried to say, but no words emerged. All she saw now was him, and he was drenched in red. Someone had given him a rag, but he had placed it over his shoulder, too concerned with Holly to wipe his own wife's blood from his face and chest. *I'm sorry*.

'Holly, you didn't save me,' Drake said. 'You saved Paloma.'

'The plant-room door,' she whispered.

'It's being watched. No one's gone up yet, but we'll hear anyone coming down.'

'Might be Vic.'

'We'll be careful.' Drake eased himself back, kneeling in front of her. His expression was slack and he could not look at anything for more than a second before glancing somewhere else. He was in shock but didn't realise it yet.

Moira stood behind him, a loaded crossbow slung from each shoulder. She nodded at Holly, and Holly nodded back, and that was all that was required between them.

'Drake—' Holly began, and the satphone rang again, startling them both. She pressed the connect button and then Vic was there, his voice low and fast, and filled with urgency.

'Holly, I got you. Listen. We won't be—' The noise of gunshots drowned him out, and Holly winced and pulled the phone away from her ear.

'Vic? What's happening?'

'Holly, we'll—' More gunshots. '—soon, just passing through Danton—' Static, cries of alarm, the thud of a heavy impact. '—soon. Okay down there?'

Holly didn't know where to begin. 'Yes, all fine. Come in the same way you got out, but be careful of the duct.'

'Say again?' Someone close to Vic was crying, long ragged sobs.

'I said the duct might not be clear, so you—' A louder scream, another shocking impact, and then the connection was broken. 'Vic? Vic?'

'They're close,' Drake said.

'Danton Rock. Maybe a mile.'

'Then we need to make sure their way down here is clear.' He helped Holly to her feet, and they stood facing each other awkwardly for a moment.

Holly opened her mouth to speak.

'Thank you, Holly,' Drake said. 'You should go and find some clothes.' He left her and shouted some orders, and two of his people started to collect the bodies of humans and furies alike.

11

The third zombie that their vehicle struck was thrown over the bonnet and smashed through the windscreen. Sean cried out and leaned back as its head struck him on the right shoulder, and the station wagon swerved but kept moving. Olivia shrieked, and as the zombie turned to face her Vic recognised Walt McCready, the friend whose house they had once partied in. Now he had no eyes.

They struck something else, and Vic was flung against

the rear of Marc's seat. He dropped the phone and it disappeared down by his feet. The vehicle skidded to a halt.

Jayne grabbed his shoulder and hauled him back, moaning with the pain it caused her. Lucy and Olivia were huddled back against the door – both of them had recognised the dead man. Lucy punched at his hand as he reached for Olivia.

Vic heard the snick of a door opening.

'Don't get out of the car!' he shouted. He raised the M1911, pressed it against old Walt's face, and pulled the trigger. His hearing was obliterated briefly but that didn't stop him from seeing. Walt was blasted against the ceiling and bits of him were scattered throughout the car. Something sharp slashed across Vic's cheek, and he wondered whether being cut by a fragment of a zombie's skull could change him.

Soon find out.

'Keep the fucking doors *shut!*' he shouted. 'Let's go!' His ears were still ringing from the gunshot as he looked around to make sure that everyone was okay. Lucy's nose was bleeding from where she'd bounced off Sean's seat. She dabbed at it, staring at Vic without expression. *Rather she was screaming*, he thought.

Someone grabbed his sleeve. Sean.

'We hit one of the bikers!' he shouted. The view through the windscreen had been obscured by the starring of the safety glass on impact, which had been held in place by its frame. Marc punched it out, and he and Sean heaved Walt's dead-at-last corpse out onto the bonnet.

Ahead of them loomed Danton Rock's first building, the small school and medical centre. Half of the school had burned down. Between them and Danton Rock was a confusion of cars and bikes, and the running dead.

Someone stood in front of the car and grabbed Walt, and for a second Vic thought it was a biker pulling the corpse away so that they could drive on. But then he saw the stained and torn summery dress, and Sean rested his rifle against the dashboard and shot the woman in the throat. She shook, her head flopping to one side where her spine had been shattered. But she did not fall.

Sean fired again. As the woman slumped back, a biker tried to stand, tugging to free his leg from beneath his crashed bike. He was bleeding from a terrible wound in his throat, the blood spurting across his chest and stomach with each heave on his trapped limb. He did not appear to be in pain.

'Close your eyes,' Sean said, but he didn't wait for the others to heed his advice. It was far worse seeing a fresh one shot.

'Give me the rifle,' Vic said. 'You've got to drive.' Sean handed it back without a word and Vic leaned between the front seats, resting the rifle's barrel on the dashboard.

'We're not even in the town yet,' Marc said, his voice higher than usual.

'Laptop okay?' Vic asked.

'Yes, but we're not even—'

'Hush it down, Marc,' Vic said softly. Marc glanced back at him, then nodded. Vic wasn't sure whether to feel comforted or terrified at the older man's brief display of panic.

Sean steered around the crashed bike and the bodies. Three Unblessed bikes roared on ahead, and Vic saw the unmistakable form of Chaney riding one of the choppers, his Remington 870 still slung across his back.

'Daddy,' Olivia said, tugging at the back of Vic's sweat-soaked shirt, 'are we going home?'

Vic pressed his lips together but did not look back at his wife and child.

'School bus still behind us,' Sean said, looking in his side mirror. The bikers had given up some of their weapons to the four adults on the bus, but Vic couldn't bear to think what might happen if even one zombie made it on board.

As the first biker passed the burned school, a crowd surged from behind its boundary wall. Chaney grabbed the shotgun from his back and swerved wide to avoid the running people. He fired, pumped the gun one-handed, fired again. The two other bikers shot their way into the town. Chaney glanced back at the approaching vehicles, and then powered away.

'Heads down, close your eyes,' Vic said over his shoulder. He smashed out the remaining shards of windscreen with the rifle barrel, then aimed ahead.

'Can't afford to run into them,' Marc said.

'I know,' Sean said, pressing hard on the gas pedal.

'I mean it. Fuck the radiator, burst a tyre, and we're—'

'I *know!*'

'Easier if they're lying down,' Vic said, and he fired. A man went down. *Didn't know him.* He fired again at another man wearing fatigues, only winging him. *Didn't know him.* Sean veered past the rushing crowd and Vic shot once more, knocking a woman onto her back. *Knew her.* It was Kate Morris, the wife of one of the mechanics down in Coldbrook. He wondered where her husband was now.

Vic shot another woman directly ahead of the car. She fell and Sean drove over her, and as she rolled between the chassis and the road it sounded as if she was hammering to get in, clawing at the metal.

Vic glanced back at Lucy where she hugged Olivia's face against her chest.

He fired again. A man went down and Vic knew his face from one of Danton Rock's bars. As Sean powered along the street, Vic bestowed the favour of true death on several other people who got in their way, two of them soldiers.

'Army,' Vic said.

'Not usually here?' Marc asked.

'No. Guess they were sent to Coldbrook when Jonah sounded the alarm.'

'Let's hope they didn't hang around,' Marc said. Vic didn't reply, but he wondered just what they would find down in Coldbrook's shallow valley.

In the town square, one of the bikes had crashed and a scrum of zombies was tearing at the biker. Chaney had parked his bike and remained astride it, firing his shotgun into the mess of bodies. Sean slammed on the brakes and Chaney looked their way.

'He needs to get a fucking move on!' Marc said. He waved through the shattered windscreen, urging Chaney to mount up and move out.

'Trying to save his buddy,' Vic said. He sighted on the struggling pile and pulled the rifle's trigger. The zombies paused in their attack, stood back, revealed the dead biker with his holed helmet leaking blood. Then they turned their attention to the car.

Chaney nodded his thanks, then roared across the square.

Vic fired again, but the trigger clicked on empty. 'I'm out.'

'Here.' Sean handed him his pistol and Marc took the rifle, digging in his rucksack for spare ammunition. They were shouting, the gunfire ringing heavy in their ears.

They crossed the square, and Vic looked back to check on the convoy. The school bus ploughed into three zombies, its wheels bouncing across several prone corpses. *Should've let them go first*, he thought. Then the driver slumped down across the steering wheel and the bus veered to the left and smashed into the police station steps.

'Stop!' Vic shouted.

'What?' Sean said.

'Bus crashed.'

'Vic, what do you think you can do about it?' Lucy asked desperately. Olivia looked up at him, scared, her eyes wet. He looked around, trying to assess the situation. Other vehicles had followed them into the square, following the bikers onto the road that led out of town and down towards Coldbrook. *Almost there!* Vic thought. But there were zombies running at the bus, and the gunfire sparking from its windows was inaccurate and panicked.

Chaney had paused on the other side of the square and was looking back. Vic raised his hand.

'Don't you dare leave us,' Lucy said.

Vic pointed at the bus. Chaney revved his bike and his rear wheel screeched as he powered back across the square, kicking up clods of turf from the green, heading for the police station.

'Keep the rifle,' he said.

'Vic—'

'Daddy—'

'Don't you dare leave us!'

'Lucy, there are kids in there,' Vic said, and in his soft voice they all heard the truth. With everything he had done wrong, leaving them behind would be one step too far.

'You said you'd never leave me again,' Lucy said.

'He won't,' Jayne said. 'He'll be back. You've seen his shooting.'

Vic kissed Lucy and Olivia. 'You need to go on,' he said. 'Get Jayne down to Coldbrook and inside. Straight down the air vent, and Holly will be waiting.'

'I could come,' Marc said, and he meant it. But he also nodded when Vic refused, acknowledging how important he had become.

Vic climbed over Jayne and slipped from the car, his M1911 in one hand, Sean's pistol in the other. For a second as the car powered away he locked glances with Lucy through the back window. Then he ran for the bus.

The sound of the other vehicles' engines faded, and the hooting of the zombies was appalling now.

'Well, come on!' Chaney shouted. He and two of his gang had reached the bus, and while Chaney fired a pistol at the advancing zombies – shotgun swinging empty from his other hand, ready to club anything that came too close – the other two men were struggling with the bus's door. The kids inside were screaming. The three remaining adults were shooting from smashed windows.

As Vic sidestepped a running dead child, wondering what he had done, praying that he would see his family again, a woman on the bus turned her gun towards him.

'No!' he shouted, but she fired anyway. He ducked down, waiting for the pain. It didn't come. Someone hit the ground behind him.

'Squatting for a shit?' Chaney shouted, and he actually laughed as he came to help Vic up. His hand was huge and sweaty.

'Not sure *what* I'm doing.'

The other two bikers had prised the bus door open, and Vic and Chaney followed them on board. One of them grabbed the dead driver and pulled him aside, a wet mess. Kids screamed and the adults shouted louder to try and calm them. The bikers seemed not to notice.

'Stray bullet,' one of them said.

'Fuck that,' the other drawled. 'Stray bullets, plural. Steering column's wasted.'

'This bus is fucked?' the first biker asked.

'This bus is fucked.'

'And here come the cops,' Chaney commented, kicking the doors closed.

Vic saw who Chaney had been referring to. Sheriff Blanks and two other cops – ex-cops now, he supposed – had emerged from the station's smashed front door and were coming down the steps. The pretty officer who'd once let Vic off a parking ticket had what looked like a fence post embedded in her abdomen.

As the adults quietened the kids, that dreadful, gentle hooting came in to fill the silence. From the several streets that met on the square, and many of the buildings around them, the dead of Danton Rock converged.

'Dinner is served,' Chaney said. And he started reloading the Remington.

12

'He'll be fine,' Jayne said. She spoke through a haze of pain and the threat of unconsciousness, the simple act of talking sending vibrations into her chest that set her bones on fire and shivers along her limbs that seemed to crush her hands.

'You *can't* say that,' Lucy said as if she was disgusted.

'She *can*, Mommy. She knows.' Olivia had sat up as soon as her father had left and was staring from the back window, even as they left the town uphill behind them.

'She can't,' Lucy said, softer this time. 'It's just something that people say.'

Jayne gave the woman and her kid a smile, even though to smile hurt her cheeks. It was worse. Much worse. The churu had never been this bad.

Lucy was staring at her daughter and Jayne wondered what they'd been through already. There were billions of stories of pain and anguish on the planet today, but fewer every second. Zombies didn't have stories – no past, no future. They were as far from human as you could get.

'He's a brave guy,' Jayne said. The wind was roaring through the smashed windscreen, and now and then she thought she could hear those hooting calls.

'I'm not sure what brave is,' Lucy said. 'He's got guilt. He loves his family. And sometimes he loves someone else.'

Jayne opened her eyes a little wider and thought, *Holly*. She'd heard the way Vic had spoken to her over the phone, seen Lucy's reaction, but back then she hadn't put two and two together.

The little girl didn't know anything about all that. Her Daddy had gone to help the kids, and Jayne had told her that he'd be back. That seemed to be enough for her, but there was no saying what she was thinking on the inside. Never was with kids.

'Well . . .' Jayne said, not knowing how to respond. She shifted and bit her lip, breathing heavily against the churu coma that she felt rising. *They need me on my feet. They need me able to—*

Sean slammed on the brakes.

'What?' Marc snapped.

'Bike.' He looked back at Jayne and saw her pain. She

grinned, breathing heavily through it. 'Won't be long,' he said.

A motorbike roared uphill and skidded to a stop on the driver's side.

'Found the place,' the biker said. 'Looked from a distance – been a hell of a fight there. Dead soldiers all around, three Chinooks outside the compound, one burned out.' He spat. 'Still got the stink in my nose.'

'*How* dead?' Sean asked.

'Very dead. Didn't see any walkers. Where's the bus?' Several other vehicles had stopped behind them, and more bikes. 'And where the fuck's Chaney?'

'Bus crashed in the town. Chaney, Vic and a couple of others stopped to help it,' Sean said. 'So the compound looks clear?'

'Think so,' the biker said, staring uphill, back the way they'd come. He scanned the rear of the car, eyes lingering on Jayne and her twisted limbs. She was curled up in pain and she hated feeling different, despised the way he was looking at her. But then she realised that perhaps he saw a saviour, not a cripple.

'We'll follow you down,' Sean said.

'Got you covered,' Marc said. He'd set aside his laptop and picked up the rifle.

'I think I saw the vent you were on about,' the Unblessed guy said. 'Cover's off. We'll park as close to there as we can, and one of us'll go down, check it out. Anyone got flashlights?'

'Dunno,' Sean said. 'Maybe we should worry about that when we get there.' He pointed away from the road and across a sparsely wooded field. There was a dead horse, its corpse swollen, flies blurring the air around it, but that wasn't what he'd seen. Beyond the field were the remains of several farm buildings, one of them a charred ruin, one partially collapsed as if something had crashed through it. And from the farm, half a dozen shapes had emerged.

The zombies spoke to the dead air and started to run.

'Yeah,' the biker said, but he wasn't looking at the farm. He was pointing behind them.

'What is it?' Jayne asked, because she couldn't bring herself to turn.

'Lots of people,' Olivia said, kneeling on the back seat. '*Those* people.'

The biker pulled away, and Sean drove off fast. He angled the mirror so he could look at Jayne, then shifted it again so that he could see behind them.

'The others?' Jayne asked.

'Following. But still no sign of the bus.'

Jayne felt the churu coma circling her again. She tried to defy it, emitting a low, quiet moan as she struggled against the dark.

Someone took her hand, surprising her so much that she opened her eyes and sat up straighter. Pain roared through her, but she was used to it. She had lived with it for ever. She let it flood through her eyes and thud in her ears, and Olivia's hand around hers, her smile, suddenly made things easier.

They passed around a low outcropping in the hillside. The road curved down into the valley, and there was the small compound that might be their new home. Its area was perhaps two acres and it had a few buildings, some informal gardens, parking areas, and a low level of security – fence planted with hedging to disguise it, single guard-house at the gate. From this distance the bodies that the biker had mentioned were specks, the Chinooks toys.

'That's it?' Jayne asked.

'Iceberg,' Lucy said. 'Lots more below than above. Main entrance is that big grey concrete building, and a road circles down from there into the garage area. But we're heading for one of the ventilation ducts.'

'Why?'

'Only way in. When it hit, Jonah locked down the whole place.'

'Okay back there?' Sean asked as he drove.

'Yeah,' Jayne said. 'For now. But I'm not sure I'll be able to walk.'

'I could carry you,' Olivia said. 'Daddy says I'm the strongest girl in the world.'

'He might well be right, kid.' Jayne grinned, feeling herself pressed into the darkness. 'Oh,' she said, and her voice sounded very far away. Even the gunshot she heard could have been in another world. And then everything fell silent, still.

. . . carry her . . .

The voice was incredibly distant, echoed with the soft snap of gunshots.

. . . go down first, I'll follow, have to tie her on in case . . .

Jayne raged against the churu and opened her eyes. She was sitting on the station wagon's hood, Sean standing close to her with his back turned, and he was looking back over his shoulder.

'Hey, Jayne,' he said softly. 'Marc is tying you to me, and I'll carry you down.'

'We're here?' She looked around at Coldbrook's compound, and saw that close-up there were many more signs of everything that had gone wrong. Bullet holes pocked the buildings, windows had been blown out, and she could see three bodies. They were horribly mutilated, and wild animals had been at them. One of them had been torn open and its innards spread around. At least they didn't move.

Past a low building, a length of the boundary fence and hedging was scorched and twisted, and beyond lay the gutted remains of a Chinook, its rotors slumped and its fuselage burned away.

Jayne leaned against Sean and rested her head on his

shoulder, looking back the way they had come. Two of the trucks had been parked side by side across the gateway. She frowned.

'Wasn't there a Ford?'

'That one didn't make it.'

Zombies were running along the road that curved down the hillside and was obscured here and there by trees. The first few had already reached the low, hedged fence, and the Unblessed guys were walking calmly back and forth, shooting them as they started to climb. But there were many, many more.

'The bus . . .' Jayne said, and then darkness took her again. She threw her arms around Sean's chest and sobbed again when she felt his hands close around hers.

'Back with us?' Sean asked. His voice sounded different: echoing, yet deadened. 'Don't struggle. I'm climbing down the duct with you, but the ladder's narrow. It's dark. Only two torches. So just trust me, and—'

'Of course I trust you,' Jayne said. Rope rubbed the skin of her back raw, but it was a different pain from that of the churu and she clung to it. It was the pain of damage, not the agony she had lived with for so long. And when she felt a dribble of blood running down her side, she traced its journey, fascinated.

From above came the muffled sound of gunshots.

'How long . . .?' she asked, her voice slurred.

'We have to be quick,' Sean said.

They descended further, and then there were more gunshots, this time from below. Sean stopped and leaned slightly out from the ladder, aiming a torch downward, and when Jayne looked she saw a deep, dark metallic throat maybe five feet across. The torch's beam shook, and she could feel Sean's sweat soaking through to her.

A head appeared below them, and she gasped. *It'll look up and see me, and know me, and then it'll hoot and they'll know where we are, and—*

'Is it clear?' Sean asked.

'Is now,' the man said, looking up. It was Thomas, the guy they'd picked up at the roadblock.

'You *sure?*'

'Yeah. One of them, hanging on to the ladder. And . . .'

'And?' Sean asked. 'For fuck's sake, *and?*'

'And there are people down here with bows and arrows.'

Bows and arrows, Jayne thought. She closed her eyes and rested her head against Sean's damp back.

'We're not out of the woods yet.' He started climbing down again, and she could feel him shaking.

13

The pressure of memories was just as great, but none of them were Jonah's own. He saw people he had never known, places he had never been, and the images gave the impression of being from some forgotten film discovered in an attic fifty years after it had been shot – scratchy, distant. Everyone he was looking at was dead, that was the only certainty. These were memories from other people and different worlds, and he wondered whether his visions would grow stranger and more remote the further he journeyed from home.

This string of universes, Jonah thought. It was a phrase that Bill Coldbrook had used to use. He'd imagined an endless thread tied in complex knots and wrapped in infinitely tight balls, each universe at a point along the string, every one overlapping every other. But perhaps there was a more regimented structure to reality, an order to the multiverse that could be called geography, one which followed that string. *If I went on, and on, and on for ever, what worlds might I find?*

He wondered if the Inquisitors would go on for ever. He shivered. And then he emerged from the breach, and what he saw was beautiful.

The landscape reminded him so much of the valleys and mountains around his own Coldbrook. The black breach behind him was nestled at the junction of two ridges on a shallow hillside. Beyond that, everywhere was wooded. The heart of the Appalachians was like this, a wild place, home to hard people and to animals that had never laid eyes on a human being. Jonah drew a deep breath and wondered what kind of life dwelled here.

There was no sign of anything man-made – no buildings, aircraft contrails, or straight lines – and it struck him that the breaches on each Earth were in remote places, beyond where humanity might have been aware of them even if those Earths had still been thriving. Breaches were evidence of a radical, daring science that the scientists had been keen to hide from view.

He started to walk, aiming downhill because that route was simpler, and soon he was swallowed by the forest.

I have almost seen enough, Jonah thought. *Almost.*

The trees were tall and healthy, mostly spruce and balsam fir mixed in with larger hardwoods, and the forest floor was home to swathes of bramble, blueberry and rhododendron shrubs. A heavier yellow fruit that he did not recognise hung in bunches from a broad-leafed plant, and for a moment he worried about trying it. Then he laughed and plucked one, popping it between his teeth and sighing at the warm sweetness.

Small blue birds flashed between tree boles, and from somewhere higher up Jonah could hear the cry of a hawk. *Sugg could tell me if that was a goshawk or a red-tail*, he thought. But Coldbrook's chef was an incomprehensible distance from him now, and probably dead.

There might be wolves and bears, coyotes and cougars, moose and caribou, and perhaps animals that he had never seen or even dreamed of. And perhaps he would see some of them if he walked far and long enough.

Something down through the trees caught his eye, a shadow that he recognised, visible against a wall of deep blue flowers. Jonah approached at his own pace. The time had to come soon, he knew. And he had a sudden, panicked thought that for every second he stalled, another world fell to the fury infection.

'I can't know that,' he said. Birds quietened around him, and something rustled through the undergrowth. How ironic it would be to die here, taken down by a wildcat or bitten by a snake, stung by a spider or mauled by a mountain bear. Ironic and tragic, because no one would ever know, in this universe or any other.

He rolled the soft trigger between his fingers, still in his pocket. It remained warm to the touch.

'Accept,' the Inquisitor told him. His voice came from beside Jonah, even though the shape he could see was at least two hundred feet away, visible past tree trunks and through the light camouflage of bushes and heavy ferns.

'Fuck you,' Jonah said mildly.

He saw the first evidence of what had become of this place. Perhaps it had been a fury, perhaps not, but the corpse, tied to a tree, was now little more than mouldy bones and scraps of leathery skin. No evidence of clothing, though the rope was wound and knotted with skill. He moved closer and saw that a spider had made its home in the cadaver's skull. The arachnid was as large as an apple, and its web was an architectural wonder: some single strands were eight feet long and stretched in all directions. He had no wish to touch one; he didn't know how fast the spider might move. But he had seen all he needed to. There was a small metal plate in the skeleton's skull, and glinting on one wrist where both had been tied behind the tree was a watch.

Another dead Earth, and perhaps centuries had passed. He would never know when that watch had stopped.

Jonah moved on. This world had been darkened for him, and yet the beauty of the scenery seemed to bloom brighter. The flowers were wonderful, their scent subtle on the air; birds flitted from branch to branch, or plucked insects from the air, or gracefully rode thermals higher up; the tree canopy shifted and swayed, alive and kissed by the wind. And he would never be able to tell anyone about this.

I've seen more than any human ever has, he thought, *travelled further, and to die right now would just feel like only one more step.* But he still found comfort in the idea that had always kept him rooted – there were billions of stars in the galaxy, billions of galaxies, and perhaps infinite universes. He meant so little, and knew next to nothing.

The figure stood beside a fallen tree, flies buzzing around but never quite settling. The Inquisitor seemed to favour his left leg, his right shoulder was a hard scab of blood against his robe, and now that he was this close Jonah was sure he could see the end of a snapped-off crossbow bolt pinning the clothing there. The man swayed slightly, and steam rose from his strange mask and from vents in his bulbous goggles. There was so much that Jonah could ask, but he didn't want to know.

'I accept,' he said, and the Inquisitor let out what might have been a sigh.

14

'We are so fucking fucked!'

'Hey, not in front of the kids,' Chaney said.

'The kids! The fuckin' kids?'

'Dude. Please.' Chaney grabbed the biker's arm and squeezed. Vic laughed out loud.

More gunfire, more falling bodies, more swearing, the smell of fear from where some of the kids – or maybe the adults – had pissed themselves, more screaming, more thudding of zombie bodies striking the bus and scrabbling for purchase, and five minutes ago when Vic had asked about ammunition Chaney had glanced at him without replying, his look answer enough.

'Five more minutes,' Vic said from where he was hunkered beneath the shot-up steering column.

'Yeah, maybe,' Chaney said.

Glass smashed, someone grunted. And then screamed.

'Stay back, stay *back*!' a biker shouted, and Vic did not look up. He was splicing three wires together, bypassing the ignition, and he had enough to concentrate on without—

'Shoot her!' the biker shouted.

'But she's Mrs Joslin, she's our—'

Gunshot, splash, a body hit the bus's floor, and the children's screaming changed. It turned crazed.

'Hurry up, dude,' Chaney said, crawling over to kneel beside Vic.

'I'm hurrying.'

'I mean it.'

'I'm hurrying! Every time you tell me to hurry I have to answer you, and that slows me down because I need to concentrate here, and—'

Chaney tapped his leg and stood, his gun blasting again.

The biker's initial assessment of the state of the bus had seemed obviously correct but on closer inspection Vic thought he could fix it. Everyone was pleased to hear that. Scores of zombies now surrounded the bus, and more appeared from around the town every minute. Many more – perhaps hundreds – had gone in the opposite direction, following the others towards Coldbrook. How they chose which way to go, or whether they *could* perform any thought process that could be described as choosing, was something that troubled Vic. But he'd dwell on it later. Right now he was using Chaney's bowie knife and a nail-grooming kit as impromptu tools, and the guts of the steering column were hanging above him. The shear bolt and retaining clips had been blasted apart, and these he could repair temporarily. The bigger problem was that the steering lock had been deformed and the starter was smashed. As he finished splicing the wires he touched them to another bare wire. They sparked, and the engine coughed.

'Done?' Chaney shouted.

'Two minutes.'

'Make it one.'

'I'll make it two!'

'Make it one and a fucking half!'

'Not in front of the kids, dude,' Vic said, concentrating on the steering lock, wondering whether he could risk wedging Chaney's blade in there to try and jimmy it straight, worried that it would snap off and lock the steering completely. As it was now, they'd have about seventy per cent of the steering capability, and to turn right would take a much longer, wider sweep.

But fuck it.

'Done,' he said. Chaney grabbed Vic's belt and pulled him out, hauling him upright in one move and dropping him into the bloodied driver's seat.

'You got the duty,' he said.

'Fine.' Vic had only glanced around briefly and what he'd seen was not good. Zombies crowded at the unbroken windows, smashing at them with fists and heads, falling away with bullets in their brains.

'Out of ammo,' one of the bikers said.

'Then piss on them!' Chaney shouted.

Kids screaming, the two adults remaining with them doing their best to calm them, and the most terrifying thing wasn't the noise of gunshots or the screaming but the soft calling of the zombies. Weren't they supposed to growl, or groan, or moan? And weren't they supposed to *eat* their victims? But there were no *supposed tos* here. This was reality.

Vic once more touched wires to each other and this time twisted them together. The engine grumbled into life. It didn't sound too happy about it. 'Come on, come on, be a good girl,' Vic said. He slid the gearstick into reverse and pressed down on the gas. The bus rocked and then moved, and in the mirror he saw several standing kids jolted to the floor. The gunfire lessened, and then the bus started bumping over fallen bodies.

'Gross,' Chaney said.

'How much ammo you guys got left?'

'Not much.'

Vic nodded and kept reversing, checking in the side mirrors and not slowing down when he saw zombies in his way. The woman cop with a fence post through her lay in the road, thrashing around like a beetle turned onto its back. Vic twitched the wheel slightly, then looked away. He hoped that she'd be grateful.

'The bus turns left, but right will be a problem.'

'Oh. I thought you'd fixed that?'

'I did what I could, given the circumstances.'

'Right. You think we'll make it?'

Vic thought of the route down to Coldbrook, going over each stretch of road in his mind's eye. 'There's one bad turn . . . but if I can bounce us off the banking . . .' He shrugged.

'Bounce us.' Chaney stood beside him, shotgun held in both hands. 'You seen *Speed*?'

'The film?'

'Yeah. These buses can do amazing things. Jump impossible gaps. Wheelies.'

'Right,' Vic said, and the two men laughed. It felt surreal to hear laughter in such a place. The ground in front of the police station was strewn with bodies, many of them still moving, and there was an open area where the bus had been parked. Rising slowly from a body heap was Sheriff Blanks. He still wore his gun, but not his hat. His left leg was crushed and he kept tilting in that direction before righting himself again, a constant sway-and-stumble. He stared at the bus.

Vic started forward and hauled the wheel to the left. *Hope this holds*, he thought as unsteady vibrations shook it.

'Get the kids down,' Chaney shouted back. 'They won't want to see this.'

The bus struck Blanks and knocked him back to the ground. Vic hoped that he'd smashed his skull, but there was no way to make sure, and no time. They ground over more bodies and continued in a tight circle, and Vic eased off the turn earlier than he would have normally. The bus straightened slowly, crossed the lawned area at the square's centre, and then he aimed the vehicle for the road leading out of town.

With the bus mobile, the zombies didn't stand a chance. A few faced them head-on, and Vic ran them over. Others leaped at the bus as it passed, some managing to grab onto frames where windows had been shattered. There were gunshots, but mostly the vehicle's occupants saved their ammunition and let the things fall away behind them.

Vic saw people that he and Lucy had socialised with – town barbecues on the square, bowling nights, evenings at the pub – and there were others he recognised from their work in association to Coldbrook. He kept telling himself that they were no longer themselves. It worked, mostly.

Coming back to you, Lucy and Olivia. The thought drove him on. The steering wheel thudded against his hand as the wheels tried to take them in a different direction, and he could feel a terrible vibration through his feet from the steering column. His daughter and wife were warm and alive. He would touch them again. They'd made it to Coldbrook and were inside, safe, protected, waiting for him to return.

As they left Danton Rock he hoped the going would be easier, though it appeared that most of the town's inhabitants were leaving as well. Some were following the road, but most of them seemed to be taking a more direct route, crossing the hillsides and passing through the wooded areas between the town and the Coldbrook valley. As though they were being called.

There was a blue Ford on its roof beside the road.

'One of ours,' Chaney said. A man and child stood beside the car and at their feet was a woman's body, still half inside the broken door. Two zombies walked past the car, and Vic thought, *They can smell their own.* The little girl ran at the bus. Vic accelerated and did not look back.

From behind him came the steady crying of traumatised children, and the deeper sobs of adults. Mrs Joslin's body had been wedged beneath two seats, but her blood on the floor was still wet. The two Unblessed had taken seats, one at the rear of the bus and one halfway down. They stared stoically ahead, neither of them catching Vic's eye in the big rear-view mirror.

'This the right you mentioned?' Chaney said.

'Yeah.' Vic edged the bus as far to the left as he could, then started a gentle right turn. As he'd guessed, the bend was tighter than the bus could take and inevitably they would hit the bank rising from the road on the left.

But where he'd remembered a sheer bank it was actually shallower. Too shallow to nudge them off.

'So . . .?' Chaney said, holding onto the back of Vic's seat.

'Best sit down,' Vic said.

A man stood on top of the bank, silhouetted against the sunlit sky. His tangled hair was a blood-soaked halo.

'You're sure this will—?'

'I want to see my wife and daughter again,' Vic said. 'There's no way that won't happen. Make sure everyone's holding on. Ten seconds.'

The bus's left wheels left the road, rumbling across rough ground, and then they started climbing the slope. *Please don't turn over, please don't flip*, Vic thought. But he didn't know who or what he was asking.

The bus tilted to the right, and Vic turned as far in that direction as he could. The steering wheel thumped at his hands, the impact travelling up his arms and wrenching his shoulders, and the noise was tremendous. Rocks scraped against the chassis, kids cried out, the windscreen starred and shattered, and then the front end slipped down the slope and bounced back onto the road. Vic wrestled the wheel as the big vehicle rocked back to the left. He banged his head on the side window, cursing. Then they settled, still moving, and—

something's wrong

—the bend eased ahead of them, and as the kids

cheered and clapped Chaney slapped him on his painful shoulder. Then Vic saw hands across the bottom of the windscreen's frame.

The man from the top of the bank reared up and came at him, pulling himself through the shattered window.

Vic pressed himself back into the driver's seat, and then the man's face exploded sideways. Vic's ears rang, and Chaney reached past him to push the body back out, grabbing the wheel as the bus drove over him, struggling to keep them straight, his shotgun wedged across Vic's lap where it had fallen.

Vic leaned forward and grabbed the wheel again, nudging Chaney aside with his shoulder. Vic was shouting – he could feel his mouth open and the pressures in his throat – but he could barely hear his own voice. He could feel a trickle of blood from his right ear.

Chaney laid one big hand over Vic's and squeezed. The gesture was intimate and gentle, and welcome.

Coldbrook came into view a couple of minutes later. And any relief Vic had thought he might feel at seeing that place again evaporated.

The compound was crawling with the walking dead.

15

'I see you coming down the road!' Holly said as soon as she answered Vic's call.

'Lucy and Olivia?'

'They're fine. Down in Coldbrook.'

Vic sighed and closed his eyes. *They're safe!*

'Jayne's here too, but she's . . . not well.'

'What d'you mean?'

'Her disease. She's in and out of coma.'

'But Coldbrook's safe?'

'For now. Drake and his people are helping us. I came up when Lucy told me what you'd done.'

'Where are you now?'

'Inside the duct housing, looking out. Vic . . . there are hundreds of furies. Those biker guys and a few others are holding the perimeter. But for every one they shoot down, two more take its place.'

'I see Chinooks. There are soldiers there?'

'Yeah. Zombie soldiers.'

'Shit,' Vic said. 'But their weapons?'

'Mostly outside the boundary,' Holly said.

Vic had flicked the satphone's speaker on and Chaney was listening in. He'd calmed the kids down and told the adults to keep watch at the smashed windows. They could see more zombies converging on them from the hillsides and back along the road, but they needed a breather so that they could pause, plan.

'So how do we get in?' Vic said. 'That fence and hedge isn't much, is it? Amazed the bastard things haven't just marched through it.'

'Me too. But aim for the gate. It's open, but blocked off with the two largest vehicles — a few of the fuckers squirmed underneath them but they were shot, and their bodies are blocking the way for others.'

'Miss, my name's Chaney,' Chaney said over the satphone to Holly. 'You know as soon as those trucks pull back there'll be a flood of 'em. And though Vic here's a mean driver, he won't be able to run them *all* down.'

'Hey, Chaney. Yeah. But it's the only way. Vic, try and pull up against the duct housing, might be able to just step across.'

'Won't be long before they follow us down the duct.'

'You'll have to be quick. But we're ready to block off Coldbrook's garage as soon as we're all inside.'

'You won't be in one of the trucks?' Vic asked, because he could already see that whoever drove them from across the entrance would be in major trouble.

'Can't. Been stabbed.'

'Stabbed?'

'Long story. Vic . . .'

'Yeah?'

'Just . . .' Everything unspoken between them for years remained unspoken, but its weight reached them both.

'Jeez,' Chaney said. 'Be there soon, miss. Open the bar.' He clapped Vic on the shoulder and turned to tell everyone what was happening.

'Yeah,' Vic said into the phone. 'See you soon.'

Holly signed off.

He started driving again, slowly, heading for Coldbrook's main gates as he had hundreds of times before. The closer he came, the more he saw of the desperate siege that the compound was under.

The two trucks were parked nose to tail across the gate. There was a man on each roof, shooting any zombie that managed to scramble up that high, and piled in front of the gates were a dozen bodies. He'd have to drive over them. More were sprawled around the perimeter fencing, and they formed a raised step from which others tried to launch themselves over the hedging. Most fell back with a bullet in the head. A few made it over to be shot inside the compound.

But how much ammunition could these bikers have been carrying?

'Chaney!' Vic shouted.

'Here.'

'I think once we're through the gate I can swerve around, then back the bus against the duct housing. Rear emergency exit should be just the right height.'

'Won't that take too long?'

'Few more seconds. Best bet.'

'Sure.' Chaney moved back down the bus. 'Okay kids, and you guys, everyone to the back of the bus, hunker down, stay low. Anyone with ammunition left, watch those broken windows. Miss? The second we stop, you pull the emergency handle and pop open that back window. There'll be someone there. You do as they say. Understand that, kiddies? Do as they say, and there'll be candy and ice cream for tea.'

'I don't want candy,' a kid said, 'I want my mommy.'

'Yeah, well. Me too,' said Chaney.

Vic ran down four adults and two children, and then the trucks across the gate drove apart and the bus bounced over the piled corpses, landing heavily. Inside the compound, he turned sharply to the left, the bus shuddering, steering wheel vibrating, and felt the back end skid around on the grass. *Yes!* he thought, because that gave him the angle he needed.

Vic glanced across at the gate he'd just come through. The trucks crashed together again, crushing several zombies between them, but the attackers had swarmed. A dozen were inside and running for the bus, several falling as the men on the truck's roofs opened fire, others reaching the vehicle as he slammed it in reverse and pulled the wheel hard to the right. Even with the hampered turning ability, he was lined up just right. He floored the gas pedal. Back past the guard building – windows smashed, door off its hinges – more gunfire erupted. An explosion. Someone screaming, and—

They don't scream!

Vic glanced forward – and wished he hadn't. One of

the trucks' gas tanks must have been punctured by a stray bullet, and now the spilled fuel had ignited and the truck was ablaze. A guy had dropped from the driver's side and was running across the compound, his clothes and hair aflame, zombies grabbing for him as he ran, tripping him, falling on him and biting even as the flames flared in their hair and transferred to their own clothing.

Vic turned away just as the second truck caught fire.

Something was scraping across the ground beneath the bus. It thudded against the chassis. He slammed the brakes and stopped them just right, tail end facing the duct housing with a two-foot gap to open the rear emergency window. Perfect.

The banging continued.

'That was some pretty fucking shit-hot driving, Sandra Bullock,' Chaney said. 'Now let's get that candy and ice cream.' He waited until Vic was up and moving down the bus, bringing up the rear. His shotgun boomed again, and Vic's ears rang.

'How many cartridges do you have?'

'At a guess, three more up the pipe.'

Vic pulled his M1911. He had no idea how many bullets remained, if any.

The rear emergency window fell away when it was opened, and the kids were helped over into the duct housing as quickly as possible. Huddled on the small platform inside, shaded from the sun, Vic could see Holly helping them.

Will the ladder inside hold us all? he thought. *What if someone falls? What if one of those things gets in before—*

Screams, shooting, and he saw a child snatched down from the back of the bus. The kids still inside the vehicle surged back, and one of the bikers – standing with one foot on the rear window frame, one propped against the duct housing building – fired down between his feet.

Kids were now screaming, crying, panicking, and Vic's heart broke for every one of them. *I hope he killed her before they bit her*, he thought as he and Chaney exchanged a quick, loaded glance.

They didn't have long. And there was nowhere else to go.

The second truck's fuel tank went up and its door smashed through the front of the bus, scything into the upright supports ten feet from Chaney and Vic. Vic felt a wave of heat and saw people burning, smelled cooking flesh. His mouth watered involuntarily, then he retched.

'Pussy,' Chaney said, one arm around him as they moved closer to the rear window. The second biker was lifting the kids and throwing them across the narrow gap. The adults had gone over, and they grabbed the kids and hauled them in, set them on the ladder, reached out for more.

The guy straddling the gap fired again and again, and then he shouted as his gun's firing pin clicked on empty.

Vic pushed past the few remaining kids and leaned out the window. He looked down between the back of the bus and the duct housing and saw bodies left and right. They were crowding to get into the gap, but the zombies that the biker had shot had formed a barrier on both sides.

'Go!' Vic shouted. The biker ducked down and stepped through the duct hatch, then turned and reached for the next kid.

A burning man climbed the pile of corpses and reached for the window. Vic shot him in the top of the head. On the back of his leather vest was the word *Unblessed*.

'How many more?' the biker asked.

Vic looked around, and for the first time he was staring into the kids' terrified faces. He managed a smile, and one of the little girls smiled back.

'Six,' he said. 'Chaney?'

Chaney plucked up a girl and launched her through the window. The others soon followed.

Vic leaned from the window and shot a woman from Danton Rock. She bore no visible wounds, but her eyes were dead. She fell and rose again, because his aim was off. When he went to shoot her again, his gun clicked on empty.

She climbed the corpses, planted a foot on the dead burning man, and leaped.

Vic ducked inside the bus and the woman smashed against the window frame, tearing her face. Her arms came through and she kicked against the metal, trying to get a hold.

'Chaney!' Vic shouted.

'Eyes and ears,' Chaney said, and Vic closed his eyes and covered his ears. The sound of the gunshot was still deafening.

'Our turn,' Chaney shouted. 'After you.'

Vic wasn't going to argue. He stepped across the gap into the duct housing. The others were already descending the ladder, and he could just make out Holly's head in the erratic torchlight.

Chaney came across, grunting when he had to bend almost double to get through the hatch.

'We only lost one,' Vic said.

'One too many.' Chaney turned and aimed his gun at the hatch. They could see through the length of the bus, across the compound to where the two trucks were now burning ferociously. And as they watched, figures lifted themselves into the bus through broken windows, scrambling towards the back.

'There might still be guys outside,' Vic said quietly.

'Yeah.' Chaney chewed his lip, his heavy beard moving back and forth. He blinked a few times, then turned and looked below them. They could hear the echoing sound of people descending, crying, and an occasional gasp as hands or feet slipped. A torch's beam lit the upper part of the duct, but lower down Vic could see the flicker of flames. Drake's people, Holly had said. He was glad she'd gone back down.

'Chaney! Chaney!' Shouting.

'Jesus. That's Hitch!' Chaney said, recognising a friend's voice.

'On top of the bus! Me and a woman, don't think there's anyone else, don't think there can be, there're fucking *hundreds* of them.'

'Got ammo?' Chaney shouted. He fired as a zombie leaped across from the bus, pumped the Remington, clicked on empty.

'Some,' Hitch said.

'Then shoot your damn way in here!' Chaney pulled Vic back from the open hatch.

Shooting. Vic heard cries of alarm from below as the explosions echoed down the metal duct. Then a woman dropped down from the bus's roof, feet propped on the bus's emergency window frame, and as she crouched and stepped across hands grabbed her legs and pulled. Her eyes went wide and she screamed, falling forward, her face striking the duct's edge with a sickening crunch. She went slack and the zombies pulled her into the bus, and as they started biting Vic shouted, 'Hitch, *now!*'

Hitch dropped down between the bus and the duct, then sprang up into the opening, a heavy pistol clasped in his left hand. Vic grabbed one arm and Chaney the other, and they hauled him inside. His jeans seemed to catch on something and they pulled harder. Then two zombies rose in front of the opening, holding on to his legs.

'Gun?' Vic said. He took Hitch's gun and leaned over his back, shooting first one and then the other zombie in the face. He didn't register who they might have been, not even their sex. They fell away and Hitch scrambled inside. It was then that Vic realised they had another problem.

He glanced down the five-feet-wide shaft. The nearest kid was maybe twenty feet down, with another twenty to go before they reached the first damper across the duct. Those lower down had already worked their way around that structure, descending the same way he'd ascended less than a week ago.

And the duct access cover was outside, buried beneath twenty bodies.

'Go,' Chaney said.

'But—'

'Go. Your family.' He snatched the gun from Vic's hand and pushed him, grasping his belt so that he didn't tumble from the small platform.

'No time to argue,' Hitch panted. He smelled of fuel and sweat, and there was vomit and blood plastered across the front of his leather jacket. Unblessed indeed.

Vic knew that every moment counted. So he grabbed the ladder and started down. Hitch came after him, and for a few seconds Vic heard Chaney grunting and cursing. The weak daylight from above flickered. Vic looked up as he climbed down, and past Hitch he could see Chaney struggling on the small platform.

'Chaney!'

'Coming.'

'Now.'

'Yeah, yeah.' More shots, and the light seemed weaker now. *Killing them as they come in*, Vic thought.

A child cried out and Vic looked down. He'd trodden on a kid's fingers. 'Go on. Quick!' Three children huddled on the damper blocking the duct, one of them clasping an electric torch, waiting for their turn to worm through to the next part.

'Shit!' Chaney shouted above them. 'Shit!' The gun fired twice more before it ran out of ammunition. 'Okay, coming down, better get your asses in gear.'

'Move!' Vic said to the kids. He jumped down next to them, trying to stand on the struts across the damper. If he put his foot through it he'd be trapped.

Two kids climbed through, and as the third went Vic grabbed the torch from his hand. He was barely eight years old. 'Candy and ice cream?' he asked.

'Yeah, buddy.'

The boy nodded and climbed down, guided by someone from below.

Hitch reached the opening and twisted through. Chaney

was descending. And then the duct grew lighter again, and Vic knew what was happening without even looking.

'Chaney, hug the ladder!' he shouted, pressing himself against the duct. Chaney grunted, and three bodies crashed down behind Vic, thumping against his legs. He turned quickly, but they were motionless, their heads ruined.

'Hoped that'd hold them longer,' Chaney said, looking up.

Sounds came from above, and Vic looked up past Chaney to see another shape launch itself into the duct. It struck the sides and started spinning, and it hit the fallen bodies head first. It slumped against the duct, then started thrashing.

Vic brought the torch's heavy end down on the zombie's head, again and again. Each time he struck it jerked and hooted, and he was terrified he'd get its stuff on him, brains or blood or spit, that would work its way into scratches on his hands or arms.

'Feet,' Chaney said. Vic stood and stamped down. It was keening softly, a high-pitched noise that seemed to fill the duct, and when the skull broke it rose into a cry.

'Dude, that's not a person,' Chaney said, dropping down beside him.

'Yeah.'

'Go. Torch.' The big man snatched the torch from Vic and pushed him towards the opening.

Vic dropped onto his hands and knees and backed through, swinging his legs until he felt someone beneath the damper grab his feet and guide him down. He was at eye level with the corpses, and the one he'd crushed looked at him wetly. It was a man, and he'd loved and been loved, kissed with those bloodstained lips, dreamed with that glistening, pulped brain.

'Chaney, come on!' Vic shouted, but then he saw the truth. Chaney could not come. And he knew it.

Three more zombies dropped from the platform. One landed on Chaney and pushed him down, and the big biker lashed out with the torch, catching it across the chin and shoving it against the wall.

'You stay to watch and I'll bite you myself!' he roared, and Vic knew that the only way to help Chaney was to go.

He slipped down into the next section of duct and clung on to the ladder. Hitch was lower down, looking up at the opening with his eyebrows raised. Vic shook his head.

'Fuck,' Hitch said. 'I've never seen that man lose a fight.'

'He hasn't lost,' Vic said. 'He's winning. Move it.'

They slid down the section of ladder, the duct lit by a torch shone from below. Another biker was standing on the next damper, lighting their way.

'Chaney?' he asked when they reached the damper.

'If he'd survived he'd be—' Vic began, and then the

biker's face broke into a grin. Forty feet above them, a pair of legs clad in stained, torn jeans worked their way through the gap. The legs kicked as the big man struggled, then one of his feet found the ladder.

'Told you he's never lost,' Hitch said.

'We should go,' Vic said.

'But Chaney,' Hitch said.

Vic looked at him, then at the other biker. 'You *know* we should go.'

'It's okay,' the guy said. 'He's—'

Chaney was through. Clinging to the ladder. Blood spattered Vic's face as he looked up, and he jerked back against the wall, spitting.

'Go!' Vic shouted, shoving Hitch at the gap. Hitch fell to his knees and went through, and the other biker followed, handing Vic his torch. *I should have gone first*, Vic thought, shining the light up.

'Chaney?'

The man did not look down. He clung to the ladder, and his blood speckled the duct's wall.

'Chaney?' Vic asked again. He looked at the narrow gap he had to go through, saw the Unblessed disappearing out of sight . . . and then something made him look up once more. A sense of silent motion, a feeling of change.

Chaney filled his field of vision and Vic jumped back, striking the duct wall so hard that he saw stars. The man landed hard and his feet punched through the damper, trapping him there, buried to his knees. He leaned forward – and Chaney was gone, scoured away by this fucking plague. Such a big man, destroyed completely.

And now he wanted Vic.

Vic kicked out at Chaney, knocking aside one grasping hand. Chaney hooted. It was an absurd sound coming from him, a man Vic had only known for a matter of hours but who was already large in his memory, and he looked so pathetic trapped here. Vic dodged left, and realised there was no way he could make it down into the gap without Chaney grabbing him.

He heard the noises from above and knew that none of them could hope to survive down here. The zombies were coming through, and in moments they'd fall upon him, and then he would become one of them.

If only he had a gun, he would take that pain away from Lucy and Olivia.

Chaney jerked forward, then grew still. Something sharp and wet projected from his left eye.

Vic shone the torch into the narrow gap leading around the damper. He thought it might be the first time he had ever seen a crossbow for real.

'Lucy.'

His wife was shaking, but her strength was clear to see. 'Hurry,' she said, and as she struggled back out of sight and the next body came down Vic followed her.

They worked their way quickly to the ground and went through the main duct into the plant room. There was no time to seal it from there: they could already hear the thuds of falling bodies. In the garage Holly was already revving the Hummer. Vic slammed the door and waved, and she reversed the big vehicle against the door, blocking it shut.

She pulled hard on the parking brake. They all heard it creak. So much depended on that.

Olivia ran to them, and Vic hugged Lucy and her as though he'd been away for ever. He heard children crying and talking, and one or two of them even laughed at something Vic couldn't see. Their voices were music to his ears.

16

Now what? someone said. Jayne wasn't sure who. There were new voices here, and she wasn't sure she recognised them. Or perhaps her pain was distorting the voices of those who had saved her, and making them strangers.

Now we find a cure.

Or try, Marc said, and there was an emptiness in his tone that Jayne could hear clearly, even with sight taken from her. She wondered if she would ever see again. The churu was playing with her, and each game was a fresh agony.

She's really immune, a new voice said, full of wonder.

It had a strange accent that she could not place, which gave it a sense of distance.

Just like your Mannan.

'Who's Mannan?' Jayne whispered. She recognised her own voice – even felt her jaw and mouth and tongue moving as she spoke – but the words came from a very long way off.

'Jayne?' Sean said. 'You're awake. Can you move? Can you open your eyes?'

'Nnnn,' she said, because she could do nothing. It had her in its grasp.

'What's wrong with her?'

'A disease,' Sean said. 'Churu. It affects her joints and bones. She can usually massage it away, but—'

'Does Mannan have the same disease?' Marc asked.

'No,' said the stranger. 'But this looks like chero-blight. My wife would have known for sure.'

An awkward silence. Jayne breathed deeply, felt hands on her that she knew were Sean's. They gently massaged her shoulders and neck. She opened her eyes to find that, mercifully, her vision had cleared.

'It was a common disease in our world,' the man said. 'Paloma would have known how to cure it. But we have books, a medical room, herbs, chemicals. We make do.'

'Then Mannan's immune for another reason!' Marc said, and he sounded alive for the first time since Gary's crash.

Jayne gazed around the room. It was quite large,

functional, with tables and chairs and a handful of comfortable sofas. One sofa was bloodstained, and some of the tables and chairs had been overturned. Air conditioning hummed. She felt the weight of the rock and soil around and above them. But she did not feel safe.

The people she had come to know during the past few days were assembled around her – dear Sean, Vic and his family, Marc looking thoughtful – and there were also some whom she did not recognise. One was a pale woman, leaning against a chair and pressing a hand to her side. Then there was the tall man dressed in strange clothes, a strong-looking black woman standing beside him, and several others. Beyond her field of vision she could hear adults and children talking, and smell cooking food, rich wine.

Jayne looked up at Sean, and his smile warmed her. 'What did I miss?' she asked.

17

Jonah had been too amazed at what he was seeing to consider what he *might* see. And from the moment when he had voiced his acceptance to the Inquisitor he had placed himself in that strange being's hands, and in his own hand lay the certainty of the Inquisitor's demise. Warm and flexible, the small trigger sat in Jonah's palm. When he rolled it, he felt a linked sensation in his chest, a twisting knot against his heart that took his breath away. There was such potential there. But not yet.

'Time to leave these unclean worlds,' the Inquisitor said, and held out his hand. Jonah looked close, and was shocked to see the clearly defined lifeline on his palm, hairs on his arm, and dirt ground into his creased fingertips. It looked far too human.

'How do you speak English?' Jonah asked. 'How do you *know* so much?' But the Inquisitor did not answer. Jonah took the proffered hand and saw the smudged tattoo on the inner arm again, its shape ambiguous, its edges bled and faded. And then he recognised it, and the shock struck him numb.

HMS *Cardiff*, Jonah thought. The circle of rope encircling a castle turret: the *Cardiff*'s crest. He had seen it before when he was younger, when he had briefly considered a career in the navy. Perhaps, in another world, his decision had been different.

'Who are you?' he asked. But the Inquisitor had turned and had started walking, expecting Jonah to follow and showing no emotion. Whether he had seen Jonah's shock or not, he was way beyond such Earthly concerns now.

The Inquisitor left that world, and then they were travelling. There was no slow transition: one moment Jonah smelled blue flowers and ferns, and felt the breeze in his hair; the next, they were *in between*. There was no sense of movement, nor of time passing, and yet worlds were being passed by. Whole oceans of possibilities, countless realities, all flitted past, and Jonah could only sense the magnitude of what was beyond, and the nothing of where they were. The breach that Coldbrook had formed through from one Earth to another had taken account of time and space, but the route they now travelled was timeless, and without space. In the breaches there had been memories, but here there was nothing. *Where are we?* Jonah thought, but even 'where' held no significance here.

In that non-place there was nothing around him but the Inquisitor, and he was the one thing that Jonah had no wish to see, or smell, or sense through body warmth. He tried to close off his senses, but they were not his own. He was a prisoner already.

The instant ended, and a bright light seemed to fill him and then bleed away. *I've come so far*, he thought. He had to watch; had to be aware. He could not ruin this.

Jonah opened his eyes.

The room felt painfully familiar – buried, windowless, with the weight of the world all around. But that was where any familiarity ended. He and the Inquisitor stood in the centre of the room on a smooth circular stone, worn down through the ages by generations of footsteps. Surrounding the stone were seven smooth metal uprights, waist-high and three inches thick. They glowed faintly, and

Jonah could hear a subtle ringing in his ears, as if the uprights were still vibrating with some mysterious echo.

Beyond them, the blend of modern and archaic confused his senses. Three desks buzzed and hummed, while the three people standing behind them were dressed in fine robes, inlaid with gold designs and glittering across the chests with flickering lights. They wore headpieces with microphones and earpieces, one wore heavy-framed glasses, and all three focused intently on their desks. Jonah could not see what they were doing, but their concentration was evident as the washed-out white light of reflected computer screens played across their faces.

Behind them, a tapestry covered one wall, a creation of obvious antiquity that showed Jesus lying in the Virgin Mary's arms, dead and not yet risen again. Another wall held a simple wooden cross, and the others were home to a collection of religious artefacts – crosses, artwork, carvings, parchments.

Jonah breathed in and smelled something vaguely spiced, an unpleasant aroma that reminded him of age and neglect. The Inquisitor removed the mask across his nose and mouth and inhaled, sighing deeply.

A woman behind one of the desks glanced up at Jonah and the Inquisitor.

'*Deus nobiscum sacri itineris,*' the Inquisitor said. The woman flicked a switch on her desktop, and the metal poles surrounding the smooth stone slid soundlessly into the floor.

'*Deus in nobis*,' she said. 'Please move along, Revered One. Busy day.'

Busy day, Jonah thought, wondering what she meant. 'Who are you people?' he asked, but it was as if no one had heard him. The poorly lit room thrummed with power. It was a nauseating feeling.

The Inquisitor took his arm and steered him across the room towards a door. It was set in an ornate archway, a beautiful structure that sickened Jonah with its intricacy and the care that must have been taken in creating and maintaining it. *They find time for beauty while doing their best to destroy*, he thought. He pulled free of the Inquisitor's grip and turned to face the three robed people, hating them for their casual manner, shaking with anger. The trigger in his pocket seemed to call to him, urging him to explode the disease through his heart and set himself to bite.

But the Inquisitor grasped his shoulder and pulled him on, and as Jonah reached one hand into his pocket the room lit up.

Again Jonah shrugged the Inquisitor's hand from his shoulder and turned around. The smooth circular stone glowed briefly and brightly, and the metal rods rose swiftly from the floor, accompanied by a gush of silver steam. As the glow died down, two shapes appeared within the metal circle, forming on the stone.

How many feet to wear that stone down so much? Jonah wondered. But then the shapes manifested some more, and all conscious thought was ripped away by shock.

This new Inquisitor was a woman, but there the differences ended. She still wore the familiar robes, the strange mask that leaked steam, the bulbous goggles that hid her true eyes, and the scalp hat which Jonah had started to believe had become a part of the Inquisitor he knew. Beside her on the stone stood a tall man. He was perhaps several years younger than Jonah, and thinner. But it was him. Face contorted with fear, limbs shaking, blood running down across his neck and chest from a wound beneath his left ear, eyes wide and disbelieving, mouth slack and dribbling. But still Jonah.

Me, Jonah thought. *That's me. Another me. A similar, alternate me.* And the first thing he did was to try and see whether this new Jonah clasped something in his pocket, something that might perhaps explode and mist the air of this wretched room with disease-laden blood.

But there was nothing except terror to this man, and Jonah wondered how much his world and life differed from his own.

'You . . . you . . .' the other Jonah said, and Jonah smiled at him.

'Don't be scared,' he said. 'Wendy wouldn't like that.'

'Wendy,' the terrified man said, and his shaking seemed to lessen.

'*Deus nobiscum sacri itineris*,' the woman Inquisitor said, and the robed woman behind her desk responded.

Jonah's Inquisitor grabbed his arm again and pulled him towards the deep arched opening. He pushed him close against the door and stood back, and Jonah lifted both hands to his face, tucking the nut-sized ball into his mouth between teeth and cheek. Because something was going to happen.

Flames erupted from holes around the fine stone arch. They stripped away his clothing, so quickly that by the time he registered that the flames did not burn they had faded away. His clothing and shoes lay in a scorched pile around his feet.

Brighter, heavier flames came, searing away his body hair and then coating him with a layer of something fluid and yet dry.

Jonah stroked the ball with his tongue, and looked down at his pale old-man's body, denuded of hair and speckled here and there with moles and other imperfections. *They won't see*, he thought, looking at the fine raised scar on his chest. *They won't see . . . and if they do, that will be my time. But if they don't, my time is not yet.*

He laughed softly, wondering what Wendy would make of him now. He'd always been hairy, and she'd sometimes called him her Sasquatch. Then he gasped as seven glass needles were fired at him. He felt the rush of something entering him at each penetration point, and a warmth spread through his body, flushing his torso and then filtering out into his limbs. The darts fell away to shatter on the floor.

'Your body is cleansed,' the Inquisitor said. 'Time now for your soul.'

The door whispered open in front of them, ancient oak sliding into the wall. Jonah closed his eyes and breathed in deeply, gathering himself, and it was memories of Wendy that he used to clasp hold of his identity. He could not afford to lose himself here, not for an instant. He could not let fear overcome him, nor weaken him. *I am Jonah Jones*, he thought, and as the Inquisitor led him from the room towards whatever might lie beyond, every memory he had ever treasured solidified in his recollection, and his determination to succeed grew stronger by the moment.

The door opened onto a hallway fifty feet across, a marble-clad area that stretched out from left to right. To his right Jonah saw the hallway fading into gloom, but two hundred feet to the left was a wide opening, beyond which gorgeous blue sky and blazing sunlight were visible. Elaborate sculpted fountains lined the centre of the hall, the musical mumble of falling water perhaps there to calm the people walking by. The high vaulted ceiling was decorated with complex and beautiful paintings – the Virgin Mother cradling her baby child, the scene at Calvary with characters named in ornate writing, a Concert of Angels, and a collage of holy men marching across lightning-streaked clouds. As Jonah realised that these holy men wore facial masks that looked terribly familiar, he registered just where the crowds thronging the hallway were coming from, and where they were going.

Doorways lined the wide space on both sides, equally spaced along the high walls, all decorated with arched openings and carved reliefs. The doors opened and closed, and each cycle introduced a new couple onto the floor.

Inquisitor – and victim.

There were hundreds of them there, all walking right to left towards the light. Inquisitors marched with solemnity, and their naked victims' reactions differed widely. Some shouted and raged, others cried, a few fought, and some walked with a blank-faced stare. Several people reminded Jonah of himself, and his heart raced as realities clashed.

Each Inquisitor, each Inquisitors' companion, represented another Earth fallen to the zombie plague, and the scale was staggering.

And then Jonah saw that the Inquisitors had faces.

He turned to the being who had been haunting him since the moment when the experiment to open the breach had succeeded. The Inquisitor walked as before – solemn, almost proud – but he had removed the strange snout appliance, and the goggles now hung around his neck on a ragged strap made of skin. He blinked against the light, and a soft steam rose from the moisture running from his eyes. Seeming to sense Jonah's scrutiny, the Inquisitor glanced at him.

His glistening eyes were of the palest blue, piercing and utterly human.

Jonah caught his breath and turned away. It had felt as if the man was looking into his soul. He made sure that the soft ball was secure beneath his tongue, then asked, 'What of your world?' His skin was crawling, his balls tingling. *Someone just walked over my grave,* he thought.

'This is my world,' the Inquisitor said.

'But your time in the navy, on HMS *Cardiff*. Were your parents proud? Mine would have been. Your father, the miner, do you think he would be proud of you now?'

'*This* is my world,' the Inquisitor said again without acknowledging Jonah's questions, 'and pride is a sin.' In his left hand he held the breathing apparatus that he had worn for so long. In his right he rolled and caressed a set of rosary beads. Jonah had the sudden urge to rip them away, tear them apart to send the beads skittering and bouncing across the marble flooring. But he had not come here to put on a display of petulance.

Once again he tucked the small ball between his teeth and cheek: warm, flexing. Ready to bite.

They followed the flow of people towards the opening

that led to sunlight and blue sky, and alongside the staggering architecture, beautiful painted ceilings that would put the Sistine Chapel to shame, and sculptures that seemed to exude a life of their own, Jonah noticed signs of the advanced technology that he knew existed here – floating lights, glimmering laser-fields, and prayers relayed into his mind without sound. The prayers' tone made him queasy. They shimmered with righteousness.

Unabashed at his nakedness, Jonah and his Inquisitor approached the opening at the end of the hall, and the wide stone arches framed Jonah's first view out onto this new Earth. For a second the sun was blinding, a comforting warmth on his skin and a prickling distraction in his eyes. But after he had blinked a few times he could see, and he was perhaps not as surprised as he should have been. He'd been prepared for this, after all. And perhaps, having already seen wonders, he had been numbed against more.

He had seen St Peter's Square a hundred times on television and in newspapers, but little had prepared him for its sheer size and splendour. An atheist all his life, still Jonah had found great beauty and splendour in religious architecture – some of his favourite buildings were cathedrals and churches, and while others were looking at the cross on the wall, he would be wondering at the tunnels, bodies, treasures and mysteries buried beneath his feet.

The square was filled with Inquisitors and their charges. They formed several lines on either side of the Vatican

Obelisk, which was topped with a globe, the Earth beautifully wrought in coloured, textured metals. The lines moved forward quickly, the head of each disappearing inside a large structure built on the steps below St Peter's Basilica. This was something else that Jonah had never seen: an intricate marble-clad building with a gold-domed roof, three main entrances onto the square, and smaller openings leading directly onto the Basilica steps. From here the line of naked, smooth-skinned people was directed up the steps and into the Basilica. Guided by their Inquisitors – in some cases helped along physically – their naked skin was stained with free-flowing blood, and even from this distance he could see that their faces looked wrong – noses snoutlike, eyes bulbous. The steps beneath them were stained black with old spilled blood, the marble having absorbed it over however long this had been happening until it looked as if the Basilica itself was bleeding, black blood running down into the square where worshippers had once sought to gather. These new worshippers were unwilling, and torture was their introduction into the ways of this world.

'Soon you will meet the Holy Fathers, and your acceptance into our Church will begin,' the Inquisitor said.

Jonah smiled, and nodded. And he knew at last when his time would be.

Friday

1

Coldbrook was full again, its air thrumming with fear, people hustling urgently from place to place, and Holly could feel the pressure of danger beyond the walls and above the ceilings. There was little sense of safety, and no feeling that they could stop running. This pause was a breath between screams.

More Gaians had been brought through to help guard the facility, and the adults – the Unblessed, and the others who'd come in with the convoy – were taking it in turns to eat and rearm. The bikers had lost their leader, but Hitch had said they were all part of a new gang now: survivors.

Many of the children slept, or curled up silently on chairs and beds brought into the large common room. None of them would sleep on their own, and no one would force them. There were twenty-four children in Coldbrook now, twenty of whom were without parents. They all had stories to tell. Holly didn't want to hear any of them.

Jonah was gone, Holly had barely seen Vic since his return, and she was more exhausted than she'd ever been in her life before. Her wound hurt, though the bleeding had stopped. And each time she blinked she saw Paloma's head coming apart and splashing across Drake's face. *You didn't save me, you saved Paloma*, Drake had told her. But she could not help wondering what he saw each time *he* blinked.

As she arrived back in Secondary, Marc was talking French on the satphone, and even if Holly had concentrated she would only have picked up one word in ten. So she set his steaming coffee down in front of him and took a seat, accessed the Net, and sipped her own mug as she surfed news sites. The taste of coffee, so familiar and usually comforting, seemed strange against the things she saw.

The BBC World News site was still being randomly updated, movie clips and photographs now seemingly uploaded by members of the public. And no news was good news. Governments were falling, communications were failing, and humanity's timeless ability to wreak destruction upon itself was being put to the test in a variety of ways. The UK were firebombing several of their main cities, recycling Second World War tactics in an effort to wipe out the furies. China was using biological weapons against their population, killing tens of millions in vast swathes in an attempt to protect a billion. Russia continued to defend its borders, even though the plague was rife across the country from east to west. Small wars flared, larger wars threatened, countries joined forces, others attempted to isolate themselves and ride out the storm alone.

'We're running out of time,' Holly said softly, and Marc threw the phone onto the desk.

'Fuck,' he said. 'Fuck fuck fucking hell.'

'What?'

'Time!' Marc leaned back in his chair and rubbed his face, covering his eyes as if to shut himself away from the views on the large screen. Holly switched them off. She had seen enough herself.

'How's it going?'

'Not good.'

'I thought you were gathering information, getting people involved. This network of friends you and Jonah have around the world.'

Marc laughed. 'Yeah. Net's already glitchy, and it's going to go down eventually. You know that, don't you?

It's way overloaded, and servers will crash. Bash, back twenty years.'

'So . . .'

'So I'm going to do my best. I am. But it's going to take me months, or years, and—'

'We probably don't even have days!' Holly gasped.

'Tell me about it.'

'But at least we have Jayne and Mannan,' she said, desperate for any shred of hope.

'Yeah.' Marc nodded at the laptop. Holly turned the screen to face him. Marc accessed his mail account, the printer in the corner started whispering, and he dialled the next number.

Will it really all go? she wondered. A world with no Net, no phone communications . . . and then she knew that yes, it would, because this had all happened before. Earth was following in Gaia's footsteps.

She left Marc in Secondary and paced through Coldbrook, afraid that if she stopped she would not be ready to run when the danger broke through. Perhaps she would never feel safe again. She wished she could see Vic. But he and his family had retreated to his old room, they needed their peace, and she was the last person to deny them that.

Surrounded by more people than she had ever seen in Coldbrook, Holly felt so alone.

She walked along the short corridor and passed

through the common room to the garage area. Even before she opened the door and saw the unsettled expressions of the two guards – Moira and Hitch – she heard muffled hooting echoing from the plant room.

'They just won't shut up,' Moira said.

'Spooky fuckers,' Hitch said. His voice wavered. He held a pistol ready in his hand.

Marc was right. They were running out of time.

2

'Still want to slit my throat?'

Marc jumped a little, then sighed and rested back in the chair. 'It's not over yet. I said I won't kill you until it's over.'

'Define "over".'

'Yeah.' Marc stood and stretched, his joints creaking. The desk he'd requisitioned in Secondary was piled with printouts, the laptop stood open, and the satphone was plugged in to recharge.

'So when will you be ready to begin?' Vic asked.

'I *have* begun.' Marc pointed at the printed sheets. 'I understand about thirty per cent of that.'

Vic flicked through papers, read lines here and there, saw formulae, tables, and some words he had never heard of – some of the phrases were in English and yet alien to him. He touched the laptop's pad and the screen lit up, revealing a dozen unread emails. He saw that they'd come in over the past few minutes.

'All these people are trying to help?' Vic said.

'It's going to take for ever,' Marc said. 'It's daunting. It's scary how much I don't know. I told Holly, and she didn't seem to accept that very well. And there's one thing I haven't told anyone. About Jayne and Mannan.'

'What's that?' Vic asked.

'I think they need to mate. Conceive. I think it's their child that might provide the cure.'

'But that's . . .' Vic said, aghast.

'I know. Maybe years.'

'I wasn't even thinking timescale.'

'You see my problem,' Marc said.

'Coldbrook won't last,' Vic said. 'They'll get in somehow. We're taking a breather, but everyone in the garage is twitchy, listening to those things in the duct. Soon we'll have to move again, and from then there's only one way to go.'

'I know that, too.'

Vic turned and looked at the blank screens, seeing himself and Marc reflected there. 'Tomorrow,' he said. 'We'll tell them all tomorrow.'

'Yeah,' Marc said. 'Everyone deserves a day of hope.'

3

Jayne surfaced slowly, eyes still closed, and she knew that Sean was still in the room with her. She felt his influence; she felt safe.

'Hey, you awake?' he asked.

'Yeah. How'd you know?'

'You've stopped snoring.'

'I do not snore.'

'Damn right you do. I thought it was an alarm, or something. Been banging the air conditioning, trying to get it to shut up. Dogs for miles around—'

'Way to labour a point,' Jayne said, and opened her eyes. Sean was sitting across from her, leaning back in a chair with his feet on a small desk. The room had belonged to a guy called Jonah who wasn't here any more, and the others seemed to hold him in high regard. There were books on every surface, and an old photograph of an attractive middle-aged woman on the desk. Sean had been careful not to disturb anything.

'How long have I been asleep?'

'Six hours. Since we got in, pretty much.'

'You slept?' she asked, but she knew the answer to that.

'Couldn't.' He shrugged.

'So what'd I miss?'

'That woman Holly came to visit. That's all. I think everyone's just . . .'

'Taking a breath,' Jayne said.

'Yeah. So how do you feel?'

'Bit better.' That was a lie. She didn't feel better at all, but she found that she could move more easily than before, straightening her limbs, pushing herself upright so that she was leaning against the wall. Holly had given her some powerful painkillers, and she'd had a restful sleep. The light comas were more exhausting than staying awake through the pain.

'So this Drake character,' Sean said. 'He's sent two of his people back over. Through. Whatever. Sent them back to fetch the drugs that might help you.'

'Marc is afraid that it'll affect his experiments.'

'And that's what you are now? An experiment?'

Jayne smiled, and for the first time in days it did not hurt her face. 'Sean, I owe you everything. Everything. And because I owe you, then I want a lot more people to owe you, too. I'm immune, and if Marc can make anything of that – a cure, a vaccine – you'll be the one who helped save the world.'

'Huh!' Sean shook his head.

'You're so sweet,' she said.

He didn't look at her, and Jayne knew why. She could see his daughter in his eyes, sometimes even when he was looking right at Jayne herself. She wasn't a replacement, not even an equal. Maybe they'd talk about it one day.

'I have to do what I can,' Jayne said. 'I'll take whatever Marc gives me, and give what he needs to take.'

'Even if it means you'll die?' Sean asked.

'Everyone dies.'

4

Jonah had never been to Italy. Wendy had always wanted to go, but for some reason something always got in the way. Usually his work. Now he was there, Roman sun warming his skin and the layer of matter that had been sprayed there through the doorway. If he looked up at the sky, with its wispy clouds and light blue depths, everything could almost be all right.

He was in line with his Inquisitor, and close-up he felt distant from all those other naked people. Some were distinctly human, others less so – higher-browed, taller, more heavily muscled. On distant Earths, along the string of universes, evolution had taken different tracks. As well as making them all appear vulnerable, the nakedness was also a barrier of sorts, making them ironically less than human in Jonah's eyes.

Perhaps part of it was that he knew he would be killing them all – soon. All these people brought from their Earths and their Coldbrooks, perhaps the last of their lines, chosen by their Inquisitors to oversee the infection of a new world, and he would turn them all into zombies. He would be wiping out so much intelligence, so much rich ambition and original thought and probing philosophy.

So it was easier to look at the ground or the sky, or the looming, grand buildings that would witness the culmination of his and Drake's plan.

The curved walls and grand columns around St Peter's Square had been covered with small writing, and he was too far away to read it. Perhaps it was scripture, or this world's perverted version of what scripture should be. Higher up he saw planes' contrails crossing the sky, the aircraft themselves moving incredibly quickly. Objects that he'd thought at first were birds hovered over the square, flitting here and there, and they glinted where they caught the sun. He guessed that they might be airborne cameras, and he averted his stare in case someone perceived his intent.

Men and women in colourful uniforms – orange, yellow, blue – stood at seemingly random points around the square, both at the edges and close to the central obelisk and fountain. They were in pairs or small groups, chatting and lounging against statues or walls, but Jonah sensed their alertness. He had seen photographs of the Swiss Guard, and even in his reality their ceremonial role was only a small part of their purpose. He imagined that here they must be a full fighting force. He turned his gaze away from these people as well. Their casualness disturbed him.

Holly would have hated this place, with its bastardisation of all she thought of as pure and precious, and Jonah craved to discover what could have gone so wrong. Despite his lack of belief, even he could see that these devout souls had betrayed their philosophy and made themselves godless. Did they really think that they were performing God's work? And how had this world's beliefs become so twisted? One of their holiest places had been turned into a factory of death, and they continued praying at the site of their greatest blasphemy. He was sad that he would never know the truth and, even if he did, that it would soon die with him. He might have been part of one of the most ambitious experiments in history – Coldbrook, and its brave, doomed journey – but some things would always remain a mystery to him.

Perhaps, as with people, there were some realities where evil was endemic.

The stone paving beneath Jonah's feet had been smoothed and grooved by the passage of countless feet, and he wondered just how long this had been going on.

A flurry of movement further along the next line caught his attention. A tall middle-aged woman stepped aside from her Inquisitor and spun around, kicking out at its head. She missed, though the Inquisitor had not appeared to move. And in the blink of an eye she was gone. The seemingly relaxed guards sprang into action, grabbed her arms and legs, and dragged her away. She started shouting, but one of them thrust something into her mouth. Blood splashed. *Cut out her tongue*, Jonah thought, and he, like all the others, turned away.

He rolled the ball in his mouth, the trigger that held the key to this twisted place's doom.

For all of you, he thought.

Jonah would be dead within minutes. And his solitary regret was that he would not stay down.

5

Holly had told Drake that she needed to be alone. She knew that he hadn't believed her, but he'd given her the time. So she'd retreated to her small room, closed the door, sat on the bed, and for a while she'd dreamed that everything was as it had been.

Inaction made her twitchy, so she plugged in the laptop on her small desk and flipped it open, and three minutes later she was patched into the Coldbrook security camera network. She scanned the facility for a minute or two, avoiding what she really needed to see.

'Please God that it's not as bad as I think,' she said. The first three cameras were out, their systems blown, and she gasped as the image from the fourth surface camera appeared.

There were hundreds of zombies in the compound above. Perhaps even thousands. The image was silent, but Holly could see that most of them were motionless mannequins standing or sitting, facing in random directions. Now and then their mouths would change shape as they made their hooting call. Some were burnt, mutilated, darkened with dried blood, and others looked almost untouched. Both extremes were horrific in their different ways. She pressed the key to swivel the camera, and it swept the compound from left to right. Fires still burned in the destroyed trucks close to the entrance, and she froze the camera on the school bus backed against the ventilation duct. The vehicle was packed full of furies, and the duct housing was almost buried beneath bodies. The image moved, shimmered and shivered. She imagined them packing the duct itself, scores of zombies piled in there so that those at the bottom were crushed beneath their weight.

Crushed, and yet still animated. She had heard them in the garage.

Holly started to shake. This could not last. Safety here was a fleeting thing, pressured to failing point just like those monsters in the ventilation shaft. Coldbrook had been built with designed-in fail-safes, some of which Jonah had triggered and one of which Vic had bypassed.

It was time to prepare her own measures.

Holly had seen these bodies before. At least she knew for certain that they were dead, though she was still unsettled as she edged past them, stepping over an outstretched arm. The repair she'd made days before was holding well, but she bypassed it and mounted a small vertical ladder set into the core housing. She shone her torch down into the space beneath her – the space surrounding the core – and even after everything she had seen the science of this place still gave her the shivers.

In the depths of Coldbrook, the core was rooted into the mountain itself.

Holly descended the ladder, and when she almost slipped and fell she held on tight, wondering what a pointless death down here would change, how many lives it might put in jeopardy or destroy. Coldbrook had always been an amazing place, which was why she'd always loved working here, with people who saw the awesome potential and importance in what they did. And now they were *all* important.

As she went deeper, so the pressure of the core impressed itself upon her. She could not feel or hear it, yet it sang in her bones. It was only when she reached the narrow platform at the deepest part of Coldbrook that she realised why that sensation was familiar – it was the same as passing through the breach.

Perhaps the multiverse was laughing at her.

Holly had no time to rest. She opened her tool pouch, flicked the torch's beam across the mess of control panels and boards, and found what she had come looking for.

Even here, she felt realities hinging on one act or object. If this screw failed, realities might change. If this capacitor was faulty, stars might crumble.

She got to work.

An hour later, after Holly had showered, she stood inside the doorway to the garage area, listening again to the sound from behind the plant-room wall. If she didn't know what was in there, she might have imagined a thousand doves cooing softly in the darkness. The Hummer was still parked tight against the door. There were two people from Gaia standing watch with Hitch and another Unseen, chatting quietly, their fascination obvious.

'We're cool,' Hitch said when he saw her watching. 'No movement from there, just that fucking awful noise. We need some Springsteen in here, drown it out.'

'Springsteen?' one of Drake's people said.

Hitch's face fell. 'Dude.'

Holly left the garage knowing that they could never be safe, and that it would take more than walls to separate them from the chaos that had smothered her world.

But she felt happier now, because she had a secret.

6

Vic snapped awake at the screeching alarm, and déjà vu screamed in with it.

Olivia sat on the bed wide-eyed, her arms hugging her knees. Lucy sat up, face grim, hair awry.

'Oh, shit,' Vic muttered, standing, tripping over his discarded boots, sitting to slip them on again, and all the while his family did not speak. The alarm thrummed into them, that awful repeating tone that could mean nothing good.

His satphone rang. 'Yeah.'

'Vic, they broke in,' Holly said. 'The garage, the plant-room wall, it was just blockwork, and it cracked under pressure. Weakened by the Hummer impact, maybe. I was there an hour ago and it was all fine, but . . . Hundreds of them. I'm in Secondary, I can see them on the camera. Being held back in the common room right now. But I can't reach Sean, he's in Jonah's room, you need to get there and—'

'What are you doing in Secondary?'

'Trying to adapt the breach. Doesn't matter – you need to protect Jayne, Vic. It's all about her now, and Marc.'

'Where's he?'

'Here with me. Drake's here, too. He said Moira and others are going to take the kids through.'

She means through there, Vic thought, and his spine tingled at the thought. 'Right. I can pick up Jayne and Sean on the way.'

Gunshots, and he wasn't sure whether they were from

outside the door or had sounded over the phone. Olivia and Lucy looked at the door, startled. Outside.

'Holly, gotta go, see you in Control in three minutes.'

'Wait!'

'Holly—'

'Loved you, Vic.'

'I'm not going through without you,' he said. 'We'll wait in Control.'

'Okay. Now go.'

'Holly . . .' *I loved you*, he wanted to say. But he didn't, because he *still* loved her, and to say that in front of Lucy would have been too much. Holly disconnected and he pocketed the phone.

'They're in,' Lucy said.

'Yeah. Okay, listen. We have to get through the breach.'

'With Jayne,' Lucy said. 'She's our hope.'

Vic grabbed his pistol; reloaded now, and with three spare magazines.

'But won't they follow us through?'

'Holly's doing something to the breach, I guess to prevent that. And we'll be ready over there when it opens again. Defend it until we're ready to come back through with a cure.'

'And what'll be left?'

Vic couldn't answer that, so he didn't try.

'Ready, princess?' he asked.

'I'm scared,' Olivia said.

'You follow close to me, keep your eyes on my back, turn when I turn. Remember how you'd follow my steps in the snow?' His beautiful daughter nodded. 'Pretend we're doing that now.'

He pulled on his boots and stood by the door. *Last time I ran from here, I turned right.*

Vic opened the door, paused at the corridor junction, checked both ways, and headed left.

7

'We'll take Marc with us,' Drake said.

Holly nodded, her heart thumping, looking from Drake to Marc. *I can't say goodbye. It might slow them down.*

'I need everything,' Marc said, picking up piles of printed material. He glanced at the laptop and satphone, frowned.

'No use over there,' Holly said. 'You need to go.'

One of the screens showed the garage, block wall tumbled from the pressure of zombies massed in the high duct behind it, hundreds of them now pressing forward against the wall below the camera where the short corridor to the common room began. Earlier, Holly had caught a brief glimpse of Hitch's slack face in the mass. The middle screen showed the common room. It was empty of kids now, and a tide of zombie bodies was flowing through the door like a slow wave. Several people – from Holly's Earth, and from Gaia – were systematically shooting any new one that managed to force its way, through, adding to the pile of cadavers. Gunshots flashed, crossbows whispered, gun smoke hazed the air. It could not last.

The fourth screen showed hundreds more zombies gathered around the parked bus and open duct. If she watched long enough, Holly knew that she would see them drop out of view on one screen and appear again, eventually, in the garage.

'Moira's leading the kids,' Drake said to Marc. 'You need to come with us.'

Marc nodded, looking around the room as if he'd forgotten something important. *He's scared*, Holly realised. She held his arms, catching his stare.

'I'll see you soon,' she said. Marc offered a brief smile.

'You're not coming?' Drake asked.

'I need to close the breach for a while, until we're . . .' She trailed off, pointed at the screens. 'Make sure Vic picks up Jayne on his way.'

Drake nodded, and behind him Moira stared at Holly. Smiled. Holly smiled back.

They left Secondary, and Holly closed the door behind them and locked it. Then she returned to the desk and sat back, placing her pistol beside her laptop. She tapped a few keys and brought up the program she needed. Deep down by the core, an electronic switch the size of her thumb waited to trip.

On the screens she saw more zombies forcing their

way through into the common room, and the defenders had fallen back from the frenzied things. One corpse crawled, peppered with bullets and bolts, reaching beyond the camera's view before staying still. Others rolled down the pile of bodies, stood, and stumbled out of sight.

Holly flicked the image to a corridor view, just in time to see Vic and his family disappearing around a corner towards Jonah's room. She wanted to call Vic, tell him to get a fucking move on, but that might distract him and slow him. So she switched cameras again, flipping through several before she saw Vic, Olivia and Lucy outside Jonah's door.

Vic reached for the handle and pushed the door open.

On another screen, she saw zombies flooding into the common room.

Holly's hand hovered over her laptop. She offered up a prayer, knowing that with a few keystrokes she would change this world. *Marc will be safe soon, he has the knowledge, he has Mannan, and if I have to sacrifice Vic and his family and even Jayne . . . if I have to kill them . . .*

There was still time for them to reach the breach. Minutes. Maybe seconds.

But time.

8

He's going to fucking shoot me! Vic thought, and then Sean lowered the gun.

'We have to go,' Vic said.

'Where?'

'Through the breach. Now!'

The gunfire had ceased, and from the direction of the common room two junctions away he heard an ominous rumbling.

'Daddy?' Olivia said, and Lucy was calming her, shushing her. *I should have sent them on!* Vic thought, but it was too late now. Much too late.

'Where's—?'

'I'm here,' Jayne said from behind Sean. She sounded weak and looked so slight, and Vic could barely credit that the future of their world might lie within her.

'Footsteps,' Sean said.

'Come on.' Vic ushered his wife and daughter towards the staircase, touching his pocket to make sure he had the spare magazines for his pistol. One in the gun, three in his pocket, thirty-two bullets, and Holly had said there were *hundreds* of zombies.

Sean and Jayne were following.

'Ammo?' Vic asked.

'Not much.'

Jayne was slow. She groaned as she tried to run, crying,

cursing, and when Vic caught her eye he saw the desperation there, and how hard she was trying. She didn't want anyone's death on her conscience.

Shapes moved behind them, and Vic paused, ushering Jayne and Sean past him. For a second he thought these were fellow survivors fleeing the zombies, because they were running so hard, arms pumping and feet pounding the corridor's floor. Then he saw the blood.

He braced, leaned forward, aimed and fired. The first man's head flipped back and he fell, tripping those behind him. They stood quickly and ran on, less than twenty feet away. Vic fired again, and again. A biker went down, face shattered, his arms bleeding from bites. The gunfire was deafening, but Vic could still hear his daughter's screams.

Sean was by his side, firing five times in five seconds, and now there were ten bodies down, twelve.

One woman jumped, and Sean shot her in the eye in mid-air. She landed and slid almost to their feet.

'Ammo!' Vic said, and he changed magazines while Sean continued shooting.

'Go!' Sean said.

'Fuck that.' Another shot, another. Fifteen down. The others had to slow now, climb, step over dead people who'd been made dead again.

'Your family!'

Vic glanced back and Lucy, Olivia and Jayne had gone,

towards Control and the breach. But he wanted them with him. He'd vowed *never* to leave them again.

'We've got time,' he said. He grabbed Sean's arm and pulled, and Sean saw the sense. He'd made his own vows, Vic realised. He'd rescued this special young woman, and in doing so had attached himself to her for ever. If a sacrifice was needed, Sean would make it without a second thought.

As they ran, someone screamed. Vic couldn't tell which direction the sound had come from and he put on a burst of speed, slamming through a set of double doors and gasping with relief when he saw Lucy and the others beyond.

'Block these!' Sean said. The doors swung both ways, making them difficult to barricade.

'Daddy!' Olivia pulled the belt from her jeans – pink with the word *Angel* written in glitter – and handed it to Vic.

'Clever girl,' Jayne whispered.

The scream came again, much quieter now. Back the way they'd come.

'Who's left back there?' Sean asked.

Vic was looping the belt through the doors' handles. 'Holly's in Secondary.' He paused, knowing that if he tied it too tightly—

The zombies crashed into the doors, shoving them back. The belt halted their movement, and three arms reached through the narrow opening. Vic and Sean leaned hard against the doors and Vic pulled the belt tighter, slipping his own through the handles as well.

'Daddy,' Olivia said, tears breaking her voice.

'Come on, sweetie.' Vic held her hand and ushered Lucy and Jayne ahead of him. *Not far now*, he thought. *Thirty seconds down to Control, then through the breach, then—*

The belts snapped and the doors burst open. Behind him, gunshots.

'Go!' Vic shouted, shoving Olivia after Lucy, turning, firing three quick shots. Five bodies fell, others were trampled. The zombies' numbers were slowing them down. But Vic knew he might not be that lucky again.

'Not far,' he said to Sean.

'I'll stay and give you time.'

'Fuck you will.' He grasped Sean's arm, pinching skin, eliciting a brief yelp. Vic laughed, high-pitched and crazy-sounding.

They ran, entering the staircase and securing the doors behind them. These were stronger; they might last longer. Down the staircase, veering around the slow bend towards Control, and when he saw the glass wall Vic put on a burst of speed, glancing through, terrified that he'd see the dead staring back. But Marc was there, standing defiantly just outside the breach containment and arguing with Drake. Several more of Drake's people stood poised, their crossbows pointed at the open doorway.

Vic stood in the doorway and winced, realising his mistake, braced for the impact of a bolt. 'We're fine!' he shouted. No one fired.

'About fucking time,' Marc said.

'Come on!' Drake waved them down to him, and Vic stood back to let Sean and Jayne pass. He snatched Sean's gun as he went by, and the older man paused only for a second.

'Vic?' Lucy asked. She grabbed Vic's arm as Olivia tugged at her other hand.

'Mommy, Daddy, we've got to go!'

'Come on!' Drake said. He was pushing Marc towards the breach, gesturing for Sean and Jayne to follow. The Gaians withdrew in a tightening circle around the breach.

He heard them pounding against the staircase doors one level up.

'Holly,' Vic said.

'Vic . . .' Lucy gasped.

'She's in Secondary. Shutting the breach for a short time. Otherwise the bastards'll run straight through after us, and we won't be ready.'

'No,' Lucy breathed, her eyes searching Vic's face. He blinked.

'I've got to help her,' he said, but they both knew that

was only part of the truth. The other part – the greater part – was that he could never leave Holly behind.

'Damn it, Vic,' Lucy said. She picked up Olivia and carried her down towards the breach.

'Daddy!' Olivia screeched. Vic watched them go. His wife's hair was dirty but still looked gorgeous, and he wanted to run his hands through it one last time.

'We'll be the last ones through!' he shouted. 'Three minutes. Don't shoot us.'

Before he ran, he tried to smile at his wife. But she did not once turn back.

9

Holly watched the group passing into the breach, but Vic remained behind.

'Shit.'

Her finger hovered over the keyboard.

There were no longer minutes left. Only seconds now. She was closer to God than ever before, and yet Vic stood between them.

Holly grabbed the satphone and dialled.

Vic left Control and she lost sight of him. His phone rang but he did not answer.

'Okay, then, Vic,' she whispered. A thrill went through her. Although the truth was painful, right then the fact that Vic was coming for her meant everything.

She watched Control on the lower level, the corridors of the main middle level flooded with zombies, and she flipped the other two views to Secondary's dedicated staircase. Clear – for now.

But the second she saw them in Control, she would type the code and press enter. Three US states was a huge sacrifice, but it was nothing compared to the cure that Marc might find.

Jonah sat here and watched me going through the breach, Holly thought. She wondered where he was now, if he had succeeded, and whether he was alive or dead. Or neither.

10

Vic could hear the zombies banging and hooting, and he could smell them, their curious dead stench filling Coldbrook and promising a similar fate for him.

His chest burned as he ran, and a deep sense of shame burned inside him.

He passed the staircase they'd just descended and the doors bowed out, creaking. As he raced around the core towards Secondary's staircase, he held the guns – his M1911 and the one he'd taken from Sean – in both hands, ready to aim them the instant he saw shadows coming at him.

Holly switched off the alarm. *Just me and her left*, Vic thought, and he ran harder.

The staircase was clear, though the zombies were pressing against the doors on the middle level. Dead eyes followed him as he dashed past, eyes belonging to people he had perhaps once known, and he looked away.

The corridor above was also clear, and moments later he was at Secondary's door. He tried the handle – locked.

'Holly!'

The lock snicked open and he shoved at the door, falling into the room, seeing the zombies on the screens, and Control was still clear.

'Holly, we haven't got a fucking second so we've—'

'I'm not leaving, Vic.' She was sitting at the desk again, gaze flickering across the screens, back to Vic, screens again.

'What?'

Holly was crying. Smiling. 'You came back for me.'

'To help. Are you done? Come on, let's get the fuck—'

'I lied,' she said. 'You never did understand the core. I *could* adapt it, but that's a long process, takes days. So I've bypassed a load of shit, rigged the containment to shut down instead. And that's manual.'

'No,' Vic breathed.

'One code away, Vic. Core exposure. And you know what that means.'

'It means no one ever comes back,' he said.

'Back to what?' Holly nodded at the screens. She could barely look at him.

'But the cure,' he said. 'Everything we've been fighting for.'

'There are other worlds to save.'

No, Vic thought. *No, no, this isn't why I came back, this can't be—*

But when Holly said, 'You should go back to your family,' Vic knew that it was. He had come back for a reason, and perhaps there was still time.

He walked to Holly and put his arms around her. She sighed, pressing her face against his. Then he lifted her from the chair and carried her towards the door.

'Vic!'

He shoved her through, kicking aside her leg as she braced her foot against the frame. She sprawled on the floor, and Vic stood for a moment listening, watching. He could hear them far away, but they weren't yet in the staircase.

'Don't you fucking dare!' Holly screamed.

Vic lobbed both guns at her as she stood, and as she winced and knocked them aside he stepped back in and closed the door.

Locked it.

Holly was on the other side, crying and raging. 'You saved your family!' she shouted. 'Stupid bastard, saved them and then threw your own life away. What good is that?'

'But I killed everyone else,' he said, raising his voice so that she could hear him.

'Self-fucking-pity?' Holly looked past him at the screens. Control was still clear.

'You might still have time!' he shouted.

'Let me in.'

'Not happening, Holly. Tell me what to do.'

She stared at him. She knew he was a stubborn bastard, single-minded. She knew that this door was never opening again.

'Damn you, Vic.'

'Too late for that.'

'Your name.' Holly stooped out of sight and picked up the pistols. 'Then press enter.'

'How did you—'

'I don't even know if it'll work!' she said, laughing and crying at the same time. Then she backed away towards the staircase.

Vic watched her go, hand on the door handle, heart thumping. As she pressed through the doors into the stairwell her expression did not change at all. But she watched him for every last moment she had.

He turned from the door and sat on the chair. It was still warm from Holly. Vic closed his eyes and took in a deep breath, smelling her. *I love two women*, he thought, but the image that screamed at him was his little girl, shrieking for him to come with her.

Olivia was through the breach now. A whole world away, and in a place he had never seen.

'Hope you've done well, Jonah,' he said. There was a box on the laptop screen, cursor flashing, and he tapped in his name: Vic Pearson. Holly's choice of code, the last words she'd thought she would ever see. The name glared at him, bright, accusing.

Two minutes later, on the big wall screens, Holly appeared in Control. *She'll stop and look at the camera, call me on the satphone, one last—*

But she ran through the breach without once looking back

Vic had never felt so alone.

'I've lost them,' he whispered. 'I've lost them all.'

A moment later the zombies flooded into Control, pursuing Holly, darkening that place like fluid from a foul, ruptured wound. The first of them was ten steps from the breach as Vic rested his finger on the *enter* key.

He relaxed, pressed down.

And then there was light.

Saturday

1

Ten days after helping to forge a path to an alternate version of her Earth, Holly was there again.

She watched dawn break over eastern hills, and the sunrise was a palette of colour. Dust in the air from the nukes, Drake had told her before, but she viewed it simply for its beauty. And she enjoyed the peace.

They'd camped in the small valley where the breach had been formed. The people that Drake had left guarding his side of the breach had brought tents and blankets, and enough food to make a small but satisfying meal for everyone who had come through. They had stood guard through the night while the survivors had slept. The tents had been cramped. Many had chosen to sleep beneath the stars, especially the children, who seemed able to accept this far better than the adults could.

Holly had slept away from the others. Lucy hadn't once looked at her. Olivia had come to her as darkness had settled yesterday and asked, 'Where's my daddy?' Holly hadn't been able to find it in her heart to tell the truth, so instead she had said nothing. And now the little girl kept glancing at her, and Holly knew that there would be more questions.

Don't they feel it? Lucy had asked Marc during the night. He hadn't been able to sleep, either. *Don't the rest of them feel the distance?*

Several small fires burned as Gaia's people cooked breakfast for the new arrivals. There were dozens of small fish from the stream flowing nearby, and the roots of the three-stemmed plants smelled gorgeous as they were roasted in seed oil. Olivia was playing with several other kids of her own age, jumping over the stream and sometimes slipping in. They were soaked, but happy.

Holly had yet to see Lucy this morning.

'He's dead,' a voice said. Holly jumped and turned, and Lucy sat down beside her. One of the Gaians stood twenty steps behind them, uphill. None of them were allowed to wander off on their own, but the time would come.

'He's . . .' Holly said.

'I'm not stupid.' Still Lucy didn't meet her gaze.

'He won't have felt anything,' Holly said. She found it difficult to speak.

'He went back to save you.'

'He didn't know what I was doing. He came to help. And when I told him he . . . shut me out. Made it so that . . .'

'After everything else, I'm not sure that he could have lived with you dying as well,' Lucy said. Her tone suggested this was the first and only time they'd talk about Vic like this. As she mourned, so she was tolerating Holly's shameful grief as well.

'Lucy . . .' Holly began, but she could think of nothing to say.

'I've lost him,' Lucy said, and she started to sob. 'Olivia has lost him. It's all so final.'

'It might be a beginning.'

Lucy looked at her at last. Holly held her gaze, determined not to look away. 'Maybe,' Lucy muttered, wiping her eyes. She looked towards her daughter. 'But I'm not sure I'll ever be able to shake this feeling of distance.'

Holly looked down into the shallow valley at the scar where the breach had been. It was bare stone now, an almost perfect circle of ground where all soil and life had been erased and replaced with a slowly cooling surface of molten rock. A moment after coming through she'd felt a thump at her back, a nudge, as if someone was urging her on a second before heat blasted out . . . and then nothing. People kept away from it now, partly because of the heat but mostly because they were scared. *Exactly where we are and a trillion light years away*, Holly thought.

'I hope the sense of distance will fade over time,' Holly said.

'I don't want Olivia to be told. Not until I'm ready. I've told her that Daddy saved us all, and he's trying to find his way back.'

'It's all so strange,' Holly said. 'Maybe that's . . .' *That's right*, she wanted to say. But tears threatened now, and she could say no more. She had no right to cry in front of Lucy, and she tried to hold back.

'Breakfast is ready.' Lucy stood and walked downhill towards her child.

The tears came, and Holly watched Vic's wife blur in her vision as she moved away.

Later, as they were preparing to leave and Drake's guards came in from where they had been keeping watch on the surrounding hilltops, Marc approached Holly.

'We need to talk to Drake,' he said. 'Just the three of us.' He was carrying reams of paper in a rucksack that had been given to him by one of the Gaians. He no longer carried a weapon. He was a scientist among warriors, and word had slowly spread about what he would attempt. Holly could tell that Marc would never be someone comfortable with attention.

They found Drake and took him to one side, walking up towards a ridge from where Holly hoped she would finally get a proper view of Gaia. Moira and another woman kept pace with them twenty steps behind, keeping watch. There was still danger here.

'There are almost forty of us,' Marc said to Drake as they walked. 'Have you thought about that? About how it might impact on your community here?'

Drake was silent for a time. They kicked through grass heavy with dew. Breakfast lay comfortably in Holly's stomach. She didn't think she'd tasted anything quite so perfect in years.

'Things have changed,' Drake said at last. 'You'll have a big impact on us. There's room, but barely. You don't know this world and its dangers, the places you can go, and those you can't. You'll be sharing sleeping quarters, and all of you will have to contribute. But you brought hope with you.'

'Jayne,' Holly said.

'The girl, yes,' Drake nodded. 'But also Jonah.'

'But how can we ever know?' she asked.

'We'll keep casting,' Drake said. 'And over time, if we find Earths that remain uninfected, we'll know that he released the infection to the Inquisitor's world. That's given us something to live for.'

'Seems to me you have plenty to live for,' Holly said. They'd reached the ridge now, and looking west she could see where the rising sun was playing across wooded hilltops and casting shadows into hidden valleys. There were furies out there, lying beneath the moss of forest floors and waiting to rise. But this was home to them all, and there was so much beauty here.

2

Tommy had spoken to Jayne as Sean had dragged her through the breach, reminding her of the years they had been together, good times and bad. She'd laughed and cried with him, raged at him and made love with him, and most of those memories had not involved her churu. Coming through at last, she had been sad to leave Tommy behind, but in a way she never would. He had saved her life and whatever she did from now on was testimony to that.

'Want me to carry you?' Sean asked.

'Want me to carry *you*, old man?'

'I'm fifty-two!'

'Yeah? And?'

'I'm not old.'

'Look old to me. Bit of a beer gut there. Greying hair, thinning on top.'

'I am not!'

'Quiet!' Moira was a few steps ahead, and she'd turned to scold them. They'd all been warned to walk in silence, and the children seemed to be doing it better than those adults who'd come through. Perhaps it was a game to the kids, but Jayne wasn't sure. Maybe for those so young, survival and adaptability to change were instinctive.

They walked slowly, mostly as a concession to Jayne. The people from Gaia looked at her with a combination of awe and fear, and she wasn't certain she'd ever get used to that. Sean had already stopped trying to persuade her to take Drake's cure. *When Marc is done*, she'd said. *He's the main man now*. They both knew to expect hard times.

As they topped the first rise and she could see further, a wave of pain washed over her. She gasped, and Sean held her arm.

'Will you look at that,' he said softly.

Jayne sighed away her pain, and saw another world that she might call home.

3

The lines snaked through the Basilica ahead of him and Jonah had finally seen the truth. The Inquisitors and their masters feigned ceremony, ascribing great weight to their pronouncements and speaking with deep solemnity. But this was little more than a processing plant.

As they entered the building, naked people were taken in front of the Holy Fathers and given their blessings. Past them in the darker corners of the building were the operating tables. Cries of pain echoed from the high stone ceilings, and the stench of blood filled the air. Between cries, accompanying the shuffling of feet, Jonah was sure he could hear the liquid gurgle of blood running through drains and into gutters.

Beyond the operating tables a ramp sloped up towards the exits at the rear. Here stumbled the new, naked, blood-streaked Inquisitors he had seen leaving the building perhaps an hour before.

He would never reach the operating tables. He would die unchanged.

Shuffling forward with the others, Jonah prepared himself for what was to come. He was old and had done so much, and yet there would be that instant when he had to bite. The moment between life and death.

It's for everyone, he thought. *Everything I know, and the infinities I don't.* He was witness to genocide on a universal scale, and he carried the means to end it. Perhaps. It made him sad that he would never know whether or not it had worked.

He thought of Wendy, his beautiful wife, and wondered what she would think of him now. And though Jonah was not a spiritual man, he felt closer to her at this moment than he ever had since her death. He had no expectation of seeing her again when he died, no belief that she existed now anywhere other than in his heart. But he held on to the idea that they were still together in memory. Death would make memories of them both. The queue moved on, and he drew closer to the Holy Fathers. Members of the Swiss Guard stood in greater numbers here. Each line passed in front of one of the old men, and the people only paused for a few moments before being urged on. He could make out some of what the bishops were saying now, could hear their utter conviction, the strain of repetition, and their weariness.

Jonah realised that these were *people*. The knowledge struck him hard, and for the first time since entering the old breach on Gaia the heat of tears threatened. The zombies gave the tragedy a monstrous face and even the Inquisitor projected the sense of a monstrous automaton, a victim indoctrinated and brainwashed, dehumanised. Here, on this Earth dedicated to killing every other, he saw at last that this was a very human tragedy.

Jonah drew closer, and closer. The old man blessing his line was short and thin, delicate spectacles perched on the end of his long nose, flowing red robes sprawled around him like a blood slick. The robes were grubby where people had walked on them, and white sweat stains marked uneven patterns beneath his arms and around his neck. Halfway through a blessing he yawned and glanced at a watch on his wrist. *His shift is ending,*

Jonah thought, and fury rose through the sadness, fresh and empowering.

'Nice,' Jonah muttered.

As the naked woman ahead of him was guided in front of the old man by her Inquisitor, Jonah manoeuvred the small sphere between his teeth and crunched it.

Set against his heart, the seed planted by Drake burst.

Jonah closed his eyes, but there was no pain. Whatever Drake had given him had been designed to mask reaction, and even then he wondered at the science of this thing. He felt warmth spreading through his chest, followed by an icy coolness, a numbness, and a distancing from his body.

His Inquisitor held his arm and steered him towards the Holy Father.

'The Word has found your world, and spoken its end.' The old man's voice was flat and monotonous. 'Welcome, heathen, to the true Church.'

Jonah looked down at the little man, and smiled.

'I hereby cast out your sins of errant belief and bless you into God's only world, and entrust you to perform God's holy work.'

No more sin, Jonah thought, and his grin grew wider. He was moving away. His vision blurred, and when he blinked he saw his wife. She held out her hand and he almost laughed, because she was as he had always remembered her.

'That way,' the man said, nodding to his left. He drew a cross in the air in front of Jonah's face, then glanced down at his chest.

'God doesn't know you,' Jonah rasped. His senses faded to darkness, and all awareness of his body withered. His mind clung on for a moment longer, and his final thought was of Wendy walking away from him, and himself holding her hand as he accompanied her, two lost memories.

'What's that?' the bishop said. 'Blood, there, on his chest!'

Jonah's mouth flooded with foul heat. He flitted away to blissful nothingness, fell forward, and bit.

With big thanks to my agents Howard and Caspian, and to my splendid editor Anna.

ALSO AVAILABLE FROM HAMMER

ALSO AVAILABLE FROM HAMMER

Woken by intense cold one night, Isabel Carey discovers an old RAF greatcoat hidden in the back of a cupboard. Sleeping under it for warmth, she starts to dream. And not long afterwards, while her husband is out, she is startled by a knock at her window.

Outside is a young RAF pilot, waiting to come in.

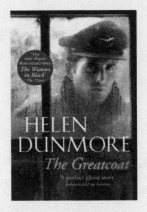

'You won't find plastic fangs or Dulux blood in Helen Dunmore's perfect little ghost story . . . this is the most elegant literary flesh-creeper since Susan Hill's *The Woman in Black*.'
The Times

'This is a haunting and exquisitely crafted tale where the line between the real and the imaginary becomes blurred.'
Glamour

'A perfect ghost story . . . This ghostly, literary war story could be the start of a beautiful friendship.'
Independent on Sunday

AN ISLAND PRISON. AN OCEAN FULL OF MONSTERS. NO CHANCE OF ESCAPE.

'One of the few fantasy authors whose new works I eagerly anticipate' STEVEN ERIKSON

THE HERETIC LAND

TIM LEBBON

Arrested by the Ald, scholar Bon Ugane and merwoman Leki Borle awake on a prison ship bound for the island of Skythe – a barren land warped and ruined by ancient conflict. Survival is tough and the colony's original inhabitants are neither friendly nor entirely still human.

But something else waits on the island, a living weapon whose very existence is a heresy. Destroyed many years ago, it silently begins to clutch at life once more.

New epic fantasy from the author of *Echo City* – out now!

Paperback: 978-1-84149-938-3
Ebook: 978-0-748-12876-1

orbit

About Hammer

Hammer has been synonymous with legendary British horror films for over half a century. With iconic characters ranging from Quatermass and Van Helsing to Frankenstein and Dracula, Hammer's productions have been terrifying and thrilling audiences worldwide for generations. And with the forthcoming film, *The Quiet Ones*, there is more to come.

Hammer's literary legacy is now being revived through its new Partnership with Arrow Books. This series will feature original novellas which will span the literary and the mass market, the esoteric and the commercial, by some of today's most celebrated authors, as well as classic stories from more than five decades of production.

Hammer is back, and its new incarnation is the home of cool, stylish and provocative stories which aim to push audiences out of their comfort zones.

For more information on Hammer,
including details of official merchandise, visit:
www.hammerfilms.com

AN EXCLUSIVE MEDIA COMPANY